Super Natalie

— ·· —

Super Natalie

Caitlin McKenna

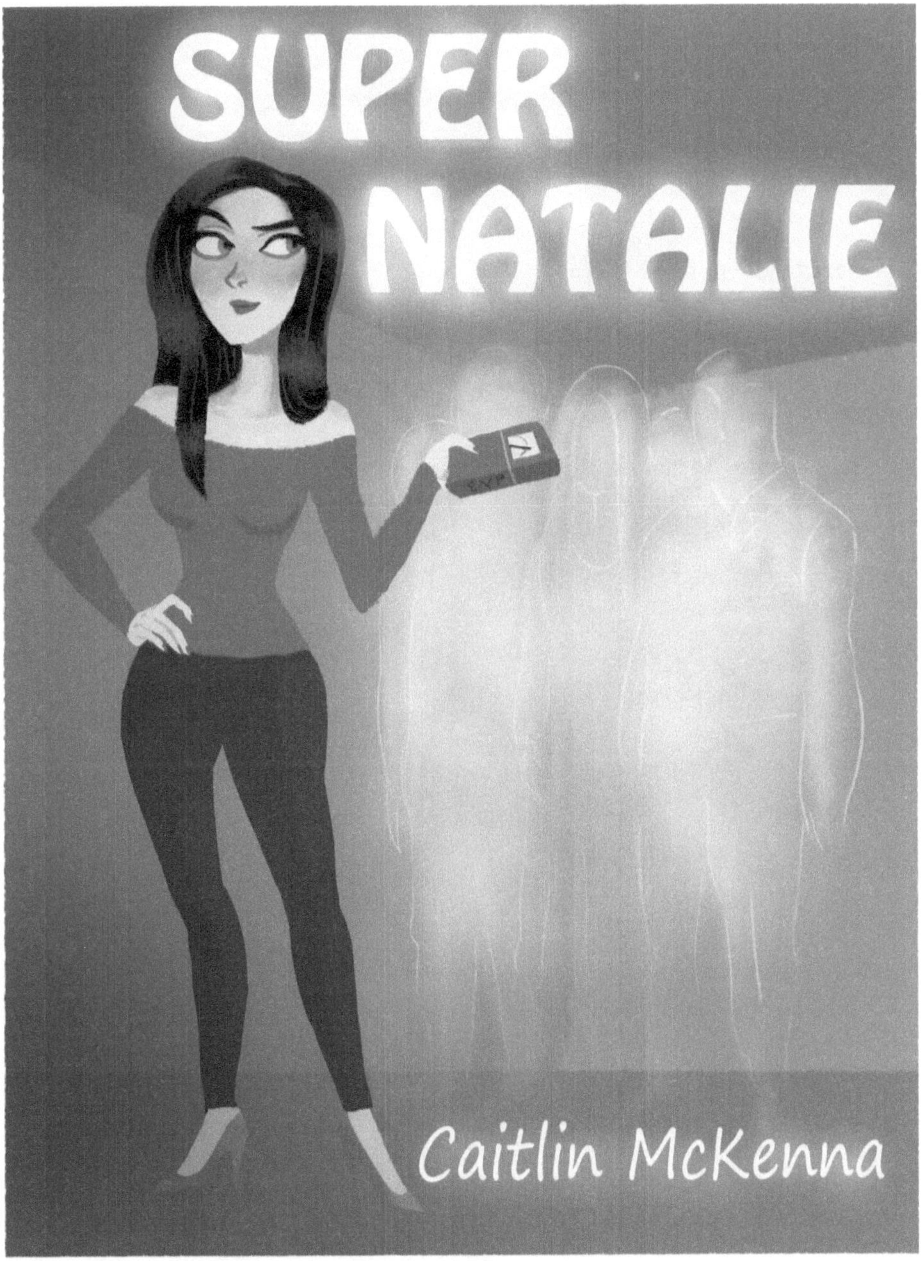
SUPER
NATALIE
Caitlin McKenna

ISBN-13: 9780692638873
ISBN-10: 0692638873

Visit the author's website:
http://www.caitlinmckenna.com/

Connect with Caitlin:

Twitter:

http://twitter.com/#!/caitmckenna

Facebook:

http://www.facebook.com/pages/Caitlin-McKenna/193255944037874

Books by Caitlin McKenna

No Such Luck

Manifesting Mr. Right

My Big Fake Irish Life

Logging Off

For Mom and Dad

Acknowledgments

I am forever grateful to my sister Lynn and good friend Anna who continue to read every version I give them. Your love, support, advice and input is truly appreciated.

A big thank you to Valerie Repnau for editing at all hours of the night so that I could make my deadline.

Many thanks to Jim Lau, Lucy Lin, Lydia Look, and Robert Spitz who helped me with research, and a huge thank you to my good friend Shane Sweet of *Sandbox* who went above and beyond to answer my many questions about rock bands while cutting his current album.

Thank you to Megan Dong for, once again, creating such an awesome cover.

Most of all, I'd like to thank my family—especially my husband, Jay, who doesn't complain when I spend weeks sitting in front of my computer. Thank you Mom and Dad and Mom and Dad Wilkinson, Aunt Cutes, Aunt Joan and Carole for your constant love and encouragement.

Thank you to all of my avid-reading friends—especially Lori Gordon, Luisa Leschin, Maura Swanson and Dianne Magambo who constantly promote my books as well.

Thank you to all of my readers who continue to buy my books. I am blessed to have such a wonderful support team.

Chapter 1

———◆———

"So, Natalie, you see dead people," Ed Cummings, the TV host of *World's Weirdest Hobbies*, asks me with quite a bit of sarcasm to his voice.

But what do I expect? *World's Weirdest Hobbies* isn't exactly *60 Minutes*. For the record, seeing dead people is not a hobby of mine, nor is it my burning desire to be a guest on this particular show, telling the whole world (or at least the part of the population who watches these types of programs) that I see things most people do not. But recent events—namely getting fired from job after job due to spirits popping in at the most inconvenient time—have left me no choice. Because of them, I have finally reached the financial status of flat broke. I'm appearing on *World's Weirdest Hobbies* only because they're paying me eight hundred dollars.

I wait for the snickers to die down before I answer Ed, who's currently brandishing a big smirk on his face, which means he's in agreement with most of the studio audience.

"Yes, Ed, I see ghosts who have remained behind as well as spirits of those who have crossed over to the Other Side."

He looks at me with all seriousness and asks, "There's a difference?"

I let out a relieved breath. For a moment, I thought this interview was going to turn into a bad Jerry Springer-type show. Instead, Ed has actually asked a valid question.

I sit up a little straighter. "Yes," I reply. "In my experience, ghosts usually haunt a location because they're emotionally tied to a property in some way and have unfinished business that does not allow them to move on. Spirits, on the other hand, have crossed over to the Other Side, which is what we are all supposed to do, but they often return to check on their loved ones, or in some instances, they cross back over to convey an important message."

Ed slowly and dramatically folds his arms and takes up a pose of intently studying me. "So, they just … appear out of thin air? Whenever? Wherever?" He leans in. "Do they get to see you naked?"

The audience roars with laughter, and Ed does too. In fact, everyone is laughing—except for the man I suddenly see, standing right next to the irreverent TV host.

"Talk about crossing over. That last comment crossed the line," the man, wearing a top hat, coat and tails, says directly to me. He has an upper-crust British accent, and yes, he is dead.

I give the spirit a light nod in agreement, then look away from him.

"Are you seeing any dead people now?" Ed asks.

"No," I immediately answer. I've been down this road too many times, and the last thing I want to do is give Ed ammunition to tear me apart.

"Do they watch you having sex?"

"I say!" The spirit sizes up Ed. "If only I had physical fists to strike this low-life scoundrel…."

I couldn't agree more with my new dead friend, but I force myself not to respond. Even though I'm being paid for this TV appearance, my contract never stated that I had to deliver a free demonstration of my abilities. I'm already being ridiculed without anyone knowing that I really can see the deceased, and I'd have to be insane to invite more mockery.

Of course the spirit, like all the other past manifestations I've encountered, has his own agenda. He moves in front of me, *directly* in front of me, and plants himself inches from my face. "Natalie, I most certainly know you can see me."

Exasperated, I glue my eyes to the spirit, telepathically sending him a message. Being from the Other Side, he has the ability to hear my thoughts; therefore, he knows full well why I'm pretending I don't see him. But my new client is master of my own game and pretends he doesn't understand me.

"Why do you feel compelled to lie?"

"Isn't it obvious?" I finally blurt out, answering the British spirit.

Ed narrows his eyes on me. "Isn't what obvious?"

I give my British friend a nasty look, realizing that he has bested me, before I turn my attention to Ed. "Nothing. Sorry. I was just … uh…."

Ed leans toward me and quietly says, "Oh, I get it. Okay. I'll play along." Ed gazes out onto his beloved audience. "She's seeing ghosts, ladies and gentlemen! Right now. In this very studio. They're all around us!" he adds with an exaggerated flourish of his hand.

"Even this pathetic sod wants you to admit it," the British spirit remarks. "Why not enlighten him, my dear?"

I hate to admit this, but my deceased friend has a point. Before, when spirits seemed to stalk me, I tried to ignore them as best I could for fear my employers would think I was a head case. Clearly my present situation is a little different. The people surrounding me *want* to hear from the Other Side—or at least see a good show.

"So, how many ghosts are you seeing?" Ed asks excitedly.

I clear my throat. "Um … one, but he's a spirit, not a ghost."

"Ghost, spirit. What difference does it make? He's dead isn't he?" Ed turns to his audience and raises his hands for them to laugh, which they do.

"This is going to be quite a thrill!" my client exclaims, and for some reason, I suddenly feel ill.

"So, one. You're seeing one dead dude. That's it?" Ed glares at me. "Are you sure you're not seeing four or five?"

I glare back. "Just one." *Trust me, Ed, one is enough.*

"Okay. Well, good. One. We have *one* spirit with us right now." Ed's eyes dart around the live studio audience. "*Where* is this spirit from the Other Side?"

"He's standing right ... behind you."

The TV host jumps out of his chair, which sets off several chuckles from the audience. "Are you sure?" Ed examines the area around his chair. "*I* don't see him."

"I suppose you wouldn't, Ed, since you're not clairvoyant."

Ed ignores the dig, sits back down, and turns to me. "So, what's spooky dude's name?"

I gaze at the spirit. He removes his top hat, sweeps it in a grand gesture toward me, and replies, "Wilson Gooding at your service."

"Wilson Gooding," I answer Ed in a calm, serious voice. "He has a British accent and looks to be from the early 1900s. Is he an ancestor of yours?"

"Gooding? Huh. Gooding, Gooding," Ed methodically repeats, dramatically tapping the side of his temple with his finger. "Well, if Gooding is long for good, he couldn't be related to *my* family." Ed erupts with a loud laugh, which spurs on the audience to join him.

"I'm most certainly *not* related to this vermin," Wilson Gooding states, clearly offended.

"He says he's not related to you," I inform Ed, over the laughter.

"What a shocker!" Ed remarks with wide eyes before he addresses his audience. "Anyone related to this bloke?"

The audience suddenly goes quiet as everyone looks around. No one speaks up, and after a couple of seconds, Ed says, "Wait a minute. Wilson. I do know that name!" He snaps his fingers together. "Wilson was the name of Tom Hanks' volleyball in *Cast Away*!"

I hear the audience explode with laughter as I glance at Gooding.

"I don't find humor in that statement. Have I missed something?" he asks me.

"No," I tell him. "It's not funny."

Ed narrows his eyes at me. "What was that? Are you talking to the dead again, dear Natalie?"

"Yes," I say dryly, above the smattering of chuckles.

"Well, if he doesn't know me, then who does he know?"

I wearily look at Wilson Gooding, wishing I could just collect my money and go.

"I know Skye," my spirit client informs me, "the young woman he's having an affair with. She's the beautiful blonde in the first row, and she happens to be my first cousin's great-great-granddaughter."

I quickly glance at the first row of seats and see a gorgeous girl in her early twenties, wearing a tight red cashmere sweater.

"Well?" Ed asks. "Don't keep us in suspense."

"Uh…." My mind is whirling. Ed Cummings had been on a hit television series a few years back, but he'd asked for a fifty percent raise before beginning the second season, so the network canned him. Back then, he was the hottest thing in Hollywood. Now, he was a second-rate actor with a dimming, disingenuous smile who wore knockoffs of expensive Italian suits and enjoyed demeaning his guests. I'd heard he married Carolyn Finch, a semi-successful independent producer who was thirteen years his senior. To my knowledge, they were still married. I zero in on Ed's left hand and take note of the gold band around his ring finger.

"Spit it out," Ed encourages. "This is *World's Weirdest Hobbies*, after all. Nothing you say will shock *this* audience."

The audience laughs. Some even throw out a few jeering comments while others begin to cheer me on.

"Ed." I lean in. "You really don't want to know."

"Of course I do," Ed replies with over-the-top enthusiasm before he gives me a you-are-really-stupid look, due to the fact that I forgot about the microphone attached to my blouse and everyone heard the comment I'd intended for Ed's ears only. "We all want to hear what the spirit said to you."

The audience starts yelling at me to tell them who my spirit is related to.

Squirming in my seat, I glance up at Wilson Gooding.

"Tell him the truth," he says.

"I can't."

"Why not?" Gooding asks me. "He deserves it, and you'd be helping Skye. Do you know that louse told her he was getting a divorce? I know for a fact that he never plans on leaving his wife."

"You can't what?" Ed pulls my attention back to the show.

"I can't repeat what Mr. Gooding told me." I glare at Ed. "Please, you won't *want* me to reveal what he told me."

"Go ahead. I ain't afraid of no ghost!" Ed begins to sing the *Ghostbusters* theme song and the audience members join in.

"It does make one wonder what Skye sees in him," Gooding adds on a sigh.

Ed finally stops and the audience settles. "Natalie, tell us. Or maybe you can't because you're a fraud."

I tried to warn him. I gave him every opportunity to let it go. I look directly at Ed. "He knows Skye—the woman in the first row who happens to be your mistress."

Ed goes pale as the audience pops with shocked gasps. The cameraman runs wild, scanning across everyone in the front row, until he lands on the beautiful blonde whose face is now stone-white with horror. Skye stares at Ed, her eyes pleading. Ed stares back, frozen with fear—or dread, or terror since I'm sure he's wondering what his wife will do to him when she learns about his off-the-air escapades.

Skye slaps the camera away from her face, then flies up the aisle and out the studio doors.

Ed turns on me, full-blown anger now blazing in his eyes. "Who put you up to this?!" he screams in my face.

I shake my head, jerking back. "No one."

"You're a liar!" Ed lunges for me as the red lights on the cameras turn off and security guards rush toward the stage. Ed drags me from the chair, shaking me violently. "Who are you? Who paid you to do this?"

I suddenly become aware of the audience, egging Ed on to tear my head off, and I wonder if they are honestly this bloodthirsty, or if they think this is all part of the show. I fight to get away, but Ed grabs onto me like some tiger shark refusing to release his potential dinner, and I worry that he might be going in for the kill.

Ed is screaming obscenities at me and he's so close to me that I can smell his horribly bad breath. I watch sheer hatred flood so fast into his face that his color changes from red to purple, and as I try to dodge the spittle flying from his mouth, I suddenly find Ed's arm pressing against my throat. I start to gasp for air. Stars begin to swim in my vision, and just when I'm about to lose consciousness, two security guards finally pull Ed off me. I fall to the floor, gasping for air, coughing and trying to catch my breath.

As for my spirit, he floats right next to me and says, "Terribly sorry, my dear. Unintended consequences." And with that remark, Wilson Gooding quickly and conveniently disappears.

———

Forty minutes later, I'm sitting alone in the producer's office of *World's Weirdest Hobbies*. I can hear a heated exchange going on in the room next to me, but I can't make out what anyone is saying. I hear the word "lawsuit" a few times and "she faked it," and I'm kicking myself for blurting out Ed's secret on national television.

Even though the show is filmed in advance and then edited before being broadcast, it might as well have been live. Practically every member of the studio audience whipped out his or her smartphone and started recording Ed's attack on me. The incident was posted all over the Internet within seconds. The most-watched recording was on YouTube with the title of *Ed Cummings Gone Wild*. Now, you can understand how I've managed to lose job after job due to tenacious spirits.

I rub my eyes with a loud groan. I've received a second notice on my late electric bill. My rent is due in seven days, my car payment in twelve, and now I'm a little panicky, wondering if they will pay me for my appearance since they were unable to finish the show. As my stomach starts to churn with anxiety, the producer's door flings open.

Darren Zephyr, a stocky guy with a rigid walk and a constipated expression on his face, slams the door shut, marches around his desk and sits down. He deliberately sets his elbows on the desk, laces his fingers together, and only then does he blow out a breath and look at me. "Miss Dalton, this is quite a mess."

Please, God, don't let me lose my paycheck. My heart begins to pound. I push my fear aside because I know I've done nothing wrong. I clear my throat, and with a confident tone, I say, "I'm sorry, but as the recorded interview will confirm, I tried to warn Ed. I told him I didn't want to say anything, but Mr. Cummings forced the issue. I did everything that was requested of me, including answering Mr. Cummings' questions."

"Yes, Miss Dalton, we are aware you fulfilled your obligation. However, as stated in section three, paragraph two of your contract, if our findings reveal that you were paid by a third party to damage or ruin the reputation of Ed Cummings, *World's Weirdest Hobbies*, this production company, or the network, all monetary compensation will be denied. Do you understand?"

"Yes." I try to keep the outrage from my voice. "When can I expect payment?"

"Soon, but right now I'd like to discuss what we expect from you in the next few days."

I tense up, tightening my grip on the armchair.

Zephyr regards me for a moment, looks toward the door, then leans in. "The thing is, Ed's wife is the executive producer of this show, and she has no idea what went down this afternoon. At least not yet. So in the meantime, we need to do damage control, which means no talking to the press, no tweeting, no comments on Facebook."

"I think you're a little late for your damage control. It's already posted all over the Internet."

He releases an impatient sigh. "Miss Dalton, you really don't know much about our industry, do you? There is always a story behind the story."

And as I begin to wonder what that "story" is, Zephyr's door is thrown open with a loud bang. I turn around and see a woman in her late forties, standing in the doorway. Her eyes, tiny slits of hatred, are locked on Zephyr with pinpoint accuracy. I can see her taking deep breaths and her nostrils are flaring like she's some pissed-off dragon ready to unleash a ball of fire that will instantly incinerate him on the spot.

Zephyr shoots out of his chair, his hands already up in defense, prepared for impending battle.

"Where's that cheating bastard?"

"I don't know."

"Stop protecting his sorry ass! I swear, Darren, if you don't start talking, I will see to it that you never get another job any higher than an unpaid intern! Now where is he?"

And this must be Ed's wife, Carolyn Finch.

"He's not here, Carolyn. I swear. He ran out of the studio moments after he attacked Miss Dalton."

Then Zephyr motions to *me*.

Yeah, thanks a lot, Zephyr. Like I really need to be in this woman's cross-hairs. My eyes grow wide with apprehension. I shake my head as I quickly get out of the chair I'm sitting in and position myself for a fast departure.

"Please, I don't want any trouble," I tell her, and Carolyn Finch's rage instantly shuts down. I'm totally baffled—as is Zephyr. We share a look, but we're both afraid to say anything.

Finch quietly closes the door. "Sit," she commands. I do as requested. She comes back over, leans against Zephyr's desk, and studies me. After a minute of silence, she very calmly asks, "Who told you about my husband's affair?"

As much as I'd like to give her a straight answer, I somehow don't think she's going to want to hear it. "Look, I don't even know if it's the truth," I offer instead.

"Oh, come on." Finch throws her head back with a sarcastic laugh. "I just watched the playback. No one missed the staggeringly stunned expression on Ed's face. The oh-shit-I've-been-caught look was real, honey. Even Ed couldn't have faked that. Now, I want to know who gave you the information."

I think about lying to her just so I can get out of the office unscathed, but she's staring at me so intently that I swear she plans to drug me with truth serum if I don't start talking.

I swallow hard, then look into Carolyn Finch's eyes, unflinching. "I knew nothing of your husband's affair until this afternoon when the spirit I was communicating with informed me of it."

The two producers just stare at me, saying nothing, and then a few seconds later Zephyr bursts out laughing. To my surprise, Finch doesn't join him. Instead, she cuts him with such a stinging glare that I think he may have peed his pants. Zephyr immediately snaps his mouth shut.

Finch puts her attention back on me. "You're serious."

I slowly nod.

"You have the ability to communicate with spirits."

I nod again.

She keeps eye contact with me, no doubt doing her I-can-tell-if-you're-lying voodoo on me, and when she's done, she paces off a few steps, muttering something to herself. I want to look at Zephyr, but I don't dare.

Finally, she turns around and says, "Do you know what I can't stand about so many of those ghost hunter shows? They go into locations that are reporting paranormal activity, they coax entities to make contact with them, and when they do, the ghost hunting team just up and leaves. They don't help these poor lost souls go into the Light or find peace or move on. They just pat themselves on the back for making contact and then move on to the next one."

Finch comes and sits down next to me and softly asks, "If you were on one of those shows, Miss Dalton, would you do that? Would you allow them to remain lost—stuck between two dimensions?"

I'm at a loss for words, too stunned to learn that Carolyn Finch not only believes in the supernatural, but she seems to have an understanding about different dimensions and trapped souls, and the need for sending them into the Light.

"Would you?" she demands.

"Of course not. I'd help them move on."

"Done." Finch springs to her feet, glances at Zephyr. "Fire Ed—from the show and my marriage. Tell him my attorney will be in contact. Arrange a meeting with my development team. I'd like to see if I can give Miss Dalton a reality series."

"Wait, what?" I interject, my face full of confusion.

"Carolyn, you can't be serious," Zephyr remarks with a patronizing attitude. "You can't possibly believe in such nonsense. I don't know how this woman found out about Ed's affair, but I assure you it wasn't from a dead person. She's a fake, a charlatan, and most importantly, a nobody without a following."

Carolyn shoots him an icy glare. "My beliefs are none of your concern, Darren, but what I *do* know is that you had better start keeping up with social media. Miss Dalton's appearance has gone viral. By this time tomorrow, I guarantee she'll be more popular than Lady Gaga." Before Zephyr can say another word, Carolyn Finch turns her back on him and says to me, "We'll be in touch."

A smile slowly takes over my face. I not only survived the wrath of Carolyn Finch, but she believed me. Someone actually believed me. "What just happened?" I ask the equally perplexed Zephyr.

Unfortunately, Zephyr is not at all happy with Carolyn's orders, and he suddenly turns nasty. "Don't think for one second that any network is going to give you a series. You might have fooled Carolyn Finch, but you haven't fooled me."

I stiffen with indignation. I'm tired of being thought of as the bad guy when all I'm trying to do is help. "I'm not a fake or a charlatan, and I most certainly don't need to be defending myself to you," I tell him, throwing his curt behavior back in his face.

"You're an opportunist and nothing more," he volleys. "There's no way in hell you're getting a series."

I shake my head in disbelief. "Did I ask for a series? I don't even like being on TV," I clarify, forcing myself to calm down. "I just want to get paid for my time today."

"And you will." Zephyr looks away, scribbling something on a pad of paper on his desk.

Right when I'm about to get up and leave, I hear a male voice directly behind me. "Demand payment now."

I glance over my shoulder and see a hunky shirtless guy wearing nothing but red swim trunks. He has light brown hair, a nice even tan, and an absolutely gorgeous body. I rub my eyes, thinking I'm seeing things. He has to be dead because Zephyr didn't react to him, but he doesn't look dead because he appears solid and three-dimensional. There's no transparency to him whatsoever, which makes me believe that he must have passed away recently.

"The guy's not going to pay you," Hunky Spirit says to me. "He's going to say you pulled a stunt to embarrass Ed, and their lawyers will say you are in breach of contract. So, go on. Tell him you want your check now."

Zephyr looks up. "We're done here, Miss Dalton. If you don't mind, I need to get back to work."

"Actually, I'd like my check now."

"You'll get it in a few weeks." Zephyr swivels in his chair and turns his back on me.

"Tell him you'll go to the press."

"I really need it now," I insist, but Zephyr doesn't answer me. "Mr. Zephyr, I want nothing to do with a new reality show. I just want to put this day behind me, and I think you'd like to do the same."

Zephyr swivels back around. "You're not in a union, Miss Dalton. You are a guest of our show, which means we are not obligated to pay you for thirty days."

"What a scumbag!" Hunky Spirit chimes in. "Don't back down."

"Fine," I tell Zephyr. "I'll just be on Facebook and Twitter in the meantime." I turn to go.

"Wait." Zephyr resentfully opens the right drawer of his desk, pulls out a book of voucher checks, and writes me a check for eight hundred dollars. He tears it out of the book and peers up at me. "I'll give you this on one condition. You will not post anything about today on any site, and you will not speak to anyone affiliated with any news organization about the stunt you pulled today. Understood?"

"I did not pull any stunt, as you put it. And as I said earlier, I want to put this behind me, so I have no intention of posting anything or talking to any reporter."

Zephyr hands me the check. "I'm sure you know the way out."

I take the check and head for the door.

"Good job, Natalie," commends Hunky Spirit.

I don't say anything. I don't look at the spirit or acknowledge him in any way, but as soon as I'm alone in the elevator (and by alone I mean not sharing the elevator with anyone who has a pulse) I turn to my latest tagalong. "Can you believe what a jerk that guy was?"

"He has a Napoleon complex and Carolyn, unfortunately, makes it worse by usurping his authority all the time. He'd be a much nicer guy if he changed jobs."

I nod, blowing out a breath, realizing Hunky Spirit is probably right. "Thanks for helping me, back there," I say with sincerity. I've rarely had a spirit help me with an issue, because it's generally the other way around. "So, what can I do for you?" I ask, cutting to the chase.

Hunky Spirit opens his mouth, I'm assuming to tell me what he needs, but then he regards me intently and says, "You really don't like communicating with us, do you, even though you're good at it?"

And now I feel guilty. "It's not exactly normal," I answer, trying to defend myself. "If you guys would just make an appointment with me, it would be much easier. Instead, I struggle to hold on to a decent job because people in your postmortem position are always demanding my attention anytime, anywhere."

"Well, you did ask for this, you know."

I furrow my brow and stare at him. "Excuse me?" The elevator doors open and I walk out with my new clingy friend.

"This gift of communicating with the dead," he clarifies, floating next to me. "We're all born with the ability to communicate with spirits, but you chose to keep it. You asked for it." He follows me into the garage.

I climb inside my car, knowing it would be better to continue this conversation in private. As soon as I shut the door, Hunky Spirit appears in the passenger seat.

"I never asked to be tortured on a daily basis by irritating, insisting spirits who should have thought about tying up loose ends before they kicked off."

"Whoa," he says. "Now there's some serious pent-up frustration. But hey, I get it. I guess it would be a little weird to be followed around by the dead, though you've got to give me some slack. I had no idea I'd go to work one day and never come home."

I glance over at my new client as I turn on the engine to get some air circulating in the car, and to hopefully lessen the overwhelming smell of the sea. "Sorry. You look ... more alive than other spirits I encounter. Did this just happen?"

"Six weeks ago."

"That totally sucks," I say earnestly. "You're incredibly talented, having learned how to communicate with me so quickly."

"I have a lot of time on my hands."

"So, I'm guessing by your swim trunks that you were swimming in the ocean."

"Actually I was a lifeguard, but I didn't die in the water. While on break, I ran to my car which was parked along Pacific Coast Highway, and bam! Some teen was texting while driving and ran right into me."

"God, I'm so sorry." I regard him with genuine sympathy. "Tell me how I can help you."

Hunky Spirit stares off into the distance with a strange look on his face and suddenly vanishes.

"Okay, take your time. You know where to find me," I call out. "Unfortunately," I add, under my breath.

I pull out onto Sunset Blvd in Hollywood, now that my spirit is gone, and I wonder if he got pulled back into the Light. This often happens—spirits disappearing with no warning. I've always wanted to ask one of them where they go so suddenly, but then I've never wanted to encourage this type of continual communication, especially since the communication has become much stronger over the last two years. When I first started to see and hear ghosts and spirits, it was more like impressions. I'd sort of see an outline of a figure or when I heard someone talking, it would be so soft that I wondered if I was imagining things.

But it seems like the more I've protested about being a messenger for the dead, the more clearly I've been able to see and hear them. I can't help but wonder if there isn't some sort of ghostly community message board on the Other Side with my name written all over it.

I merge onto the 101 Freeway. I'd like to pretend that Hunky Spirit was lying when he said I asked for this "gift" but he wasn't. I did ask for this. Not intentionally, of course, but the outcome is the same. I remember the event like it happened yesterday.

It was the summer of 1998. I was twelve and I went away to summer camp in Minnesota with my sister Stephanie—only we stayed in different cabins because she is three years younger than me. While Stephanie was off swimming and hiking and learning how to shoot a bow and arrow, I ended up getting stuck with a camp counselor who seemed … well … a little off.

One night, we were all sitting around a campfire, roasting marshmallows and telling ghost stories, when Angelina, a snooty girl from Park Avenue in New York, spoke up. "These stories are stupid," she snipped. "Why don't we do something constructive, like talk about our futures?"

Heidi, our cabin's counselor, who had a head full of dreadlocks and a body full of piercings said, "Far out, Angelina. Let's go around the circle and share with the group what we all see ourselves doing in ten years."

Naturally, Angelina started. She was going to be the richest woman in the world. Melissa, the girl next to Angelina, wanted to be a rock star. Carly dreamed of winning the gold for figure skating in the Olympics. Sarah was going to start her own bakery, and my friend Camille was planning on having a career in the fashion industry.

"What about you, Natalie? What do you want to be?"

"I don't know," I told her, shrugging my shoulders.

"Hey man, that's okay," Heidi remarked. "We'll help you figure it out. What are you drawn to? The Arts, the medical profession, travel?"

"I don't know," I repeated, as I started to feel a little uncomfortable. The other girls were staring at me and I was sure they were judging me.

Heidi's mouth dropped open. "Well, you have to know *something*," she replied in a strained tone that suddenly didn't sound like her.

"I'm only twelve," I defended. "I haven't really thought about it."

"Wow," Heidi replied, with an exaggerated roll of her head. "Well, I hope you figure it out soon, little girl, otherwise you'll end up wandering around this world clueless and lost. You'll be on the streets, get forced into prostitution. Maybe you'll start shootin' up heroin while you drift from one boyfriend to another, desperate to find anyone who will love you because you need to fill that hole in your miserable, empty life. But you won't find the love you're looking for because you'll never seem to get a break, so you'll forget with drugs and you'll use so much one night that you'll almost die, and you'll be rushed to the emergency room where some sympathetic sap will get all clingy with you after you come to, and she'll then think you are her new life mission. She'll think she's going to help turn your life around. So she'll get you a job at a summer camp teaching bratty rich kids things that will NEVER have any use in the real world!" Heidi dramatically flung herself on the ground and started rolling around, laughing hysterically.

Too stunned to say anything, we all just sat there, staring at her, and then everyone's eyes drifted toward me, as if I had somehow caused our counselor to go temporarily insane.

I got up and backed away from the circle of craziness just as Heidi started up again, spewing out all the mistakes she'd made. I was filled with terror, thinking that I could be staring at my own future if I didn't figure out my life that very instant. So I started talking out loud. I was screaming, really—to God, the universe, or whoever could possibly be listening—that I did not want to end up like Heidi. I needed to know right then and there what I was doing here on earth. I begged the heavens to tell me my life's purpose, no matter how strange or foreign or unlikeable it might be. I begged to be told that instant, so I didn't have to wander around looking for it!

I fell to my knees, still hearing the camp counselor ranting, and when I opened up my eyes, I saw a shooting star. And as the star faded into the night, the energy around my body felt electric. It felt alive. I stared at my hands and I could see my own aura.

I looked up at the rest of the group, their attention split between my pleading like I was crazy, and crazy Heidi thinking she sounded normal. Then I squinted and rubbed my eyes a few times because I could clearly see an older Native American man standing in the flames of the campfire—only his body was transparent and no one else seemed to notice him.

I gasped when I realized that I was seeing a spirit. I couldn't believe it. I didn't want to believe it. I convinced myself that I was seeing things because we were telling ghost stories earlier. I closed my eyes, assuring myself that I wasn't seeing anything, when I heard, "This is your life's purpose—to help heal the living and the dead."

My eyes shot open to see the Native American spirit standing right next to me. He looked directly into my incredibly shocked eyes. He smiled this knowing, wise smile and then he vanished into thin air.

I sank to the ground—only no one noticed because two other camp counselors quickly descended on everyone to corral us away from crazy Heidi, and I couldn't help but wonder if I shouldn't go with her.

The next morning I'd convinced myself it had all been a bad dream. But then later that day, I saw a deceased little girl with a pale complexion and blue lips who had drowned at the camp's lake some fifty years prior. This girl suddenly reminded me of an earlier childhood memory I had tucked away, hoping to forget. It was of a boy I'd seen when I was eight. He had blue lips too and hollowed eyes, but back then I thought he was a classmate playing a horrible trick on me. I'm not sure what I saw when I was eight, but I now knew what happened to me the night before was very real.

So, my life's work is to communicate with the dead, I thought to myself. *Great.* I couldn't be a veterinarian, a yoga instructor, or a financial analyst. No, my life's work was going to be … difficult to explain.

I remember staring out onto the lake, thinking that I could still somehow have a normal existence. This little extra ability wasn't going to prevent me from having a normal job, a normal family, or a normal life.

When I left summer camp, I was convinced that I was as normal as anyone else. Of course, it wasn't long before I realized that in dealing with the paranormal, I'd never be normal again.

Chapter 2

———✦———

Before I go home, I stop by the ATM and deposit my check. It'll keep my lights on and my landlord off my back for another month but that's about it. First thing in the morning, I know I'll need to hit the pavement and start looking for work yet again. Maybe I'll try the Starbucks over in Toluca Lake. My friend Luisa told me they were hiring.

Now that I think about it, working in a coffeehouse might just be the perfect job. My boyfriend Dean and I hang out in coffeehouses all the time, and I've yet to see a spirit or a ghost.

Speaking of Dean, thank God he's in Seattle right now. He works for Wells Fargo bank and has to travel out of town several times a year. We've been dating for nine months now. He's been hinting that our one-year anniversary was going to be unforgettable, which makes me think he's going to pop the question, and I'm not sure how I feel about that.

I love him. Of course. Dean's a great guy. Very practical. He's obviously great with his finances, something I can seriously benefit from once we're married. I just wish we could live together first. You don't buy shoes without trying them on first, so I don't see why that logic can't apply to relationships. Living together would be kind of like a dress rehearsal or a dry run. You'd think with Dean being so practical he'd totally go for the idea. But no. He quickly shot me down the second I brought it up on our six-month anniversary.

My mom says him being old-fashioned is a good sign that he will always treat me with the utmost respect. I'm sure she's right, even though he said he didn't want to live together because he needed his space. Apparently he often gets claustrophobic.

I don't think my best friend Lucy likes Dean because he insists on going Dutch every time we get together with her and her boyfriend, Matt. Dean points out that Matt drinks a lot more than any of us and Lucy likes to order several plates of food to share with everyone at the table, some of which Dean doesn't eat. Because we all share the food, I think we should just split the bill evenly, but Dean insists that everyone pay their proper share according to what each of us consumes. Matt always pays for himself and Lucy, and I often pay for Dean because I'm a little embarrassed. Dean also insists on going Dutch when it's just me and him. It bothers me a little, but what can I say? That's a banker for you.

Aside from Dean's money issues, we are perfect for one another. We've even fallen into a routine and oftentimes people think we are already married. On Saturday mornings, after we've slept in our own beds at our separate apartments, we meet up at Starbucks or Coffee Bean & Tea Leaf, grab a muffin and coffee and relax for an hour or so. He reads the paper and I check my email. We'll then hang out at either his place or mine. Dean likes to catch up on his sports teams, of which he has many, and it would take me way too long to list them all. Sometimes we'll catch a movie before I make us dinner. Dean doesn't cook, but he cleans, insisting that he do his proper share.

If I were marooned on a deserted island, I'd definitely want Dean with me because he thinks of everything and then he thinks everything through. We dated four months before we slept together, just because he wanted to make sure we were compatible. I didn't mind waiting. I'm a little reserved myself. Truth be told I'd only been with two guys before Dean, and if I were to rate them as lovers they'd both receive an "F".

Dean isn't "F" material. In fact, he's actually quite good, but he is a little fussy. He likes things organized. For our first time together, he actually assembled an intimacy tray. Placed in the center of the tray were two condoms. He had no intention of using both, the second condom was for backup, in case the first one broke. Also on the tray was a tube of lubricant (should we need it), a warm washcloth, a towel, and two chilled bottled waters. In addition to the tray, he had washed his sheets and *ironed* them! If I had just met Dean, I would have flipped out and left immediately. But since I knew he was a neat freak, I realized this probably wasn't out of his realm of normal.

After Dean and I took off our clothes and hung them up, he began kissing me and talking softly to me. In a very seductive voice, he asked me to lie down and get comfortable, so I did. But then he started announcing what he was going to do.

"I'm going to kiss you now, if that's all right with you. I'm going to touch your breasts, if you're okay with that."

At first I was worried Dean was into S&M and would, at any minute, be pulling out whips and chains. But when I told him to stop asking me for permission, he got very quiet and confided in me that he was still a virgin.

Wow. A good-looking guy who was twenty-eight and still a virgin. Of course, I was twenty-seven and, as previously mentioned, I had only been with two other guys before Dean, so I'm not one to talk. However, seeing as how I had the most experience in the room I tried to take charge and get him to loosen up, but it shut him down if you catch my drift, so we went back to him being in control.

I let him take his time, and I was worried about freaking him out again, so I just lay there, and afterwards he told me it was the best experience ever.

Over the months, I've gotten him to be a little less structured, and he's finally learned to do so, and now we both have a good time. Still, some things are a little weird. When we shower together at his apartment he always washes my feet, not because he has a foot fetish, but so he knows my feet are super clean before I climb into his bed. There's also the hair requirement when snuggling. Dean's good at snuggling, but I have to keep my hair up in a ponytail, so there aren't any loose strands that can inadvertently get in his mouth.

Other than that, our relationship is great. Dean tells me he loves me every day, and it's not one of those off-the-cuff I love yous. He always cups my face in his hands, looks deeply into my eyes, and only then does he tell me he loves me. And that is how I know he means it.

Of course I love him too. How can I not? Especially since Dean shared with me how special I really am to him. He wasn't a virgin for lack of opportunities. He'd purposely been celibate for so long because he used to be a serious germaphobe. He told me I was the first girl who didn't repulse him when we kissed. I know that sounds like a backhanded comment, and maybe it is, but Dean and his therapist have come such a long way. He has his germaphobia under control now, especially since his fear of identity theft has taken much of his attention these days, and to be honest, I can't blame him. Like germs, identity thieves are everywhere, ready to strike an unsuspecting victim, and I have to say I'm developing a fear of them too, though my fear is warranted since a complete stranger just last week tried to rent a car under my name.

Aside from his little idiosyncrasies, Dean and I are so alike. We share so much together. He really likes my family, though he thinks my sister is a society deadbeat. He enjoys hanging out in my apartment, except when I get busy and don't have time to clean, and then it's just too messy for him to tolerate. He thinks it's character building to have so many different jobs, and he really is very supportive every time I have to look for a new one.

We pretty much know everything about each other except for one thing. Dean doesn't know I communicate with the dead. I have had a few spirits contact me when I've been with Dean, but I've managed to talk to them without him noticing, which was rather difficult because Dean notices *everything*.

I know I shouldn't keep this secret from him, especially since our relationship appears to be marching onward, but I think the truth might send him over the edge. I don't know this for a fact, and I know

I shouldn't pretend to be someone I'm not, but Dean has suffered through so many phobias that I'd feel horrible adding the fear of ghosts to his list.

And what's truly great about Dean being away on business is that he will never find out about my appearance on TV. He hardly ever watches TV. He thinks YouTube is a serious waste of time and brain cells. So, if everything else falls apart after today, at least my love life will remain intact.

I turn the key in the security gate of my apartment complex in North Hollywood and make my way over to the mailboxes where I find more unpaid bills waiting for me. *Just what I need.*

"Whoa, check it out!"

I glance up to see two teenage guys staring at me.

"Are you the ghost chick?" the one on the left asks.

Oh, no. Carolyn Finch was right. The video has gone viral. Why did this have to happen now? If any stranger could ID me as "the ghost chick," how will I ever be able to find another job? It's bad enough to receive ridicule from ex-employers, from ex-friends, but not from strangers who don't know anything about me. "Sorry, no."

The guys huddle around an iPhone, which is replaying *Ed Cummings Gone Wild*, and I am cringing.

"Dude," he says to me. "It *is* you!"

He turns his phone around so that I can once again relive what I have titled *When TV Hosts Attack*. "That's not me," I emphatically state.

"Dude, you're wearing the same clothes!" The guys crack up as I look down at my blue and white striped blouse, the one clearly seen in the video. I let out an exasperated sigh.

"You really see dead people?" the other kid asks me excitedly.

"Kind of," I mutter, not wanting to get into it.

"That's awesome!"

Awesome? Did I hear him correctly? This guy not only believes me, but actually thinks my ability is awesome? First Carolyn Finch and now this guy. Maybe things in the seeing-dead-people world were looking up.

"So, do you think you can connect with my turtle? He died last week."

"She sees dead people, not dead turtles," his buddy chastises him.

"But you see animals too, right?"

"Once in a while," I explain, suddenly feeling a little more confident. "But I've never exactly had pets seek me out."

"Why not?"

"Don't know." I shrug. "Maybe because animals don't hold grudges or leave things left unsaid, like people do."

"Well, if you see my turtle around, will you let me know? I live in two-eleven."

"Yeah, sure." I watch them walk away, still a little stunned that they didn't make fun of me. Maybe I've had such negative responses in the past because I haven't met enough people who believe in ghosts. Maybe the horrible incident today might end up changing things for the better.

I make my way over to the elevator just as the doors are opening. I see that it's going up so I get on and push the number four button. There's a couple already in the elevator and I can't help but notice that they won't stop staring. I'm assuming they've seen the video too. I offer a smile, hoping I get the same positive reaction that I received from the teens. But I don't. The girl whispers something to her male companion and when the doors open on the third floor, they rush out. *Great.* I guess not everyone who's seen the video is open-minded.

Right when I get settled into my apartment, my cell rings. I pull it out of my handbag and see BLOCKED on my caller ID. It's either my mom or someone calling back from one of the many job applications I've been filling out all over town. I have no choice but to answer it. I put on a bright, cheery voice and say, "Hello?"

"Natalie?" I hear a strained, concerned female voice on the end of the line and I know it can only belong to my mother.

"Hi," I answer briskly, hoping she thinks I'm in the middle of something. I love my mom but sometimes my phone conversations with her end up being a lot of work on my end, involving a pen, a blank sheet of

paper, and five minutes of taking down dictation. Whether it's a new recipe she's just heard on the radio, or the address to a new restaurant that
has received rave reviews, or the name and author of a must-read book,
my mom prefers to call me, instead of writing down the information on
any of the hundred different notepads I've given her over the years, or
better yet, taking a moment to enter it in her iPhone. "What's up?"

"What's up? That's what you have to say to me?"

"That's what I normally say." *I know I'm going to regret asking this
but....* "Is something wrong, Mom?"

"No, Natalie. Nothing at all could be wrong—just that my own
daughter has gone on national television and told the whole world she
sees ghosts!"

*Okay, so maybe taking a few minutes to write down a new recipe would
have been the easier conversation.* "Where did you hear that?"

"I saw it on YouTube, like everyone else."

"You go on YouTube?"

She lets out an annoyed grunt. "Why wouldn't I? I may be in my
forties, but I don't live in the Dark Ages."

"You're in your fifties, Mom."

"Don't change the subject. This is serious."

I hear the buzzer ring and run to the intercom. "Mom, I've got to go."

"Natalie, we need to talk."

Knowing I can't just hang up on my mom, I buzz in whoever is waiting downstairs, hoping it's someone with great news like the Publishers
Clearing House saying I've won a million dollars, or maybe it's my old
boss coming to beg me to return to work. I'd even be happy to see my
friend Lucy, bringing up a pizza for us to share. "Let me call you back,
Mom. I just buzzed someone in."

"Who?"

"I don't know. That's why I've got to go."

"You buzzed someone in without knowing who it is?"

"You can stop worrying about me, Mom. I can take care of myself,"
I reply as I open the door and try to see who has stepped off the elevator.

"That's debatable," she says, disconnecting her phone, as she walks right towards me.

"Hi, Mom."

"Talie." As soon as she steps inside my tiny one-bedroom apartment, she heads to the kitchen and immediately notices the dirty dishes in the sink. "I thought you had a dishwasher."

"It's broken."

"Goodness." She takes note of the unfolded laundry in my laundry basket sitting by the couch, the stacks of newspapers piling up on the kitchen table, and more dirty dishes left on the coffee table. I have to admit it, my apartment is unusually messy. Because I have to keep it so clean for Dean, I tend to really let it go when he's out of town. "When was the last time your housekeeper was here?"

"Uh … never." I pick up the dishes off the coffee table and take them into the kitchen, which is only a few steps away. "I don't have a housekeeper."

"Well, that explains it." My mother sets down her purse. "Would you mind getting me a cool glass of water?"

I pull down a glass from the cabinet as I watch my mom inspect the tiny scratches in my wooden end table. "You know, if you take a used black tea bag and rub it on these scratches, the tea will stain the damaged area and make this look like new."

My mom is a travel agent. When most travel agents went out of business as Expedia and Travelocity and all those book-it-yourself travel websites came along, she doubled her client list because she knows little details that those sites do not. In almost every tourist destination, she's an expert on where the great out-of-the-way places are that only the locals know about—the best restaurants, the gem beaches, the exciting day trips. She's in the know on how to get premier hotel rooms for almost nothing. She educates her clients on who offers the best upgrades, and she instructs all of them on how to deal with travel emergencies.

My mom expertly handles the minor inconveniences we all face when traveling: how to get wrinkles out of clothing without an iron, how to pack clothing from three suitcases into one, how to remove lipstick off a white shirt. Needless to say, her tips and remedies extend well past her job, which makes me wonder if she's currently thinking she has a quick and easy remedy for me.

I get my mom some water and myself a Coke, while I watch her scrutinize my one and only houseplant that is limp and turning brown. I hand her the glass of water and she dumps it over the plant. "Can I have another, please?"

Without arguing, I go back into the kitchen as my mother notices spilled candle wax on the carpeting. "You know, if you take a brown paper bag and iron it over this wax, it will come right out of the carpeting."

"Seriously?"

She gives me an exasperated look. "Why don't you call me about these things?"

"I don't know," I sigh, wondering the same thing myself. I spent an hour the other night, trying to take the wax off each carpet fiber with my fingernail and finally gave up. I know I should have picked up the phone to get some good housekeeping advice from her when it happened, but I didn't want to add another mistake to my growing list of lifetime failures. "You should write a book."

My mom squawks with laughter.

"I'm not kidding. You could be Martha Stewart on a budget."

Before my mother can answer, her cell rings. "Yup, she's here," my mother says to whoever is on the other end, and then hangs up.

"Who was that?"

"Your sister. She's on her way over."

"What? Why?"

"Well, obviously you need our help."

"I don't, Mom." I hand her another glass of water, which she actually drinks this time. "I'm perfectly fine."

"Hardly. I heard what you said to Ed Cummings." She brushes cookie crumbs off my couch before sitting down. "You don't honestly believe that you can see ghosts, do you?"

I don't want to talk about this with my mom, but it's a little hard to deny it now. "I do and I can."

My mother gets all misty-eyed, then mumbles, "My eldest is having a nervous breakdown."

"I'm not having a breakdown," I hiss, though I often think I'd have an easier time of it if I did.

The buzzer sounds and I push the intercom button. "Yes?"

"Talie, it's Steph. Let me up."

I grudgingly push the button, then open my apartment door. A couple minutes later, my younger sister appears. She's super skinny and has on a pair of straight-legged jeans that are so distressed they look like they've been in a fight with a bobcat. She's also wearing a tank top that's so small, it barely clears the bottom of her bra. Needless to say her midriff is showing, allowing everyone to see her double-pierced belly button. Even though my sister dresses too grunge for my taste, she's really very pretty. She has raven black hair which flows beautifully down her back. She could easily be a hair model if she hadn't colored a very wide portion of her gorgeous hair with a blue streak which only reminds me of seeing a skunk in weird blue moonlight. I'm about to say something, when I see her boyfriend, Peter, (also rail thin and the exact same height as Stephanie) running down the hallway to catch up with her.

"This is just great," I grumble to myself. Peter's studying at AFI to be a filmmaker, specifically one who sheds light on taboo subjects. No doubt he thinks I fall into this category.

"Hey, Sis." Stephanie comes in and makes herself at home.

"So you talk to the dead, or *think* you talk to the dead," Peter says to me while he judgmentally looks me over. "Are you on any medication? Do you feel this could be some kind of psychotic break?"

I roll my eyes at Peter, glance down the hallway to make sure no one else is coming for this intervention, then I shut the door.

Stephanie goes to my fridge, takes out two Cokes. She tosses one to Peter and keeps the other for herself.

"Look, I appreciate all of your concern, but I'm not crazy. I see ghosts. Other people see ghosts. It's really not a big deal."

"How long has this been going on?" my mother asks, opening up her home remedies file on her iPhone.

"Wait a minute." Peter takes out his camera from his shoulder bag. "Let me get set up first."

"Peter, please, I really don't want to be recorded right now."

"Oh come on. This will be great."

"Pete!" Stephanie glares at Peter with wide eyes and motions him to put the camera away.

I sit down, resigned to the fact that I'm not going to get rid of anyone until I fully explain my situation. Truth is, I tried to tell my family years ago, but my father said it was all in my head and if I continued to talk that way, I wouldn't amount to anything good.

Of course, he wanted to hear all about it when his business partner, Blake, died from food poisoning days after one hundred thousand dollars went missing from their construction company. Blake did indeed visit me, but it was to tell me that he'd gotten sick from a catering truck that needed to be shut down. The money never turned up, but my dad's main foreman suddenly quit and disappeared, so no mystery there.

"Okay, here's the truth." I steady my eyes on everyone, making sure I have their attention. "I've been seeing spirits ever since Stephanie and I went to summer camp."

"The camp was haunted?" My mother's face is aghast.

"Yeah, but that's not the reason. Something happened there, something that allowed me to see them. Steph, do you remember when my cabin counselor went crazy?"

"Oh, yeah. That was intense. She just wigged out," she recounts to Peter. "They had to take her away in an ambulance."

"No way!" Peter exclaims with an excited laugh.

"It totally freaked me out," I add. "*She* freaked me out. Heidi said I was going to end up just like her because I didn't know what I wanted out of life. I was so terrified of Heidi and was so afraid my future might end up like hers, that I begged to be shown my life's purpose right then, right there. And all of a sudden I could see spirits."

Stephanie and Peter regard me with blank expressions, but my mother seems particularly disturbed by my story. I can only assume she thinks I'm insane.

"It's the truth," I insist.

"It's a little thin," Peter, "the Filmmaker," replies.

"Well, that's how it happened!"

"How come I don't remember that?" Stephanie squints at me with a stern, dubious expression.

"Because I didn't tell you," I confess. "I'm the older sister. I'm the one who's supposed to know everything. I'm the one who's supposed to protect you. Back then you were afraid of your own shadow. I don't think my informing you that ghosts really did exist would have helped you out in that department."

Peter scoots forward on the couch. "So, one day you were perfectly normal, and the next minute, poof, you can see ghosts?"

"Yes, I guess that's what happened."

Peter shakes his head. "Something's missing."

"Excuse me?" I say, rather indignantly. "Since when are you the authority on my life?"

"I didn't mean it like that," Peter amends.

"Well, what did you mean?" Stephanie asks, crossing her arms the way she always does when she's taking my side.

"Can it really happen that way?" he questions. "Can someone suddenly become psychic in an instant?"

"I did," I say defensively.

"If you say so," he responds in a sing-song type of voice, which only tells me that he's not convinced. "But if I were shooting this as a movie, I'd make you rework the beginning."

"That's how it happened!" I yell at him again.

"No, it didn't." My mom, who has been unusually quiet, finally speaks up. We all cast our eyes on her and wait for her to explain. "I think you've ... uh ... always seen them."

"See there. Just as I suspected." Peter sits back with a cocky attitude, satisfied he's right.

I dismiss Peter with a shake of my head and glare at my mom. "Spill it."

My mom lets off a nervous little laugh before her eyes meet mine. "I refused to believe it back then," she says in this tiny voice I've never heard before. "I forced myself to forget about the times you would see them when you were little." My mother offers a weak smile.

Stephanie, Peter and I are staring at her, holding our breath. "Go on," I encourage.

My mom fidgets with the buttons on her blouse, looks off in the distance, clearly uncomfortable. "It happened mostly when we were out of the house. Something would catch your attention, something that your father and I couldn't see. You'd follow it with your eyes and you'd lock onto whatever you were communicating with. You seemed to be listening intently, because you'd laugh or cry or remain fixated on what was in front of you. When you could walk, you'd run after your imaginary friend. Then when you were five or six, I'd often hear you talking to someone beside you, someone who could only be seen by you."

As my mother recounts part of my childhood, I vaguely remember having a lot of "friends" appear out of nowhere—some kids, some adults. I even had a golden retriever follow me around for a week. "I remember," I reply with surprise in my voice. "I definitely viewed them as friends."

"And all children have imaginary friends," my mother points out. "I figured you were no different. But when Uncle Bill died and you were telling me things he said, things you couldn't have possibly known, I began to realize it wasn't a phase."

"Why didn't you tell me this before?"

"I thought it went away." She shrugs. "You had just turned eight and almost overnight you didn't seem to be distracted anymore. It's like you stopped noticing things that weren't there."

"I was eight?"

My mother nods. "We were living in Chicago."

"I was in third grade," I add, suddenly recalling the layout of my homeroom class. We had five rows with five school desks in each row facing the blackboard and the teacher's desk. I sat in the row closest to the large picture windows, which ran the entire length of the room. And that was where I saw him.

"Did something happen to you I don't know about?" my mom asks.

I think back on the winter days and how I loved to watch the snow fall. It helped me to forget that my parents were fighting a lot, and that I didn't have many friends at school.

There was one day in particular that stood out from the rest. It was still morning, third period, when the snow began to fall faster— so fast that I could no longer see the playground. Someone from the principal's office made an announcement that school had been cancelled for the rest of the day, and the classroom erupted in hoots and hollers. Everyone hurried to put on their coats and mittens, stored by the door, and as I was zipping up my coat I saw a boy my age, staring into the window. He had blue lips and hollowed eyes, and he was fixated on me.

I screamed, and all the kids turned around and glared at me. I pointed to the boy who wasn't going away, but no one saw him, or they pretended that they didn't see him. They all laughed at me and called me a freak, and I was sure they were playing a cruel trick on me.

From that point on, I refused to look at anything I saw out of the corner of my eye, and if I did see someone or something supernatural, I pretended it wasn't there. I completely shut down my ability—until, of course, my time at camp.

"I saw a ghost at school and was teased about it," I finally reveal to my mom. "I think that's when I started to block them out."

"I wish I had known," my mother says, empathy in her voice. "I could have helped you."

"How?" I question. "Can you see them too?"

"No, but the psychic gene runs in the family."

My eyes quickly dart to my sister. "Not me." Stephanie shakes her head. "Though I wish I were psychic. It would be so cool."

"It isn't," I tell her, still feeling the sting from my homeroom class laughing at me. "It's the complete opposite."

Stephanie turns her attention to Mom. "How come I'm not psychic like Talie?"

"I don't know," my mom simply answers. "But I think it's because you don't have deep blue eyes. For whatever reason, those who have deep blue eyes in our family are the psychic ones."

Peter instantly takes a picture of me before I can protest, then studies it. "Whoa! Your eyes look violet! That's freaky, Natalie."

"No, it's not," Stephanie retorts. "The actress Elizabeth Taylor had deep blue eyes which often photographed as violet."

"Hey, you know, you kind of look like her," Peter notices, eyeing me. "Same color eyes, same color hair...."

Stephanie gasps. "Nana has deep blue eyes and she reads people's fortunes!"

"Seriously?" I look at Stephanie. "Something else you haven't told me?" I glare at my mother.

"When you were growing up, your grandmother kept her fortune-telling under wraps. Only now, she talks a lot about it to her friends in the home, and will give someone a reading if they ask."

"Yeah, if you visited her once in a while, you'd have known about her sixth sense," Stephanie chides me.

My sister's been going along with my mom whenever she visits my nana, who recently moved into assisted living. At first, I thought Stephanie had finally grown out of her selfish phase until I learned that my nana's place is five minutes from a cheap but lavish spa my sister often frequented when she had a full-time job. Now my mother and

Stephanie make a day of it—a visit with Nana, followed by a light lunch and a spa treatment.

"If I wasn't out searching for a job instead of still living at home like you, I would," I throw back.

"I don't need a job anymore. I'm in a band."

"On the weekends. What about the other five days of the week?"

"Girls, please," Mom interrupts.

I take a breath, settle down, and realize I need to clarify why I haven't visited Nana. "Listen, Mom, I tried to visit Nana, but I couldn't get past the front door."

"It's not a depressing place like you think it is. She's happy there."

"That's not the reason."

"Ghosts?" Peter asks with wide eyes.

I nod, looking away, recalling my first attempt to see her. It was a few months ago, when she had first moved in. I had parked in the visitor's parking, walked into the lobby, and saw so many spirits it looked like a Halloween convention. I immediately turned around and ran back to the car before any of them knew I could see them.

"Okay, so maybe it's more depressing than we can see," Stephanie offers, "but Mom is right. Nana doesn't mind being there because she's made a lot of friends and she's the center of attention."

"I'll go see Nana tomorrow."

"She'd like that," my mom says.

"So, I guess this means you're not bananas after all," Peter remarks.

I smirk at him as Stephanie's face lights up. "Wait a minute! Why aren't you using your gift to make money?"

I'd asked myself this very question hundreds of times. So many people were making a living as an intuitive or a psychic medium, why wasn't I? It's not like I feared I wouldn't be able to connect with the spirits. To my knowledge, I connected better than most. While some mediums explained how they could only get a sense or a feeling, or maybe hear one word or one phrase from a spirit, I was having complete conversations with them. I could hear and see every spirit I came into contact with—loud and clear.

And maybe that's why I hadn't fully acted on it. As it was, they were making contact with me at work, at home, when I was getting a physical, of all things. If they bombarded me this much now, what would happen if word got out that I was officially open for business?

"I don't know how to turn it off," I finally answer my sister. "And frankly, I don't want to be seeing dead people every second of the day."

"So, maybe Nana can teach you how to control it," Stephanie suggests.

"I thought she just read tarot cards."

"Nana does that for fun," Stephanie clarifies. "But her true gift is much more complicated. She knows what people are going to say before they say it. She knows who's going to pass away a few days before they do. She knows who's coming to visit, and I'm not just talking about those of us who are alive."

I shake my head, a little stunned to hear all this. "Why did you keep this from me?" I ask, my eyes shifting from Stephanie to my mom.

"Well, I wouldn't have, had I known that seeing the deceased was the reason you haven't been able to hold down a job."

"Or why you hardly have any friends," Stephanie adds.

"Thanks for the reminder, Steph."

"Hey!" Peter interrupts. "Can you predict the lottery numbers? It's up to ninety mill."

"I see dead people. I don't see the future."

"That blows." Peter slouches, then suddenly stiffens. "Are there any here now?"

"No, I made sure all previous tenants had moved out before I moved in."

Peter lets out a relieved breath.

"You definitely need to have a long talk with Nana," my mother insists. "At the age of eighty-eight, she has finally embraced who she is. It's time you did the same."

Chapter 3

———•———

*M*y ghost intervention turned into telling ghost stories for the rest of the night. It was a lot of fun for me but creeped out my sister and Peter when they realized the female ghost who appeared in their room at the Hotel del Coronado in San Diego was probably real and not a figment of their imaginations brought on by heavy drinking.

When everyone left at around eleven, it was then I realized I hadn't heard from Dean. He always sends me a text when he's out of town. If he wants to talk, he sends me an email with a lot of I love yous and smiley faces to which I then pick up the phone and call him. Lucy was the first to point out that he never calls me. It is a little strange, but I think it has to do with his therapy and trying to break his neediness patterns.

I refresh my email, but nothing comes over. It's so unlike him that I really should call to make sure he's okay. I grab my phone and dial his cell.

Dean answers on the third ring. "Hello?"

God, he sounds like he's half dead. "Are you okay?"

He hesitates, but then finally says, "Yeah."

"You don't sound okay."

"I'll be back in town tomorrow night. We can talk about it then."

"How about we talk about it now?" I ask, a little guarded, wondering if he's been afflicted with another phobia I'll have to adjust to.

Dean lets out a long, troubled sigh. "Why did you keep this from me?"

I stay neutral, knowing for a fact that my ghost communication is the only thing I've kept secret—that and the bite-sized Snickers bars I have hidden in the back of my pantry. "Can you be more specific?"

"I know." His tone is filled with shame and despair.

I feel like screaming at this point, but I know it will accomplish nothing. "What are you referring to?" I ask in a gentle, even voice.

"Your appearance on *World's Weirdest Hobbies.*"

There is NO WAY he could have seen the clip. "You watch *World's Weirdest Hobbies?*"

"Don't be ridiculous," he retorts. "You remember Clive?"

"Yeah, he works with you."

"Right, well Clive can't go fifteen minutes without looking at his phone. After he reads his email, he checks out the latest cat videos on YouTube and when he's done with that, he sees what's trending. Apparently, Ed Cummings is trending because he went postal on a guest. Imagine my surprise when, in between meetings, Clive informs me that Ed's guest was you."

Hmm. This might not be as bad as I think. Sounds to me like Dean is angry because I was on a show he hates, not because I see ghosts. But I must find out for sure. "Did you watch the clip?"

"Enough of it to make me sick. Why did you do that, Nat?"

Okay. That was a little uncalled for. "Unlike you, Dean, I don't have a full-time job. I needed the money."

"You did?" Dean immediately softens. "Why didn't you tell me? I would have given you whatever you needed."

I am stunned by this revelation. I never felt I could lean on Dean, especially when it came to financial issues. I take back all the reservations I've been having about him. "Really, Dean? You honestly would have given me money?"

"Of course, babe. I will always lend you whatever you need, no matter the amount. And no matter how high the interest rates go, I'll only charge you one percent interest."

He didn't just say that, did he? No. It has to be a joke. I wait for him to break out in laughter. But he doesn't.

"Nat, are you there?"

I finally find my voice. "I tell you I'm having a serious financial crisis and you respond by saying that you'd charge me interest?"

"One percent is nothing, but it is enough to teach a person responsibility."

"You don't think I'm responsible?"

"Nat, it's not your fault. Just look at your family."

"And what's wrong with my family?"

"Nothing. It's just that your mother's divorced, so there's something a little broken there. Your sister's an *artiste*, which is really synonymous with the word loser, so of course I can't blame you. You're surrounded by a bunch of bad role models."

"I can't believe what I'm hearing."

"Nat, this is why I didn't want to talk about it now. This type of conversation is much better served in person."

"Actually, Dean, for your sake, this conversation is better long distance. If you were here, I'd deck you for talking bad about my family."

"I'm sorry," he quickly apologizes. "I mean no disrespect to your family, though with regards to that whole ghost bit, tell me, whose bright idea was that anyway? Stephanie's? Or maybe it was your friend Lucy's. She seems like the type."

"Neither, Dean," I reply tersely. "I actually do see ghosts."

He laughs hard, and when he realizes I'm not laughing with him, he finally stops. "You honestly don't believe that, do you?"

"It's the truth," I say flatly.

"Oh, whoa, whoa," he pipes through the line. "Babe, ghosts don't exist, okay? But there's no need to panic. As you know, I've had my share of dealing with … issues. Help is on the way. I will see to it."

"I don't need to be fixed, Dean. There's nothing wrong with me."

"We'll leave that to the doctor. My therapist, Dr. Hanson, is amazing. She's a god, really. I'll give her a call right now and set something up for tomorrow. I'm there for you, babe. I won't let you go through this alone."

"I'm not going to see your therapist," I say as simply as I can.

"We'll take it slow. Admitting to the problem is the first step, and I can hear you're not there yet."

"I'm not crazy."

"Repeat after me: There is no such thing as ghosts. It really helps to vocalize it. There is no such thing as ghosts."

I let out an exasperated sigh. "I can't do this."

"Sure you can. Look at how far I've come."

"No. I mean I can't be in a relationship with you anymore."

"Nat, I know how scary this is. Seeing ghosts is an extension of the real problem. It's probably some kind of phobia that developed in your childhood, and I know from experience that it can turn your life upside down."

"I don't have a phobia!" I scream. "Except maybe I'm developing one of you."

Silence.

"You don't mean that," Dean tells me in this really small voice.

"I'm sorry." I can't say I didn't mean it because I suddenly realize how much weird crap I've had to put up with from him and how often I make excuses for him. Why do I do that? For what? Okay, there is that little fear—well, actually big fear I have that I will never find someone who will understand and be able to handle my always-open ghost helpline.

"Babe?"

"Dean, I don't like how much of myself I've had to change for you. It's not healthy and it's not fair to you or to me."

"What are you saying, Nat? I hope you're not saying what I think you're saying, because I broke my celibacy for you. Do you know how long it took me to accept your germs? Do you have any idea how much love I have for you in order to be with you? We're meant to stay together."

Oh, wow. This is so out of my comfort zone, way way past seeing dead people. "Dean, I'm sorry."

"And?"

"And nothing."

"Nat?"

You know, I never liked him calling me Nat. It reminds me of gnat and I told him months ago I didn't like it, but he always seems to "slip" when he's angry.

"Look, Dean. Because I love you, I'm going to help you here by telling you something you might not yet understand. Not only do you have a fear of germs and closed spaces and thieves, but you also have a fear of intimacy and in my opinion the only way you're going to overcome that fear is to be intimate with someone ... *anyone* other than me."

"You're not a doctor, Nat. Your advice is absurd."

"Well, why don't you leave that for Dr. Hanson to determine."

"So, you're saying goodbye? You're walking away from me? Just like that?"

"I'm afraid so."

Silence again. And now tears. This is killing me. Dean has always shared with me what's on his mind. He has no fear of telling me his opinions or asking for help when his therapist deems it necessary. I kind of liked that I had a boyfriend who really opened up. But his crying is like no other. It's not a quiet, solemn, manly cry. It's all-out bawling—which is what he's doing at the present moment.

I say nothing—I couldn't if I wanted to because his wailing would just drown me out, so I remain on the line and wait. Five minutes later, he's gotten it out of his system and finally he's done. I still don't say anything because I know what's coming next. The unrepentant anger.

"I hope you get some help, Nat, because YOU REALLY NEED IT!" he screams and hangs up on me.

Even though the anger part was abrupt, it was mercifully short. I sit there for a moment and take in what's happened. I've just ended a co-dependent, nine-month relationship with a guy I thought I loved.

And I've never felt better.

———————

The following morning, I head out to see my nana who now lives about thirty minutes away from me. On the drive over I can't help but review what has happened to me in the last twenty-four hours. They say your life can change in the blink of an eye. Pretty sobering to know a mere few seconds can change a life, but it's true. Ask an Olympic gold medalist or a person who survives a bad car accident, or someone who meets their soul mate because they missed their train by a few seconds. In a way, I guess this is what's happened to me. Those few seconds on national television have forced me to accept who I am. And now all those ghost memories I'd suppressed are finally resurfacing.

The biggest one, of course, was when I'd seen the dead boy outside my classroom window. At the time, I really had thought kids were pulling a prank on me. I remember wondering how they did it, but more importantly, why. Was it because I'd seen an old deceased man one day after school, when I was walking home with my best friend Hannah and I told her about it? I thought she was cool with it. But then she started to ignore me when other kids were around, and later she stopped talking to me altogether. We moved to New Jersey shortly after that, and then to Wisconsin, and I don't have any recollection of seeing anything unusual until that fateful night at summer camp in Minnesota. Now I'm hoping my nana can fill in some of the blanks for me.

I pull up to Willow Creek, my nana's assisted-living retirement home which sits on five acres out in Calabasas. It seems like a decent place to live. The property has a well-manicured lawn with several shade trees, wide walking paths, and plenty of benches and tables to sit and visit with families and friends. The building itself seems fairly new, maybe ten years old. It has a Southern Plantation feel to it, with huge white columns in the front of a grand three-story manor. There's a wraparound porch with rocking chairs and several hanging flower baskets above the railing.

And, of course, there's the dead people. Still. Lingering around— trying to blend in with those who are very much alive, which is really absurd if you could see what I see. One guy is dressed in a red velvet smoking jacket, another man is wearing fireman gear from head to toe, and a young woman has on an old-fashioned bathing suit and swimming cap. Then there are those who don't seem out of place, until you get a closer look at them. Their complexion is a little too grey or a little too white. And some seem to have hollow eyes.

"Okay," I say to myself. "I can do this." I push back my shoulders, hold my head high, and make a beeline for the front entrance. I'm about fifty yards away when an older woman, a deceased older woman, moves up the path to the left of me, and we accidentally make eye contact.

Oh, crap. I falter, and then I'm frozen in my tracks because this woman is now smiling at me, coming over to me, and how can I turn my back on someone who was probably very sweet when she was alive?

"Natalie?"

My head snaps toward the front entrance. "Nana!" I run to her and give her a sorely needed hug. "You have perfect timing."

"I always do." She gives me a knowing smile and pats my hand.

"Nana, I'm so sorry I haven't come to see you. I feel just horrible."

"Well, you're here now, and that's all that matters. Would you like to see my apartment?"

"I'd love to."

I walk slowly with my nana since she uses a cane, but she does so with grace. She was a professional ballet dancer, and because of such rigid training for so many years, she has always maintained good posture and a healthy weight. At the age of eighty-eight, my nana is still gorgeous. We share the same deep blue eyes that run in our family, but with her silver grey hair, Nana's eyes always look violet.

As we walk through the lobby, there is no shortage of spirits. There's a young woman in a blue dress with white polka dots who stares at me, followed by an African American man dressed in a cream-colored three-piece suit. He tips his hat to me as he walks by. I glance at my nana who seems to be wearing a serene, pleasant smile on her face, and I'm not entirely sure if she noticed them. Before I can ask her, we're standing at her front door.

When I step inside, the first thing that hits me is how bright and clean her apartment is, and how it reminds me of a hotel suite since she doesn't have much of a kitchen. Because the residents are required to have all their meals in the main dining room, the apartments are only furnished with a sink, a small refrigerator, a microwave, and a coffeepot.

Nana's living room is nicely decorated with large vases and silk flowers. She has a caramel-colored leather couch with a matching reclining chair, and a flat screen TV. She has two sliding glass doors and a large picture window that looks out onto a peaceful pond lined with willow trees. Down the hallway, I can see her bedroom and bathroom—both easily accessible.

"This is really nice, Nana. Much nicer than I had pictured."

"Yes, and now it has a five-year waiting list."

"Honestly?"

"My friend Doris, who lives across the hall, came to look at this place when it first opened and gave it rave reviews."

"You really like it here."

She nods. "With your grandfather gone now twelve years, I needed a change of scenery."

I follow Nana back into her kitchenette.

"Would you like some tea or coffee? I also have those shortbread cookies you used to devour as a child."

I laugh. "I'd forgotten about those. I just ate, but I could use some water." I help my nana make herself a cup of tea and then we both sit down in her living room. I've always been comfortable talking to my grandmother about anything, but seeing ghosts wasn't a normal topic of conversation. I take a few sips of water, thinking about how I can open the subject.

My nana drinks her tea, then helps herself to one of her shortbread cookies. "I saw you on YouTube last night."

I choke, staring at my grandmother.

"Are you all right, dear?"

I nod, getting control, then I finally say, "Nana, I cannot believe how hip you are."

"What else is there to do in retirement? I read my books on a Kindle, I play blackjack on my computer, and I even hone my motor skills on the video game *Martian Attack* with my friend Florence."

"*Martian Attack?*"

"Women can have fun blowing up aliens too."

I laugh. "Nana, you are an inspiration to all of us."

"Well, I like to be an inspiration and a help, especially to you." She sits back, crosses her legs at her ankles, taking me in. "Your mother told me that your gift is far more advanced than we suspected."

I give her a surprised look. "So, you knew too?"

"You saw your first spirit when you were five months old. I know this because I saw him as well." She offers me a cookie, and this time I accept.

"Nana, how come you didn't tell me or talk to me about this?"

"Your father forbade it. He never believed in anything he couldn't see."

I think about growing up with my dad. He wasn't around much. Being in the construction industry, he often left the house at six in the morning. And when he came home thirteen hours later, he'd still be working. My dad was practical, a problem-solver, and didn't have time for excuses, missed deadlines, or lazy people. My mom divorced him when I was fourteen. It's not that she didn't love him. She just got tired of never seeing him.

"Yeah, I can see Dad saying that. Mom said he was very protective over 'his girls.'" I take a bite out of the shortbread cookie. "How come Stephanie doesn't seem to have any psychic ability?"

"She did at one time," my nana corrects. "All children have a great sixth sense, but most, like Stephanie, grow out of it. When children are told that what they are seeing is their imagination, or that ghosts are as real as the Easter Bunny, it's understandable why so many eventually lose their psychic abilities. Since your sister stopped seeing spirits so early on, your mother and I assumed that's what happened to you."

"I think I blocked it out for a while. But now I see them all the time."

"You can control it. You just have to find your psychic on/off switch." Nana takes a sip of her tea. "Did you notice how those two spirits in the lobby looked at you and not me?"

"So you did see them!"

"I did, but I kept myself closed off to them."

"How?"

"It's a matter of controlling your energy. Think about how you feel when you're walking alone at night and no one is around. You keep your purse tight to your body. You have your keys in hand, and you walk with a purpose to your car, correct?"

"Yes."

"Now contrast that to when you come home from a long day at work. You kick off your shoes, your shoulders relax, and you let down all your defenses."

"That's true. I do."

"Well, it's basically the same thing. If you allow yourself to be open, people will flock to you. If you're depressed or angry, or even indifferent, you will give off the type of energy which will keep people away."

"Makes sense." I brush the cookie crumbs from my fingers onto the plate. "But, Nana, I couldn't possibly be inviting them to talk to me. Not when I spend most of my time trying to avoid them."

My nana studies me for a moment, then says, "Are you constantly wondering if any souls are near you? Are you often thinking about when you will see one next?"

"All the time. How can I not? It seems like all I do is run into one of them at the absolute worst time."

"That's because you are connecting with them. In your efforts to avoid them, you first have to know where they are, so your energy is seeking them out. You've been drawing them to you like a magnet."

I gasp. "No wonder they keep showing up at work! And it's always two to three weeks after I start working. Right around that time, I've settled into the routine of my new job, I feel comfortable and I think, well, a spirit should be showing up right about now to blow this for me."

Nana chuckles. "I used to do the same thing."

"So who else in our family has this ability?"

"Right now, only you, me, and your great-aunt Bonnie."

"Aunt Bonnie?"

"Just try and keep a secret from the woman." Nana makes a small sound of amusement and the look on her face tells me she's tried. "Aunt Bonnie's not a psychic medium like we are," my nana explains, drinking her tea bit by bit. "But she is one of the best intuitives around."

"And she has deep blue eyes," I recall. "What's with the whole deep blue eyes connection, anyway?"

"No idea. Seems whatever gene makes our eyes so blue also makes us extra sensitive to energy."

I take a swallow of my water. "Do spirits and ghosts pester you like they do me?"

"Oh, I don't know if pester is really the right word." She nibbles on another cookie. "If you'd been wandering around, desperately trying but failing to communicate, and then you finally found someone who could help you, would you leave them alone?"

"No, I suppose I wouldn't."

"The poor things are just trying to get a message through to their families. Now, if you want to talk about annoyance," Nana bubbles with a laugh, "let us talk about those left behind."

I share my nana's laugh. "Trying to talk to the living relatives is the toughest part of the job. I once had a guy throw a shoe at me!"

"Oh, dear." She shakes her head, chuckling.

"After that, I found myself dodging spirits and pretending I couldn't see or hear them."

"That will only make their desire to contact you stronger."

"So I've discovered," I grumble.

My nana finishes off her tea and sets it aside. "It's difficult, Talie, to approach the remaining family members, especially the skeptics, which is why I always ask the spirit to tell me something that is not public knowledge, so the family has proof I'm not making it up. With your lovely smile and your kind, gentle disposition, I've no doubt that people will eventually warm to you."

I spend another two hours talking to my nana. She says I shouldn't fight it. If I give in to my ability, my life will run so much smoother.

As my nana takes me through the lobby again, I pull in my energy as she's instructed me to do and it works! Not one spirit takes notice of me. "You seem to have an unusually high number of spirits hanging around here, Nana."

"Well, when you get to be my age, you lose a lot of friends to the Other Side. Some choose to remain here until the loved ones they left behind pass away too. Do you see that man over there?"

I look over and see a short, thin man, probably in his nineties, with a full head of white hair, standing behind a woman who also looks to be in her nineties. "Is he her husband?"

"Brother. He passed three days ago, and her daughter is coming to tell her."

I watch a dark-haired woman, my mom's age, enter the lobby and make her way over to the woman.

My nana gestures to the young woman by the window who looks to be from the 1920s. "The flapper is Mrs. Evans' younger sister, and the man standing next to her belongs to Mr. Podolsky."

I turn and see a man wearing all purple with a flower coming out of his top hat. "Whoa. Who was this guy?"

"Not was, is. That's Mr. Bauman and he's off his rocker." My nana walks me out. "Call me anytime with questions and please come see me more often."

I give Nana a big hug and kiss. "I will, Nana, thank you."

Chapter 4

I am definitely walking a few inches taller. I can't believe that in a matter of minutes, my nana was able to teach me how to lower my spirit antenna. I shake my head in disbelief when I think about all the years I've been suffering. Now that I'm able to control the communication, I might not mind having it. Maybe now I can find a good, decent job and actually be able to keep it. Maybe I can live a normal life, and maybe, just maybe I'll be able to meet someone who'll understand.

Feeling euphoric for the first time in ages, I decide to drop in on my best friend—especially since I know she's going to flip out when she hears the news about my break-up with Dean.

Lucy and I have known each other for close to eight years now. We went to UCLA together but didn't get to know each other until we were both talked into being hand models at a cosmetology convention over a long weekend. We ended up sitting next to each other in the same booth for ten hours each day and hit it off immediately.

Even though I consider Lucy to be my best friend, she doesn't know about my exceptional communication skills. I was going to tell her, about a month ago, when one very animated spirit wouldn't stop talking to me while I was trying to carry on a conversation with her. I broached the subject of ghosts, and she quickly dismissed it, saying that ghosts were as real as the earth was flat. Needless to say, I wasn't going to lose yet another friend over trying to convince her of their existence. But now, with the YouTube video and Dean's refusal to believe I can speak to the dead, it's time to let Lucy in on my secret that's not so secret anymore.

I finally arrive at Lucy's apartment and push the buzzer. There's a loud crackle over the intercom before I hear, "Yes?"

"Hi, Lucy, it's Natalie."

"Hey! Come on up."

I take the stairs to the second floor, knock on the door, and wait. I can hear Lucy and another female speaking Chinese loudly. I'm about to knock again, assuming she can't hear me, when she cracks open the door.

"Bad timing?" I ask.

"Never. But my grandmother's here. She's uh … superstitious, so don't be offended."

Before I can ask Lucy what she means, a very short, tiny woman yanks open the door and stands next to Lucy, glaring at me. "What happened? Have you been whistling or walking under trees at night?"

I crinkle my brow in confusion. "I'm sorry?"

The little woman pushes past Lucy and waves her finger at me. "You should never clip your nails at night, either. Best way to attract spirits."

Lucy says something to her in Mandarin, which spurs on another excited exchange, until Lucy finally says, "I will. I'll tell her. Don't worry, Grandma. Go rest. I'll be back soon, and then we'll go see a movie. Okay?"

Even though I don't speak Mandarin, I know Lucy's grandmother has agreed to the plan. The tiny woman again glares at me suspiciously, as Lucy grabs her handbag and keys then shuts the door.

"What was that all about?" I ask as we head down the stairs and out the door.

"She's lived all her life in Taiwan. The Taiwanese can be very super-stitious. She thinks you're attracting ghosts."

"Why does she think that?" I ask innocently, even though I already know.

"Well, we were about to eat dinner last night," Lucy begins as we walk down the street, "when one of my grandmother's friends sent her a video clip of her favorite show *World's Weirdest Hobbies*. Wondering what was captivating my grandmother's interest, I took a look for myself and screamed when I saw you. I told my grandmother we were friends, and she became very concerned for you. Since she's convinced everything on that show is real, now she thinks you're haunted." She gives me a sideways glance. "So, why didn't you tell me you were going to be on TV?"

"Oh, uh … well, because of the show's theme," I say, watching her closely.

"Ghosts? That clip was hilarious." She laughs, and we walk into Café Latte. "Though it didn't look like the show's host was in on the joke."

Great. Lucy thinks the show was staged. "It wasn't a joke," I quickly amend before I lose my nerve.

"I think the host will agree with you." She chuckles, misunderstanding me. "He wasn't at all happy about being punked. You know, you're very photogenic," Lucy says, changing the subject.

"Thanks," I reply. "So what was your grandmother saying to me about walking under trees and whistling?"

"Oh, they're just old Chinese superstitions. Some people believe you shouldn't walk under trees at night because that is where ghosts hang out. If you whistle at night, you will attract them and they will follow you around."

If Lucy only knew…. I force a laugh as we get in line.

"Yeah. A little far-out, right? I told my grandmother to stop worrying, that *World's Weirdest Hobbies* is a show all about sensationalism, and that they hire non-actors like you and me to read from a script."

"I didn't read from a script," I tell her.

"No, you obviously didn't." Lucy's eyes widen. "Guess that's why the host attacked you."

Grr. She's not getting it. How am I supposed to convince her that I see ghosts when I revealed it on a show which has no more credibility than a tabloid magazine? I mull this over as Lucy and I order our coffees. We grab them when they are ready and sit outside at a table by the front door.

Lucy pops the top off her coffee. She adds sugar, stirs, then clicks the top back in place. "So, what were you doing on that silly show anyway?"

Say it. Just blurt it out. Do it! I open my mouth. *Crap. I can't.* "I needed the money," I say instead. "I'm unemployed again."

"Oh, Talie, I'm sorry." Lucy has true concern in her voice. "What happened this time?"

A window cleaner who'd been dead over a year was still showing up for work. "Oh ... uh ... I cc'd the wrong people in an email," I quickly throw out. "But it doesn't matter now. I have much more interesting news."

Lucy stops sipping her coffee and gives me her undivided attention. "Dean and I broke up."

"What?" A huge smile takes over her face. "Finally!"

If anyone else had reacted like this, I would have been really hurt, but Lucy's very straightforward. She's smart, practical, cares deeply for her friends and family, and has a protective streak in her that can sometimes be misread.

"You disliked him that much?"

"No," she says backpedaling, then she stops herself. "Yes, I did. I'm sorry, Talie, but Dean was so wrong for you."

"I know." I give off a half sigh, half laugh. "It took me a while to admit it, but he was."

She's now glued to me. "So, what finally did it?"

"He saw the same video clip you saw and completely freaked out."

Lucy sits back, rolling her eyes. "So typical of him. Let me guess. He hates those types of shows, feels he shouldn't be connected to them in any way, which means you cannot be connected to them. Am I close?"

"Shockingly close," I reply, opting not to tell her the entire truth. It would be too awkward if she were to have the same reaction as Dean. "He said I should have come to him for money instead of going on that show."

She gawks at me. "Mr. Tightwad would have loosened his purse strings?"

"Oh, sure," I say enthusiastically. "He told me he would have lent me the money with one percent interest."

"No way!" Lucy's jaw drops open. "He wanted interest?"

"Yup."

Lucy bursts into uncontrollable laughter. And I can't help but laugh along with her. It really does sound so absurd and I can't believe I made excuses for him for so long.

Lucy wipes her eyes, trying to get control of herself. "I can't wait to tell Matt. He's just going to die."

"So Matt's not a fan, either?"

"Matt told me he had more fun getting a root canal than talking to Dean at dinner."

"Why didn't you guys tell me?" I ask, a little exasperated.

"Because you seemed to be in love with him. You excused his bad behavior all the time, so we knew you saw it, but for whatever reason you chose to ignore it."

"I know. I did. I'm sorry." I take a swallow of my coffee.

"Why *did* you choose to ignore it?"

I'm not ready to tell her I felt so abnormal seeing spirits that I didn't feel like I could judge Dean's abnormal behavior. "I don't know," I answer instead. "I haven't had the best track record with boyfriends. I guess I feared if I broke up with Dean, I would end up being alone forever."

"Oh, Talie, you are not going to end up alone, so get that out of your head right now. My prediction is that you will end up with someone far better than Dean."

"Thanks."

Lucy giggles to herself.

"What?"

She shakes her head. "I was just picturing Matt. He said if Dean asked you to marry him, he'd tackle you in the church aisle and not allow you to go through with it."

I smile. "I'm glad I have friends like you, especially since I think I'm one of those women who gravitate toward emotionally wounded guys."

"We've all done it. As you know I did. Remember Terrance?"

I groan. "That guy couldn't tell the truth if his life depended on it."

"Well, once you meet a normal guy, you'll never go wounded again."

I laugh. "Yeah, I have to say Matt's pretty awesome."

"My grandmother even approves of him, and she didn't approve of my own father."

"Nothing like getting her seal of approval," I reply. "Of course, what's there not to like about Matt? I sure wish he had a twin brother."

"Well, he does have a new tenant, Ryan, living in the other half of his duplex. Cute. Single. Funny." She slurps her coffee.

"Funny is good. How cute?"

"Very."

"Then why is he single?"

"Because he just moved here from Florida."

"Oh, really." My brow rises. "Wait. What am I thinking? As much as I'd like to forget about Dean as fast as I can, I really should take time to decompress."

Lucy nods, agreeing, but then I see the cogs in her mind turning. "Okay, how about this? My grandmother's leaving tomorrow to go visit my brother in New York. I'm thinking about having a small dinner party Friday night, if you're available. I'll invite Ryan, and if you two hit it off, great. If not, well, then there's no pressure."

"Sounds like fun, as long as this isn't a blind date in disguise."

"Talie, I told you after loser Harrison that I wasn't going to help you with your love life anymore, and I meant it, so just relax. Like I said, no pressure." She peers at me over her coffee cup.

I take a deep breath, considering. "I could use no pressure for a while."

"Great," Lucy punctuates as if the whole thing is settled. "I wish I could stay longer, but if I leave my grandmother alone too long, she will feng shui my entire place."

I laugh. "Plus you've got to take her to that movie you promised her, though I'm guessing you won't be seeing a scary one."

"A romantic comedy is more her speed. She has three boyfriends waiting for her back home."

"Seriously?"

"What are we going to do with our older generation?"

I laugh, shaking my head.

"I'll call you tomorrow."

As I watch Lucy head back to her apartment, I finish off my coffee, debating whether or not to order another one, when the lifeguard spirit suddenly materializes in front of me. I jump, a little startled.

Because I've been in this situation before, I take out my cell phone, lay it on the table, then I put on my Bluetooth headset, so people around me will think I'm talking on the phone instead of talking to myself—or worse, a dead guy.

"Take the job," my dead hunky lifeguard demands.

"Excuse me?" I study his face—hazel eyes, prominent chin, full lips. "Are we related somehow or are you one of my spirit guides?"

"Neither."

I look away and see two guys the next table over eyeing me. I shift in my chair, turn my back on them, and lower my voice.

"I need you to take the job," he says to me, a little desperate, and I can only assume my near-future employment will allow me to finish whatever he's left unresolved.

"I'd love to take any job," I confirm, "but none has been offered."

The hunky lifeguard vanishes just as my cell rings. I quickly glance over at the two guys who are now giving me really strange looks since my cover of being on the phone has just been blown. I get up, answer my cell, and walk down the street.

"This is Natalie."

"Hi, Natalie. This is Adam Reed with Finch Productions. Ms. Finch would like to set up a meeting with you."

"Regarding...."

"The reality show."

He couldn't possibly be talking about the ghost reality show, could he?

"Are you still there?"

"Yes, sorry. Uh. I'm free tomorrow."

"How's eleven o'clock?"

"I'll be there." I disconnect the call and walk back to my car.

Could Carolyn Finch seriously be considering doing a reality show with me? *No, that's ridiculous.* This meeting has to be about *World's Weirdest Hobbies.* By now, Zephyr has worked out the "story behind the story," which means I'll have to be part of it somehow. I guess I could go along with whatever they've concocted—as long as it doesn't make me look more like a freak than I already am.

———◆———

At eleven o'clock sharp, I enter Finch Productions. I actually arrived fifteen minutes earlier, hoping Hunky Spirit would appear and explain if this job was the one he was referring to, but he never returned. Not that it really mattered. I had to assume that this meeting was only going to procure a one-day job, most likely involving me in a studio, reading off some script which would logically explain why Ed tried to strangle me.

I check in with the receptionist, then sit down in the lobby. The phone is ringing off the hook, and I can see a group of people behind a glass-enclosed conference room. I close my eyes to see if I can feel any spirits near me, one in particular, but everything seems "normal."

"Natalie?"

I open my eyes to see Carolyn Finch towering over me. I quickly stand. "Ms. Finch."

"Call me Carolyn. Come on back."

First name basis? This is a good sign. I follow her down the office corridor lined with framed one-sheets of her past hit shows. Her earlier projects had been sitcoms, but her recent ones are either talk shows or reality series. *World's Weirdest Hobbies* has only been on the air one year, though I imagine they'll never run out of material.

We finally reach the biggest office at the end of the hallway and walk inside. "Sit," Carolyn commands as she moves around her desk.

I take a seat, happy to see that no one else is in the room—living or dead.

"My staff has done quite a bit of digging on your background." Carolyn shuffles through a stack of papers. "You've had over twenty jobs in the last sixteen months. You were a receptionist for an insurance company, but you were fired when several employees complained about your strange behavior. You delivered the mail for a technology corporation downtown, until your boss caught you talking to a wall. You worked in a local paint store, but were repeatedly having conversations with yourself, and last month you were a salesperson at a greeting card store in the mall, where co-workers would often see you violently gesticulating to thin air in the storeroom or when you were on break." Carolyn meets my gaze. "More ghosts?"

No doubt Carolyn's attorneys and Zephyr will be holding a press conference where they'll explain how I've been unstable my entire life, and then they'll provide testimony from all these former employers who can back up their claims. And then a far worse thought occurs to me. *Will they demand I return the eight hundred dollars?*

I clear my throat, pushing down the fear. "As I said before, Ed insisted I reveal the information I was being given. I never intentionally set out to make him look bad."

Carolyn stares at me like I'm clueless, which apparently I am. "I'm not talking about what happened with Ed. I thought I made myself clear the other day. My interest in you is for a possible reality series."

I scoot forward in my chair, certain I'm not hearing her correctly. "You mean the one you mentioned off-the-cuff?"

"Yes, of course." She sits back, studying me. "Why else would you be here?"

"I thought maybe I was supposed to help fix Ed's damaged reputation."

Carolyn laughs hard. "He no longer has a reputation."

I am so confused. She couldn't possibly be thinking about creating a reality show for me. Could she? I slump in my chair, shaking my head, at a complete loss for words.

"Natalie, I guess you don't know about *my* reputation, but when I make a decision, it's a done deal. There is no second chance for Ed. And when I told Darren Zephyr to look into creating a ghost hunter reality show involving you, I meant it."

"You're serious. You're actually considering working with me?"

"Why not? Ed's gone, *World's Weirdest Hobbies* is going on hiatus, and most importantly, the Paranormal Network is looking for new content."

I truly want to believe Carolyn—that she's offering me an amazing opportunity, but it seems too easy. There has to be a catch. "There are hundreds of psychics, mediums, and intuitives who would die for the chance to have their own show. Why would you want to risk your reputation on someone like me?"

"What risk?" Carolyn clicks her pen impatiently as if we've gone over this a hundred times. "You already have a following, and we already have the first episode."

I give her a look of utter confusion, and then the light bulb goes off. "Oh no. You mean me with Ed?"

"Nothing like putting the raw truth out there." Carolyn swivels back and forth in her leather chair with a satisfied look on her face.

I pin her with a scrutinizing glare. "This is a real job offer."

Carolyn stares at me—her expression dumbfounded. "Have you not gone onto Facebook or YouTube?"

"I told Mr. Zephyr I wouldn't."

Carolyn dramatically throws her hands in the air. "No wonder you're a little slow. To tell you the truth, Zephyr talked me out of my reality series idea about ten minutes after you left his office," she confides. "But then later, something happened."

Carolyn grabs a remote control sitting on her desk and aims it at a TV monitor. "I was watching the playback again with my assistant. Of course I was watching Ed, but Adam was watching you, and he noticed something very strange."

The monitor turns on next to me with a blank screen. She hits a few buttons on the remote and my interview with Ed begins to play.

"Here's your reaction to the ghost, I mean spirit, appearing to you." Carolyn points to the screen, even though I can clearly see my reaction for myself. "Now, look at what's happening in front of you."

I lean in and spot a few orbs of light that suddenly appear. Then a very light, smoky, transparent image begins to take the shape of a man. I gasp. "You caught him! That's Wilson Gooding!"

"Adam caught it too. He immediately took to tweeting, only to discover that others had already noticed it."

My eyes are transfixed on Carolyn's monitor. "Oh my God."

"Is this strange mist what you saw?" she asks, curiosity peaking. "Is this how he appeared to you?"

"No, I actually saw him with the same detail that I see you. I could make out his clothes, his facial expressions." I continue to watch the whole scene play out. "But this is incredible!" The video ends and I lock onto Carolyn. "You have evidence of the paranormal."

"Not really." She sighs. "At least, not according to all the paranormal debunkers out there."

"What do you mean? He's right there!" I gesture to her monitor, suddenly finding myself enraged at the thought.

"He's also appearing on a controlled production set with a studio audience, and the topic of the day happens to be ghosts."

"Please tell me you're kidding. You have proof, real proof. How can anyone refute this evidence?"

"The skeptics and the debunkers are saying we faked it." She shrugs. "Can you blame them? We are filmmakers, after all, with high-tech equipment, directors, and editors. If this hadn't come out of my own studio, I would have assumed it was fake as well." Carolyn leans in, laces her fingers together. "But the good news is that the believers outweigh the non-believers four to one—hence your new fan club." She relaxes back, stretching her arms behind her head with a confident smile.

I rub my forehead. "Four to one?"

"A fairly high number when you consider the massive volume of hoaxes these days. Then again, everyone's intrigued by a good mystery, and good mysteries are great for ratings. Just look at how many shows have been devoted to Bigfoot and UFO sightings. There's no question that people want to know more about this clip, and that's exactly what we're going to do with the pilot. We can have you narrate the episode, tell the folks out there watching exactly what you saw. We can even have you undergo a lie detector test, and then we'll bring on experts—those highly respected in the parapsychology field, as well as special effects technicians who can deny any claims that the ghost image we captured was in any way fabricated. We can make this an amazing pilot for a new series dealing with the supernatural." Carolyn gasps, inspiration striking, and slaps her hand down on the desk. "We'll call it Super Natalie!"

"Super Natalie?" Could this really be happening? Could I finally have a chance to explain to people that I'm really not crazy? If I agreed to do this series, I wouldn't have to be embarrassed anymore. I wouldn't have to come up with lies to cover up my odd behavior. I'd finally be able to embrace who I am.

"Have you ever wondered why you have this gift, Natalie? Maybe you haven't been able to hold down a typical job because a ghost hunter-type series is what you're really supposed to be doing for your career."

I think back on what the Native American spirit at camp had said to me about this being my purpose in life. It would certainly explain my lack of interest in any particular field. And, of course, I can't help but wonder if this is the job Hunky Ghost wanted me to take. "Is that how it happened for you as a producer?"

Carolyn smiles. "You tell me. You're the psychic."

"Psychic medium," I correct, "which means that even though I'm slightly more intuitive than the average person, most of my ability pretty much rests with the dead—so to speak." I study Carolyn who seems so sure of herself, so in control of everything. I'm clearly not a mind reader since she would have been the last person I'd have thought was interested in the paranormal. "So, do you truly believe in the supernatural, or do you believe in it for ratings?"

Carolyn breaks out with a loud laugh. "You and I are more alike than I realized." She gets quiet a moment or two before she says, "I lived in a haunted house when I was a kid. Back then, it was a taboo subject, but I would have given anything for some paranormal group to come in and get rid of the disturbances."

"Did you live there long?"

"Three years." She fixes her eyes on me. "My two brothers, my mom and I were convinced there was something paranormal going on only weeks after we moved in, but it took my father a lot longer to come around."

"Did something happen to convince him of it?"

"An entire shelf of books came flying at him, one by one."

"That would do it for me," I say with a light laugh. "And now you are left with wanting answers."

"Like I said, mysteries intrigue everyone."

"Is that the way you'd like to present our show, as a mystery?"

"Partly. I'd like to provide probable theories if not concrete evidence. I also want this to work on a visceral level. I want people to experience this the way you and I have. I'm thinking documentary-style, one camera, your perspective, which will also be the audience's perspective, and of course that will also make it scary."

"Like *Blair Witch*."

"Exactly!" She slaps the desk again. "I know we will scare a lot of people, namely those who already believe in ghosts, but I hope we can also be taken seriously."

I think back on all the jobs I've lost and how I thought by being honest with my employers, that they'd understand. Of course, it didn't happen that way. "Or we can end up being a laughing stock," I throw out.

"We might be, but remember, we are not forcing people to tune in. Those watching our show must at least question the existence of ghosts, if not believe in them entirely."

"I never thought of it like that."

"Natalie, this could be a really good show. I'm excited about this, and I'd love for you to join me."

I smile, shaking my head, still not believing what I'm being offered. "I've been embarrassed, ridiculed, shunned, and labeled crazy because I can see spirits. It can't get any worse for me, and maybe I can change this misguided perception. "Yes," I finally answer. "I'd love to work with you."

"Wonderful!" She beams. "I'll have your contract drawn up this afternoon. Come by anytime tomorrow and we'll get you squared away." Carolyn stands and shakes my hand. "Welcome aboard, Natalie."

Chapter 5

———◆———

Only minutes after I leave Carolyn's office, I wonder if I shouldn't continue with my employment search. Offers can fall through. What if Carolyn thinks she has final say, but there's someone else above her who rescinds her offer to me? What if they call me tomorrow and say, "Just kidding. We were seeing how psychic you were, and the joke's on you. There is *no* job!"

I pull out my phone and look up my interview on YouTube. Over a million views! It really has gone viral. That's just crazy. Then again, I'm sure it's because Wilson Gooding was captured on film. Not to mention the fact that a TV host went mental on me. *Doesn't Carolyn know that I'm not really the one who's creating this frenzy?*

But back to the financial part of this. Carolyn said I'd be involved with pre-production meetings starting on Monday. Did those meetings come with a paycheck? I knew I'd be getting paid to do a day of voice-over work needed for the pilot, but that was probably a few weeks away since the editor first needed to recut the show. I'd run out of money again by the end of the month. *Crap. I need to get payment clarification.*

I start heading back to the office when my phone rings. I glance at the screen on my phone to see who's calling. It's Lucy, so I answer. "Hey."

"You're still coming for dinner tomorrow night, right?"

"Yeah, what time?"

"Say around seven?"

"Do you need me to bring anything?"

"Just you. See you tomorrow!"

And then Lucy hangs up on me, which is weird because she never calls for a five-second conversation. If there was a contest for who could talk the longest, she'd win hands down. She's a speech therapist. Her entire career is about talking, and believe me, she's really good at it.

No, Lucy purposely cut our conversation short. Something is up. I call her back but get her voicemail, which means she's ignoring me. "Humph." I know her odd behavior couldn't have anything to do with her job because she doesn't work on Thursdays. It could be about her boyfriend Matt, but I get a nagging feeling that it has something to do with me—specifically me and tomorrow night.

As much as I'd like to say that being a psychic medium helps me, it doesn't. Even psychics who strictly rely on their own intuitive abilities don't seem to have any edge over knowing their own future. I'm sure there's got to be some unwritten rule that we all must agree to before being born.

"I'm going to give you an incredible sixth sense," God probably tells us, "on one condition. Well, actually, three conditions: 1.) You cannot see into your own future. 2.) You will never be given the winning lottery numbers, no matter how many times you ask. 3.) You will have to search for your soul mate like everyone else."

I wonder how many psychics truly enjoy having a sixth sense. I mean, what's the fun in knowing the future if it doesn't serve your own self-interests? *Oh, right, there is that be-selfless-and-serve-mankind reason.*

With a sigh, I realize I must stop panicking. I decide to skip going back to the production office, and I give up on trying to figure out Lucy's call. I know I just need to let it go. However, it would be nice to get some advice on this potential new career of mine. And I know exactly who I must see.

———————

It's lunchtime when I arrive at my nana's place. Before I get out of the car, I close my eyes and visualize roots growing out of the bottom of my feet to ground myself. I then put white light around my body for protection. Not that I need protection from any of the sweet souls I might encounter, but it's good practice, and Nana says not all old people are sweet. After I do this, I pull in my energy and step out of the car.

Because it's only a little past noon, I decide to check the dining room before going to her apartment. Sure enough, my nana is sitting at one of the tables with three other residents.

"Now, Margaret," my nana begins in a very authoritative voice, "you need to eat at least half of your green beans and all of your chicken. You're losing weight too fast."

"Oh, Pauline," the older woman huffs, "I appreciate your concern, but I'm fine."

And right away, I see an older gentleman wearing an argyle sweater bending down to talk to my nana. "Tell Margaret that if she doesn't eat, I'll have to divulge all the embarrassing moments she's had over the last fifty years, beginning with her cousin's wedding."

"Her cousin's wedding?" Nana asks.

Margaret lets out a sharp "Oh!" She holds up her shaky hand and feels the air next to my nana.

"Is Gene here?"

"Why yes, he is," my nana declares. "And he says if you don't start eating, he's going to spill all of your secrets."

"I love hearing secrets," the sweet woman sitting next to Margaret says, licking her lips. "Did you know Arnold Sorrento, that nice old man in 205, has been in prison? He robbed a bank back in 1966."

Margaret tuts, then grudgingly eats her green beans.

Suppressing a smile, I touch my nana on the back. "Hi, Nana."

Her face lights up when she sees me. "Oh, Natalie, what a pleasant surprise!"

When I bend down and give my nana a big hug, I notice the older man sitting to the right of her staring at me.

"Pauline, you never told me how gorgeous your granddaughter is," he comments. "You are the spittin' image of the late Elizabeth Taylor, when she was young of course."

"Why, thank you." I smile at the elderly gentleman. "You're the second person who has told me that this week."

Margaret stares at me. "You do look a little like her."

"Must be my eyes," I speculate.

"They're violet," the elderly man observes. "Just like Liz's and just like Pauline's." He regards my nana with affection. "Violet eyes can beguile any man."

Amused, my nana waves him away. "You are the biggest flirt, Marvin, and our eyes are deep blue, not violet."

"They look violet to me," Marvin remarks.

"They are definitely violet," the woman in between Marvin and Margaret adds. "I used to be an interior decorator. I know my colors."

"Well, I'm sure Natalie didn't come all this way to talk about our eye color." My nana wipes off her mouth and pushes back from the table.

"I don't want to interrupt your lunch," I step in.

"I'm finished, dear." She stands and takes hold of her cane.

"How come you don't have to eat everything, but I do?" Margaret asks with a pouty face.

"Because I don't have a deceased husband hovering over me insisting on it."

"Humph!" Margaret exclaims. "That man can no longer tell me what to do."

The spirit named Gene blurts out, "She cheated on her typing exam to get her first post."

"Margaret, eat up," Nana warns. "Gene is telling me something very interesting about your first job as a typist."

Margaret goes red in the face, picks up her fork and doesn't say another word.

"Let's go sit outside," my nana suggests.

We leave her table mates behind, and we slowly start walking toward a side exit.

"I see you've been working on lowering your psychic antenna," my nana observes.

I open the door for her. "I did what you showed me and it seems to be working. Gene didn't see me, and the deceased caretaker we walked past a moment ago didn't seem to take notice of me, either."

We walk around the porch to the back side of the property and sit down on two rocking chairs facing the pond. I watch a family of ducks paddle around.

"You're doing remarkably well." My nana pats my arm. "And if you keep working on directing your energy and focusing your thoughts, you will be more in tune with everything, not just the dead."

I watch the family of ducks suddenly look in my nana's direction, and all at once, they get out of the pond and start waddling toward her. "Oh my gosh, Nana. Are you telepathically talking to them?"

"Haven't tried." She takes out a bag of bread crumbs from her purse and starts throwing the stale bread to the ducks. "They know the routine."

I laugh. "You've got them trained."

She hands me half the bag, stealing a glance at me. "Something's troubling you."

"Is that what you mean about being in tune?" I ask, and she nods. "I wouldn't say I'm troubled, but I'd sure like your advice."

"I'm all ears."

"I've been asked to be on a TV series involving ghost hunting."

She stops throwing the bread and looks at me, her face lighting up. "That's wonderful."

"Is it?" I toss bread to the smallest duck.

"Why wouldn't it be?"

"I don't know. I mean, I'd like to do the show, but what if they ask me to fake it, or what if it turns out terrible? What if I anger a lot of spirits?"

"So it's a reality series, like *Ghost Hunters*?"

"Yes, only it's just me and a handheld camera."

"Sounds exciting." She smiles. "How could they fake that?"

"Oh, they can do a lot of things with special effects or visual effects after it's shot."

"Are you getting a sense from them that they'll want to embellish the truth?"

"The producer doesn't, but I really don't know anyone else." I run out of bread, so I sit back and rock. "I guess I'm just worried that if no ghosts show, they'll either ask me to pretend I see them, or they'll add them in the cutting room to make the show suspenseful."

My nana turns to me. "If ghosts are present in the locations you'll be investigating, I have no doubt you'll make contact."

"Thanks for your vote of confidence."

Nana is quiet for a moment, then, "Will you do something for me?"

"Of course."

"I'm very happy you'll be working with your gift, but this is now a little different. Instead of spirits and ghosts seeking you out, you'll be seeking them. Please make doubly sure you have placed protection around yourself before you step foot on the property. As you know, spirits have already crossed over, but ghosts have not. If they are confused or angry or vengeful, you'll need to keep them at a distance—not to mention the entities who have a much darker nature than the ordinary human who is merely lost."

"You mean demons?"

"Precisely."

"Have you ever encountered them?"

"Yes, and I don't recommend it." She gives off a nervous little laugh. "Leave them to the demonologists."

I stiffen, now worrying about running into darker energy, and my nana picks up on it.

"Have you already had a bad experience with them?"

"Once," I tell her, rubbing my hand over the back of my neck. "I can't say for sure if it was a demon, but I sensed something very dark and very powerful."

"Recently?"

"In high school. Do you remember hearing about a Ross Richardson?"

"I can't say that I do. Was he in the news?"

"Yeah. He was a varsity football player, a straight A student, and had girls clamoring over him all the time. But something happened during our senior year. He started skipping school, missing football practice. He became withdrawn, anti-social. Everyone thought he got into drugs, except for me. I knew it was something else. There was something dark around him. I saw him talking to himself one day, and I could have sworn I'd seen some kind of black mist enveloping him. When I walked past him, he looked directly into my eyes—only it wasn't Ross. It was … I don't know. Creepy. For those few seconds, I felt instantly sick. That night Ross killed his parents. Shot them both in the back of the head while they were watching TV. He claimed he had no memory of it, and I was the only one who believed him because I then knew he had been possessed."

My nana rocks back and forth. "I remember him now. Tragic. With what you're describing, it does sound like he was under the influence of an evil spirit. But you don't have to worry about getting possessed. You already know that no spirit can enter without being invited."

I nod, because I do know this, but it doesn't seem to comfort me much.

"Talie, no need to worry. I have a very good feeling about this show. I imagine you'll be helping lost souls move on, and for those times when you don't encounter any spirits at all, then at least you'll be shedding some light on the possibility of spirits and other dimensions, something I wish people had been open-minded enough to think about when I was in my twenties."

"Did Grandpa believe in things he couldn't see?"

"Oh, Lord, no."

"Really? Even when he knew you could?"

"He didn't want to know about my abilities. I broached the subject one day when he caught me talking to a spirit, and he refused to listen. I started explaining that I had been communicating with a deceased friend of ours, and he flat out cut me off. He said he wouldn't hear of it, and that I'd better keep those loony thoughts to myself or some stranger might have me committed."

"How horrible, Nana. I always thought Grandpa and you had such a close, loving relationship."

"We did. It was a different time then, and your grandfather just couldn't wrap his mind around such a wild concept. He was a good man and still is."

"Have you seen him since he's passed?"

"The day after he died, he came to me, hat in hand, and asked for my forgiveness."

"Oh, Nana, how wonderful. Have you seen him recently?"

"He stops by from time to time."

"Please send him my love."

"I will." She pats my leg. "Now, what's this show of yours called?"

"Super Natalie."

My nana rolls with a laugh. "Quite appropriate. I've no doubt it will be a tremendous success."

The second I wake on Friday morning, I check my cell and find two messages from the show. My stomach drops. *Crap. I knew it. Too good to be true.* I hit my voicemail icon.

"Hey, Natalie. It's Adam over in the production office. Your contract is ready to sign. Come on over when you get a sec."

Really? I quickly hit play on the next message. "Hey, Natalie, Adam again. We have a definite green light and the schedule's been pushed up. Need to hear from you ASAP."

I hop out of bed and dial Adam as I hurry into my kitchen for some coffee.

"Production," someone answers briskly.

"This is Natalie Dalton returning Adam's call."

"Hold please."

A second later, I hear, "Natalie! Thank God. We thought we lost you."

"Why?" I ask, equally curious and confused.

"Well, you didn't answer your phone."

I look at the time on my microwave; it's only eight in the morning. "I turn it off at night."

"Probably shouldn't do that anymore. Hollywood, like New York, never sleeps."

The advantage of having so many jobs is that I'm very good at reading between the lines. No doubt, with my new position, there is no clocking out.

"So, we have your contract here," he chirps. "Do you want me to messenger it or would you like to stop by?"

"I can be there in an hour."

"An hour is great. I'll let Carolyn know you've resurfaced, and she can stop looking for another paranormal investigator."

I stiffen at his words. "She was—"

"Kidding!" He forces a chuckle. "She really wasn't, but definitely keep that phone on," Adam says as more of an order than a suggestion. "Sadly everyone is replaceable in this industry," he admits before he lowers his voice and whispers, "Just look at Ed."

I swallow hard. "Good to know. Thanks for the tip. I'll see you soon."

Thoroughly panicked that somehow I was an unknowing contestant in an odd version of *The Amazing Race* where the psychic who reached the production office first would get the contract, I skip breakfast, take a fast shower and fly over there.

I am immediately sent to legal where I sign a contract for ten episodes at two grand a week! Wow! The contract didn't specify how many hours or how many weeks I'd be working, but I don't care. This will be the most money I've ever made in my life!

As I leave the production office, which is clearly in high gear, I think about what my nana and Carolyn have said to me over the last few days. Maybe being on this series really is my true calling. Like it or not, television shapes our culture. It influences attitudes, opinions, it exposes people to topics not normally encountered in their own personal lives. Some will enjoy our series and believe that what they are seeing is real, and some will find it absurd. But either way, it opens up a dialogue and puts forth the one burning question so many skeptics still seek to answer: Is there life after death?

Even though I'm relieved to have signed a binding contract, it still doesn't alleviate the financial crunch I'll feel before I receive my first check. I let out a loud groan. As much as I don't want to do this, I need to ask my mom for a small loan.

I climb into my car, pull out of the production office garage and head to my mom's. My jaw clenches—a natural reaction when I think back on the one and only time I had to borrow money from her.

I just turned seventeen and for my birthday, she gave me my first credit card. Because my card was really just an additional card added to her account, I swore to her that I would be responsible and only charge what I could afford. I had made a fair amount of babysitting money over the last year—two hundred and twelve dollars to be exact. I was quite certain that nothing I bought would ever be more than that. Of course, that was before London Forbes came into my life.

London was the most popular girl in high school. We'd been assigned as lab partners in biology, and because I ended up doing most

... well, all of the work, I guess she felt like she owed me. So one day after school she asked me if I wanted to hang out with her and her friends, Aubrey and Colette—two equally popular girls.

Feeling friendless most of my life, I jumped at the chance. When I piled into London's car with the rest of the girls, I figured we were going to her house to hang out. But London, Aubrey and Colette all came from rich families. While kids like me were doing homework and chores after school, they were shopping—and that's exactly where London took us.

I knew I couldn't afford anything, but I could at least look, and it wasn't long before I found myself mesmerized by a two-hundred-dollar pair of Kate Spade hot pink pumps. The girls oohed and aahed so much that I had to buy them. London also talked me into a three-hundred-dollar clutch that matched my pumps perfectly, so I couldn't say no.

Needless to say, when my mom saw the bill, she hit the roof. It took me eight months of endless chores to pay her back, and it totally wasn't worth it since a very drunk London threw up on my excruciatingly expensive Kate Spade pumps only hours after I began wearing them.

Shaking off the horrible memory, I pull into my mom's driveway and go inside. "Mom?" I walk down the hallway and into the kitchen. The lights are on, but she's nowhere in sight. Then I hear the start-up to another song coming from the one-car garage located in the backyard.

I head out to find my sister playing with her band. She actually has a really good voice, so I'm not entirely sure why she's decided to scream through most of the lyrics. Maybe it's because her band is all guys and she feels she needs to be more butch, or maybe she thinks it's cool. I don't know. I'm not even old and I find myself agreeing with what my father used to say, "It just sounds like noise to me."

I lean against the doorframe, waiting for them to finish, and with a clash of the cymbals, they are done. "Hey, Steph."

She opens her eyes and sees me. "Oh, hey! How do you like our new song?"

"It's uh … loud."

She comes over. "Yeah, that's what the neighbors say. We're not allowed to play at night anymore."

"Maybe you should try … um … quieter, sexier songs, you know, maybe a blues-type song. You have the voice for it."

"Yeah, maybe," she says. "Have you met my band?"

I look over at the guys. Her scrawny guitarist is shirtless, wearing black leather pants, and her drummer is a pudgy guy with a big stain on his T-shirt and smudged glasses. I don't want to judge, but I just can't see this band being in the Top 40. Ever.

Stephanie gestures to her guitarist. "Antonio, Natalie. Mikey's on the drums."

"Yo." Antonio nods to me.

"Whatup?" Mikey asks.

"Hey. Uh … you sound … wow." I force a smile and quickly turn my attention back to Stephanie. "Have you seen Mom?"

"She went to the store. Should be back any minute. We're having tacos for dinner. Are you staying?"

"Can't. Going to Lucy's. See ya." As I turn to go, Mikey starts playing a tune on a harmonica, which suddenly gives me chills all over my body, like I'm getting a sense of déjà vu or something. I look back at him, and I get this quick visual flash of the three of them in a recording studio. For a moment, I'm frozen. I've never experienced something like this. I wonder if I'm getting more in tune with my psychic abilities like my nana said I would.

"Let me break out my banjo," Antonio says, chiding Mikey.

"You can still kill it," Stephanie says to Mikey, enjoying his riff.

Shaking off the weird moment, I go back inside and find my mom unpacking the groceries. "Need some help?"

"Oh, hi, sweetie." She hands me one of the bags. "Those go in the pantry."

I take the grocery bag and notice that my mom has already poured herself a glass of wine, which means she's had a really bad day."

"I heard you and Nana had a good talk the other day."

I take the instant rice, spaghetti, and cereal out of the bag and place them on the shelf with the other starches. "We did. I stopped by again today. Nana's given me all kinds of great information, exercises and a few books to help me learn as much as I can about the sixth sense."

"Exercises?" my mom asks, curiosity taking over. "What kind of exercises?"

"Oh, you know, how to control my energy better, how to protect myself, how to strengthen my own psychic abilities so that I can receive important information in other ways than from the deceased."

She nods in approval. "Sounds fascinating."

"As Nana reminded me, everyone has a sixth sense including you, Mom. It's like a muscle. If you don't use it, you lose it."

"Well, maybe you and Nana can teach me so I can be prepared for days like today." She finishes unpacking the last bag, opens the cabinet and takes down another wine glass. "Would you like a glass of wine?"

I really don't since I need to get going, but I can't deny my mom. She clearly needs to talk about something. "Sure, but just a half glass. I can't stay long."

My mom pours me a half glass, and we sit down at the kitchen table.

I study her face, which seems troubled and somewhat sad. "What happened?"

My mom inhales deeply and says, "Sherry informed me today that she's downsizing. Because of the sluggish economy, she can no longer afford to have five travel agents working for her, so she's letting three go. Me, Jim, and Marci … the oldest three."

My jaw drops. "The most experienced three." I cannot believe what I'm hearing. "You're her number one agent *and* her best friend!"

My mother takes a large gulp of her wine. "Apparently friendship is overrated."

"Oh, Mom, I'm so sorry. Please tell me she was honorable enough to give you a severance package."

"Enough for two weeks' work."

"That's pretty cold."

She tips her head back and finishes her glass. "Especially since I was the one who kept her in business when all the travel websites sprang up."

"I know you did." I sit back, thinking this through, and then an idea comes to me. "Maybe it's time you started your own travel business. You could do it right from here."

My mom pours herself a second glass, shaking her head in defeat. "I'm a dime a dozen and more importantly, I'm not a web designer."

"You don't need to be." I lean in and take hold of her hand. "You're someone who cares about her job. You're the only person I know who thoroughly researches the places your clients are going. You're a cut above the rest." And then I'm struck with inspiration. "That's what your new travel website should be named—A Cut Above!"

My mother's shoulders slump forward. "Talie, I'm too old to start my own business."

"What are you talking about? You may be in your fifties, but you have more energy than people my age."

She lets out a little laugh. "I sure don't feel that way today. I suddenly feel like I'm eighty."

"Well, you're not," I insist. "You're too good to quit. I bet three-quarters of Sherry's clients stay because of you."

"I am good at research," she humbly admits. "Do you really think I'd get clients if I put up a website?"

"Absolutely. And you can drive people to your site by posting all of your great travel tips and emergency remedies that actually work."

A small smile slowly forms at the corners of her mouth. "It does sound kind of fun, and I wouldn't have a forty-minute commute anymore."

"It could be a great adventure," I encourage her. "And I don't know anyone who enjoys adventures more than you."

My mom suddenly jumps up, runs to her handbag, and pulls out a business card. "I just remembered that I met a nice young man at Starbucks the other day who does web design for a living."

"How perfect is that?" I let out a light laugh.

"Kind of a weird coincidence," she says, staring at the card.

"It's meant to be."

"Thank you." My mom gives me a big hug. "Thank you for being such a great daughter." She pulls back and suddenly gasps. "Oh! Why didn't I think of this before? Be my business partner! You're out of a job, I'm out of a job. We can do this together!"

"Oh, wow. Mom, I'm touched you'd want to go into business with me. Yesterday I would have taken you up on your offer, but I actually have some great news for a change. I landed a job."

"What?" She seems a little deflated but quickly rallies. "When?" she asks excitedly. "What is it? When do you start? Tell me everything." She tops off my wine glass.

I take out cheese from the refrigerator, crackers from the pantry, sit down and begin to tell her all about my new ghost hunter series. Two hours later I leave a mom who is in a great mood. I'm in a great mood too until I remember the reason I went to see my mom in the first place—to borrow money. I obviously couldn't ask under the circumstances. I could have easily asked Stephanie but she never has money, so there was only one person left. My dad.

In spite of the nasty divorce my parents went through, I still have a good relationship with my father. He moved to Arizona eight years ago where he began a new construction company, and he's been doing incredibly well ever since. He's remarried now, to a thirty-one-year-old woman named April, and she seems to spend his money almost as fast as he makes it.

I've never asked to borrow money from my dad, but seeing as how he's very generous these days, he might not mind my asking. At least that's what I'm hoping. I haven't spoken to him in over a month, mainly because I'm embarrassed. It seems like every time he calls, I've just lost another job, and though he's never said he's disappointed in me, I can hear it in his voice.

Of course, this time will be different. I have a job. *But how can I tell him about it?* My dad thinks people who believe in ghosts are idiots and that the paranormal is all a bunch of nonsense. *I'll just leave out the details.* Before I lose my nerve, I dial his cell number.

"How's the hunting going?" he asks me in a very flat tone.

Oh, crap. Does he know? Did he see that viral video like everyone else?

"Natalie, are you there?"

"Yes, hi Dad. I'm here. I was just ... uh ... driving through an area with bad cell service, but I can hear you now."

"Have you found a job yet, or are you still hunting?"

Oh, whew! He meant job hunting. "I actually found a job. Just signed a contract today, as a matter of fact."

"Excellent! What is it?"

"It's uh ... it's with a TV production company."

"Hey, that's great." He sounds genuinely impressed. "Do they produce anything I'd know?"

"Uh ... well, they do reality shows, but what I'll be working on is a new series."

"Does it pay well?"

"Yes, and I have guaranteed work for a minimum of ten episodes."

"Honey, that's fantastic." I hear him melt. "I'm so proud of you. What's your position?"

"I'm actually going to be on camera. I'm like the narrator, or the spokesperson."

"Really!" He laughs with this proud kind of laugh. "I had no idea you were interested in that line of work. When did this happen?"

"I just kind of fell into it. But I think I'm going to like it much more than any of my other jobs. I don't start for a few days and then I won't receive my first check for two or three weeks, which is um ... why I'm calling. I really hate to ask you this, Dad, but can I borrow some money? I can pay you back as soon as I get my first check. It's just this month is a little tough. My car insurance is due and my health insurance has gone up another fifteen bucks a month."

"Of course you can. Whatever you need. I'm just happy to hear at least one of my daughters has a real job in the real world. You need to talk some sense into that younger sister of yours."

"I will."

"Call me later with your bank information and I'll wire you whatever you need."

"Thanks, Dad." And suddenly I really miss him. "When are you going to come for a visit?"

"Maybe we can all get together this Christmas, or better yet, you and Stephanie can come out here and stay as long as you wish."

"We'd love to," I tell him excitedly, though I suspect April won't feel the same. "Thanks again, Dad, and I'll talk to you soon."

Chapter 6

———⋆———

Because I stayed at my mom's an hour too long, I find myself scrambling to get over to Lucy's. I know I'm late but not terribly late. It's twenty past seven when I knock on Lucy's door.

"Hey, Talie!" Lucy greets me with a broad smile before she notices the small bouquet of sunflowers I've brought her. "Oh, they're gorgeous! Thank you!"

I follow Lucy inside, expecting to see her other guests already there, but the place is empty. "Am I the first to arrive?"

"Er ... yeah." Lucy avoids eye contact and hurries into her kitchen. "Wine?"

I nod, following close behind, sensing she's holding back. "What's up?"

"What do you mean?" She gives me an innocent, wide-eyed look.

"You're acting strange. You sounded weird on the phone too."

Lucy quickly cuts to the chase. "Here's the deal." She squares her shoulders, ready to defend herself. "I had planned on having eight for dinner, but four can't make it."

Which leaves.... "Tell me this is not a blind date."

"No! Of course not! No." Her words are flying fast out of her mouth. "Ryan knows he's just meeting you because you are a friend of mine."

I glare at Lucy with narrow eyes. She thinks her calling is match-making, and though she'd like to believe she's good at it, she isn't. Okay, so Lucy had one amazing success story. Her first matchmaking endeavor has recently blossomed into a marriage, but all of her other so-called matches have been … well … more like match misery.

Alisha and Guy made it two dates, Rachel and Zach made it three, but the zinger was Jasmine and Don. Lucy was certain they would totally hit it off, and they did, for almost six months. Then Don had a complete meltdown, confessed he'd been living a lie his entire life, and Don is now known as Donna.

You'd think that such a matchmaking debacle would have deterred Lucy from trying to be Miss Matchmaker.com, but no. It made her all the more determined, so she moved her attention on to single me. She decided to match me with a guy named Harrison, and to be frank, he was a complete ass.

Lucy puts her hands up as if she's trying to shush me, only I'm not saying anything. Okay, so maybe I'm shooting daggers at her with my eyes, but I have good reason to do so.

"Natalie, I know what you're thinking, but Ryan is not another Harrison. I promise. Not even close."

"How could you do this to me?" I admonish her. "Especially since I just broke up with Dean."

"It's because you just broke up with Dean. What kind of a friend would I be if I allowed you to date another guy like that? I've put a lot of thought into this, Natalie, and I've come to the conclusion that you, me, and Matt need to work on this together."

"Since when did my decision on who to date become a group activity?"

"Think of Matt and me as your support team. With us, you can't go wrong, especially having Matt on board. He will see to it that you don't ever date another Harrison or Dean."

I blow out a breath. "Having Matt involved does give me some comfort." I eye my matchmaking friend. "Harrison was worse than Dean. You at least have to admit that."

"He had the potential to be worse. That's all I'll admit to."

My mind instantly flashes back to when I first met Harrison. It was a Friday night, four years ago. Shocking as this sounds, Lucy had arranged for a blind date without informing me. She felt I'd freak out if I knew, especially since Jasmine was still suffering from her dramatic split from Don—I mean Donna.

That night, Lucy suggested we hang out in Old Town Pasadena. The last time we were out there, we'd discovered a great pizza place on Green Street which was cheap and really good. Lucy kept glancing at her watch, saying we had to go, even though it was supposed to be a casual, no pressure, no schedule evening.

As soon as I got to the restaurant, I knew. Harrison "just happened" to be there. I cast a suspicious glance toward Lucy as we joined him.

"This is Harrison," Lucy beamed, introducing us.

I couldn't tell much about him except that he was cute. He had brown, curly hair, a ski jump nose and a tiny mouth. I sat next to him and the conversation between the three of us was pretty easygoing, until....

"So, how do you and Lucy know each other?" Harrison asked me.

"We went to UCLA together."

"Oh yeah?" He seemed a bit surprised. "I went to USC for journalism."

"Cool," I replied. "I was a business economics major."

Harrison let out a snotty laugh. "And how's that working out for you?"

"Fine, thanks," I bristled and shot a look at Lucy who was suddenly avoiding my gaze.

"Well, good for you," Harrison added. "Especially since the hot careers are in technology and engineering. All my buddies are computer systems analysts, biomedical and software engineers...."

"So, why didn't you get a degree in a 'hot career' as you put it, instead of journalism?"

"I'm a people person. I like doing investigations, finding the story. As long as there's corruption and greed in the world, there will always be news."

"And there will always be businesses driving our economy," I remarked with a tinge of disdain to my voice.

After that, I didn't have to worry about fighting with him because I couldn't get a word in edgewise. Harrison was thinking about moving to New York because, after all, he was a serious journalist and not some lightweight, Ken-doll-looking entertainment news reader who reported on nothing but fluff.

I'd like to tell you that things got a little better when Lucy changed the conversation from career to family, but they didn't. Harrison was the brightest of four kids. He was valedictorian of his high school class in San Francisco. He was allergic to cats and dogs, and even if he wasn't, he'd never own anything that could carry fleas. Harrison was interested in marriage but only to a woman who would give him no less than six children. According to Harrison, his genes were too good to go to waste. And to top it off—Harrison was a major skeptic when it came to anything paranormal, so no ghost-believer there.

An hour later, I was exhausted listening to the guy talk about himself, and I insisted Lucy come with me to the bathroom. "Lucy, I love you, but you need to end this nightmare date nicely or I'll end it Clint Eastwood-style."

"You're packing a gun?"

"No," I said, rolling my eyes. "But if I had one, I might be forced to use it just to put him out of our misery."

"I'm so sorry," Lucy's apology spilled out of her mouth. "I don't remember him being this arrogant."

"I just want to know what you see in me that made you think I'd be even remotely interested in a guy like that?"

She shook her head and was lost in her own thoughts, trying to figure out what she'd missed. "We've been in the same yoga class for a month now, and he seemed so easygoing."

"Lucy." I took her by the arms and forced her to look at me. "You're still not answering my question."

"Well, Talie." She sighed. "If you really want to know, you get a little uptight regarding the opposite sex. You become guarded and clam up. Harrison's a talker...."

"So the whole 'opposites attract' theory."

Lucy gave me a sheepish grin.

"Okay, well I'm ending this date now. Promise me you'll never do this to me again."

Lucy made an "x" over her chest. "Cross my heart."

And that brings us back to the present and why I am currently glaring at Lucy. "Before I commit to staying, I want to know how you can confidently say Ryan is not like Harrison or Dean when you barely know the guy?"

"Because Matt is very picky about his tenants. He turned down over twenty-five applicants and lost two months' rent before he chose Ryan. You know Matt is a good judge of character."

"Yes, he is."

"Then have a little faith."

"Okay, fine," I grudgingly answer.

"And whatever happens tonight, remember there's always a reason for everything."

I raise my brow to Lucy, questioning her.

"Remember when I didn't want to go to our alumni party three years ago? If we hadn't, I would have never met Matt."

"All right. I see your point. So tell me about this guy."

Lucy lights up with a smile. "He's—"

"Hey, Lucy, we're here!" Matt calls from the front door, and I immediately get nervous.

"No worries," Lucy says quietly as I wipe my suddenly sweaty palms off on my pants.

"Hey, sweetie." Matt lumbers in on his six-four frame. He's built like a professional basketball player, whereas Lucy is five-two and model thin. Matt kisses Lucy then picks her up like she weighs ten pounds and gives her a long embrace, as if he hasn't seen her in months. He finally releases Lucy and gives me a peck on the cheek. "Hey, Talie. This is a new buddy of mine, Ryan Emery."

Ryan steps out from behind Matt. He's also very tall, maybe six-one or six-two. He has messy light brown hair, a golden tan, and a friendly warmth about him that instantly pulls me in.

"Nice to meet you, Natalie," he says, meeting my gaze.

"Likewise." I offer a warm smile. "I hear you're living right next to this guy." I playfully punch Matt in the arm.

"Yeah." Ryan chuckles. "The place is pretty sweet."

"What would you like to drink?" Lucy asks the guys. "A nice glass of wine? Soda? Beer?"

Ryan and Matt exchange looks and say at the same time, "Beer."

I laugh as Lucy grumbles, "It's tough to sophisticate them, Talie."

"At least I left my caveman club at home," Ryan teases.

"Here's to progress." I raise my wineglass to him.

The four of us meander into the living room where Lucy has bite-size quiches, an artichoke dip, and mini egg rolls for us to munch on.

I'm shocked to hear myself say this, but Lucy described Ryan pretty well. How can I not find him attractive? Aside from his good looks, Ryan seems to have an easygoing personality. He fits right in, and as he and Matt start telling us a funny story about the day Ryan moved in, I can't seem to stop smiling.

"Of course, I wasn't laughing when Ryan pulled up in a U-Haul and unloaded a bunch of sound equipment." Matt pops a quiche in his mouth. "I thought I had leased the place to a rocker who'd be sharing a common wall with me."

I let out a big laugh. "My sister's in a band. I know how loud their 'quiet' practice sessions can be." I turn to Ryan. "But you're not in a band?"

He swallows a swig of beer. "Film production."

"That's cool," I remark. "So, I'm guessing you're the one who records the sound?"

"Yup. I've done both sound and camera work for commercials, documentaries and a few films." Ryan grabs a quiche off the tray. "I work on location, so I can be gone a lot, which is why I was specifically looking for someone with a duplex who could keep an eye on things when I'm away."

"Lucy was telling me that you just moved here."

"Yeah, from Florida." He eats the quiche and continues, "I did a lot of commercial work there, mostly as a location sound mixer, but with the documentaries, I'm everything—the director, cinematographer and sound mixer. I now prefer being behind the camera, and I'm hoping to get into television."

"Well, Hollywood is obviously the place to be for that," I reply, scooping artichoke dip onto a tortilla chip.

"Natalie and I have a college friend who's doing fairly well as an actress," Lucy chimes in. "She's been in a few things, but it took her a while because she had to join the actors' union first. Do you have to be in a union, too?"

"Unfortunately, which is why I'll be doing non-union gigs until then."

Matt grabs an egg roll and pops it in his mouth. "You have a decent résumé, so it shouldn't be too tough to land something."

"Actually, I just did an hour ago."

"Right on!" Matt puts his hand up and Ryan slaps it.

"Is it a commercial or a film?" Lucy asks.

"It's for a new TV series on the Paranormal Network and Natalie, you'll get a kick out of this. Their working title is *Super Natalie.*"

My eyes grow wide as saucers.

"How about that, Talie?" Lucy laughs. "A series named after you."

"Oh, I get it. Supernatural … Super Natalie. Clever name," Matt adds with a snort.

I try to hide the shocked look on my face, but Lucy catches it. "Do you know about this series, Talie?"

Am I ready to tell my best friend about my secret life—one she doesn't believe in? And how weird is it that Ryan and I might be working together? "Um … I kind of know about it," I confess, averting my eyes. *And let's just leave it at that.* I turn my attention to Ryan. "Congrats, Ryan. That's awesome." I clink my wineglass to his beer bottle.

Ryan is smiling this gorgeous smile at me, and Lucy is flat-out staring. I know that look of hers. The cogs are turning in her mind, trying to figure out why I appeared so shocked and what I meant when I said that I kind of knew about the series.

"Oh my God!" She gasps.

Crap.

"This has something to do with that interview you had on TV, doesn't it?"

I let out an embarrassed sigh. There is no denying it now. "For some reason the producer from *World's Weirdest Hobbies* wants to do a show with me."

"No way!" Matt interjects.

Lucy's mouth drops open. "That's incredible, Talie. Why didn't you tell me?"

"I just found out a little while ago," I stammer. "To be honest, I didn't think it would happen in a million years, but apparently I already have a following, so the network will have a guaranteed audience for the series."

"They're right about that. You have a *huge* following," Matt informs me as he pops two quiches in his mouth. "That YouTube thing was crazy good."

"YouTube thing?" Ryan leans in, his eyes jumping between the three of us.

"Dude, the clip I was telling you about before we walked in," Matt reminds him, reaching for his phone. "I'll show you."

"Hon, no toys," Lucy politely tells Matt.

"Right." Matt puts away his phone. "I'll show you later."

"It's a clip of Natalie, right?" Ryan asks, trying to keep up.

"It's of me with Ed Cummings from *World's Weirdest Hobbies,*" I explain since Ryan is still in the dark.

"Oh, just show it already," Lucy acquiesces.

"Sweet!" Matt grabs his phone and within seconds he and Ryan, and even Lucy, are watching the clip of me.

"Whoa!" Ryan looks over at me since I'm not watching it. "That host really went after you."

I take a healthy gulp of my wine. "Yeah, fun times."

"So, I don't understand something," Lucy speaks up. "What does this clip have to do with a new series on the Paranormal Network?"

Here goes. I steady my eyes on Lucy and say, "During the interview with Ed, they caught a spirit on camera—the very spirit I was talking to."

Everyone falls into silence.

After what seems like eternity, Lucy asks, "You really believe that you were ... talking to a ghost?" she balks slightly, still staring at me like I've lost it.

"Yes. Well, technically a spirit," I say, trying to make light of it. "But yes."

"I thought it was a joke." Lucy looks like she's been hit by a truck. "I told my grandmother the whole thing was staged."

"It wasn't," I inform her. "I tried to tell you the other day."

"I thought we were laughing about it being a practical joke."

"I know." I shrug my shoulders. "For some reason we weren't clicking."

"Wow." Lucy slowly sits down, takes a drink of her wine.

"Let me see that." Ryan asks for Matt's phone, and then plays the clip over. "I see what you're talking about," he says. "There's some kind of black mist in the frame."

Matt looks over Ryan's shoulder. "That is so awesome!"

"This is a special effect," Ryan states with great authority.

"It isn't," I correct him.

"Hmm." Ryan plays it again. "The mist seems to come out of nowhere. I'd definitely have it analyzed."

I join Lucy on the couch, feeling defeated. "It's not a special effect." I tip my head back and finish off my wine.

"No wonder it's gone viral." Ryan finally gives Matt back his phone. "So, how did you end up on that show anyway?"

"Well, I fit the theme of the show. I see ghosts."

"Honestly?" Ryan gives me a dubious look.

I glare at him, a little confused and a little irritated. "When you got called for the job, didn't they tell you what the series was about?"

"Yeah, a ghost hunter show. But all those types of shows are faked."

"Maybe some of them are, but not all," I argue. "The spirit caught on camera during my interview is real," I say again, even though I know I'm wasting my breath.

Lucy turns to me. "But *you* don't believe in ghosts, do you?"

"Um … yeah," I reply apologetically, once again feeling embarrassed about my ability. "I can kind of see them."

"See them like in *The Sixth Sense*? Like the I-see-dead-people kid?" Lucy asks, incredulously.

I force myself to meet her eyes. "Yeah."

And now everyone is staring at me again, just like my past co-workers and employers have done when they've caught me in mid-conversation with someone they can't see themselves. Lucy, Matt, and Ryan are frozen, unable to fathom that what I'm telling them is true, and even though I can't hear their thoughts I imagine Lucy is thinking, *My best friend has gone over the edge.* Matt is probably right behind her with, *Wow, what a nutter! At least she's a cool nutter.* I don't know Ryan at all, but I imagine his inner dialogue is, *How can this chick believe in ghosts? She's old enough to know better.*

I'd love to share some of the experiences I've had with them, but I know I'll just make myself look crazier. Instead, I try to go for the logical, scientific approach.

"Is it really that difficult to believe in something you can't see?" I look at Lucy who slowly shakes her head, and I assume by the sudden sadness I see in her eyes that she's thinking I need to seek out professional help.

"Yeah, you know, I never thought about that," Matt chimes in, lightening the mood. "We can't see the air we breathe, but it's there. Billions believe in God and no one can see Him. We all believe in love…." Matt sits down and puts his arm around Lucy, trying to shake her out of the trance I've put her under.

I love optimistic Matt. He really is a gem. As I feared, Lucy isn't taking it so well, and I can't help but wonder if her grandmother's beliefs have had a negative effect on her in some way.

"Great artichoke dip!" Ryan says, so over-the-top that we all laugh, including Lucy.

I know this isn't going to be the end of the discussion between Lucy and me, but at least the guys moved us off the subject and on to sports. Within minutes, everyone is back to having a good time.

I thought I was going to get through the rest of the evening without talking about it, but when Lucy and Matt go into the kitchen together and leave me alone with Ryan, it suddenly gets very quiet.

After a few minutes of uncomfortable silence, a trill of bells goes off, rather loudly, from the bottom of my handbag, alerting me to a new text. Two seconds later Ryan's cell alerts him too. We both grab our phones, read our texts, and look up at the same time.

"Production meeting," I announce.

"Monday morning at nine," Ryan replies.

"So I guess the series is really happening," I say brightly.

"It looks that way."

"Congratulations on your new job."

"You too."

And then more silence. *Awkward.* I think about getting up and running into the kitchen, insisting I should help Lucy with the dishes, but Matt is already helping her and I'm not entirely sure if my going in there will be of any comfort. "So, I take it you don't believe in ghosts."

"Uh … no …," he says, trailing off, as if he wanted to say more but changed his mind at the last minute.

I could just leave it. I've obviously made him feel uncomfortable with my up-close-and-personal relationship with the dead. But I'm going to be working with this guy. And let's be honest here. We are all skeptical until we experience something paranormal. "Have you ever experienced anything that couldn't be explained, or seen something out of the ordinary?"

"No."

Okay. No chance here. I immediately think of Harrison and Dean and wonder if I will ever meet a guy who isn't a skeptic. Now, this is seriously awkward. "Well, not everyone has to believe in the same things to work on a show together," I say enthusiastically.

"I totally agree." He looks at me, studies my face. "I'm actually glad you believe."

I lean back from the table in surprise. "You are?"

"Well, yeah." He shrugs. "I know you now, and I'd hate working on the show if I knew you were a total fraud."

I squint at him in confusion. "But you just said you didn't believe in ghosts."

"I don't, but the optimist in me thinks that if someone like yourself believes in something so strongly, then anything can happen."

A skeptic with an open mind. I like that. "Well said." I flash him a smile. I think back on the beginning of the evening, and ask, "So, even though I freaked you out earlier, you're excited to take the job?"

"Very." He nods, and then his mouth twists into this funny grin. "This morning I talked to a buddy of mine in Florida who's working on a new series too. *It's a Mortician's Life.*"

"Eww."

"Exactly," he says. "That could have been me."

"Talking to the dead is way better than burying them," I proudly proclaim.

"What will Hollywood think of next?"

"Hmm. We haven't had sitcoms that take place in Heaven or Hell."

Ryan chuckles. "We could have a military show where superhuman doctors patch up angels and demons coming off the battlefield."

I laugh, and I'm so relieved that I won't have to hide or be ashamed about my ability around him.

"So, have you worked on other TV shows?" Ryan asks me.

"No, this will be the first. I'd never been in a TV studio until I went on *World's Weirdest Hobbies*."

"So we're both going into unknown territory." He eyes me with a playful smile.

"Seems like it." I hold his gaze.

"Well, if you have any questions on where to look or how to stand, or how to appear natural on camera, I can help you with that."

"Thanks, and if you have any questions on how to film spirits, or how to get rid of one when it touches you, I've got you covered."

He chuckles as Lucy and Matt finally come out of the kitchen, bringing dessert.

"Okay." Lucy sets down a cake platter and a large bowl. "I've got angel food cake and fresh strawberries. Who wants what?"

Ryan and I exchange looks and with a shared smile, we graciously accept both.

Chapter 7

————•————

*M*onday morning at a quarter to nine, I drive into the production office's underground garage, and just as I'm about to turn off my engine and go inside, Hunky Spirit appears in the passenger seat. I jump with a start.

"You look like you've just seen a ghost." He laughs.

"Do you have any idea how old that joke is?"

"Sorry. I'm new."

I focus on my client. "Before we go any further, what's your name?"

"Tyler," he says. "Tyler Scott. I'd shake your hand, but...."

I can't help but laugh. "I have to say, it's refreshing to work with a spirit who has a sense of humor. Most in your postmortem position who die prematurely are not real happy about it."

"Oh, I fit into that category right after it happened," he informs me. "I was out of control with rage. I swore I'd hunt down the kid who did this to me and haunt him for the rest of his life."

"What made you change your mind?"

"He's ... uh, here with me. He already paid the ultimate price for texting while driving."

"That's sobering," I remark. "I'm very sorry ... for both of you."

"Thanks."

I turn toward my client. "So, Tyler. I don't understand something. If you died out on Pacific Coast Highway, how did you find me in a TV studio in Hollywood?"

"Your name is on a ghost bulletin board."

I gasp. He laughs, and I realize he heard my thoughts the other day. Another difference between ghosts and spirits is that spirits can know what we are thinking and ghosts do not have that ability. "Ha, ha," I reply.

"Couldn't resist," he says, then gets serious. "Remember when you were out in Santa Monica, listening to your sister's band in that dive bar?"

I nod. "Three weekends ago."

"Before you went into the bar, you were walking on the very beach I watched over as a lifeguard. I was there too, on PCH where I had died, staring at a super bright portal of light—one that felt insanely warm and inviting. But I just couldn't go into it, you know, because of the whole unfinished business bit. I forced myself to look away from the Light because I still needed to figure out how I could get a very important message to someone. And that's when I saw another ghost by the water. She was running, crying hysterically, and then she ran right through you. You instantly turned and yelled, 'I can help you.' I knew then that you could see us."

I study Tyler. "If you knew I could see ghosts, why didn't you make contact with me that night?"

"I tried. I was yelling right next to you, but you didn't hear me."

"Sorry. I guess I was preoccupied with the other ghost."

He shakes his head. "It wasn't you. I wasn't good enough at directing my energy, and for some reason, I couldn't follow you into the bar. Frustrated, I went back to my spot on PCH, the Light came back, so I gave in and crossed over. Once I was on the Other Side, I suddenly had knowledge of where to find you."

"I'll have to remember that," I tell him. "The next time I run into stubborn ghosts, I'll let them know that if they go into the Light, they'll receive a free Omniscient app."

Tyler laughs. "You might also—"

And he's gone. *Damn.* I'm dying to know why they vanish so quickly. Is it God calling a meeting and all spirits are required to attend? I must get the answer to this the next time I see him.

Now that Tyler has disappeared, I suddenly notice Ryan staring at me. He obviously pulled into the garage and parked next to me while I was … engaged. I force a smile and wave before we both get out of our respective cars.

"Hey, Ryan," I say, and can't help but notice how sexy he looks with tousled hair.

"Morning."

He comes over to me and I notice that he smells good too—a very clean fresh scent, like lilacs and vanilla, and I wonder if this guy is into aromatherapy soaps. I picture him in the shower, seeing if I can psychically pick up on the answer, and bam! I'm hit with an image of his stunningly gorgeous body. Muscular arms and legs, a beautiful butt, a washboard stomach and "Oh!" I slam my eyes shut, immediately stopping the x-rated movie in my head.

"Natalie? Are you okay?"

Two plus two is four. Four plus four is eight. When I open my eyes again, Ryan is gawking at me. "So … um … we're here!"

"Well, I am … at least."

I laugh, really hard. Ryan must think I'm a total head case. Not only am I acting like a complete spaz, but he probably saw me talking to Tyler. "How long have you been sitting in your car?"

"I pulled in right behind you."

I nod and say nothing. I have a feeling he wants me to give him a non-paranormal explanation for the animated conversation I was having by myself, but I'm not a good liar, so I shouldn't even attempt it.

"I saw that you were … on the phone?" he asks.

"So to speak." I clear my throat.

"You ride-share with them?" he asks jokingly.

"Uh … well … sometimes," I say in all seriousness, and Ryan gives me an incredulous look. "Spirits can attach themselves to objects, to people…."

Ryan stifles a laugh, and I know he's having a hard time believing me. "Sorry."

"You asked."

"I was actually kidding," he confesses.

"I wasn't," I say flatly. *Why start sugarcoating now?*

Ryan looks around with a dubious expression on his face.

I try not to smile. "Still coming?"

Ryan pushes back his shoulders. "Of course." He opens the door for me and we walk inside.

A spry girl with super short platinum blonde hair and big blue eyes meets us in the lobby. She's carrying a bunch of folders, and I can only guess that she's part of the production team. "Morning, Natalie, Ryan. I'm Haley. Grab yourselves some coffee. Meeting's about to begin in the conference room." Haley's cell rings and she answers it on the go.

I scan the area for my spirit friend Tyler as Ryan and I get our coffee, but he's nowhere to be seen, and my guess is he might not show for another day or two. From past experience, when spirits involuntarily vanish, they don't come back right away.

Of course, I can't help but wonder what message he has that's so important and who it's for. I just hope I can get it taken care of during my off hours. It always seems like the persistent spirits are the ones who have me travelling far distances to deliver their message, and often the messages are not well received. I remember, with one case, I had to go back to this old woman's house six times before I could convince her that I was not trying to "steal her blind," that I was only passing on a message from her recently deceased husband. It's the reluctant and the skeptics that have made me often regret that night at summer camp so long ago, where I learned about my ability.

"Hi guys. Come on in," Carolyn calls to Ryan and me as we enter the conference room and sit down with the others. The only person I recognize is Adam, Carolyn's assistant, who's so skinny he would disappear if he wasn't tricked out in tech. He has two cell phones attached to his belt, a Bluetooth earbud jammed inside his ear, and an iPad sitting in front of him. Head down, Adam's bony fingers furiously type away on his iPad.

"I see you two have met," Carolyn says to us.

Ryan and I quickly make eye contact, and I know he's thinking the same thing. "Yes," I answer. "Just now in the parking lot."

"Excellent." Carolyn turns to the others who are already seated. "Ryan Emery is our camera operator and location sound mixer. I'm sure you all know that this is Natalie Dalton, America's soon-to-be favorite ghost huntress."

There are a few chuckles from the others as Carolyn starts with the very good-looking, well-built, forty-something guy sitting closest to her. "This is Geoff Atchison, our field producer and production manager." She gestures to a pudgy guy, in this thirties, with super curly black hair and a friendly face. "Carlos Padilla is our story producer who will also be out on locations." She motions to Adam. "You all know Adam Reed, my efficient assistant...."

Adam briefly peers up at us without his fingers missing a beat.

Carolyn gestures to Haley who Ryan and I met in the lobby. "Haley Pierce is our researcher and clearance coordinator. She is already doing research on the property of our first location."

Haley gives everyone a little wave before Carolyn glances back at, "Geoff?"

"We're a small crew," Geoff begins, "which is fine for what we're trying to accomplish. We want to shoot this like a documentary. Single camera. Handheld. We'll need to prove ourselves before the network will loosen the purse strings and allow us to hire more people. Because of this, we'll all be wearing several hats, so we need to work together seamlessly.

We don't have time and more importantly we don't have enough money for egos here. We are a team, so speak up when you have a suggestion."

"When you have a good and constructive suggestion," Carolyn corrects, and we laugh before she motions to Haley.

"Okay," Haley begins, putting on her trendy, purple-framed glasses in order to read her notes. "Our first location is a California landmark, The Gorham Theatre in West L.A. It was built in 1945 and has seen hundreds of Hollywood stars grace its stage throughout the years. It's also been a location for tragedy. A stagehand fell to his death off the catwalk during a performance of *Dracula* in 1949. An actress by the name of Lily Watters committed suicide in 1961 by slitting her wrists in the dressing room after receiving poor reviews of her performance as Hedda in *Hedda Gabler.* And in 1992, a young actor hanged himself, in the same dressing room, after being excoriated by his director. Several cast members, over the years, have reported seeing these apparitions." Haley looks up for reactions or comments.

"Sounds like a colorful location," I remark.

"From my viewpoint, I think it would be a great first place to investigate," Carlos offers up as he grabs a doughnut off the breakfast tray sitting in the center of the conference table. "The theatre has a rich history and it's in our own backyard."

"I like it," Carolyn agrees, "but I do have one concern. It's a theatre, and another place where ghosts can be created."

"I don't think that will be an issue," Geoff throws in his two cents. "Skeptics will always point out the obvious, no matter where we film, no matter how we cut the show. Besides, everyone knows we don't need a theatre to create a ghost when we can get far better results with CGI."

"How's accessibility on our first location?" Ryan asks. "Is it still a working theatre?"

"Yes, but it's not as busy as it used to be," Haley informs us. "They no longer have a set season of shows. It's become a rental theatre for independent productions. I just spoke with the manager who said they closed a production last night, and as of right now, they don't have any-one currently renting the space."

Carolyn and Geoff exchange looks, then Carolyn announces her decision. "Let's get in there before someone else does."

———

The rest of the day is spent prepping for the show. Geoff and Ryan are busy going over the equipment needed and figuring out with Haley what can be used where, with regards to the location, while I sit with Carolyn and Carlos trying to understand the flow they'd like to achieve on the show.

"Even though it's reality TV," Carlos explains, "it still needs a beginning, middle, and end."

"And naturally we need lots of dynamics and suspense in the pro-cess," Carolyn points out.

I lean back, taking in everything we are discussing. Because I'm not an actor, all this talk of how to present myself and the situation becomes a little dizzying. The fact that Carolyn and Carlos were wor-rying about how they'd have to do several takes with the non-actor clients just adds to my stress.

"I'm not an actor, either," I remind them, speaking up.

"True," Carolyn agrees, "but you've been on TV and handled your-self well."

"Once," I clarify, suddenly feeling a little panicky.

"I worked on a sitcom last year," Carlos says, "and you have no idea how many 'actors' ended up looking like a deer in the headlights."

I'm starting to feel a little like a stunned deer myself. *I can't believe I'm doing this. I'm not only going to be on a reality series, I'm going to be the star of the reality series.* What if I become that deer in the headlights too? What if I can't speak without continually messing up? What if I keep missing my mark when I'm walking around? What if I lose my connec-tion to the spirits?

"For this series to work, realism must outweigh everything else," Carolyn insists, "which is why you are so perfect, Natalie. An actor would ham it up, probably pretend to be possessed like the now disgraced psychic medium, Derek Nezbie."

This gets a chuckle out of me. "I've seen him," I tell Carolyn. "And I always thought it was an act. He was too over-the-top to be real."

"Why don't you explain how your process works?" Carolyn suggests as the door opens and in walk Geoff, Ryan, and Haley.

"Great timing," Carolyn remarks. "I think everyone should hear this too."

Ryan smiles at me as he, Geoff and Haley sit on the other side of the conference table.

A smile is good.

"So tell me how it works," Carlos asks, opening another file on his iPad. "I might be able to weave it into the story."

I put my focus back on Carlos. "Uh, well. I don't know exactly," I reply honestly. "It's not like I know what you had for dinner last night, and I can't tell you what you'll be doing next week. The information I receive mostly comes from ghosts and spirits who connect with me when they choose to and not the other way around."

"And ghosts are different from spirits," Carolyn supplies.

"At least in my experience, they are," I clarify.

"How so?" Geoff asks, grabbing a bottled water from the center of the conference table.

"Ghosts haunt a location," I explain. "They have not crossed over to the Other Side, so they do not possess any of the 'perks,' if you will, from being on the Other Side."

"What are the perks?" Carlos eagerly asks.

"Freedom to appear anywhere at any time, omniscience, understanding the big picture—that type of thing. Ghosts are usually bound to a location or an object. They have a difficult time communicating with us because their viewpoint is still so narrow. They are as they were in life, which means they can be happy or sad or angry or downright spiteful."

"Oh." Haley seems surprised.

I glance at Carolyn, who is sitting back with a satisfied smile on her face, then I continue. "Spirits, on the other hand, have gone into the Light. They've crossed over. They can return anytime they like. They are not tied to one location, and they have knowledge about the past, present and future that they were not privy to when they were alive. They get the big picture because they have been reconnected to God, to the Source. Spirits come back because they need to help someone still living. They also come back to partake in their loved ones' joyous celebrations."

"I'd much rather be a spirit than a ghost," Haley admits.

"Me too," Geoff agrees. "I'm a perk man myself."

This gets a laugh out of everyone.

I turn my attention back to Carolyn. "I'm assuming that because we'll be investigating locations that have reported disturbances and paranormal activity, we'll be running into more ghosts than spirits."

"That's an accurate assumption," Carolyn states.

Carlos pecks away on his iPad keyboard. "Do you see them, hear them, or feel them?"

"I usually see and hear them together. Sometimes, I only see them. If there's no acknowledgement on their part that they see me, then I know it's a residual haunt."

"That's when you pick up on energy from the past," Carolyn adds proudly, but looks to me for verification. "Correct?"

"Yes," I confirm. "It's like a film loop of the past that's played over and over. A residual haunt is usually experienced where a traumatic event has occurred. The emotional energy of the event is so charged that it leaves an impression on our dimension. The living can see it, even though the spirit has moved on. The battlefields in Gettysburg have several residual haunts. Also, it's worth noting that with a residual haunt, the loop itself can often be of the soul before the trauma occurred."

"You lost me," Ryan interjects.

"If, say, a woman lives in a house for fifty years and gets brutally murdered in her bedroom, the loop might not be of the murder but of her cooking in the kitchen hours before the murder took place. If I were to experience this residual haunt, I would see the loop of her in the kitchen, but she wouldn't see me because she wouldn't really be there. It's only her residual energy that would be imprinted so strongly on the location that I'd pick up on it."

"Makes sense," Geoff says as he focuses on Carolyn. "Rita's energy will probably remain here after she's gone."

"Who's Rita?" I ask.

"She's the sandwich lady," Carolyn tells us. "She comes by every Tuesday and Thursday, selling her gourmet sandwiches. She's always singing a little tune, dancing to the music she listens to from her iPod. She's very lively."

I smile, trying to picture the woman, and then get a bit of a jolt when something catches my eye. It's Tyler. I'm surprised to see him back so soon, but what has me really baffled is why my client is not focused on me. He's fixated on Ryan with a shockingly intense gaze on his face.

Chapter 8

————◆————

The next morning, I'm scouring the Internet, watching as many episodes of *Ghost Hunters* and *Destination Truth* as I can, hoping I get a feel as to what will be expected of me. One thing that's going to be different with our show is the number of people. I'll be the only paranormal investigator. Since we're shooting it with one camera, we've decided the format should be like a video diary where I'll talk into the camera and explain what I'm feeling, sensing and seeing. Ryan will be the only crew member going in with me. Will we have enough footage to make an hour-long show exciting?

The other thing I'm worrying about is whether ghosts or spirits will contact me. After all, I'll be searching for them instead of the other way around, and if my failure in trying to contact the spirit of Tyler Scott is any indication on how the show will go, I'm going to be a total flop.

Thinking about Tyler, I decide to look him up on the Internet. I come across a tiny blurb about his death on PCH. I skim the article. TYLER SCOTT, 23, WAS ON DUTY AS A LIFEGUARD....

My eyes continue to fly over the article. It says nothing about his family or friends. I search the public records and find close to fifty Tyler Scotts in their 20s. *Shoot.*

I enlarge his photo and sit there studying it. There's something familiar about him. I can't put my finger on it and it's driving me crazy. *Why is he back? Does he have a message for someone or not?* I've had a few spirits attach to me in the past, but they generally make their reason known fairly quickly. *And what is Tyler's sudden fascination with Ryan?* If Ryan had been working at the production office, it would make sense that he'd been haunting Ryan instead of me. But he wasn't.

"Tyler?" I call out. "Are you hanging around?"

Ring, ring! My cell suddenly goes off, making me jump. Fearing I might miss an important work call, I changed my ringtone to the sound of an old-fashioned European phone. Wow, was it loud!

I quickly see who's calling and answer. "Hey, Lucy."

"I think you freaked out Ryan."

"What do you mean?"

"I just got off the phone with Matt. He said Ryan didn't sleep all night because he kept hearing weird sounds in his room, and he felt like he was being watched."

"Great," I groan. *What is Tyler up to now?* "I think I should go over there and talk to him."

"I'll pick you up in ten."

I race to change out of my dingy sweatpants and into a pair of jeans and a T-shirt. I quickly reapply my makeup and run a brush through my hair. I stop to wonder why I'm acting like a teenager. I can't allow myself to like Ryan, because he doesn't believe in what I do. It's fine to work with him, but passing on messages for the dead is supposed to be my life's purpose, so ultimately I need to be with someone who understands that.

Damn, why does Ryan have to be totally hot? Not only does he have an amazing body, but he has an extremely handsome face. I couldn't stop staring into his smoldering grey eyes when I'd first met him at Lucy's. And of course I couldn't help but notice how perfectly shaped his mouth is, one I wouldn't mind kissing.

I quickly shake away the thoughts I'm suddenly having and grab my handbag just as Lucy calls me on my cell to tell me she's waiting downstairs.

"Hey." I climb into Lucy's convertible and shut the door. "He knows we're coming, right?"

"No, but Matt does." Lucy looks in her rearview mirror and pulls into traffic.

"Wait a minute. I can't go over there and ambush the guy—especially since he doesn't believe in the paranormal."

"We'll ease into it," she recommends. "Work it into the conversation, which won't be that difficult seeing as how you two are on a show about ghosts."

And what exactly is she expecting me to tell him? "You know, we never talked about the other night. Did I freak you out too?"

She offers me a guarded smile. "You surprised me."

"I'm sorry," I say. "I should have told you."

"No, I'm the one that's sorry." She takes a breath. "You want to know the truth of it all? The reason I react so strongly whenever the subject of ghosts comes up is because ... I'm scared to believe in them."

I give her a slightly perplexed look. "Why?"

"Because if you believe in something, you give it power." Her voice sounds a little shaky.

I turn toward her, concerned. "Lucy, have you had a paranormal experience?"

A shadow crosses her face. "I don't know. Maybe."

"Do you want to tell me about it?"

She gives me a quick sideways glance, and I can already see fear in her eyes. "Before I transferred to UCLA, I attended Cal State University Channel Islands for my first year. Did you know it used to be a mental hospital?"

"No, I didn't. And not the most brilliant move, if you ask me," I remark with a lighthearted tone since I can see that Lucy is petrified just talking about this.

"I had to change rooms, you know." Her hands tighten around the steering wheel.

"Sorry to hear it was that bad," I say gravely. "What happened?"

She blows out a quick breath. "It started out slow. Objects falling off the shelf, books moving, doors slamming. Then one night a woman screamed in my ear. But no one was there and my roommate was sleeping soundly." She lets out a nervous laugh. "My heart was beating so fast I thought it was going to come out of my chest, and my roommate was snoring." She shakes her head. "I thought I was losing it."

"We all feel that way when we first experience the paranormal. What happened after that?"

"My sheets were pulled off me the following night, and then it began escalating very quickly. I started getting scratched, and a few nights later I felt like someone was trying to strangle me."

"God, Lucy, how horrible. Did you do research and try to figure out who the ghost was?"

Lucy gives me a wide-eyed cynical look. "Our school used to be home to the insane. I'm not sure it would have mattered."

It would have, but I don't tell this to Lucy. Some people aren't programmed to deal with this type of thing and I assume Lucy is one of them. "Is that when you moved to a different room?"

She nods, keeping her eyes on the road. "But it had already changed me, you know? I've always believed in God and that there is an entire spirit world we cannot see, but I never thought spirits could physically harm you."

"Unfortunately, some can."

"Kind of debunks the stereotypical scene of parents tucking their children in for the night. In reality, parents should be saying, 'Why yes, Kendra, there are such things as ghosts and evil spirits. And, gosh, maybe there really is some monster in your closet or under your bed.'" She glances at me with a wry smile and I laugh. "Have you ever experienced a malicious spirit?"

Caitlin McKenna

"I've come across a poltergeist and angry souls who died violently. I did know someone who had been possessed by something evil, but for me personally, I've never been touched by malicious spirits or anything darker than that."

Lucy shudders. "There's something darker than malicious spirits?"

"Oh you know, demons," I say a little flip. "But I don't think the spirit you ran into was evil. She was probably a lost, confused soul who'd been tortured and treated unfairly at the asylum."

She glares at me as if I've lost it. "She tried to strangle me."

"She could have been a sane person in life, fighting against some horrible orderly, and that's what she was trying to tell you."

"How about writing me a note next time?"

I smile. "All ghosts were once people and usually quite harmless."

Lucy takes in a deep breath, considers my words. "You think that's what she really was? A confused ghost?"

"I'm willing to bet on it." I watch her shoulders relax. "Thank you for telling me."

Lucy releases a long sigh, as if she's letting go of any fears she has from her bad experience. "I don't know how or why you want to do this."

"It's what I'm supposed to do, and believe it or not, I'm finally beginning to feel comfortable with it."

"Have you always been psychic?"

"I've always seen ghosts and spirits, but as for the rest of the psychic stuff, not so much—though my nana is teaching me how to access all of my sixth sense skills."

"Is your nana psychic too?"

"Very. She's much better at it than I am."

"I wonder if she could read Matt." Lucy gasps with excitement. "Actually, that's a great idea! I *should* have her meet Matt. She could tell me if she sees an engagement ring in my future."

I laugh. "Don't you want to be surprised?"

106

"Sure. As long as I'm wearing a flattering dress and my hair and makeup are perfect and there's a photographer nearby to capture the moment."

"You crack me up." And suddenly I hear Sandbox, my new favorite band, come on the radio. "Oh! Turn it up."

Lucy raises the volume. "I love this song!"

Even though it's September, it's eighty degrees on a beautiful day in sunny Southern California. Lucy has the top down. The wind is blowing in our hair and feeling like we don't have a care in the world, we both start singing along to *Streetlights* as we head down the road.

———

When we arrive at Matt's, he calls Ryan to come over. Five minutes later, Ryan walks in and I can't take my eyes off him.

Just out of the shower, Ryan's hair is still wet, and he must have been in a hurry drying off because part of his T-shirt is soaked through, which only clings to his sculpted arms and well-defined chest. I instantly remember the vision I saw of him in the shower.

"Hey," Ryan says, surprised to see me, and I quickly move my eyes back onto his face. He doesn't seem to have noticed that my gaze was lingering on his body, maybe because he's expecting me to say why I'm standing there with Matt and Lucy and why we're all staring at him.

"What's going on?" he asks Matt, and Matt continues to stand there without saying a word.

Ryan moves on to Lucy who pointedly says, "Natalie needs to talk to you."

I glare at her with a how-is-that-subtle look. Seriously. Just how am I supposed to work "you're being haunted" into casual conversation now?

I sigh and turn my attention to Ryan. "I heard you had a bad night."

Ryan glares at Matt with a what-the-hell expression. "Dude."

Matt then glares at Lucy. "I thought we had this all worked out?"

"Oh, right," Lucy answers, then eyes me. "Natalie, don't say anything to Ryan because we're all just going to hang out together and if it comes up in conversation, great. If not…." Lucy shrugs, glances back at Matt with a look that tells him how ludicrous this all is.

"Oh, for God's sake." I shake my head in disgust, then turn my attention to Ryan. "You might have a spirit attached to you," I say, cutting to the chase.

"What?" Ryan gawks at me as if I had two heads.

"The noises, the disturbances you experienced last night—"

"That's nonsense," Ryan groans. He briskly paces off a few steps. "What I had last night was an overactive imagination brought on by all the ghost talk for the show."

And Ryan walks right through Tyler who has just shown up. "Um … actually your imagination has nothing to do with it." I stare at Tyler who is now standing roughly three feet to the right of Ryan. "Unfortunately, no one else sees him, so it looks like I'm staring at nothing.

"Oh, my God! Are you seeing a ghost right now?" Lucy asks, throwing her hand over her mouth.

"Don't encourage her," Ryan replies.

"Tyler, why do you keep leaving so abruptly?" I have to ask before he disappears again.

"Sorry. Can't help it. I expend a ton of energy in order for you to see me, and when it's gone, I get sucked back."

"Are you talking to a ghost?" Matt asks quietly.

I ignore him and continue with Tyler. "To the Other Side?"

"Yeah, and it's so amazing there that it takes all my willpower to come back here."

"Why *are* you coming back?" I ask. "Maybe you're just supposed to stay on the Other Side."

Tyler glances at Ryan who is staring at me with an incredibly skeptical look on his face. "I can't. Ryan is—"

"Damn, he's gone again!" With a frustrated growl, I turn around to see my friends frozen. But I don't care. They need to know the truth and deal with it. "I can't believe this! He was just about to tell me and he's gone." I march to the window, frustrated as hell.

Silence.

Finally, Lucy has the courage to speak up. "Who's gone?"

"Tyler Scott." I turn around, forcing myself to calm down.

"So you're on a first name basis with a ghost?" Ryan's tone is fairly sarcastic.

I ignore the dig. "Do you know a Tyler Scott?"

"No. I don't know any Tyler living or dead." Ryan starts to leave.

"Look, Ryan, I know this is—"

"Just stop," he says, turning back. "If you want to do your magic show for the network, that's fine. But don't try to play me." Ryan sends Matt a warning look to butt out, then exits, slamming the front door.

"I'm sorry," Lucy says to Matt. "I didn't think he'd be so uptight about it."

"Me neither." Matt is still staring after Ryan. "I've never seen him so angry."

"That wasn't from being embarrassed," I maintain. "I mean, obviously I don't know the guy, but I'm willing to bet something else, a lot deeper, set him off." I focus on Matt. "What do you know about his personal life, about his family?"

"He's lived his entire life in Florida. He grew up there, he graduated from Florida State University, and then he moved in with his girlfriend. Soon after, he began working on commercials."

"What happened to his girlfriend?" Lucy inquires.

"They broke up," Matt informs us.

"Why?" I ask. "Because he decided to move out here?"

"Don't know." Matt shrugs. "But I can find out. Why is it so important? Do you think she died?" His eyes suddenly grow the size of saucers. "Is she Tyler Scott?"

"No, Tyler's a guy. He was twenty-three," I supply, remembering the article I read. "How old is Ryan?"

"Twenty-seven." Matt grabs three beers out of his refrigerator, and we all sit down trying to figure out the mystery.

Lucy takes a sip of beer. "Maybe this Tyler guy worked with Ryan, but Ryan didn't know his name. Did he say if he was in the film business?"

"Not sure if he had a second job," I tell her, "but at the time of his death, Tyler was a lifeguard and was killed on PCH a couple of months ago."

"That's brutal." Matt's eyes dart around the room. "Has he come back?"

"No. Since he's a spirit instead of a ghost he was probably yanked back to the Life Source." I stretch my arms, take a deep breath, and thoughtfully stare at the ceiling. "Do you know what's troubling me? I think it's really strange that Tyler is not hanging around with his family. Instead, he's here with Ryan, which can only mean that Tyler's message is extremely important."

"Then how can Ryan not know Tyler?" Lucy asks.

"That's what I'm trying to figure out. The look on Ryan's face told me that he really didn't know who Tyler was."

"Maybe Tyler saved his life," Matt offers up.

"A guy saves your life and you neglect to get his name?" Lucy remarks.

"That theory doesn't work anyway." I shake my head. "Ryan just moved here and Tyler died a couple of months ago. Arrgh! None of this makes sense."

"Where did you first meet Tyler?" Lucy queries.

"At the production office the day I was filming *World's Weirdest Hobbies*. I assumed he was related to someone who worked there, but a few days ago Tyler told me he had seen me on the beach in Santa Monica right before he crossed over."

Lucy leans back, rubbing her chin with a Sherlock Holmes-type expression on her face. "So, maybe Ryan has something to do with this message, but the message is really intended for you."

"It isn't," I state adamantly.

Matt chugs half his beer. "How can you be so sure it's for Ryan?"

"Because of what Tyler was about to say. Just now when I told Tyler that maybe he was supposed to remain on the Other Side, he said, 'I can't. Ryan is' and then he disappeared."

"No wonder you're frustrated," Matt remarks.

"Maybe Tyler is a friend of the family," Lucy interjects. "Does he have any siblings?"

"No, he's an only child," Matt adds.

I drum my fingers on my cheek. "Maybe Tyler knows a good friend of Ryan's."

"It *has* to be something like that," Lucy adds, and Matt starts laughing. "What?"

"Listen to us. It's like we're solving a real-life mystery."

"We are," I say, giving him a strange look.

"No. We're talking about a dead guy who's communicating with you and following my friend around."

"Sounds pretty normal to me," I tell him. "You'll get used to it."

"I think I already am," Matt finishes off his beer, "which is kind of weird."

Chapter 9

———◆———

Over the last few days, I've practically been living at the production office, with all the prep and the production meetings regarding our first on-location shoot. We're also dealing with post production for the pilot, which will focus on the portion of my interview with Ed when the spirit of Wilson Gooding manifested.

On my first full day of work, we spent the afternoon shooting in the studio. I talked into the camera and explained what I saw and heard when the spirit made contact. This footage is being cut into the pilot which will set up my video diary format for the rest of the series. At first it was a little uncomfortable looking into the camera. But when I started talking about how I connected with Wilson Gooding and how I saw him versus how everyone else saw him, I felt like I was talking to a good friend.

I have to say Carolyn has been true to her word. She's given the show an investigative feel. It's very fact-based, and of course, half of the show will be devoted to analyses validating that the spirit image caught on camera is authentic. Everything about this series is exciting. I can't believe how much I love my new job. My opinion is valued here, which is so foreign to me. For the first time in my life, I don't feel like a freak.

My relationship with Ryan, on the other hand, is pretty much nonexistent. He's completely closed off now and hasn't said a word to me except for when he's had to ask work-related questions. He's always professional, so I know no one has noticed that there is tension between us, but it's very obvious to me. During our production meetings, he avoids eye contact and he sits as far away from me as possible. I'd hoped that Tyler would return, so that I could finally get some answers. I don't exactly know the connection between the two, but I'm certain the message will be life changing for Ryan or whoever he's supposed to give it to.

It's Thursday afternoon and the *Super Natalie* team is heading off to our first on-location paranormal investigation. We pull up to the Gorham Theatre at half past three. A woman with over-teased platinum blonde hair and super long fake eyelashes greets us outside the entrance.

"I'm Marjorie Sanders," the woman says in a voice that sounds like she's spent the last few years drowning her sorrows in a bourbon bottle. "I'm the current owner of the theatre."

I immediately take her in. She's at least sixty-five but is no doubt trying to appear younger, though it's not working because she has stuffed herself into leopard-print pants two sizes too small and is teetering on three-inch gaudy gold heels. Her shirt is a crisp white blouse, unbuttoned and tied off at the waist. The collar is wide and turned up to frame her thick gold chain, dangling down into her wrinkled cleavage. She's had so much work done to her face she makes Joan Rivers look like a cosmetic surgery virgin. Marjorie's eyebrows are practically in her hairline, and her lips are so swollen from lip filler injections, I almost ask her if she's recently been mugged.

I steal a glance at Geoff, who looks equally alarmed, and I can't help but wonder if he's thinking that she could be the first candidate on a reality show titled *Emergency Makeover.*

Regaining his composure, Geoff makes the introductions before he pushes Carlos forward to get Marjorie's history, so that he can speak with me privately. "It goes without saying that we need to spend as little time with Marjorie as possible."

I peer over at Marjorie who seems to be flirting with Ryan. "Agreed."

"Now, I just got off the phone with Carolyn, and instead of the show appearing to be your point of view the entire time, we are only going to make it your POV for the scary moments which will be the investigation at night."

"Sounds great," I reply. "That will make it easier on all of us."

"I think so too." Geoff hands me a list. "These are some of the questions you should ask her. But right now, let's concentrate on the first question, which is for Marjorie to show you the areas of the theatre that have seen the most paranormal activity."

I nod, following along, when Marjorie suddenly lets out a loud laugh resembling that of a hyena.

Wide-eyed Geoff stares at Marjorie. "We might have to do a few takes."

Thirty minutes later, our affable hair and makeup person, Shani Peyton, has finished with my makeup and is convincing Marjorie to change into black pants.

"They'll make you look super skinny," she explains, and Marjorie's face suddenly lights up. Shani then convinces her to wear lower heels, for safety reasons, and though Marjorie settles for one-inch heels, they are still gold.

Ryan walks back over to Marjorie with her radio mic. "If you could do me a favor and attach this microphone to your blouse…."

Marjorie runs her eyes up and down Ryan. "Why don't you do it, honey? That thing is so tiny and I'm all thumbs." She sticks out her chest in Ryan's face.

"Uh … well. If you could button up your shirt, then, for me."

"That's new," she purrs. "Most men ask for just the opposite." Ryan turns a few shades redder as she continues to try to flirt with him, but when Ryan refuses to be anything but professional, she acquiesces.

"Looks like you're all set," Ryan says to her, quickly turning away before she asks him for something else. Marjorie ogles his ass as he comes over to me.

"And you thought the ghosts were going to be the scary part," I say, which at least gets a chuckle out of him.

"Listen, about the other day," Ryan begins. "I'd just gotten off the phone with my mom who didn't give me very good news."

"Everything okay?" I ask, concern filling my eyes.

"My parents are getting a divorce."

"Oh, Ryan. I'm so sorry."

"It was quite a shock—still is—so when I came over and was hit with another shock, I guess I overreacted."

"I shouldn't have come unannounced, and Matt only said something because he was trying to help."

"I figured as much." Ryan secures the wireless transmitter/receiver pack for the mic to the back of my jeans as I attach the radio mic to my shirt. "How does that feel?"

"Good. Thanks." I study Ryan, and I can see that he's already moved on in his head. I have a feeling he chose to say something to me now because we wouldn't have time to talk about it any further or to discuss why I was there in the first place.

Of course, I want nothing more than to continue with the conversation. If I could calmly explain to him that Tyler's spirit was only around to deliver an important message, then maybe Ryan would be willing to help me figure out their connection. But for now, at least we were talking.

"Ryan?"

Geoff takes Ryan aside to discuss the shooting changes for my initial introduction to the client. Since we're on a shoestring budget, we don't have a director, so Geoff will be filling that role while relying heavily on Ryan's cinematic expertise.

"All right, everyone. Let's get going!" Geoff grabs me, and we walk over to Marjorie. "How are you feeling, Marjorie? Are you ready to do this?"

"I'm always ready for the camera," she growls, then coughs to smooth out the rasp in her voice that only comes from years of smoking.

Geoff eyes Ryan, who joins us, then instructs, "Let's take it from Natalie pulling equipment out of the car. Marjorie, when you see

Natalie approaching the door, come out, shake hands, and say, "You must be Natalie. Please come in."

Marjorie nods, and I head toward the theatre's parking lot.

I stand by the already open rear lift gate of a black SUV (that is supposed to be my car) as Marjorie goes back into the theatre and closes the door.

Ryan looks through his viewfinder, makes adjustments.

Geoff, who's sitting to the side, stares at the playback monitor, scrutinizing the picture. A moment. Everyone settles. Geoff yells, "Action, Natalie!"

Haley, the research assistant and clearance coordinator, is also Ryan's assistant when needed. She comes in next to me and holds up a slate. "The Gorham Theatre, Scene 3, Take 1." She hits the sticks together and moves out of frame.

I reach into the SUV, pull out my camera, and head toward the entrance of the Gorham Theatre with Ryan filming my every move.

Ryan pulls back into a wide shot to get the entrance of the theatre into frame.

Two seconds later, Marjorie dramatically opens the theatre door and steps out with an exaggerated smile on her face. "You must be Natalie," she says to me in this sexy siren-type voice, which would have totally freaked me out had she not been looking directly into the camera.

"Cut!" Geoff calls out. Ryan removes his eye from the viewfinder as Geoff hurries up the walk. "Don't look into the camera, Marjorie. Act as if we're not even here."

"Shouldn't I have a rapport with my audience?" she asks innocently, batting her false eyelashes at Geoff.

"Uh, no," Geoff says firmly. "You will only be speaking to Natalie who is here to help you because you've been experiencing a lot of paranormal activity in your theatre."

"So, I'm unsettled by it."

"I would be," Geoff replies, "if unexplained things were happening in my place of work."

"I have it now," Marjorie tells all of us. "Back to one?" she asks Ryan, referring to us starting over.

"Yes, back to one." Ryan shoots me an exasperated look which says this could be a very long day.

Haley slates once more and we begin again. I pull out my camera as I did before and head up to the theatre just as Marjorie whips open the door, out of breath.

She stares at me wide-eyed with terror. "Natalie! Thank God you're here! Save me. Please save me!"

"Cut!" Geoff drags his hand over his face just as Carolyn arrives on set. He gets up and pulls Carolyn to the side for a pow-wow.

I walk over to Ryan. "I wonder if any of the other ghost hunter shows have difficult clients."

"She seems a little desperate, doesn't she?" he remarks as we both glance over at her. Marjorie's checking her appearance in a compact mirror.

Haley comes running up to Ryan and me. "I'm so sorry, guys. She seemed perfectly normal when I met with her a few days ago."

"We'll make it work," I assure her, remaining optimistic. "I bet she'll be great in this next take."

Haley hurries away to speak with Geoff and Carolyn, and though I'd like to say I know what I'm talking about, I don't. After five more disastrous takes, Marjorie is forbidden to speak, and when she can't look normal by refraining from doing exaggerated facial expressions, we all know she'll either need to be replaced, or we'll have to scrap the show.

Lucky for us the manager, Blair Roberts, arrives at the theatre. He's a quiet, lanky guy in his early twenties wearing round wire-framed glasses and a Renaissance Festival T-shirt. He seems calm, together and astute, so Geoff and Carolyn ask him to step in for Marjorie.

"But I'm camera shy," Blair tells them, pushing his glasses up on his nose.

Geoff and Carolyn exchange a look and then Geoff says, "You're perfect."

For the eleventh time, I grab my camera out of the SUV, and make my way up to the theatre entrance just as Blair opens the door. "You must be Natalie," Blair says in a normal, non-dramatic tone. "Please come in."

Yes! One-take Blair. I follow Blair into the old theatre's lobby. It's a bit dusty and dingy. It has well-worn red carpeting and a few banged up built-in benches. Dozens of crooked black and white photos from past productions adorn the walls along with old theatre posters that are curling and yellowed on the edges. Anybody can see this theatre has fallen on hard times.

"Let me show you the first hot spot." Blair escorts Ryan and me to the main dressing room. "In 1961, Lily Watters, a well-respected stage actress at the time, slit her wrists after receiving poor reviews for her portrayal of Hedda in *Hedda Gabler*."

"Has her apparition been seen by many?" I ask as I pull out a small notepad from my camera bag.

"No, but actors have heard a female weeping, and we've found unexplained drops of blood on the makeup counter."

I nod, looking around, trying to pick up any paranormal energy.

"Also in this dressing room, an actor hanged himself."

"What happened?" I ask.

"In 1992, we had just extended a very successful run of *Equus*. The actor playing the lead role ended up in the hospital one night, so his understudy, Marty Bressler, went on. He had only delivered his first few lines when he froze. Suddenly terrified, he looked out at the audience and couldn't speak, so he ran off the stage in the middle of his performance. The director marched into the dressing room and tore him apart. Everyone quickly cleared out, but the cast could hear the director telling Marty to get it together and get back out there or else his career would be ruined. Right before the curtain went back up, Marty was found hanging from this pipe." Blair points above us to a thick steel pipe running the length of the dressing room.

"What are some of the experiences that have been reported?" I ask in a neutral voice.

"Actors have heard a male voice yelling, which many believe to be that of the director. Several company members have felt cold spots here." Blair holds out his hands, then looks above his head. "This is where Marty was hanging. One actress swore she saw him one night before the curtain went up."

I finish jotting down some notes, then I glance at Blair. "So, the director has passed away as well?"

Blair nods. "He basically drank himself to death. Ruined his liver. Died seven years ago."

"And what was his name?"

"Phil Wycoff."

I nod, scribbling down his name, then follow Blair onto the stage and the next site of paranormal activity.

"Above me is the catwalk where we hang lights for our productions. Legend has it that a stagehand fell to his death on opening night of *Dracula* back in 1949."

"Do you know his name?"

"Sorry, no. We had massive flooding in the mid '80s and a lot of the theatre records were lost."

Blair continues on and shows me the last hot spot, a theatre seat where a woman in white can often be seen watching the shows. (Why is there always a woman in white?) After that, I wrap it up with Blair who seems more than happy to get away from the camera.

"Seems like this place should be ripe with your ghost friends," Ryan ventures with playful sarcasm as he removes my mic and battery pack.

"We shall see," is the only thing I can say.

I'm secretly praying that Ryan is right. It would be very helpful to me if ghosts proved my point to Ryan before I talked to him about Tyler. Not to mention, I'm a little worried we might not get much activity since I haven't felt any strange energy around the theatre. Normally, if a place is haunted, I feel a heaviness to the air, or a presence, like if I turned around someone would be standing right behind me. But I haven't felt any of this.

We spend the next few hours setting up stationary cameras throughout the theatre and making sure that the areas we'll be working in are safe. Because we'll be using a night vision camera in an unlighted theatre, we need to clear away stacked up furniture and props, so that we can walk through the theatre without tripping or running into objects in the dark.

While the crew continues setting up, I meet with Carlos. "Here's your script." He hands me a bunch of typed-up pages. "I know you're not an actor, and I realize you probably won't have time to memorize this, but this should help guide you. As you will see once you read through this, I tried to make it sound like you're more of an investigative reporter."

I quickly skim the lines he's given me and, oh, wow—it's totally cheesy. I really like Carlos, and I know he's been doing this a lot longer than I have, but I don't think I can say a lot of this with a straight face. Do I tell him? "Thanks." I muster a smile. "This will be a good ... guide as you said."

"I recommend saying the lines out loud, over and over," he instructs. "Before you realize it, you will have memorized a good chunk of it. Carolyn would like you to stick to the script as much as possible. At least for the opening, but then, obviously, if you experience something paranormal, then by all means, say what you need to say."

I secretly pray a ghost shows up the second Geoff calls action. "Okay, great." I force another smile as I walk away, wondering how I can sell this naturally. Clearly Carolyn has been working on *World's*

Weirdest Hobbies for far too long if she thinks this sounds real. I glance around for her. "Haley, where's Carolyn?"

"She had to go back to the office. She only stopped by to see how it was going. Do you want me to get her on the phone for you?"

"Uh … no that's okay. I can talk to her later."

Before I know it, everyone is ready to go. To lessen any human interference, Geoff will remain outside with the rest of the crew, watching the video feeds. Aside from the camera recording me, Geoff, Carlos, and Haley will be monitoring the stationary cameras that are set up throughout the theatre. Geoff will be communicating through an earbud to Ryan, but not to me. I can't have Geoff talking in my ear when I'm trying to listen for ghosts doing the same.

After I center myself and put protection around both myself and Ryan, I take my mark. Remembering that Ryan is getting instructions from Geoff, I wait for Ryan to cue me. A moment later, he signals me and Ryan begins rolling on a shaky handheld camera, very close to my face, so the audience believes I'm the one holding the camera.

Into the camera I say, "Good evening!" *Wait. Did I just do a really bad Dracula imitation?*

I can see Ryan listening to Geoff, then he relays, "Uh, Natalie, can we do that again, with uh less Bela Lugosi?"

I laugh. "Sorry. I have Dracula on the brain." I glance down at the script in my hand, shove it back in my pocket and try again. "Good evening," I say minus my exaggerated Transylvanian accent. "If you're watching me, you must be a believer in ghosts, which is good, because this show is not for the fainthearted."

Uh-oh. I can feel the urge to laugh out loud. *Keep it together.* I really wish Ryan was not the camera operator. He's making me nervous. I mean, his very job requires him to be focused on me like a laser, watching my every move, and at an uncomfortably close distance. I'm told I have a horrible poker face, which means he will see my every thought, my every feeling.

Focus! I put my eyes back on the camera. I know, by looking into the lens, I'm supposed to be talking to the audience, but in reality I'm staring directly at Ryan, therefore I'm talking to him. And this dialogue isn't me. I'd never say this. How do actors do it?

Just say it! "Are you ready for the thrill of a lifetime? Come along with me as I investigate places that are infested with ghosts and entities, and all things that go bump in the night!" I quickly look away and burst with a laugh. "I'm sorry. I can't say this with a straight face. No offense, Carlos."

"S'okay," he says, a little hurt.

Ryan stops filming as Geoff gets up and comes over to me with that same look he was giving Marjorie.

"Look," I tell him defensively, "this needs to be as real as possible. Like in the other ghost hunter shows, the audience will get a rundown of the place we're about to investigate. It doesn't make sense to begin the investigation with this dialogue because we open the show getting facts about the property from our client."

"We still need to remind the audience about those facts throughout the show, but I understand what you're saying," Geoff replies. "We could tone it down a little. Do you need time to tweak this with Carlos?"

"How about if I just say what comes to mind? If it doesn't work, then I'll ask Carlos for help."

"Whatever makes you feel comfortable."

That was easy. I scan the script. "Can I also drop this whole thing about how I'm the only one going in there? I don't see why the audience can't know I have Ryan with me."

"It won't be as scary," Geoff insists. "Let's just try it out tonight, and if it becomes a problem, we'll take that part out in post."

"All right," I agree, and everyone takes their places.

Geoff calls action, and I look directly into the camera. "I'm about to begin the investigation of the Gorham Theatre. In order to rule out any unintended noises or interference, I'm leaving my production team out here, and I'm going in alone."

Ryan, pretending to be me, quickly pans off me and on to Geoff, Carlos and Haley, who are sitting in front of the monitors.

Off camera, I say, "We have set up stationary cameras throughout the theatre, so that if any paranormal activity happens when I'm not there, our cameras will catch it."

Ryan stands to the side of me and moves the camera back onto me, again to make it appear like I am holding the camera myself.

I hold up the EVP recorder hanging around my neck. "This is an EVP recorder. It will pick up any voices that cannot be heard with the human ear." I glance at my watch, then back into the camera lens and say, "It's a little after 10 p.m. on Friday, September 13th. This is my first investigation of the Gorham Theatre in Los Angeles, California."

Ryan and I cautiously walk into the pitch-black theatre. I turn on my flashlight to help lead the way into the lobby, which now takes on a creepier feel. The dark stains on the carpeting come across as dried blood, the banged up benches show deep long scratches in the wood, like someone was clawing at it. The theatre is deadly quiet, so quiet, my own breathing sounds very loud.

I suddenly realize Ryan has the night vision camera back on my face. I worry I appear taken off guard, which I was. I actually tried to film myself with Ryan's camera earlier because I felt a little uncomfortable lying to the audience, but I couldn't even frame my face. Plus, I realized that if I spent all my time concentrating on trying to do a good job filming, I might miss out on spirits trying to contact me. It's safe to say that Ryan's job of camera operator is very secure.

I focus, and then I talk into the camera with a hushed tone. "Because there aren't any reports of paranormal activity here in the lobby, I'll begin in the main dressing room."

Ryan moves the camera off me and films the hallway as we quietly make our way toward the main dressing room. I tap Ryan's shoulder, my sign for him to move the camera back to me when I need him to.

Quietly I say, "This dressing room is where both Lily Watters and Marty Bressler committed suicide. Right above me is where Marty

Bressler hanged himself." I look up and Ryan gets a shot of the dusty steel pipe.

As I turn, Ryan films the floor and switches over to shoot from my point of view. I stay right next to the camera as he shows the audience the dressing room, careful to avoid the mirrors and an unintended reveal that I am not alone.

"Is anyone here with me who'd like to make themselves known?" I wait. I don't move, I don't speak, and to the left of me I hear a loud bang, as if something has fallen off a shelf.

Ryan's camera whips around and slowly pans across a clothes rack full of costumes.

"Lily Watters or Marty Bressler, was that you? Are you trying to get my attention?"

I'm met with silence. I have to say the silence makes it much scarier, as opposed to the other ghost shows where investigators are talking to one another all the time.

As we inch our way toward the costumes, we walk around the rack and notice that behind the rack are shelves. On the floor is a single man's shoe.

"Marty, are you here with me?" I ask, and though I can tell Ryan is a little unnerved, I'm not. I don't feel any paranormal presence at all. In fact, I think I can even explain how the shoe fell off the shelf. To get more space in the cramped dressing room, Ryan and I had pushed the clothes rack closer to the shelves earlier.

But the audience doesn't know that. Like Ryan, I'm sure they will be thinking that I've made contact with Marty Bressler because a man's shoe is now on the floor. I know I could really play it up, but I don't because ghosts really exist. If I pretend I made contact when I haven't and am later found out, then I will blow my credibility as well as do harm to the reputation and validity of psychics overall.

I wait silently, hoping to experience some paranormal activity, but after a couple of minutes of not getting any response, it's time to move on.

Ryan, pretending to be my point of view, takes us out the dressing room, down a darkened hallway and to the backstage area, right above the catwalk. Ryan films the catwalk as I remind the audience about this hot spot.

In a hushed voice I say, "The catwalk above me is where a stagehand was hanging lights for a production of *Dracula* when he suddenly fell to his death. This spirit has reportedly been seen by many cast members over the years."

Ryan puts the camera back on the catwalk as I call out, "Is there anyone here who'd like to communicate with me?" I wait for a response, even though I know I'm not going to get one. I don't feel any paranormal presence whatsoever.

I remove a thermal imaging scanner from my vest pocket and Ryan zooms in on it. "This is a thermal imaging scanner. When entities are present, the temperature in the room often drops. That's why there have been so many reports throughout the years of people feeling cold spots in a haunted location. This thermal imager will go off if it detects any shift in temperature. Right now it's reading seventy-four degrees in here."

As we navigate our way through backstage, Ryan films prop tables and several disassembled set pieces neatly stacked in the corners.

"I'm talking to the stagehand who tragically died here. Are you here with me?" I call out as we make our way into the left wing of the stage.

Ryan films the many ropes that lead up to the catwalk. And just as he gets to the top, there's movement above us. I hear a sharp inhale from Ryan and though I'm waiting for a sudden drop in temperature around us, or a sickly feeling to overtake me, nothing does.

"I hear you," I say in full voice. "Can you make another noise or show yourself? I'm here to help you, so you don't need to be afraid."

And just as I finish my sentence, there is a scraping sound coming from above and another metallic clank of some kind.

Ryan whips his camera around and tilts it up toward the sound just as we hear the fast clicking of high heels running away, and though I can't see them, I know they are gold.

With a groan, Ryan cuts.

I focus the flashlight in front of me. "Marjorie, you can come out now." I make my way around the curtains and light up the area.

Marjorie is scrambling toward the exit to get out of sight, but her gold high heels ensure that she doesn't make it in time. "Please," she pleads, turning around, squinting into the beam of my glaring flashlight. "Don't rat me out. The theatre is barely hanging on as it is."

I walk over to the side of the stage, pop on the backstage lights, before turning back to Marjorie. "Then why would you do this?" I ask, truly deflated.

"For the publicity, of course. Everyone loves a good ghost story, and so many more people are fascinated by ghosts these days than by those of us who are still living! It really is haunted, you know."

"If that's the case, then you wouldn't have tried to rig our investigation," Ryan points out.

"That's not true," she emphatically states. "Just because ghosts don't show up on cue, doesn't mean they aren't here."

Ryan shakes his head in disgust, then looks to me.

"I haven't seen or felt any spirits," I say to Ryan and to our crew outside who is listening. "As much as I'd like to disagree with Marjorie, she is correct. A haunted location can go months without a single incident because ghosts don't always show up on cue."

"Give me another chance," Marjorie begs.

Ryan and I exchange looks. "Wait here," I tell her.

After a long discussion with Geoff outside, we all agree to continue filming, as long as Marjorie never leaves Geoff's side. We shoot for another three hours. Sadly, I never once saw, felt, or heard anything paranormal. And as expected, none of us caught any ghosts on film, EVP, or on the thermal imager. We did have a few unexplained noises, but nothing anyone except Marjorie would categorize as paranormal.

It's six in the morning when we wrap and I'm exhausted. I'm making my way back to my real car, my 2003 Prius, and not the tricked-out sixty-thousand-dollar SUV, when Ryan catches up to me.

"Congrats on finishing your first episode," he says with more enthusiasm than I'd expect from someone who's been working all night on a failed project.

"Not a very successful one," I say disappointedly.

"You haven't seen what a good editor can do. Believe me, there were enough scary moments to entertain an audience for an hour."

"Well, I was hoping for more, or should I say, I was hoping more would show." I stop and look at him once we reach my car. "This is me."

Ryan nods, fidgets, casts his eyes to the ground, and then after a few moments, he finally meets my gaze. "Natalie, I just wanted to say that I'm sorry."

My brows furrow. "For what?"

"For kind of being a jerk the other night. For thinking you were a fraud. There were plenty of opportunities to make something paranormal out of the few unexplained occurrences we had tonight and you didn't."

"Carolyn said to keep it real, and even if she hadn't, I always will," I tell him honestly.

It seems like he wants to say something else, maybe about Tyler, maybe about his parents. I don't know, but it starts to feel a little uncomfortable. "Who knows?" I say with a teasing tone. "Maybe before this is over you might just believe in ghosts."

"You mean the ghosts created by old ladies wearing gold heels?" he throws back.

"Okay, Mr. Skeptic. Let's see what you have to say come episode ten," I challenge with a half smile.

"Bring it on."

"Oh, I will," I reply with great certainty. "I've got a hotline to the Other Side."

Ryan shakes his head with a light chuckle. "We'll see, Super Natalie. We'll see."

Chapter 10

———◆———

The following week everyone gets to see a rough cut of the first investigation. The picture editor, Marcus, manages to put together a pretty decent show. The video diary format works really well and heightens the suspense. It's similar to *The Blair Witch Project*, and the show comes across very scary even though it doesn't yield any paranormal results.

Our lack of evidence is no doubt on everyone's mind and it's Ryan who's brave enough to bring it up. "What if every episode is like this?"

"Again, my apologies," Haley jumps in. "I'll be checking out the paranormal claims and our potential clients more thoroughly so we don't end up with another Marjorie. But whether ghosts decide to show will be out of my control."

"I know of a place that's very haunted," I offer, and everyone turns to me. "My grandmother's retirement home."

"Unfortunately, we can't film there," Haley speaks up before anyone gets excited.

"Why not?" Carlos demands.

"Because we can't exactly relocate all the elderly residents for one night."

"Haley's right." Carolyn rocks back in her chair. "We've come to learn that we need a secure location, without human interference, and that's not possible with any location currently occupied."

"That takes out my second most haunted choice," I moan.

"Which is?" Ryan queries.

"Emergency rooms."

Geoff stiffens. "I'll keep that in mind the next time my wife wants me to do some volunteer work at the hospital."

"Hey! I just got an email," Haley announces. "We are clear to shoot at a location I've already been researching, and it seems very promising."

"Let's hear it." Carolyn takes a sip of her coffee.

Haley pulls up another file on her iPad. "The Musgrave Inn, located just up the coast about five miles north of Santa Barbara. In 1859, the structure was built by Edward Scofield for his new bride, Elizabeth. She drowned in the ocean only two weeks after they arrived at their new home. Distraught, Edward shot himself in his study a few days later. Then in the early 1920s, the home was turned into a state-run orphanage, but the place burned down from a kitchen fire and thirteen children lost their lives. It was rebuilt in 1927, sold, and has been in the Musgrave's family ever since."

"What type of activity is being reported?" I ask.

"People can hear children laughing and whispering. A man in a dark suit is seen in the study and a woman in white roams the gardens."

"Another woman in white," I mutter to myself.

"How soon can we get in there?" asks Geoff.

"I can set it up for the day after tomorrow, if we can be ready in time." Haley looks around the table.

Of course we all agree. Everyone is eager to move on to another investigation which will hopefully produce real paranormal evidence. I'm especially excited to begin another investigation because I want to see if I can obtain information through my intuition. I've been spending a couple hours each day doing the psychic exercises that my nana gave me. One exercise I've been working on is holding a personal object from someone who is either living or dead, and then seeing if I can pick up impressions or information from it.

Lucy was a great help with this exercise over the weekend. She has over twenty-five close relatives who have given her items over the years, so needless to say I ended up getting a lot of practice, and I was able to receive a decent amount of information. My favorite item was a personal letter from Lucy's aunt. When I held the letter in my hand I saw Lucy's aunt in the hospital having knee surgery, which was correct. The other great item was from Lucy's oldest brother. He had given her his old notebook computer and I was able to accurately describe the inside of his house even though I've never been there. I look around the conference table and wonder how much information I'll psychically know about my co-workers before the series is through.

"Before we get going I have an announcement," Carolyn rises and catches Geoff's eye as Ryan, Haley and Carlos quiet down. "The Paranormal Network saw our pilot for *Super Natalie* and they loved it. They're going to advertise it as a Halloween special and air it on the thirtieth in prime time.

My jaw drops as everyone high-fives each other around the table.

"Of course, this keeps the pressure on us to deliver. Depending on the ratings and how well our pilot does will determine if we keep our prime-time slot, and though I'm not psychic...." Everyone laughs. "I think we're going to kick ass."

I glance around the table at all the happy faces and start to feel a little panicky. "I hope they're not expecting to catch a ghost on camera in every episode," I mention, bringing down the room. "We didn't get any evidence at the Gorham Theatre, and I just hope they realize that what you caught on *World's Weirdest Hobbies* doesn't happen every day."

"We do have an amazing pilot," Carolyn replies, not at all buying into my anxiety. "So of course it has raised the stakes. But I'm confident that we'll be able to deliver an exciting episode each and every time."

"I do too," Geoff interjects. "And to your point, Natalie, we didn't catch anything at the Gorham Theatre—no ghosts at all, not even an EVP that we could offer up. But the way Marcus is cutting it makes the episode damn scary."

"Geoff's right," Ryan agrees. "The rough cut scared me and I was there."

Everyone laughs.

"So no need to worry, Natalie," Carolyn assures me. "I have a funny feeling the spirits and ghosts will always be on your side."

———

Three hours later, after our small crew has packed the equipment for tomorrow, Ryan and I leave together. I could have sworn that I'd seen Tyler trying to materialize while I was doing audio checks with Ryan, but he never made contact. The whole situation with Tyler is very confusing to me, and now I need to figure out his connection to Ryan without bringing him up.

"Hey, you want to grab a quick bite to eat?" I ask Ryan as we head to our cars. "There's a café just down the street—about a half a block down."

"Sure." He puts his bag in the trunk of his car, and we start walking out of the garage.

I throw the strap of my handbag over my shoulder. I'm glad the tension between us is gone. I just wish I knew how Ryan feels about me. It seemed like we had chemistry the other night, but ever since then, it only feels like we're co-workers. Sadly, I think my ghost whispering has killed yet another potential relationship. "How do you like L.A. so far?"

"I haven't really had much time to explore it, but I love the weather."

I stare at him bewildered. "You have great weather in Florida."

"We also have humidity and it can be brutal."

"Yeah, I guess it can be." I swear I can ever so slightly feel Tyler near. Does he know I'm trying to make the connection on my own? "Did you live by the ocean?"

"No, Orlando, but my parents used to take me to Myrtle Beach in South Carolina every summer, and we were always right on the water."

"Nice," I reply. "I'm guessing since you moved into the valley you're not a surfer."

"I tried surfing when I was a kid and almost drowned, but I like hanging out at the beach like anyone else."

He almost drowned? What if Tyler used to live in Myrtle Beach?

We reach the café, go in and sit down. As we're looking over the menu I can't help notice how cold it's become in the restaurant. I glance up at the ceiling, certain the air conditioning is on full blast, but there's not an air vent anywhere near our table.

"What wrong?" Ryan asks, noticing.

"I was just trying to figure out where the cold air was coming from."

"I don't feel it. Maybe there's a draft. Why don't you switch with me?" he suggests.

And then it dawns on me. Tyler has to be near. I can't see him or hear him, but I can certainly feel him and something tells me to get back onto our earlier conversation. "Thanks, but I'm okay. I don't feel the cold air anymore."

"Can I get you something to drink?" a model-type waiter asks before he gives me a second look. "Do we know each other? Have we been on an audition together?"

I quickly eye Ryan, who's suppressing a smile. "Uh … no," I reply. "I'm not an actor."

"Oh," is all he says, and I can tell he's trying to figure out how he knows me.

"I'll have an iced tea," I order.

"Same," Ryan adds, and our waiter walks away.

"No doubt he saw the video," I remark, automatically feeling like I should be embarrassed about my gift again.

"Which will be really good for the show."

I smile, pleasantly surprised by his comment. "You're right. It will be."

Ryan scans the café. "I wonder if tourists who visit here go home with an inferiority complex."

I glance up from the menu. "What do you mean?"

"Check out all the waiters."

I turn and look around the restaurant. There's a gorgeous blonde girl taking an order at the table by the window and an equally beautiful girl at the cash register. Another waiter comes out with hot plates who is short but built and looks a lot like Matt Damon. I laugh. "They must all be actors, waiting for their big break."

"Yeah, I guess so."

I feel another cold blast of air blowing down my neck, and I suddenly feel like I need to get back on the subject of his childhood. "Have you lived in Florida your entire life?"

"Yup. Even in the same house."

"So, why Myrtle Beach for summer vacation? Do you have relatives there?"

"No," he remarks casually. "My dad's in sales. His territory includes Florida, Georgia, North and South Carolina. He's always had a lot of business accounts in Myrtle Beach, so when I was a kid, my mom and I went to the beach while he went off working."

Instantly the temperature around me drops again. Tyler is definitely trying to tell me something. "Must have been tough on you. Did you make a lot of friends at least?"

"Sure, but most of the other kids were there for summer vacations like I was."

The waiter brings us our drinks. I stir sugar into my tea, continuing with my questions, determined to figure out the connection. "So, you didn't know anyone out here?" I ask, sipping my tea through a straw. "You just decided to pack it up and come on out?"

"Why not?" Ryan gulps half his tea, leans back in the booth. "I'd just broken up with my girlfriend, work had started to slow, and two of my best buddies moved, one to New York and the other to Louisiana."

"Sounds like a perfect time for you to move too."

"Have you decided?" Our waiter comes back over with pen and pad in hand.

Ryan and I quickly scan the menu again. "Uh ... I'd like the chicken club, please." I hand over my menu.

"French fries, potato chips or coleslaw?"

"Chips."

"And for you?" he asks Ryan.

"I'll take the turkey sandwich with fries." As soon as our waiter leaves, Ryan asks, "So, have you always wanted to be a ghost hunter?"

I do take note that he doesn't ask how long I've had the ability to communicate with spirits, which pretty much tells me that he's not yet convinced I can."

"Never crossed my mind until Carolyn offered me a job as one."

Ryan gives me a strange look. "But you were being interviewed as one on *World's Weirdest Hobbies*."

"No. As the title suggests, my ghost communication was only viewed as a hobby and not taken seriously."

"Then why did you agree to the interview?"

"To pay the rent. I never thought anyone ... real would be watching. I was told I'd be asked questions about what I can do and that would be it. I never dreamed a spirit would practically show up on cue, and a very insistent one at that."

Ryan looks directly into my eyes, "You really saw a spirit that day?"

"You saw it too."

"How do you know that a producer other than Carolyn didn't create that black mist so you would react to it?"

"Because I didn't see a black mist. I saw the apparition in solid form."

"Like you see me?"

"Pretty much, except he was partially transparent."

He shakes his head in confusion. "Explain."

"Well, you've seen a double exposure photo, right?"

Ryan nods.

"It's like that."

Ryan stares out the window for a brief moment, then puts his eyes back on me. "So, in the studio, when you were being interviewed you could see him and hear him?"

"Yes." I force myself to suppress a smile. So far, Ryan and I are very good at interrogating each other.

"Did you make anything up or embellish what you saw and heard, feeling the pressure of being on TV and in front of a live audience?"

"Not at all," I assure him. "I actually tried to block everyone out, including the cameras, so that I could concentrate on the information I was being given."

Ryan lets out a big sigh, and I can tell he's as frustrated with my answers as I am with his.

"It's okay if you don't believe me."

"I'm not saying I don't," he amends. "It just seems too easy. I mean, how come you can hear them so well?"

"As opposed to...?"

"Just yesterday, I was flipping through channels on my car radio and I heard a psychic on some morning show. The psychic sure had to ask the caller a lot of questions. If she were real, it didn't seem to me that she could hear the spirits very well."

"I don't know if she had true ability or not since I didn't hear the interview. But most psychics only get an impression or a word or a phrase."

"But you say you can get so much more. Why? How?"

"I think because they seek me out and are desperate to have their messages heard," I tell him honestly. "If I were on a morning show trying to pick up on a caller's life, I might fail miserably. I don't know. I can't explain it. Maybe my sixth sense uses 4G while everyone else is on dial-up."

Ryan laughs as our food comes. We start eating and before I know it, we've been sitting in the café for two hours talking about our favorite bands, movies and books. I have yet to make the connection with Tyler, and Ryan has yet to be convinced that I speak to the dead, but it doesn't matter. We're enjoying each other's company.

And just as I've completely forgotten about Tyler, he slowly materializes right next to Ryan.

With wide, urgent eyes, he shouts, "Ryan's my—"

And he's gone.

"No!" I yell because he just can't go again and leave me hanging.

Ryan is staring at me like I'm some total nut job.

"Sorry," I say, my mind racing for a normal, logical, no spirit involvement explanation for my outburst. "I just realized that … I forgot to pay a very important bill!" *Yeah, that's good.* "Give me a sec."

Silently cursing myself for acting ghost crazy, I let go of my frustration and whip out my phone, as if I'm paying the "fake" bill online. With my head down, I concentrate on Tyler and send him a quick telepathic message. *Focus, Tyler. Give it all your energy. Please don't leave again without telling me your important message.*

"Done." I put my attention back on Ryan. "Now what were you saying?"

As Ryan begins to tell me a funny story about a commercial shoot he was on with a spitting camel, I can see Tyler trying to take shape out of the corner of my eye. I can't help but be reminded of the 1960s *Star Trek* series, when they'd sometimes have trouble beaming back on board *The Enterprise.*

I avert my gaze for a second and concentrate on Tyler. *I can hear you without seeing you,* I explain telepathically. *Please, just talk to me.* I hold my breath, praying he gets my message.

And he does. A moment later I very clearly hear, "Ryan is my brother."

——•——

How? I think to myself while I sip coffee in Starbucks, waiting for Lucy. *How can they be brothers?*

"You called for Operation 007?"

I glance up to see Lucy plonking herself into the chair next to me.

"Had to." I scoot the coffee I ordered for her in front of her nose.

She checks her watch. "I've got ten minutes before I have to meet with another client. Give me the highlights."

"Tyler said Ryan was his brother."

Lucy's eyes widen. "Tyler, as in dead Tyler?"

"Do we know another Tyler?"

"And he told you they were brothers?"

"Yes."

"I didn't think he had a brother."

"According to Ryan, he doesn't." I slurp down my coffee. "Hence the need for Operation 007."

"I'm not sure if spying on the guy is going to yield any answers. Besides, why would you take the word of a dead guy?"

"Because he has no reason to lie."

Lucy sips her coffee. "Okay, so maybe Tyler is Ryan's brother and Ryan doesn't want to talk about him for some reason. Why don't you just ask him?"

"I did, remember? I asked him if he knew a Tyler and he said he didn't."

"Then he doesn't," she emphatically tells me. "Look, Tyler can't be his brother because they don't have the same last name."

"That's true, they don't," I grumble, wondering why I hadn't thought of that. Lucy and I sit there for a moment, trying to think this through.

"Maybe Tyler was adopted," Lucy suggests.

"That theory would work if he were older than Ryan. It would be unlikely for Ryan's parents to give Tyler up for adoption after they already had Ryan."

"Right." Lucy sighs. "We should probably recruit Matt into this investigation. They've become good friends. He might have better luck at getting to the truth."

"Do you think Matt will be up for it?"

"Absolutely. Because of you, he's now on this anything-and-every-thing-paranormal binge."

"Good. Have him call me with whatever he finds out."

"I will." Lucy stands, checks her watch again. "So, are you usually this determined to help other spirits, or might there be a little more between you two besides work?"

"Not sure. I like him, Lucy, but I have no idea how he really feels about me. I also don't think he'll ever be convinced that I truly talk to spirits, let alone believe in them."

"Hmm. Minor stuff. When you want to kick this relationship into high gear, that's something I can definitely help you with. Thanks for the coffee."

I watch Lucy leave, then glance up to the heavens. "Cupid, look out. Lucy's gunning for your job."

———

As soon as I get back into my apartment, I sit down, clear my head, concentrate on my breathing and focus in on Tyler. "Can you hear me, Tyler?"

I wait for any sound or drop in temperature to let me know that he's around, but nothing happens. I picture Tyler in my mind, remembering what he looks like, and I suddenly realize that his eyes are the same as Ryan's which is why he seemed familiar to me.

My gut tells me that they are brothers somehow, someway. I close my eyes and in a flash I see a young pregnant woman. She is very pregnant, as in ready to deliver. She's being wheeled into the hospital. She's holding the hand of a man who I assume is her husband, but I can't see the man's face. Is this Ryan's and Tyler's mom? It has to be.

No, that can't be right. Ryan is older than Tyler. Ryan never said his parents got divorced, and he never indicated that he had a stepmom. Maybe Ryan's dad isn't his biological father. I open my eyes, more confused than ever, and know I'm not going to figure this out until I have another conversation with Tyler.

My buzzer suddenly rings, making me jump. I press on the intercom button. "Yes?"

"It's Steph. Let me up."

I open the door and when she steps off the elevator, it looks like she's brought pizza. "Hey!"

"Hungry?"

This is a first for my sister. She never brings food when dropping by. In fact, she normally comes over to see if I can feed her. "Is everything okay?" I have to ask.

"Why wouldn't it be?" She comes in and immediately settles on my couch.

I grab two Cokes out of the fridge, two plates, and a bunch of napkins before joining her.

"What did you do to Mom?" Stephanie opens the pizza box and we dig in. "She's like a wild woman with a computer."

I laugh. "That's good. That means she took my advice and is going to try to make a go of her new online travel agency."

"Why would she do that when she already has a job?"

I stop chewing and stare at Stephanie. "She didn't tell you?"

"Tell me what?"

"Sherry laid her off."

"What?" Stephanie appears totally shocked. "Why? I thought they were best friends."

"Apparently because they are best friends, Sherry thought Mom would understand."

"Remind me not to have *those* types of friends," she says with her mouth full. "Well, this sucks."

And I can just see my sister's thoughts spinning around in her head. No more free lunches or spa treatments or a free place to stay. "You might have to think about getting a real job now," I recommend.

She rolls her eyes. "Like you have a real one … talking to dead people."

"It comes with a paycheck. How many real gigs do you book that actually pay you and your band members?"

"We get a percentage of the door."

"After they sell a certain number of tickets, and then you have to split it with the band. Can't amount to much."

"So I'm just supposed to give up my dream?" She glares at me, all ruffled.

"No, but maybe you should fine-tune it," I suggest gently. I take a drink of my Coke, waiting for her to settle down, then, "Steph, if there's one thing I know it's energy, and the energy you have around your band is that you guys get together and play for fun. So, tell me, is it just a hobby?"

"No!" she hisses with indignation. "Well, maybe Antonio thinks that, and maybe Mikey feels a little like that because he'd rather play the harmonica over the drums, but not me. It would be totally awesome if I could make a living with music."

"So, maybe you need to rework your style, or at the very least have a talk with the guys and see how committed they are. If you don't take yourselves seriously, no one else will."

"The guys have full-time jobs. It's not as easy as you think it is."

"Then, make it your full-time job to be the manager of your band. See if you can get booked into a real place instead of some hole-in-the-wall."

Stephanie finishes off a second piece of pizza and chases it with her Coke. "If I can get us into a decent place, we'll just be the backup band for someone better."

"Not someone better, someone more popular. Everyone needs to start out somewhere. If you want to be in a band and make money at it, then it needs to be a full-time commitment, and you need to treat it like a full-time job."

My sister goes quiet. She is staring at the floor which means she's actually listening to something her big sister is telling her, for once. "You don't like my music, do you?"

"I liked what you used to play better. You have such a beautiful voice. Those southern rock, bluesy songs showcased your voice much better than the hard rock you perform now. Why did you change?"

"We lost two great band members and added Antonio, so Mikey and I decided to try something different."

"Mikey plays the harmonica really well, and if I remember correctly, you can take apart a fiddle."

She smiles proudly. "I can, can't I." Stephanie takes a swig of her Coke, and then she laughs.

"What's so funny?" I work my way through my third piece of pizza.

"I was just thinking about when we were kids. Remember our tea parties and all the vows we took?"

I think back on when Stephanie and I, along with our teddy bears, Charlie and Fred, would drink tea and proclaim our future. "I'm going to live with the faeries," I remark, remembering one of mine.

"And you kind of are," Stephanie says. "Ghosts, faeries, what's the difference?" She snorts. "I said I was going to dye my hair purple."

"And you kind of did. Purple, blue? What's the difference?"

We both laugh and fall back onto the couch, totally stuffed with pizza.

"Those were good times," I tell her, still remembering how, back then, I thought anything was possible.

She peers at me. "For a big sister, you sometimes have good ideas."

"Sometimes?"

"Well, the time you asked me to help TP the head cheerleader's house and we got stuck in the tree wasn't so bright."

"It would have been if we'd brought a ladder like I suggested."

"She thought we were weirdoes peeping in her window."

I let out a sharp laugh. "The look on her face was worth it."

"And the firemen who rescued us were hot!"

"See, the idea wasn't so bad after all."

Stephanie smiles, gazes off in space again, then turns back to me. "Talie, I know we're not kids anymore, but let's promise each other that we'll really go for it this year. Let's go for our dream careers."

I stare at my sister. "Are you feeling okay?"

Stephanie polishes off her Coke. "What makes you say that?"

"Well, you don't talk like this. You're great at being in the moment, but since when did you decide to plan ahead?"

She sits back up. "When you said you talked to the dead."

"I don't understand. You knew about Nana's gift. Why is my ability affecting you so much?"

"I don't know. I think maybe I didn't entirely believe everything about Nana's ability because she's old and old people are eccentric, but you're not old. And then I got to thinking about how we will all die. I've been able to avoid a lot of things, but I'm not going to get out of that."

"Yeah, kind of sucks that immortal vampires aren't real."

"Right?" She nods, then gets serious again. "You know what I think? I think you're going to be the Donald Trump of the supernatural world. You'll go into ghost-infested locations and cut them loose left and right. 'You're fired,' you'll say. 'Be gone!'"

I laugh hard.

"Seriously though, after you finish with the TV series, you could charge a ton of money and become super wealthy."

I sigh. "I don't know. It feels weird."

"It shouldn't. Not everyone can be a brain surgeon. Look at all the pro-golfers, pro-basketball players, the pro-football and baseball players. The good ones are millionaires, and for what? Playing with a ball? Do you think they feel guilty?"

"Probably not."

"And they shouldn't because people are interested in sports. You shouldn't feel guilty because people are interested in the paranormal."

Stephanie sits up and holds out her pinky. "So, let's do this. Let's make a vow. I'm going to have a great career as a singer, and you're going to have a great career as a paranormal investigator, and we're both going to make a ton of money."

"I like that." I smile, take my pinky and hook it in hers. "Agreed."

Chapter 11

———◆———

The following day, the Super Natalie Team is driving to our next location, the Musgrave Inn. Ryan and I are riding in separate SUVs which is better for me because I need to concentrate on centering myself and raising my psychic antenna, so to speak. I can tell my nana's exercises are really working because I've started to pick up little facts about my co-workers, something I'd never been able to do before.

I gaze at Carlos, who is busy rewriting a few questions, and I instantly see him in the dead of night tiptoeing to the refrigerator. He slowly peers over his shoulder, and then he opens the door, takes out leftover fried chicken, and bites into a leg.

I suppress a smile before I glance at Sam, the show's editorial assistant, who is now part of the investigative team because he is also our video equipment expert. I know absolutely nothing about Sam since I only met him this morning, which is a better test for me to try and psychically gather information on him. After a few minutes, I see Sam in his kitchen. He's in a T-shirt and shorts and I can't help but notice that he has very hairy legs. He lines up six little plates on the counter, puts canned food on each, then places them around the house. Then I see his cats. How cute.

I wonder if I'm correct with these snippets I'm picking up. I can't ask Carlos, but I can ask— "Sam, do you have cats?"

He turns around in his seat and looks alarmed. "Has something happened to one of them?"

"No. Not at all. I just sensed that you had six cats who loved you very much."

He breaks into a smile. "Yeah, they're great. Only I have five."

"Five cats?" Carlos asks. "Better you than me, man."

That's weird. I saw six bowls.

"They're my girlfriend's," Sam sets the record straight, all macho-like. "I tolerate them."

I suppress a smile, knowing the truth, and am so excited about my new ability that I quickly concentrate on Haley and suddenly I see some guy sucking on her toes. "Oh!" *TMI, TMI.*

"What's wrong?" Haley asks me.

"Nothing. Everything's fine. All good here!" I nervously laugh as I quickly look away. *Mental note: Ask Nana how to filter!!!* I lower my psychic antenna as fast as I can and stare out the window for the rest of the ride.

An hour later, we pull into the inn and immediately the hairs stand up on my arms. It's a well-kept gingerbread-style manor with an immaculate lawn and two borders of colorful flowers lining the walkway up to the front door. *Hansel & Gretel* instantly pops into my head. The inn might look inviting, but I can feel other energy there—energy of deep sadness, of grief, of absolute fear. I know before we begin, that this location will not disappoint.

Remembering what my nana said, I put protection around myself right before I step out of the car. I peer up at the house and am drawn to the big picture window on the first floor. The energy of a presence is so strong that I half expect to see an apparition standing there. But I don't. Still, I can definitely feel someone staring at us.

"You're picking up on something, aren't you?" asks Geoff, who is now standing by my side.

I nod, without breaking contact from the energy I'm reading from the window.

"Ryan!"

Ryan hurries over with a camera and without discussing anything with Geoff, I quickly put on my radio mic and begin my video diary. "I've just arrived at the Musgrave Inn." I point to the window. "A man's spirit is staring at us right now. I can't quite make out what he looks like, so I'm going to try and see him another way."

Ignoring the camera shoved in my face, I close my eyes and concentrate on connecting to the ghost's energy. A few moments later, I see a man forming in my mind. "This man is around forty or forty-five," I tell the audience. "He's short, maybe five-six or five-seven, average build. He has some grey in his beard and around his temples. He has on black trousers, a white shirt and a black vest. He is stuck here, in this house."

I open my eyes and begin walking toward the inn when the front door opens and immediately the connection is severed. Out step the owners, a middle-aged couple, to greet us.

"Hi, I'm Natalie Dalton with *Super Natalie*," I introduce myself, extending my hand.

"Miles Musgrave," Miles says, shaking my hand, "and this is my wife, Denise."

"Thank you for coming." She greets me with a warm smile. "Let us show you around."

And then we cut. We have to cut because the Musgraves aren't properly miked, but wow! What an improvement over the gazillion-take Gorham Theatre episode.

Ryan gets them set up with radio mikes and Carlos goes over the questions with me and the clients, so they have a chance to think about what they want to say.

As they're getting ready, I psychically read the couple. They are honest, hard-working people who are a little freaked about what has been happening in their inn. Unlike our last location, where Marjorie wanted the publicity of her theatre being haunted, this family wants the disturbances to stop. I instantly think about what Stephanie said, how I should be the Donald Trump with ghosts and fire them. Suppressing a smile, I decide that's exactly what I'll be doing.

After Shani puts a little makeup on the Musgraves and touches up mine, we are officially filming. We do the introduction again, and then the Musgraves show Ryan and me into the kitchen. I immediately sense otherworldly energy faintly hovering around the four of us, as if we're being curiously observed.

Denise holds her hands in front of her. "We've known about the history of this place but never experienced anything paranormal until we started remodeling."

I glance around the kitchen and receive one-second glimpses of it on fire. "When did the remodel begin?"

"Two years ago," Denise explains. "We started with the bedrooms upstairs. Because we were remodeling one bedroom at a time, we were still taking in guests. Quite a few complained of hearing kids laughing and running up and down the hallway at odd hours."

"We don't have kids," Miles interjects.

"Even though we were hearing about other guests' experiences, Miles and I were still skeptical because we hadn't experienced anything unusual ourselves. Then we tore down this section of the kitchen." Denise motions to the right of where I'm standing. "When we removed old cabinets, we discovered burned brick behind them. Soon after, we could hear a child screaming, sometimes late at night."

I study the area behind the new cabinetry.

"It's really disturbing." Debbie gets misty-eyed, and I can see she's trying to keep it together. "It breaks my heart to think that children died here in a fire, and it's even more disturbing to think they might still be reliving it."

As much as I want to comfort Debbie, I know I must remain objective. I gently ask, "How often do you hear the child?"

"A couple times a week," she says, looking to Miles for confirmation and he nods.

"I'll set up an EVP session in here and see if I can get you some answers," I assure the Musgraves who seem very relieved.

Carolyn had cautioned me about promising anything to the clients. Actually it wasn't Carolyn but more the legal department who needs to make sure the production company doesn't get sued. Of course, the legal department doesn't know that I truly can talk to the dead, so I'm not worried.

"Are you having trouble anywhere else?"

"In the study," Miles replies.

"Lead the way." I follow Miles and Denise into the study where I'm instantly hit with a heavy sadness.

Miles walks to the back of the room. "This is where Edward Scofield took his life with a pistol shortly after his bride had accidentally drowned in the ocean."

I'm instantly drawn to a group of pictures on the wall. In the middle is an old black and white photo of a young woman—pretty, early twenties—standing with a man in his forties. I study the man's face and know immediately that this is not only Edward Scofield, but the ghost I saw earlier. "Is this Edward Scofield?" I ask.

"Yes, and his wife Elizabeth. This was taken the day they arrived," Miles informs me.

"Mr. Scofield still resides in this house," I explain to the Musgraves who look a little stunned.

"Is he here right now?" Denise asks timidly.

"No, I saw him earlier." I walk over to where I felt his energy. "He was staring out this very window."

Denise comes over to me. "From where you're standing, guests have reported seeing a woman in white walking through the gardens."

I gaze out the window and see if I can feel anything, but I don't. "Have either of you seen her?"

"No," Miles speaks up. "Just the guests."

"Have any of them given any more description of the woman except for her being dressed in white?"

Both Denise and Miles glance at each other, then shake their heads. "Anywhere else?"

"The hallway upstairs," Miles replies as Denise, Ryan and I follow him to the second floor.

The hallway is wide, with hardwood floors and a large window at the end, allowing in plenty of light. There are four bedrooms on each side of the hallway.

"We've stopped remodeling and taking in guests until we can get some answers," Denise states with hope in her voice.

"I will do everything I can," I tell her and Ryan cuts.

———————

Carlos sits with the Musgraves to collect any new information not given to Haley over the last few days. The rest of us set up stationary cameras in the study, the gardens outside, the kitchen and hallway upstairs. Because I will also be investigating the gardens, the command post has been set up in a van in the guest parking area where Geoff and the rest of the crew can monitor the stationary cameras, along with my investigation.

After the Musgraves leave for the night, I go and sit inside one of the SUVs and take twenty minutes to center myself. I know this is an active location and I need to ground myself again and reinforce the protection I placed around myself, as well as put protection around Ryan and the rest of the crew. I'm actually excited about this investigation. I finally have live clients along with dead ones. With a deep breath, I open the SUV door, ready to begin.

"There you are," Ryan says to me and does a double take. "Wow. Your eyes are really violet right now. You should see them."

I smile thinking about my nana and how incredibly violet her eyes appeared after she had been psychically working. "It's from my energy work."

"Ah," Ryan says, nodding, and without hearing his thoughts I know he's thinking, *Yeah, right. Whatever you say.* I'd like to tell myself that this doesn't bother me, but it does. Is Ryan going to be like this on every investigation?

"You know this is an active location, right?"

He plugs my radio mic into a new battery pack. "If you say so." Ryan hands me the new pack with a totally innocent look on his face, like he wasn't being condescending, even though I'm pretty sure he was.

"Ready to do this, Mr. Skeptic?" I throw back in a rather needling way.

He gives me a dumbfounded look. "What's that supposed to mean?"

I know I shouldn't get all riled up, especially since I spent so much time centering myself, but I just can't let this go. "I saw Edward Scofield before we set foot in the inn. You can't deny that."

"I know you believe that," he says. "But I didn't see anything. Sorry."

I breathe out my irritation with a quick exhale. After all these years I still have a hard time remembering that other people can't see what I can, especially when some of the ghosts are so clear to me. Now I'm secretly hoping several ghosts will show, causing Ryan to run screaming out of the inn like a little girl. It would serve him right. Besides, Ryan was the one who said, *Bring it on!* If only....

The back doors to the van are open and I see Geoff sitting closest to the exit. "Are you ready?" he asks as he sees me approaching.

"Very," I tell him.

"I have a good feeling about this one, Natalie. I mean, how often does it happen to other ghost hunters that they have an experience before filming begins?"

See, now Geoff here proves I'm not being irrational about Ryan. He's a completely normal, down-to-earth guy. He's never seen a ghost nor experienced one, but he takes it on faith that they exist. And here we are, working on a show that could very well capture irrefutable evidence that ghosts really exist.

"I wish you could have experienced the ghost too," I say to Geoff while glaring at Ryan who is now standing next to me.

"I'm sure we will all see something soon," Geoff remarks. "Right, Ryan?"

"Yeah," he happily agrees.

Geoff puts his attention back on me. "Do you know what's so great about our show? You have a true ability, Natalie. Whereas many of the other ghost hunters have the passion, they don't have the gift, so go in there and do your magic!"

"Thank you, Geoff," I say with great sincerity. "I won't let you down. Coming, Ryan?"

Ryan follows after me. "You know, Geoff used to be a basketball coach. He gives great pep talks." Ryan flashes me a mischievous grin, and I realize he's been messing with me this whole time.

"Oh, is that right?" I say with a half smile. "Well, Mr. Skeptic, you're going to need that little pep talk from him when you run like a scaredy cat after seeing your first ghost."

"Never gonna happen."

"Care to make a wager?"

"Sure."

"Okay," I say. "*When* you see a ghost, if you're able to hold it together, I'll buy you dinner wherever you like, no matter the cost. However, when you see your first ghost and you completely lose it like I know you will, my choice and your treat."

"Oh, this is going to be so easy," he says with a laugh and shakes my hand, making it official. "I already feel guilty, making you pay, since I'm going to be eating like a king in the most expensive restaurant I can find."

"Don't worry about it, since it's never gonna happen," I retort. "Would it be rubbing it in too much if I posted a picture of you screaming your head off?" I ask, suppressing a grin.

"Don't worry about it, since it's never gonna happen," he throws my words back at me.

"We shall see," I say, taking my position on the walkway up to the inn.

Ryan puts in his earbud so he can communicate with Geoff, then stands an arm's length in front of me since he is now going to be filming the rest of the evening as if it's from my point of view.

We're both staring at each other as we wait to begin. After a minute or so, it feels like a staring contest, and we both start laughing. I break eye contact and look away, trying to get it together quickly because I have undone most of my energy work. I center myself again and reinforce the protection I put around myself as Haley comes up, slate in hand.

Ryan begins filming, and Haley holds up the slate between Ryan and me. "Exterior Musgrave Inn, Night Investigation, Scene 9, Take 1."

I gaze directly into the camera. "This is my video diary of the Musgrave Inn. My team and I have set up several stationary cameras throughout the property. They are monitoring those cameras from a van parked at the entrance. The owners have left for the night." I glance down at my watch. "It's five after eleven, and I'm ready to begin my investigation."

I turn on my flashlight to illuminate the walkway. Ryan and I reach the front door and walk inside. I stand for a moment in the foyer. Ryan has me in extreme close-up. It's dead quiet.

In a very soft voice I say, "I'll start in the study where Edward Scofield shot himself." Since I saw his ghost earlier, I'm fairly certain he will show himself again. At least that's what I'm counting on.

As Ryan and I make our way into the study, Ryan takes the camera off me and slowly films the entire room. The study that was warm and peaceful earlier in the day, is now cold and creepy, and with the night vision camera, I don't have to be staring through the lens to know it looks as scary as it feels.

Ryan films me as I pass my flashlight over the photos hanging on the wall. They appear eerie and odd, like the photos themselves are haunted.

"Mr. Scofield, are you here with me?" I remain perfectly still, seeing if I can sense him.

Of course, this would be much easier if I could turn on the lights. I know it's scarier to be surrounded by complete darkness, but this puts me at a disadvantage. His ghost could be standing at the window where I saw him earlier, and like everyone else who doesn't have much of a sixth sense, I'd never know it.

I close my eyes for a moment and have an overwhelming sense that Mr. Scofield is indeed standing by the window. I focus my eyes and I can barely make him out.

"Are you by the window?" I ask, sending Ryan a message on where to film.

Ryan pans over to the window where I suddenly see fast movement—a shadow fleeing from the window. *Damn! I knew it! Did we completely scare him off?*

"Was that you, by the window?" I wait quietly, not moving at all. I tap Ryan to put the camera back on me, and I tell the audience in a whisper, "He's still here. I just saw him for a split second, and I can still feel his energy near." I look around, searching the room. "Can you make some sort of a noise to let me know where you are?" I wait for a response, not moving at all. I focus my energy, reaching out to him, and in the very far corner I find him.

And now I'm torn. Do I tell Ryan where he is and chance that he gets scared off again? Or do I help him first?

"Mr. Scofield, my name is Natalie and I'm here to help you. There's no need to be afraid. I can help you move on."

Since Ryan cannot see or sense Mr. Scofield, he begins panning the room again, and as soon as his camera sweeps across the corner, I feel Mr. Scofield's energy fade.

I tap Ryan who puts the camera back on my face. "He's gone," I tell our viewers. "I'm going to continue my investigation into the kitchen now, but I'll return here later and see if I can make contact again."

Ryan and I try to move as one across the hardwood floor while I remind the audience about this next hot spot. "The kitchen area is where the Musgraves have heard the sound of a child screaming."

I stop just inside, so that Ryan can pan off me and sweep the kitchen with his camera. And just like the study, the bright, cheery kitchen I stood in earlier now appears dark and dangerous. Using my flashlight, pitch-black areas light up, briefly casting long freakish shadows onto the walls. As I stand there, remaining silent, I get a strong smell of smoke. Ryan does too because I hear him take a deep breath.

"I smell smoke," I say, passing Ryan's inhale off as my own. "It's so strong that if it were real, my eyes would be burning and this room would be on fire."

I touch Ryan's arm and have him move with me further into the kitchen, and I tap him again, so he knows to put the camera back on my face.

"I'm going to start an EVP session with my recorder."

Normally, I would explain that EVP stands for Electronic Voice Phenomena and that the recorder can detect sounds the human ear cannot, but I will explain that as a voice-over, so as not to interrupt the tension and flow of the investigation.

"Is someone here who would like to speak with me?"

I stand perfectly still. The smoke smell has not gone away. In fact, it's getting stronger and without warning I hear a very faint, almost distant, child's scream. The temperature in the room suddenly drops ten degrees, and I most definitely feel a presence. I quickly hit Ryan, who begins panning the room again. I know he's filming in the wrong direction because there's a little girl standing right in between us.

"What's your name?"

In a very tiny voice I hear, "Abigail."

"Hello, Abigail. I'm Natalie. Do you know why I'm here?"

Very faintly I can hear, "No," and I'm praying the EVP device is recording her voice.

"I'm here to help you. Are there other children with you?"

I wait for a response, but I don't hear one, and I wonder if she's distracted by Ryan who's slowly moving the camera over the kitchen. I'm sure he's being directed to do that by Geoff, and I realize this idea of me appearing I'm alone is not going to work. I need to be able to communicate with Ryan. In a matter of a few seconds I know he's going to put the camera on me which might frighten Abigail, so now, there is only one way I'm going to be able to communicate with Ryan.

"Abigail, I'm going to point a camera at you, but don't be afraid. It's just so I can see you better, okay?" I tap Ryan and say, "I apologize in advance if my camerawork is shoddy, but right now Abigail is holding on to my leg."

Ryan jumps back. I see a split-second glimpse of blonde locks and a navy blue frock. Ryan screams, dropping the camera.

And Abigail is gone.

"Crap," I say.

"Shit!" Ryan spits out.

I fumble for the kitchen lights as Ryan picks up the camera to see how much damage he's done.

"Shit, shit, shit," he says, which I can only assume means that the camera is toast.

Geoff comes running in and before Geoff can say anything, Ryan blurts out, "Geoff, I'm so sorry. I have never dropped a camera in my life. It was an involuntary response. I'll pay for it."

"It's okay, Ryan," he answers quickly so that he can get back to the matter at hand. "We saw her!" Geoff announces, amped up. "My God, we saw that little ghost girl on our monitor. She was only there for a second, but we all saw her!" He runs his hands through both sides of his hair which makes him appear even wilder with excitement. "Come look!" Geoff's about to run off when he realizes he needs the camera. "Oh, God! Is the digital chip damaged?"

"No, just the lens." Ryan hands him the camera and repeats, "I'll pay for it."

"That's what insurance is for," Geoff remarks, excited again. "Come on!"

I lock eyes with Ryan, who suddenly seems embarrassed, and we both know Mr. Skeptic can't deny he saw her too. "I'll let you know where you're taking me to dinner." I suppress a laugh and am about to brush past him when I notice that he's still freaked out. "You okay?"

He's fixated on the very spot where Abigail was standing. "There's got to be a logical explanation."

"Seeing a ghost isn't logical?"

Ryan pins me with a don't-be-ridiculous look. "There's no such thing. It must have been the fact that it was dark, and your power of suggestion just got to me is all."

"Why don't we go take a look at the power of suggestion?"

Ryan and I walk out to the van where everyone is huddled around Geoff's playback monitor, and the screen is blank.

"Go back," Geoff says to Sam who's manipulating the playback. "There!" Geoff yells as the playback goes blank.

Sam slowly rewinds, and I'm holding my breath, praying the camera's footage is not damaged.

The video begins to play. Very briefly we see a jittery image of blonde curls resting against a dark dress with a white collar. Haley gasps.

Carlos puts his hand over his mouth and whispers, "Oh, my God."

"We caught her. Hot damn!" Geoff yells. "We have her on digital!"

Ryan just stares at the images before him and says nothing.

I'm smiling, too moved to speak.

"This is what you see all the time?" Geoff asks excitedly, and everyone shifts their eyes from the monitor to me.

"I see various degrees of this, yes."

"That's so incredible," remarks Carlos while Sam plays it again.

I glance at Ryan who's intently studying me, and I can only hope that he's finally seeing me in a different light. He shakes his head, and murmurs, "That's crazy."

I smile and say, "Welcome to my world."

———•———

As soon as we all come down from the high of capturing Abigail on digital, reality sinks in.

"People are going to debunk this," Ryan comments as we watch the clip for the fifth time.

"Why do you say that?" Geoff asks.

"Because in an effort for Natalie to communicate with me, she warns the audience her camerawork will be bad, which it is by my shaking hand, and then we lose the signal, which really seems like a setup. I can read the posts right now. 'If there really was a ghost, why didn't she hold the camera steady so we could all see it clearly?'"

"Ryan's right," Haley grudgingly admits.

"Which is why we need to drop the idea that I'm going in alone," I offer up. "It's still going to be scary with just Ryan and me."

Geoff rubs his hand over his mouth, still staring at the frozen image of Abigail's hair on-screen. "Okay."

"And here's one more suggestion you might not like. I need a bit more light in there."

Carlos groans as does Haley, but at least Geoff hears me out.

"I know it looks scarier if I'm walking around in the dark, but I can see spirits. When you turn the lights out on me, I can't see them anymore."

"But you can still feel them, correct?" Geoff inquires.

"Yes, though having two senses working is better than one," I explain. "Can you imagine what would have happened if the light had been on in the kitchen? We would have caught her on camera for more than just a split second."

"Or the light would have kept her away entirely," Geoff contradicts. "I don't know, Natalie. If you're standing in a well-lit room talking to someone none of us can see, it's not going to be scary to the viewers. At least when you're in a pitch-black room, people think they can't see who you're talking to because it's dark."

"I can keep working in the dark, but you are literally making me blind and shutting down one of my senses."

Geoff thinks about it for a moment, then says, "Okay, but it has to be soft, dim light that doesn't flood the entire room. Just enough light for you and nothing more."

"Great," I say. "I'll see what they have in the inn. And if it's too bright, we'll continue to shoot in the dark."

We all take a fifteen-minute break, and then we resume. Ryan grabs the second camera, and we go back into the kitchen. I turn on the pantry light, cracking the door. It doesn't give off much light to the rest of the room, but it will definitely allow me to make out shapes more clearly. Ryan looks through the viewfinder to see how it reads on camera. Because it's all the way across the room, it barely registers, which is perfect. I will appear like I'm still in the dark.

We are ready to go again. Haley slates. This time Ryan pulls the camera back much farther than arm's length, and I explain to the audience what has happened.

"I might be able to communicate with the dead, but I've been fired as a camera operator. In my efforts to film Abigail who was holding on to my leg, I had to put the camera at an awkward angle and I dropped it. Anyway, Ryan, our camera operator who is so good at filming the first half of our show, will now be filming the entire show. Thank you Ryan."

I turn away from the camera and walk back into the kitchen. "We are back in the kitchen. I no longer feel the presence of Abigail. I've probably scared her away, but I will try to make contact again."

I sit down at the breakfast nook by the door. "Abigail, are you still here?" I wait, listening for a sound from her. I close my eyes to see if I can feel her presence, but the energy in the kitchen doesn't change. "I'm sorry if I frightened you earlier, Abigail. I mean you no harm. I'd like to talk to you and help you. Will you come talk to me?" I wait for another minute and realize that she isn't coming back.

And just then my walkie-talkie goes off. "Natalie?"

I pick up my walkie-talkie and talk into it. "Go for Natalie."

"A door to the first bedroom on the second floor just opened," Carlos reports.

"On my way."

I hurry out the kitchen and up the stairs with Ryan following close behind. As soon as I get to the top landing, I confirm Carlos' report. The door is slightly ajar. I walk over to close it and notice the floor is uneven.

"Ryan, does it feel like there's a slope in the floor here?"

Ryan hands the camera off to me, and I film Ryan stepping on and around the threshold. "There's a definite slope into the room." He closes the door, or at least it appears closed. I keep the camera on the door and about thirty seconds later, the door slowly opens. "It sticks," Ryan explains. "So someone might think it's closed and it isn't."

I hand the camera back to Ryan. Into the camera I say, "Door opening on second floor has been debunked."

And that's when we hear a door downstairs slam. We run back down the stairs and see that the double doors to the study are firmly closed. Ryan gasps, and I look directly into the camera. "Mark this footage. We need to keep going but when this is played back, I'm pretty sure the doors were open as Ryan and I came out of the kitchen and ran up the stairs."

I open the double doors and slowly walk inside. The study is freezing. Before we began filming in the kitchen, we turned on the desk lamp, in case I had time to come back in. The lamp is only fifteen watts but enough for me to make out shapes, and I clearly see Mr. Scofield staring out the bay window.

"Ryan," I whisper softly, "Edward Scofield is standing by the window."

Ryan focuses on the window through the viewfinder and holds it there.

"Can you see him?" I ask.

"The camera isn't picking him up."

"Mr. Scofield?" I gently say his name as I take a few steps closer to him. I'm not sure if he can hear me because he doesn't acknowledge my presence. "Mr. Scofield, do you understand that you have passed away?"

He doesn't move.

"You don't belong here."

And slowly Mr. Scofield turns to meet my gaze.

"Why do you remain in this house?"

I can see his mouth moving but I can't hear him, which sometimes happens with ghosts. In my experience, spirits are much better communicators than ghosts. I can only hope that the EVP recorder will pick up what I can't hear.

"Mr. Scofield, you need to move on. You need to go into the Light." For the audience, I quietly say, "I can see his mouth moving, but can't hear him, so just now I was watching his mouth, and I think he said the word 'children.'"

I address the ghost. "Do you watch over the children?"

He nods.

"Then you need to take them into the Light with you."

He turns his back on me.

"There is nothing to fear. Will you allow me to help you?"

I hold my breath, thinking he will look at me again, but instead he just slowly fades away. Still feeling the emotional heaviness in the room, I take a moment to see if I can sense him lingering by. After a few minutes, I say, "Mr. Scofield is gone, but he did not go into the Light."

I'm so depressed in the study that I need to leave. Ryan and I walk around outside in the garden to see if I can contact the woman in white, but I don't sense her at all. And though I'm certain I'll make contact again with Mr. Scofield or Abigail, nothing else happens for the rest of the night.

Outside the inn where I began, I gaze into the camera and say, "It's four in the morning and time to wrap things up. Tomorrow my team and I will review all the evidence." I gaze up at the inn and Ryan cuts.

"I'm wiped," he says, wearily eyeing me. "I can't imagine how you feel."

"Drained," I answer honestly as we head back down to the van. "Physically and emotionally drained, and disappointed that I wasn't successful in getting Mr. Scofield to move on."

"So, you saw him the whole time we were in the study?"

"Yeah, and he was talking, but I couldn't hear him. I've never used EVP recorders. I hope they work."

"Amazing night," Geoff remarks as he continues to pack up the equipment with the rest of the crew.

"Doesn't seem like we got much evidence, though," I say disappointedly. "I wish I could figure out a way to make ghosts more cooperative. Maybe the Musgraves will allow us to film another night."

"Let's review everything first," Geoff replies. "We might be pleasantly surprised."

Chapter 12

———◆———

So the most difficult part of my new job is not the ghosts or the clients—it's staying up all night. Luckily our hotel is only five minutes from the inn. I climbed into bed at six in the morning. It's now half past ten. My alarm goes off for the third time and I am still horizontal. I feel like lead is weighing down my body. I can feel myself starting to drift back to sleep when my cell goes off. With an irritated groan, I answer.

"Natalie?" I hear Haley's excruciatingly chipper voice on the other end.

"Hey," I croak.

"Just wanted to confirm that we'll be analyzing all the footage and audio recordings starting at noon in Room 319. Also, they stop serving breakfast at eleven if you haven't been down yet."

"Really?" I grumble. "I better get down there."

"Do you want room service instead?"

My eyes fly open, "Seriously?"

"Yes. Whatever you like."

"Anything?"

"I just ordered for Geoff." Haley laughs. "It's not a problem."

I perk up. The only time I've ordered room service was with my mom and sister when I was sixteen. My mom had been divorced for two years and was paying all the bills, so we couldn't afford much. She took us to Disneyland and California Adventure for three days. To make it feel more like a vacation, we stayed two nights in the Disneyland Hotel, and we started each morning with breakfast in bed. It was so cool.

"Uh, if it's not too much trouble, can I get pancakes, bacon, orange juice and coffee?"

"Sure. Anything else?"

"No, that's good. Thanks, Haley."

"Anytime."

———————

After a hot shower and a great breakfast, I finally feel normal again and head down one floor to help Ryan, Carlos and Haley wade through the hours of footage and audio recordings. Not only do we need to go through everything Ryan and I shot, but we also have to view the footage from the stationary cameras that were recording during the entire investigation.

After hours of review, to my disappointment, we did not catch Mr. Scofield at all on camera. No orbs, no smoky mist, nothing at all to confirm that I hadn't just been talking to thin air.

While Carlos and Haley continue to analyze the footage from the stationary cameras, Ryan and I begin listening to the EVP sessions. Ryan takes the recorded conversation I had with Abigail while I search the second session with Edward Scofield. Eyes closed, we are both intently listening but hearing only my voice.

Finally, Ryan elbows me and says, "I think you might want to hear this."

I pause the recording I'm listening to and take off my headphones. "What did you hear?"

"A child's scream."

Excited, I take his headphones and put them on. Sure enough, there's a scream. "Oh my God." I play it again, closing my eyes. I hear the scream and then I hear something else a second later. "No way." I listen to it again, not believing my ears. "There's also two children laughing!"

I pass the headphones back to Ryan, who listens and nods right as he hears it. He doesn't say anything. He shakes his head and passes the headphones on to the rest of the group, so they can hear it as well.

I sit there thinking about this audio clip, and I suddenly visualize two little girls running around the kitchen. One throws water on the other who screams, and then they both laugh hysterically.

"Wow!" Haley laughs as she hears it for herself.

I come out of the fog. "You know what I'm thinking?" I address the group. "I think this might be the scream that Mrs. Musgrave's been hearing. If it is, she's going to be relieved to know that the scream was not from a child trapped in the fire, but from one who was having fun playing."

"Pretty cool," Carlos says, listening to the clip again. "I can barely hear the laughter, but it's definitely there."

I excitedly put my headphones back on to resume listening to my conversation with Edward Scofield. I close my eyes, concentrating, and right after I ask him, "Why do you remain here?" I swear I hear the word "guilty."

I gasp. "I think I just heard something!"

Ryan takes a listen. He furrows his brows, adjusts the gain and plays the clip again. "I can hear him. Scofield says one or two words, and then it sounds like guilty ... a few more words and ... sue something."

"Let me hear it." Carlos takes the headphones, puts them on and adjusts the volume. I watch his head bounce to the rhythm as he plays it over and over. "Because something ... guilty, something ... suicide! He said suicide!"

I quickly listen to it again. "You're right, Carlos. I hear it now. Haley, in your research on Scofield, does it say if he was religious?"

Haley pulls up his file on her iPad, scans it. "He was a Catholic."

"And suicide is considered a sin," Carlos says bluntly.

I rest my head in my hands. "Can the sin be forgiven if he asks for forgiveness?"

"It depends," Carlos replies. "I think you'll find arguments on both sides."

I drum my fingers on my cheek. "So if Edward Scofield believes he has committed a sin and has not asked for forgiveness, or even if he has asked for forgiveness, he might not believe he's worthy of entering Heaven."

"That's sad," Haley says.

I sit up. "I've got to tell him. When we go back to talk with the clients, I need to tell him." I throw the headphones back on to see if I can make out anything else, and to also ignore the silence that has taken over the room.

I continue to listen to the part where I thought Scofield said the word "children." I hear myself say, "Do you watch over the children?" I back up the recording before my question and turn up the volume. Scofield says something I can't make out, but then he definitely says, "for the children."

"Sweet! I knew he said 'children.' Listen!"

I excitedly hand the headphones over to Ryan who cups his hands around each phone and closes his eyes like I did. He nods, smiling, listens again. "Sounds like 'I'm here for the children.'"

"Yes!" I exclaim.

"I don't understand something." Carlos regards me quizzically. "The children died years after Edward Scofield, so how could he be there for the children?"

"Often adult ghosts will look after children ghosts," I explain. "So if Edward Scofield is afraid to move on because he committed suicide, he would have been there before the children died. Perhaps after they died, he felt it was his duty to look after them."

I glance at Haley and Carlos who seem to understand. Ryan, on the other hand, simply looks blown away.

———————

It takes us the rest of the day to wade through all the evidence, so we decide not to go back to the Musgrave Inn until the following morning. The clients are shocked when I present them with the evidence. When Mrs. Musgrave confirms the scream we caught is the one she hears, I play her the rest of the audio clip of the girls laughing and she is brought to tears.

Though the Musgraves feel satisfied with my investigation as does Geoff, I don't. I know there is unfinished business, so I ask if I might try to contact Edward Scofield one last time—without the cameras and paranormal equipment. The Musgraves are happy to assist, and though I'd like to take Ryan with me, I don't.

I enter the study, shut the doors behind me, and sit on the couch near the bay window. I close my eyes and take a few relaxing breaths, centering myself. I ask for protection and put white light around myself. I open my energy, concentrate on Edward Scofield, and after a few minutes, I feel a heaviness to the room. I suddenly get overwhelmed with despair, depression and fear. I open my eyes and see Scofield's ghost before me. He is staring out the bay window in his usual fashion. Even though he isn't looking at me, I sense he can hear me.

"I want to help you," I calmly tell him, and he continues to stare out the window. "I can only imagine how hard it must have been for you to lose your beautiful bride. I know you were driven to despair and I'm sure God knows that too. I would never pretend I know what's in your heart. I also can't tell you for certain what's on the Other Side, but I can tell you one thing. All my life I've been communicating with spirits who tell me there is nothing but love in the afterlife. So I ask you, how can there be anything to fear?"

Scofield slowly turns to me.

"Have you seen a bright portal of light?"

He nods.

"Does it seem scary?"

He hesitates, then slowly shakes his head.

"Then go into it. Go home. Take the children with you and go live in love."

He stares at me for a few moments more, then he turns his back on me. My heart begins to sink. He did this earlier with me, right before he faded away.

"Go into the Light," I softly say again, and as I'm holding my breath, I see an orb appear next to him, and then another.

He gazes upwards as a third moves next to him. The first orb grows bigger and in the center of it, I can barely make out a face with curly hair. *Abigail?* Edward Scofield continues to look up, and then he smiles. Tears suddenly sting my eyes as I watch him and the orbs shoot up through the ceiling and disappear.

The heaviness in the room is gone, and though the light hasn't changed, it seems a lot brighter. A strong feeling of elation washes over me. My Native American spirit was right. I am helping to heal the living and the dead.

I can't wait to tell my sister since she's already proclaimed me to be the Donald Trump of the supernatural world. I laugh out loud. I'm sure if she were here, she'd say, "Right on, Talie! You just fired four."

———•———

It's Saturday afternoon. I'm back home. We returned on Thursday, and I must have slept twelve hours straight. I had to go into the office on Friday to record two more voice-over lines for the pilot, and as I was leaving, I ran into Ryan. He looked worse than I did, though I think I saw him perk up when we made eye contact.

As good as I'm getting as a psychic, I can't seem to gain any insight into him. He's very guarded, making him impossible to read. I still need to talk to him about Tyler, but it has to be the right time, which is difficult to find since I'm sure Ryan needs a break from ghost talk. Hell, *I* need a break from ghost talk.

My mom invited me over to dinner tonight. I wasn't going to go since I still feel like I need to recharge from all the energy work I did at the inn, but my nana's going to be there, so I told her I'd really try to make it.

As I'm about to hop in the shower, I get an instant chill. I quickly grab my robe and put it on before Tyler appears. He's more transparent now, and I can't see his feet at all. "Really? This is the time you choose to speak with me?"

"Sorry, Natalie, but you said to talk to you when you're alone, and now you're alone."

"I was alone five minutes ago too, when I had clothes on!"

"I'm not a peeping Tom. When you become a pure spirit, you'll understand that we no longer think about things like that."

I tighten my robe around myself all the same. "Glad to see you're coming in loud and clear again."

"Me too. Sorry I've been MIA."

"That's all right." I lean against my bathroom counter. "Ryan and I were busy with ghosts."

"I know," he says. "This series is good for him."

"How so?"

"It's going to challenge him, make him analyze what he truly believes." He looks at me and smiles. "It's actually going to change his life in more ways than one."

"Am I part of that change?" I can't help but ask. Now that Tyler is a spirit instead of a ghost, he is privy to knowing everything.

"He likes you, you know. He's very attracted to you."

"Could have fooled me."

"His last girlfriend really screwed with his head."

"I guess that's why he's so closed off."

"He's being cautious. And he has a tough time talking about things that are painful."

"Is that why he pretended not to know you?"

"He doesn't know me. I'm actually his half brother."

"What?" I falter. "You couldn't have shared this with me before?"

"I was having serious connection problems. I've told you this information hundreds of times now, but unfortunately you weren't hearing me."

"Right." I blow out a breath, processing. "So, do you share the same biological mother or father?"

"Father."

I nod, thinking about it, then give him a puzzled look. "I still don't understand something. How can you be younger than Ryan if Ryan's parents are still married?" And just as I fix my eyes on Tyler, I figure it out. "His dad ... your dad had an affair?"

"Why do you think they're getting a divorce?"

My cell rings. I quickly glance at the screen. It's an 800 number, so I ignore it. When I look back up, Tyler is gone.

"Dammit, Tyler!" I'm beginning to think he's doing this on purpose. What is it about spirits and their half-cryptic messages? Why does it feel like I'm always having to solve a mystery with them? Agatha Christie must be a superstar in the afterlife.

———◆———

My mind is reeling the entire time I drive over to my mom's. How much does Ryan know? Did his parents tell him why they were divorcing? Was Ryan's dad leaving his wife for Tyler's mom? Does Tyler know Ryan's dad well? I am certainly not going to get these answers from Mr. Closed-off Ryan, so I have no choice but to wait until Tyler appears again.

I pull into my mom's driveway right behind my sister. Stephanie gets out and hollers, "Whoo-hoo! Now we can seriously have a girls' night like we used to." She hurries around to the passenger side to help my nana out of the car.

"Hey, Nana." I give her a kiss, wrapping my arm around hers so Stephanie and I can help her up the front steps.

"Ma, we're here," Stephanie calls out.

"In the kitchen!"

"I'm so glad you could come," my nana says, as I hand over her cane. "Your mother wasn't sure. She said you've been working around the clock with your series."

"I have. It's going great, and I can't wait to tell you all about it." We walk into the kitchen, and my mom's eyes light up when she sees me.

"Talie!" She reaches for her laptop that's sitting on the counter off to the side. "Check out my new website!"

My nana and sister park themselves on two bar stools while I look over my mother's site. On her home page is this gorgeous picture of a beach in Fiji with *A Cut Above* written in a serene-looking font that hangs over the palm trees. Off to the side, a column displays my mom's Travel Tip Of The Day.

I skim the tip and read it out loud, "If you are traveling with some-one, each of you should pack half of your clothes in the other person's suitcase, so that if one suitcase gets lost, both of you have something to wear." I smile. "Great idea, Mom."

I click on the other tabs and see her bio, rave reviews from clients, shared photos of vacations, and even a little travel blog. "This is amazing. When did you launch this?"

"Two days ago, and I already have several new clients!"

I read through some of the great comments and recognize a lot of the names. "And look how many clients stayed with you instead of Sherry."

"I know. I can't believe it."

"This is fantastic, Mom."

"Couldn't have done it without you." She gives me a squeeze.

"Am I hearing the call for Nana's famous champagne cocktails?" I ask.

"Bring them on!" Stephanie hoots, and my nana laughs.

"Champagne's in the fridge," my mom indicates, as she goes back to slicing up several cheeses. "And the Grand Marnier is in the cabinet behind you."

I remove four champagne glasses from my mom's china cabinet and set them on the kitchen counter. "How much Grand Marnier again, Nana?"

"Half a shot," she says. "And for me, a little more."

We all laugh.

I make the drinks, then pass them around, giving my nana the one she custom-ordered. "To Mom, who's still the best travel agent around," I toast and we clink glasses.

"And to Natalie, who has finally embraced who she is." My mom raises her glass to me.

We clink glasses again and dive into the cheese and crackers.

"Here's you're favorite Brie, Mom." My mother shows Nana. "Goes well with these potato crackers."

"Wow, this cheese here is really good," Stephanie says with her mouth full. "What is it?"

"Tres Leches," Mom informs us. "My neighbors recommended it."

"It's very good," I agree, taking a bite of the cheese. "And the champagne really makes the flavor pop. I can see why everyone loved it when you entertained, Nana."

"I might have to get these drinks started at Willow Creek." Nana grins, taking another sip of her champagne. "So, tell us about your TV show."

"Well." I pull up a bar stool. "I've only done two investigations, but the last one was amazing. The exercises you gave me have really sharpened my intuition, and I actually helped four lost souls cross over."

"Four?" Stephanie's eyes widen. "Damn!"

"Was it scary?" my mom asks.

"Just the opposite. I felt completely comfortable ... which is weird."

"Especially since you fought this gift of yours for so long," my mom points out.

"Of course, it does help to have a job that encourages me to talk to ghosts."

"Tell me about Ryan," my nana says out of the blue, and I gasp.

"Who's Ryan?" Stephanie asks, as her eyes jump back and forth between my shocked face and my nana smiling.

I take a sip of my champagne. "You amaze me, Nana. Your gift far exceeds mine."

"I've had more years of practice," she toots. "That boy has his eye on you."

"You have a boyfriend and you didn't tell me?" Stephanie asks, sounding a little hurt.

"No," I quickly amend. "We work together and that's all." I steal a glance at my nana who seems quite amused.

"Okay, Nana. What do you know?"

"He's a very nice boy." She slowly nods. "Good manners, good ethics. He's sweet on you." She takes a drink of her champagne.

"Well, he sure doesn't show it. He's never asked me out. He doesn't seek me out when we're at work. He doesn't seem that interested in me at all. I sense nothing more from him than I do with any other co-worker. In fact, I can't seem to read him whatsoever!" I say with complete frustration bubbling over.

"You really like him," my mother chimes in.

"No, I don't," I say defensively. "Besides, how can I like someone who doesn't believe in what I do?"

"He told you that?" Stephanie asks.

"Not in those exact words, but he doesn't believe ghosts exist, therefore he doesn't believe I'm talking to them."

"I don't think *you'll* have to say a thing," Nana interjects.

"Meaning what?" Stephanie asks, and my nana regards me as a teacher would a student.

I think about how Ryan reacted with Abigail and I smile. "Seeing is believing."

"Nana's right." Stephanie gobbles a slice of cheese. "Maybe you can ask one of them to turn up their energy in the visibility department, so Ryan can see what you see."

"I don't need to."

My mother gasps. "Did he already see a ghost?"

I nod. "A little girl—but only for a split second."

Stephanie gives me a confused look. "If he saw a ghost, then how can he still doubt they exist?"

"It's amazing how quickly Mr. Skeptic denied the evidence," I say with a sarcastic bite. "He can't explain it, but he's positive there's some kind of logical, non-spiritual explanation that will present itself soon."

Stephanie snorts with a laugh. "Denial could be more of a guy thing."

"Well, with the show and your sixth sense ability, I've no doubt there will be many more opportunities for him to see something that he can't explain away," my mother points out, as she puts cheese on a cracker and eats it.

"And he'll soon learn that not everything real can be backed up with facts." My nana giggles into her champagne glass like she has a delicious secret. "Love will cure him of that."

I sit with this information, sipping my champagne with Nana. *Could she and Tyler have it right about Ryan?*

"You've closed yourself off too," my nana astutely observes.

I am stunned by this revelation. "I guess I have. The stress of spirits popping in at work was overwhelming. I couldn't allow myself to think how bad it would be on a date."

"Two closed-off people who are afraid to admit they have feelings for one another." My nana giggles again before she downs the rest of her champagne, then motions me to pour her more. "This is going to get interesting."

"Already is," I tell her, adding Grand Marnier on the top. "He's a client of mine and he doesn't know it."

"What do you mean, 'client?'" my mom asks.

"His half brother died a few months ago and has contacted me."

"Oh, I'm sorry to hear that." My mother's voice is full of concern. "Ryan must be devastated."

"He doesn't know he has a half brother. His father had an affair."

My nana bursts with a loud, sharp laugh. "You can't make this shit up."

"Mother!" my mom exclaims, chastising her while Stephanie laughs her head off.

"Boy, you sure have amazing, entertaining spirits," my nana remarks.

"That, or they have a sick sense of humor," I say. "I think they're getting me back for trying to ignore them all these years."

"Well, I've got to hand it to them," my nana says. "This series will force you to rely on your spirit guides more than ever. But we all have faith in you. And know this, Talie, if you can convince a skeptic that ghosts and spirits exist, make him believe that you've been having heart-to-heart conversations with his dead half brother, *and* get him to fall in love with you, then there is nothing, absolutely nothing you can't handle." Nana raises her glass to me.

"Better you than me, Sis," Stephanie says, still laughing. "I think I'll stick to being in a band.

———

It's one in the morning and I'm driving my nana back to her place. "We need to do this more often," I say, as I peer over at her in the passenger seat. "Did you have a good time?"

"The best. And I'm so proud of you." My nana smiles, patting my leg. "You seem so much happier."

"I am," I confess. "It really is liberating to do what I'm meant to without negative consequences. I don't know how you dealt with your gift for so long without having support from anybody."

"Different world back then. As your grandfather says, 'Our generation was the last one where life was simple.' In a way, he's right. Everything seems so complicated these days."

"It is because life moves a lot faster. My generation must always be flexible and know how to multi-task. Seems like everyone works longer hours, and often from different locations. Families are spread out all over the globe. Technology has taken over our lives…."

"And kids your age would rather have three hundred people they've never met as friends on Facebook, than one true best friend who'd donate a kidney if need be."

"You're right about that, Nana. Though aren't you also on Facebook?" I steal a quick glance.

"Of course," she boasts. "I have to stay hip, you know."

I laugh.

"Your grandfather finds it absurd."

"I'm sure he does. When was the last time you saw Grandpa?"

"This afternoon. He's hanging around quite a bit these days."

"He is? Why?" I ask a little alarmed.

"Oh, you know. I guess I'm just getting old."

"Is there something you need to tell me, Nana?"

She chuckles. "No, but I'm no spring chicken, Talie."

"Nana?" I pull over the car, my heart suddenly racing. "Are you leaving us?"

"No, dear." She chuckles. "Not to my knowledge."

"Then why is Grandpa constantly around?"

"You'll have to ask him."

I fix my eyes on Nana. "What aren't you telling me?"

She lets out a long sigh. "I'm losing weight, and I've been a little more tired over the last few days. But that's all. I'm sure it's nothing to worry about."

"Well, you need to get a thorough checkup immediately."

"I already did yesterday. Your grandfather insisted on it." She shakes her head, disapproving of his overprotective behavior. "Everything looks fine, Talie," she assures me.

I want to believe her....

"How many grandmothers do you know who stay out and celebrate until one in the morning?"

I smile. "You are the life of the party, you know."

"As I've always been."

I chuckle, pull back out onto the road and continue to her retirement home. I drive in silence because I can see my nana is deep in thought.

A few minutes later, she shares, "You should have seen me in my twenties. Your grandfather and I won two dance contests. If he were still alive, I'd sign us up for *So You Think You Can Dance*."

"I've no doubt you'd win that too," I say with a laugh.

She looks over, studying me. "Talie, don't allow any spirit or your ability to get in the way of your love life."

"Done that already, but I won't let it happen again. And I'm glad you didn't let it interfere with you and Grandpa. You two seemed so perfect together."

"We were." She gives off a soft giggle. "Your grandfather was definitely a keeper."

"Yes, he was." I smile, remembering how Grandpa spoiled Stephanie and me when we were kids.

"I have a good feeling about Ryan. Just be yourself. Let him accept you the way you are."

"But you didn't do that with Grandpa."

"And I should have. I would have saved myself years of worry." She pats my leg. "At least your generation is much more open-minded than mine ever was. I know you don't think that includes Ryan, but it does. Mark my words, Talie, that boy is a keeper, just like your grandfather."

I smile. "I sure hope you're right."

"I usually am. Just ask your mother."

I chuckle as I pull into my nana's place and help her out of the car. I hand over her cane, and we start walking to her apartment.

"It's bingo night on Tuesday, if you want to come by," she says.

"I'd love to. If I'm not on an investigation, I will."

"Good. And bring Ryan with you. No sense wasting time in getting to know my future grandson-in-law."

"Oh, Nana." I shake my head, smiling. "You're something else."

Chapter 13

————————

"Hey, Lucy." I cradle my cell on my shoulder as I throw in a load of laundry, put in my quarters, and start the washer. "Are you and Matt still going tonight?"

"Yeah," Lucy says excitedly. "Where's your sister playing again?"

"House of Blues, on Sunset."

"Oh, right. She's on at nine?"

"Yeah. I'll pick you guys up a little after eight."

"Great, but go to Ryan's first."

"Why?"

"So I can have an extra five minutes with my hair. Gotta go!"

And she hangs up on me, which she seems to be doing a lot of these days. I can't help but wonder if she's hatching another matchmaking plan for Ryan and me. This time, I'm not minding it so much. I get butterflies in my stomach every time I'm near him, which pretty much tells me that my heart is liking him more than my head thinks I should. I really hope my nana and Tyler are right about him because it will really suck if this ends up being a one-way attraction.

As instructed by Lucy, a little after eight I make my way over to Ryan's. I ring the bell and wait, and I can already feel my heart beating faster than it should.

"Oh, hey." Ryan gives me a big smile as he opens the door. "Gotta get some shoes on. Come in for a sec."

As I walk inside, Ryan disappears down the hallway, so I have myself a look around. It's sparse, like a typical single guy's place usually is. The only two items he has sitting on the kitchen counter are a coffeemaker and a roll of paper towels. In the living room is a well-worn couch, one end table, and a good-sized plasma screen TV. By the window, Ryan has one of those huge home gym pieces of equipment, along with a full set of weights tucked in the corner.

"So, how long has your sister been in a band?" Ryan asks, as he comes back in fully dressed, and begins to close the windows and sliding glass door.

"About a year now," I answer, taking him in. He's wearing dark jeans, a white casual shirt and loafers. He has a definite tan now, which makes him seem very relaxed, and damn, he's good looking. "Were you at the beach today?"

He smiles, and I'm immediately sucked into his very cute dimples. "Yeah, I might have overdone it."

"No, you look good," I tell him, and he finally stops buzzing around his place to focus on me. I'm wearing a short casual dress that's clinging to my every curve, and at last he notices.

"You look great," he says, "without needing the beach."

"Thanks," I easily throw out, as if I look this way every day, though in truth, I spent two hours earlier getting a mani-pedi and my legs waxed.

And as if he read my mind, Ryan seems to be enjoying my legs. His eyes then travel up to my face, and he stares at me without saying a word. In a bit of a daze he finally says, "You're a stunner, Natalie. How did I not know this before?"

I smile, a hint of embarrassment coloring my cheeks. "Well, we've both been in the dark lately."

He laughs at my double meaning. "Actually, I just realized the reason. In my mind, I made you off-limits because we work together. Also I've felt like Lucy's been pushing us together, and I hate that."

"I did the same thing," I confess. "And don't get me started on my matchmaking friend. I love Lucy, but sometimes…." I let out an exasperated sigh.

"Why do friends do that? I know they mean well, but don't they realize that it has the opposite effect?"

"That's what I tried to tell her."

"I immediately thought, I wonder what's wrong with Natalie, for her friend to be pushing her on me so much?"

I laugh. "I thought the same thing. And then to find out we'd be working together."

"And that you talked to ghosts." His eyes widen in a crazy expression.

"And I said to myself—"

"Forget it!" We both say at the same time and immediately start laughing.

Ryan takes a step closer to me. "Are Matt and Lucy coming over here or are we supposed to go over there?"

"We'll pick them up." I find myself staring into his smoldering grey eyes.

"You really are a stunner," he whispers, and I suddenly feel his warm lips on mine. They are so soft and tender. He keeps kissing me as his hand gently glides through my hair. I rest my hands on his waist, quickly getting lost in the moment. Without warning, I hear AC/DC's *Back in Black* blaring between us.

Startled, I jump back. "Your ringtone is AC/DC?" I ask incredulously.

Ryan gives me this charming smile as he pulls his cell out of his pocket. "It's Matt," he tells me, then answers, "Hey, buddy." Ryan turns away from me to regain his composure while I try to regain mine. "Okay. Be right there." He disconnects the call. "Matt says they're waiting outside."

"Oh." I sound disappointed and surprised at the same time.

"He said he'll drive, so you don't have to."

"Oh, I get it." I laugh, realizing Lucy has arranged it for me to be able to concentrate on Ryan and not the road.

"Your matchmaking friend is good." Ryan smiles.

"That she is."

He picks up his keys, and we head out the front door.

"Hey, Talie," Matt says, as I climb into the back of his SUV.

"Thanks for driving." I say, and look over at Lucy who is grinning from ear to ear. I smile back, rolling my eyes.

Ryan closes the door, gets settled next to me and without hesitation, he holds my hand. I'm suddenly giddy inside. He's holding my hand, and I feel like I'm back in high school going to my senior prom.

"So, Talie, I think it's great how you're supporting your sister," Lucy remarks. "Do you have any siblings, Ryan?" Lucy catches my eye, and I instantly realize I haven't filled her in on the latest since she's still working on Operation 007.

"No," he informs her. "What about you?"

"I have one sister and three brothers," Lucy comments. "And they're all pretty cool. So, no brothers, huh?"

"Nope."

"Not even one?" she questions suspiciously.

Ryan gives her a funny look. "Uh ... no, not even one." He then eyes me, and I take a deep breath and give him a look which says that sometimes my friend is a little quirky. "I don't have one, either," I say, and Ryan laughs.

"Matt, if Lucy is asking this because you need me to be your brother for some function, I will."

Lucy's jaw drops and she pretends to be offended.

"Very astute, Ryan," I commend. "See, Lucy, even Ryan knows you're a schemer."

"At least I scheme for love. And, no, Ryan, I wasn't asking for Matt. I just had this overwhelming sense you had a brother."

"Maybe you should join Psychic Natalie here. I hate to admit it, but her overwhelming sense has been remarkably right."

"Gasp!" Lucy says, putting her hand over her mouth. "The non-believer has dropped the 'non.'"

"I wouldn't go that far," Ryan corrects. "But I wouldn't mind taking her with me to Vegas one weekend." He regards me with an amused twinkle in his eye. "Maybe you and your psychic powers could win us some money." He kisses the back of my hand.

Damn, that even has an effect on me. "For you, I would if I could," I reply sweetly. "But unfortunately it doesn't work that way."

"Really?" he questions disappointedly.

"Yeah, buddy, we already asked." Matt glances at Ryan through his rearview mirror. "And what did you say, Natalie?"

"If psychics could win money with their gift, Vegas would be bankrupt."

Ryan chuckles. "Yes, I guess that would be the case."

"But all is not lost," Lucy tells him, peering over her shoulder. "You know the saying, 'Unlucky in cards, lucky in love.'" Lucy ping-pongs her eyes between Ryan and me.

Ryan looks at me and we both laugh.

———

When we arrive at the House of Blues, I'm glad to see that there's a long line to get in. While we're waiting, I take note of the crowd, which seems to be very eclectic. Some are serious hard rock fans with their black leather pants and leather-spiked wristbands, all standing around in a cloud of smelly hair spray. Others are wearing cowboy hats, cowboy boots and rattlesnake belts, which means not all of the bands playing tonight are hard rock.

When we finally get inside, I see it's fairly packed, and I'm already getting nervous for my sister. This is the first time her band is playing here, and she told me it was tough to get in.

Taking my talk to heart, Stephanie has been working every angle. She developed a friendship with the lead guitarist in a more established hard rock band, asked if she could open for them, and the booker agreed. Now this is her chance to prove she can hang with the big boys.

As I watch Stephanie, Mikey and Antonio set up their equipment, I notice a crusty, weathered-looking old guy with a long beard and mustache hovering around Mikey. He's definitely a spirit, and he's talking to Mikey, but Mikey can't hear him.

At least that's what I think. Subliminally something registers in Mikey because he suddenly pulls out his harmonica from his bag before going over to talk to Stephanie and Antonio. Stephanie seems to be listening but Antonio flat out says no. He shakes his head and walks away. Mikey disappointedly pockets his harmonica and goes back to setting up his drums. The spirit then starts pacing on the side of the stage, and I wonder what can be so important.

Five minutes later, after the band seems ready to go, I see a guy come out from the wings. He and Stephanie exchange a look as he continues to the microphone. The audience somewhat quiets down and I hear, "Ladies and Gentlemen, Rock on Fire!"

"Whoo-hoo!" I yell, clapping loudly. Lucy and Ryan join me as Matt whistles.

With her guitar in place, Stephanie steps up to the mic. Mikey hits his sticks three times over his head, and the band begins to play. I don't remember the name of the song, but I've heard it before. It's one of her cooler, hard rock songs. I just wish it showcased her voice better.

I look over at Ryan since he seems to be into hard rock, and I can tell he's not liking the song. He must feel my gaze on him because he eyes me and mildly smiles. Matt and Lucy are talking to each other, so I can't tell what they think, but it doesn't matter. When I glance around at everyone in the club, no one is paying attention. In fact, everyone starts talking louder, like they're at some party and the music is merely background noise for their important conversations.

The song ends and the respect for the band is even less. I think we're the only four clapping and showing our appreciation. My sister looks nervous, obviously noticing that the conversation level has become much louder than when they began, so they immediately go into another song, which sounds similar to the first one.

As the crowd continues to talk louder, my eyes are drawn to the spirit who is angrily jumping around and screaming at Mikey. If the guy wasn't already dead, I would think he was going to have a heart attack from the way he was acting.

I try to connect with the old man's energy. "What are you saying to Mikey?" I ask, and the spirit immediately appears by my side.

"Tell your sister to sing the song Mikey was talking to her about."

"Does she know it? Has the band ever played it?"

"Yes, but only a few times, which is why Antonio's afraid to play it."

Their second song ends and not only is the crowd louder, but I hear a few snide remarks about them. My sister backs away from the mic, and the band members are exchanging looks.

The spirit gets right in my face. "Tell her if they play the song, it will be a huge break for them."

I open my mouth to question him further, but he cuts me off.

"Now! Before it's too late!"

I push through the crowd, trying to get to Stephanie as I see the guy who announced them come back on stage, most likely to give them the boot.

"Stephanie!" I scream at the top of my lungs. "Stephanie!" I frantically wave my arms.

She comes to the front of the stage and bends down. "What the hell, Talie?"

"Play the song Mikey wants you to play!" I yell above the roar of the crowd.

"How do you—"

"Just do it!" I scream like some lunatic, which gets her to stop asking questions.

"I hope you're right!" She shouts and quickly goes back to the guy who's trying to shut them down.

So do I. I nervously watch her, and I know she's doing some serious dancing to try to keep them on stage.

"Come on, come on, come on," I encourage under my breath, and the guy finally retreats into the wings.

Stephanie has a quick word with her band, then steps back up to the mic. "Thanks, everybody. We're Rock of Fire!"

"Whoo-hoo!" I yell. Ryan, Lucy and Matt cheer along with me, but the rest of the audience doesn't care. They continue to carry on their conversations.

Then, in an instant, the stage goes completely dark. Everyone falls into silence as they look up to see what's going on.

Over the hushed crowd, we hear the sound of one chord from the guitar, then two, and a third slowly being picked by Antonio, and my mind is transported back in time to the Old West. A blue light snaps on, a single onto Stephanie who is sitting in front of the mic. She has a fiddle on her lap, which I barely notice because in the most bluesy, soulful voice I hear her slowly sing:

I've got to go,
Because I cannot hide.
I've got to go,
Before it turns to night.
I've got to go, gotta go, gotta go, go, go.
I've got to ride, I've got to ride, I've got to ride, ride, ride.

Stephanie looks over at Mikey, a red spotlight floods over him, and he plays the harmonica like it's on fire.

The audience goes wild. The rest of the lights snap on. Antonio kicks in with his guitar as Stephanie continues to sing:

Love's on my side,
That's why I've got to go.
He didn't start the fight.
For I received the first blow,

So he drew his gun fast,
And sent five below.
Now we've both got to go,
They've set the lawmen loose,
We've both gotta ride,
Else we'll be swingin' from the noose.
We've got to go, we've got to go, we've got to go, go, go.
We've got to ride, we've got to ride, we've got to ride, ride, ride.

Stephanie joins her band with her fiddle ripping up the stage. The tempo of the song picks up again, and the band jams to one of the best southern rock songs I've ever heard. I watch the old geezer of a spirit jamming along with the band, and I think whoever believes that the living and the dead can't hang together, hasn't witnessed something like this.

With three big strums of the guitar and three slides on the fiddle, the song ends and the audience goes crazy.

I look over at Ryan, and he is clapping like a madman. "Wow!" he yells to me over the crowd. "They're incredible!"

"Yes, they are," I proudly agree. "Yes, they are."

———————

"I can't get your sister's song out of my head," Ryan says, as we walk into his place.

"That's a really good sign." I set down my handbag and follow him into his kitchen.

"A spirit really told you what song they should play?"

"Yeah. I think he was related to Mikey."

"Mikey has a ghost muse," he remarks and I laugh.

So far, it has been a fantastic night. My sister totally rocked it with her band, then Matt, Lucy, Ryan and I went out for dinner and had a great time. Lucy and I were even laughing in the restroom about how I'd have to marry Ryan and she'd have to marry Matt because the four of us were just too perfect together. It goes without saying that I'd like to continue this fantastic night with Ryan's perfect lips on mine.

"Beer, water, iced tea?" he offers.

"Whatever you're having." I can't help but stare at him with a big smile on my face.

"What?" he asks, doing a double take.

"You don't seem so uncomfortable anymore when it comes to the subject of spirits."

He grabs two beers out of the fridge and hands one to me. "That's just because I can't seem to get away from it. Work. You," he clicks off, and then realizes how it sounds. "Not that I want to get away from you," he quickly amends, looking mortified. "That came out wrong."

"I know," I say with a light chuckle and head out into the living room.

As Ryan turns on some music, Tyler pops in and sits down next to me. "Seems like a good time to tell my bro about me, don't you think?"

"No, I don't," I reply as quietly as possible, but it's not quiet enough.

"You don't what?" Ryan asks.

"Uh … I really don't like this song."

"Oh." While Ryan fiddles with the station, I mouth *GO AWAY* to Tyler. *Crap!* Ryan catches me. "You okay there?"

"Just doing some mouth exercises."

He smiles, amused. "Are you planning a kissing marathon with me or something?"

I am so embarrassed. I instantly turn red and have to look away from Ryan, especially since he comes over and sits on Tyler.

"Check it out! We're the exact same size," Tyler states, noticing how his ethereal body fits exactly into Ryan's. "I'm like one of those hitch-hiker ghosts at the end of the Haunted House ride at Disneyland."

Stop it! I yell at him with my thoughts.

"Did you say something?" Tyler glances at me.

"Am I making you nervous?" Ryan asks.

"Not you," I reply before I can think clearly, and unfortunately Ryan understands my meaning.

Ryan jumps up. "Please tell me the old dead guy didn't come back with us."

"No," I confirm. "Not him."

Ryan stiffens, looking around, "Then who?"

I let out a loud sigh. Why now? Ryan is totally hot. I can't remember the last time I went out with a totally hot, decent, down-to-earth, considerate, smart guy. *Why, why, why can't I be left alone one frickin' night?*

"Okay." I stand up, clasping my hands together. "There's nothing to freak out about. Let's just sit down and calmly talk about this."

I can tell Ryan wants to bolt, but I'm sure he'll soon figure out that he's in his own place, so where would he bolt to?

"Come on," I encourage. "I'll explain everything." I sit farther down on the end of the couch, hoping Ryan will join me, but instead, he sits right back down where he was—on Tyler. *I can't do this. I can't talk to Ryan with Tyler playing games.* "Not there," I say to Ryan as calmly as I can, and Ryan jumps up like he's spring-loaded.

"Tyler, stop it," I scold. "If you want me to deliver your message then hover somewhere else."

"Yes, sorry. Please continue," he says and slips behind the couch.

"Tyler?" Ryan questions me. "The same Tyler from a few weeks ago?" And then Ryan looks as if a light bulb just went off in his head. "Did this Tyler person live here before me? Is that it? Did Matt rent me this place and not bother to tell me it's haunted?"

"No!" I firmly tell him, standing up. "Tyler did not live here."

"Then who the hell is this guy ... and why won't he leave me alone?"

"He insists he's your half brother."

"What?" Ryan stares at me like I'm insane. "What are you talking about? I don't have a half brother."

"According to Tyler, you do."

"Well, he's wrong. You're wrong." Ryan marches off a few angry steps.

I glance over at Tyler who now looks as tense as I feel. "Tell him about his dad."

"Ryan, I know this is none of my business, but did your parents tell you why they were getting a divorce?"

He stops pacing and glares at me. "You're right. It is none of your business."

Okay, that hurt. I now know I've completely lost any chance of this night turning out to be a romantic one.

"Please tell him," Tyler begs, suddenly very serious.

I keep going. I have to. I know I need to help Tyler with his unfinished business. Plus, I'd really like for him to go away permanently. "Tyler says you two share the same biological father."

"Wrong again. My dad's never been married before."

"I know. I did the math and I assumed that to be the case," I say evenly. "Your half brother was younger than you. Tyler died a few months ago at the age of twenty-three."

Ryan won't look at me, but I see that he slightly softens at this bit of news. "If that's really true, I'm sorry to hear that."

"Ryan, this only leaves one explanation," I continue. "Your father must have had an affair."

And Ryan's anger quickly returns. "That's ridiculous," he snaps. "In fact, this whole thing is ridiculous."

"I'm just passing on what I've been told."

Ryan lets out a little laugh and shakes his head in disbelief. "Yeah, okay thanks. Look, it's getting late so…."

I stand there for a moment, hoping Ryan will just take a step back and calm down, but he doesn't. "Right." I pick up my handbag, glance over at Tyler who's staring at Ryan looking very worried, then I quietly walk out the door.

———

"I'm so depressed," I sulk, slouching halfway down Lucy's couch. "We were totally hitting it off."

"I know," Lucy agrees, coming over with a bowl of popcorn and placing it on the coffee table. "I was watching the two of you at dinner. Even Matt saw how attracted you were to each other."

"And once again my life's been ruined by a dead guy."

"Ryan can't stay mad at you forever, Talie. You guys work together."

"What if he quits?" I gasp and sit bolt upright. "What if he's already quit and I never see him again?"

"He's not going to quit," Lucy says, rolling her eyes at me.

I stare at her. "I see dead people, our job is all about dead people and though Ryan might now believe dead people can roam freely, he doesn't want to deal with them. Ever."

"Okay, so maybe Ryan will quit." She takes a drink of her soda. "But if he does, he still lives right next door to Matt and Matt had him sign a two-year lease."

"This sucks." I sigh loudly. "Have you seen him? Has Matt seen him?"

"Uh, no, Talie. Not since we all saw him," she eyes her watch, "fourteen hours ago."

I grab a pillow off the couch and put it over my face.

"I do have some Operation 007 info, though."

I peer up at her.

"Matt and Ryan were watching the football game the other night and Ryan opened up about his ex, Nicole."

"Nicole? Seriously?" I sit up straight. "What did he say?"

"They'd been together for two years and had been living together for six months when Ryan started to notice things were disappearing."

"What do you mean?"

"Matt said Ryan's Bluetooth vanished the day after he bought it. A hundred-dollar Amazon gift card he got for his birthday went missing, and then he started to notice, quite frequently, that he had less money in his wallet than he remembered."

I give her a curious look. "Nicole was a thief?"

"Apparently."

"Did she have a drug or gambling problem?"

"Ryan thinks it might have been drugs, but he will never know for sure. He was away on a four-day commercial shoot, and when he returned, the entire apartment was cleaned out."

"No!" My mouth drops open. "How horrible."

"He's never seen or heard from her since."

"And you would think you'd know someone after two years."

"There really are a lot of psychos out there." Lucy takes a handful of popcorn.

"This doesn't help," I point out. "I don't think Ryan's going to want to go from a girl who cleaned him out to a girl who acts and looks crazy while talking to the dead."

"But at least he now believes, right?"

"Who knows?" I watch Lucy eat one kernel of popcorn at a time. "We all tend to believe what we want to believe and see what we want to see. I can't force him to accept that he caught a ghost on camera, or that an old geezer of a spirit coaxed my sister's band into playing a possible hit song, or that his half brother has been trying to contact him from the Great Beyond."

"No, you can't, but Ryan's a smart guy," she reminds me. "He'll figure it out."

"And if he doesn't?"

"He will," she says confidently. "I just know you guys are going to work it out."

I offer a sarcastic laugh. "That's because you're the consummate matchmaker."

"Yes, I am." Lucy smiles. "I can't help it." She fixes her eyes on me. "Maybe I should set you up with my friend Alex. He could give Ryan some serious competition."

"Oh, Lord," I say to the heavens. "Rein her in, will you please?"

"Just looking out for you."

"As you said, Lucy, it's only been fourteen hours since we've seen Ryan. Let's give the underdog a chance."

"Good idea." Lucy smiles and flips on the TV. "Now, what movie do we want to watch?"

"A comedy, please. I need a good laugh."

Chapter 14

———◆———

Tuesday morning, I get a call from the production office. Our third investigation of an abandoned hospital is being pushed back due to an emergency call Adam received from a family that lives in his Long Beach neighborhood. Apparently they are having quite a bit of paranormal activity. They have two little kids who are scared out of their minds, so Carolyn promised we'd be out there in the afternoon.

Adam didn't mention that Ryan had quit, so I'm fairly certain I will see him soon. It's no surprise I haven't heard from him. However, it would have been nice to have seen Tyler. Shocking—that I'm now wishing to talk to spirits, but I have to say this one-way communication is a little annoying. I find it a bit unfair that spirits can contact me whenever, wherever, but when I have a question or two, I get nothing. Nada. And now, with no further information to pass on to Ryan, I know it's going to be a little awkward with him when I see him. But my nana's right. He's just going to have to accept me the way I am.

Nana! I just remembered I told her I'd come to bingo night. I grab my phone and dial her number.

On the fifth ring, she picks up. "Hello, Natalie, dear."

"Hi, Nana. How are you feeling?"

"Fit as a fiddle. Are you coming to bingo night?"

"I wish I was." I groan. "But I've been called in to work."

"Oh," she says, and I can hear the disappointment in her voice. "Are you going on another investigation tonight?"

"Yes, and I guess it's kind of an emergency. A family in Long Beach is having a lot of trouble with something in their house."

"Oh, dear. Never a dull moment," she replies. "Be sure to put extra protection around yourself."

"I will," I promise, and my voice trails off.

"Is there something else you'd like to talk about?"

I take a big breath and let it out on a sigh. "It's Ryan. He isn't speaking to me."

"What happened?" She sounds surprised.

"I told him about his deceased half brother, the one he didn't know about, and I'm pretty sure he thinks I'm a crackpot."

"Hmm," Nana responds, mulling it over. "Was he angry or did he laugh it off?"

"He was angry."

"Good. That's actually better," she assures. "It means he believes you, but he doesn't *want* to believe you."

"Not sure how that's better," I mumble, "if he directs his frustration toward me."

"It's only temporary, dear. Trust me. He'll learn the truth soon. His half brother will see to it, I'm sure."

"I hope you're right," I sigh. "I really like him, Nana."

"I know you do. I don't have to remind you that the toughest part of the job is not the dead, but the living."

I groan. "Just once I'd like someone to say, 'I believe you. Thanks for the message.'"

She chuckles. "So would the spirits."

"Thanks, Nana. Sorry I won't be there tonight, but I'll see you soon."

"I know. Be safe, and I hope your work tonight is successful."

"Love you."

"Love you too."

———————

I arrive at the production office a little after two and pull into the parking garage. Geoff is there loading the gear into the show's van along with Haley, Sam, Carlos, Shani and Adam. Carolyn is even helping out, which has me a little nervous. Are we one crew member short?

"Hey." I get out of my car, walk over, grab an armful of cables, and hand them off to Carlos who's standing just inside the van. "Where's Ryan?"

Carlos shrugs. "He should be here by now. Hey, Adam, is Ryan coming?"

Adam looks at his watch, grabs his cell—no doubt calling Ryan.

I watch Adam out of the corner of my eye as I pick up a camera case and give it to Sam. "Hi, Ryan. It's Adam, just checking to make sure you're on your way. Call me back if there's a problem."

Great. My heart starts to beat a little faster. What if he just up and quit? What if he got on a plane and went home without telling anybody? What if I never see him again?

"Do you know where he is?" Geoff asks me.

I try to hide the shocked look on my face. Do they know that we've seen each other outside of work? "No," I finally answer. "Why would I know that?"

"Well, you're psychic," he simply states.

Oh, right. Yes, the whole psychic bit. The edge I have over others that TOTALLY CRAPS OUT when I need it to work on people I love. I mean "like." Arrgh. I'm adding this to the top of my complaint list. A list I will be more than happy to share with God the second I get to the Other Side. He has GOT to rework these unwritten rules for psychics. It's just not fair.

"Are you picking up on something?" Geoff asks, forcing me out of my head.

"Uh ... yes," I reply with great relief, as I spot Ryan's car entering the garage. "He's here."

Geoff turns around to see Ryan pulling into a parking space. "Wow, you're amazing."

I laugh, realizing Geoff doesn't get that I saw Ryan's car coming down the ramp. "Not really, I—"

"I thought I was going to have to send out a search party," Geoff calls to Ryan, completely ignoring me.

Ryan shuts his door and starts walking over to us. Well, actually he's coming over just to see Geoff. I stare at him, and Ryan doesn't look at me—even for a second.

"Sorry, Geoff, I ended up getting a flat tire." He grabs the last equipment case and loads it onto the van.

"All right, everyone," Geoff shouts. "Let's get crackin'!"

My heart suddenly sinks. Ryan still hasn't acknowledged me. Now I'm regretting that we work together. How am I supposed to concentrate? The guy hates me. He seriously hates me.

I hop into the SUV with Carlos, Haley and Shani. I know I should be centering myself and putting light around my body for protection, but I just can't. I can't stop thinking about the feel of Ryan's lips on mine, and how I might not ever feel that sensation again. I don't understand why I'm so attracted to him.

Okay, he's absolutely gorgeous, and he's an amazing kisser, and he can be funny. But we have nothing in common—except for work, and him knowing my best friend, and him being buds with my best friend's boyfriend, but other than that, nothing. I don't even know why I'm thinking about him at all. Guys like him are a dime a dozen.

Before I know it, we've arrived at the Brascias' residence. Since we're running behind schedule, due to an accident on the 405 Freeway, Geoff goes in to meet the owners while Shani puts makeup on me and Carlos fills me in. "Mary and Patrick Brascia have two children, a boy and a girl, ages eight and ten, and a dog who won't go in the house anymore."

Immediately hairs stand up on the back of my neck as I get a quick flash of knickknacks sailing through the air and crashing to the ground. "Has anyone been hurt?"

"Mary Brascia was scratched by something unseen. Mr. Brascia was pushed off a ladder. The children were sitting on the family room couch when it moved across the room, and the dog has often been heard whimpering in the middle of the night."

I shake off the bad feeling lowering on me. "When did the activity start?"

"Two months ago," Carlos explains, scanning his notes. "It began the day after they moved in."

"What's the history of the place?"

"Nothing unusual. No deaths on record, no sordid past. Built in 1985. The only thing a little strange is that this house has had a high number of owners. Twenty-one, to be exact."

"Yeah, that's a lot. Too many, if you ask me."

"You're all set," Shani says as she packs up her makeup kit.

"Thanks, Shani." I put my attention back on Carlos. "So it's just the four of them and their dog?"

Carlos nods.

"Okay, thanks."

After Carlos leaves, I raise my psychic antenna to try and get a read on the house, and all I get back is a feeling of suffocation. "Great," I mumble under my breath. I close my eyes to not only ask for protection but to visualize it and lock it into place around myself, Ryan, and the rest of the crew.

"Here's your mic."

I open my eyes and see Ryan standing in front of me, holding out my radio mic and battery pack. "Thanks." I take it, and finally he looks me in the eye.

"About the other night…." He stops and seems increasingly uncomfortable. "I don't want to get into a whole thing here."

"No, of course. We're at work." I fold my arms in front of me.

"And I'm not saying that I believe Tyler exists." He runs his fingers through his hair.

I stand there, without saying a word, noticing how he alone is "getting into it."

"I mean, that's just ridiculous, right? No offense," he says, eyeing me. "But the existence of ghosts isn't logical, and though I'm not sure how you knew about my dad, when *I* didn't know about my dad, I just can't take that huge leap to believe a ghost told you."

I focus on him, a bit confused. "What about your dad?" I ask, helping him to be a little clearer. "Do you mean you found out about his affair?"

He groans, and stares at me like I'm clueless. "What do you think we've been talking about? Yes!"

So far the score is: Dead Tyler who apparently doesn't exist-1. Logical, skeptical Ryan who really shouldn't be so skeptical after all he's seen-0.

"Did your dad tell you?"

He shakes his head. "My mom."

Which means he still hasn't talked to his dad about Tyler. I really want to ask him if his mom said anything else—along the lines that Ryan has a half brother, but I don't want to push it.

"Divorce is tough on everyone involved," I say instead. "My parents divorced when I was fourteen."

"Sorry to hear that, Natalie. I can't imagine. I would have flipped out if they split when I was still a kid."

"I think it's a shock at any age. But we're all fine and my parents are happier apart."

Ryan nods, taking in what I've said, then it's as if he remembers where he is. He glances at my battery pack and says, "Need help with that?"

I clip it onto the back of my pants, then turn around for Ryan to inspect it.

He gives it a tug. "Seems secure."

I turn back around. He helps me position my radio mic without asking, and I can feel how the tension between us is starting to dissipate.

"You guys ready?" Geoff asks, clapping his hands together.

I catch Ryan's eye and he smiles. "We're good to go."

Five minutes later, everyone else is set. Haley slates, Geoff calls action, and I walk up to the house as the Brascias greet me at the door. I introduce myself, shake hands with the couple, then we walk inside.

I'm immediately hit with a dark heaviness to the place, and I sense something else—something cruel, something unclean.

Mary Brascia shows us into the living room, and I sit down with them while Ryan films us.

"When did the disturbances begin?" I ask, taking out my notepad.

Mary glances at her husband Patrick. She looks genuinely frightened, as if telling me will make the disturbances happen all over again. "The day after we moved in," she timidly replies. "We heard knocking coming from inside the walls."

"In here?" I gesture.

Patrick takes hold of Mary's hand. "Everywhere. Throughout the house."

"Doors started to slam, books and framed pictures would fly off the shelves, furniture would move on its own," Mary reveals.

"We've now had two occasions where this very couch has moved to the center of the room," Patrick explains. "I was sitting on it when it occurred the first time. Last night, it happened to our children."

I jot down a few notes. "Have your children experienced anything else?"

"Our daughter, Alexa, started having nightmares. Kept saying the boogie man was in her closet." Patrick hangs his head. "I didn't believe her."

Mary rubs his shoulders, then stares at me with fear in her eyes. "Three nights ago, Patrick was away on a business trip, and I was making hot dogs for the kids. They were playing here, watching TV. I'd just checked on them, and I hadn't been in the kitchen for more than a second when Alexa and her brother Anthony started screaming. I turned back and all the books from the bookshelves were stacked on top of each other, floor to ceiling. I took a picture of it." Mary pushes the photo towards me.

It's a freaky picture. The books are at all angles and different directions, like a house of cards. It seems impossible, and yet, there they are in the photo.

"These all happened in the past week." Patrick hands me two more pictures.

I see soup cans placed perfectly on every step leading up to the second floor. In the kitchen are knives stuck into the ceiling in a perfect circle.

Patrick and Mary huddle together as I examine the photos. "Mary took the kids and our dog, Bella, to my mother's this morning," Patrick informs me. "We just can't bring them back until this ends."

I try to continue the interview, but Mary is too upset, so Geoff has them leave for the night. Ryan films close-ups of the photos. "They could have done this," he says, and though I agree, I can't shake the feeling that whoever, or whatever is in this house, isn't just a lost soul in a bad mood.

———————

Because there's been reported activity all over the Brascia house, the crew and I spend an extra two hours setting up as many surveillance cameras as we can. I again put protection around myself, Ryan, and everyone on-site. Still, I don't feel like it's enough. I already have a cross around my neck, but something tells me to give one to Ryan.

"Hey, how about if you keep this in your pocket?"

He looks down to see I'm holding a cross, and I can tell he's trying not to laugh at me. "How's that tiny thing going to help? If you haven't noticed, I'm a pretty big guy. I'm fairly certain I can protect myself."

"Ryan, we're not dealing with a bunch of punks. If we run up on something nasty, trust me, this will help." I offer the cross again.

"Bring it on," he challenges, trying to lighten the mood. "I can handle a little nasty."

"Don't ever say stuff like that," I warn him. "Especially when you don't know what you're challenging."

"Sorry," he says when he realizes how concerned I am. "You know, if you don't want to do this investigation…."

"These people need help, and how can I turn down Adam's neighbors?"

"Well, hopefully your superpowers can find the offending party quickly and make this investigation short and sweet."

I look up at the foreboding house. "From your lips to God's ears."

———

"It's almost midnight," I say into the camera lens. "I'm about to start my investigation in the Brascia home." I begin walking toward the front door and get an overwhelming sick feeling. *Crap. This is not a good sign.* I take another step forward and find it difficult to breathe. I also sense something powerful that doesn't want me there. I glance at Ryan who doesn't seem to be affected at all. *Am I imagining things? Time to call on those in the know. God, Angels, Spirit Guides, anyone higher who's listening, please put extra protection around me, especially if I'm being a total moron and walking into something I cannot handle.*

With trepidation, I push forward and head inside. I feel that powerful presence again. "We are not alone," I say into the camera. "There's a heaviness in the air. It feels constricting, depressing, unsafe." I focus on Ryan, but he doesn't seem to notice it, so I continue. "Whoever is here, make yourself known," I call out to the entity.

Almost immediately Ryan and I hear a scraping sound coming from the kitchen. We hurry toward the sound. Ryan scans the kitchen with his camera.

"Who are you and what do you want?" I demand, staying close to Ryan's side.

Bam! Bam! Bam! Several doors slam upstairs.

Ryan and I race up the steps to the second floor. All of the bedroom doors are wide open.

Ryan puts the camera on me as I say into the camera, "Mark this footage for later review. All of these doors were originally closed before I started this investigation. So, which doors just slammed shut?" I begin searching the hallway as I address the entity, "Whoever you are, you don't belong here. You are not welcome in this house and you need to leave."

And right as those words spring from my lips, there is a very loud crash downstairs. We go flying back down the stairs and come to a complete stop. I hear something rolling in the kitchen.

I shine my flashlight into the kitchen, and this time I'm the one who gasps. The refrigerator door is open and all the contents are spilled out onto the floor. On the counter, there are three items: a ketchup bottle, a fork, and a mayonnaise jar, and they are stacked in that order end to end.

"What the—" Ryan cuts himself off. He zooms in, filming the impossibly stacked items at every angle.

And that's when I catch something out of the corner of my eye. But when I try to focus on it, I can't see anything.

"You need to leave," I demand again. "You are not welcome here." I begin to notice a black mist forming from out of the pantry. "Who are you? Show yourself!"

In an instant, there's this pungent stench, and I feel like I'm going to be sick. I can't help but cough. Ryan must smell it too since he begins to cough as well.

"There's a sickly stench, like rotting flesh," I tell the viewers, covering my mouth and nose with my sleeve.

The hairs on the back of my neck stand on end as I slowly turn. Behind me is something ungodly with scaly, burnt, black skin. It's standing upright, not much taller than me, on thick black hooves. For a moment, I'm frozen in terror as menacing, cunning eyes stare back at me, and before I can collect my thoughts, it skitters past Ryan with lightning speed.

"Ahh!" Ryan yells.

I throw my flashlight on him. "What's wrong?"

"My back is on fire." He slowly lifts his shirt.

I shine the flashlight onto his skin. There are three distinct bloody scratches all the way down his back. I grab his camera to document it. "Ryan, my camera operator, has just been attacked."

"What the hell was that?" he asks in a trembling voice.

I open my mouth to answer but am cut off by a threatening, low growl coming from the other side of the kitchen, followed by the oven door opening and closing in fast succession, creating a loud racket. Ryan hesitantly moves closer, filming it.

"Look out!" I yell, as a decorative vase sitting on top of a cabinet falls, nearly hitting Ryan in the head. Fearing another attack, I push him toward the front door. "Ryan, get out. Get out of this house now!"

Ryan doesn't argue. He hurries toward the exit with me close behind.

And just as we step out of the house, Geoff comes running from the van. "Holy, shit! This place is seriously haunted. Are you okay, Ryan?"

"No, he is not," I answer for him. "And neither am I. We're done here." I march towards the van.

"What do you mean?" Geoff follows closely behind. "We just got started."

"You know, I'm fine with talking to someone's late Aunt Edna, I'm even fine with talking to Casper the Friendly Ghost, but I don't do dark." I take off my radio mic and hand it to him.

Geoff looks at me really confused. "Explain 'dark.'"

"Demons, Geoff. Ryan was just scratched by one."

"By a demon?" He laughs. "You're kidding."

I peek my head into the van. "Let's go, everyone. We're shutting down and packing up."

The crew starts wrapping it up with Ryan leading the charge.

"Hold on a minute," Geoff says to the group. "Natalie, we can't just leave. What am I supposed to tell the Brascias?"

"Tell them to call a realtor."

Geoff physically stops me and holds me by the arms. "Natalie, please. Just calm down for a minute. We can't leave."

"We can and we are. You can call our clients from the road, and tell them not to come back here until we can get a demonologist in for them."

Geoff staggers back in total surprise. "Seriously?"

"Did you not see what we were filming? The little display of power in the kitchen, the physical attack on Ryan?"

"Yes, of course. The footage of the stacked items, the banging oven door and the falling vase were absolutely incredible, which is why we can't walk away. I've never seen anything like this. Natalie, this is irrefutable proof. I'd think you'd want to be part of the team who presents this to the world."

"Not if one of us is harmed in the process. I'd think you'd want the same thing."

"I do. I'm not saying I want you and Ryan to go back in, but maybe we can monitor things from out here."

I take a big breath, calm down, and try to explain this to Geoff. "If it were simply a noisy ghost or an angry spirit, we could. But demons feed on fear. They're not going to play unless they get something out of it."

"I hear you, Natalie, I really do. It's just … before I make the call to Carolyn and tell her why we're shutting down, educate me on how you know it's a demon instead of a ghost."

"Its hooves and black scaly skin have something to do with it."

"God, really?" He looks a little shocked. "You saw that?"

"It's not human, Geoff, and it never was."

Finally, Geoff seems concerned. "Okay. We'll leave, but we need to get our equipment first."

"We'll come back for it tomorrow," Ryan suggests.

"I can't leave those expensive cameras behind."

"I thought we had insurance," Ryan reminds him.

"Why don't I go grab them?" Geoff suggests.

"Not a good idea," I tell him.

"It'll take me two seconds," he assures us. "I'll leave everything else." Geoff heads up to the house and as he's about to walk in the front door, it violently slams in his face. Geoff spins on his heels and high-tails it back to the crew. "I like tomorrow," he says, running past me. "Tomorrow's good."

Chapter 15

On the way back to the production office, I ride with Ryan who seems a little shell-shocked, and truth be told, I'd be seriously freaked out myself if I wasn't pre-occupied with worrying about him.

"I didn't think ghosts could hurt you," Ryan says in this monotone voice that doesn't sound like him at all.

"They can't, but malevolent spirits and demons can."

"I thought you put protection around me."

"I did, but you challenged it."

He finally turns his head to look at me. "No, I didn't."

"Yes, before we went inside, you did."

He puts his hands over his face and rubs his eyes. "This is so insane. How can demons exist?" We all sit in silence, and then Ryan glares at me.

"Oh," I reply. "I thought that was a rhetorical question. Well, demons exist—"

"It *was* a rhetorical question," Ryan says flatly. "I don't believe in them."

Haley laughs.

"What's so funny?" Carlos asks.

"I don't know. Guys in general." She shakes her head. "You think if you don't believe in something then it can't possibly exist. It's kind of arrogant. Sorry, Ryan."

"It's actually denial," I point out to Haley.

"Well, women do it too," Ryan says defensively. He sits up and in a high voice he says, "Oh, Officer, I didn't see any stop sign at all. Are you sure there's one at that corner?"

We all laugh.

Carlos asks, "So, if a tree falls in the forest and no one is around to hear it, then I guess it fell after all?"

"Yes," I emphatically answer.

"Demons really exist?" Carlos queries.

"Yes."

"What about angels?" Haley asks, always looking on the bright side.

"Most definitely, yes."

She gets excited and turns around to look at me. "How many have you seen?"

"Oh, I don't know," I say on a slow exhale. "A dozen or so … that I know of."

"Seriously?" Haley's eyes light up. "Do they have huge wings?"

I chuckle. "I've only seen them in human form."

"Why would they look like us if they could have wings instead?" Carlos joins in, and I'm starting to feel like I'm "Anything Spiritual 411."

"Angels are walking among us, helping us, watching over us," I explain to them. "They have to take human form, otherwise we'd freak out if we saw what they truly looked like."

"I wouldn't," Haley declares. "I'd love to see them in their real form."

"You'd faint from the sight," Carlos says, laughing.

"I would not!" she says indignantly, slapping him on the arm.

We're all joking around by the time we get to the production office. Even Ryan seems like himself again.

Geoff gets out of the other SUV and comes over to Ryan and me. "I got hold of the Brascias. They understand and will be staying out of their house. Carolyn knows of a great demonologist and has put a call in to him. Hopefully, he can meet us at their house sometime tomorrow. Natalie, I know you don't want to be involved, but Ryan, we'd love to have you continue filming if you're up for it."

Ryan looks a little uncomfortable, but says, "If you need me, I'll be there."

"Geoff," I step in. "Do you think you can hire another camera operator for the day?"

"We can but...." He looks to Ryan, expecting him to protest, and he doesn't.

"It would be best," I simply say to Geoff.

"Okay, well...." Geoff is momentarily at a loss for words, no doubt surprised I didn't have a change of heart once I was away from the house. "You guys get some rest. Ryan, have someone take a look at those scratches." Geoff puts his focus back on me. "We're going to be busy with this case for the next few days, but if we need you for voice-over or video diary inserts, I'll have Adam or Haley give you a call."

"Sounds great. Thanks for understanding, Geoff."

Ryan and I head to our cars. "Thanks," Ryan says to me. "I could have continued the investigation, but I really don't want to go back to that house again."

"I don't want you to go, either."

Ryan smiles. "I'll walk you to your car."

As we pass by his car, Ryan does a double take. "You've got to be kidding me."

"What?"

Ryan inspects his tire. "My tire's flat again."

That wasn't just an excuse for being late? "I thought they fixed it."

"So did I. Dammit!"

"Come on. I'll take you home. You can deal with it tomorrow."

I unlock the car, clear a bunch of papers off my passenger seat, and Ryan scoots inside.

I suddenly don't know what to say to him without bringing up subjects I'm sure he's tired of talking about. Ryan isn't exactly chatting it up either, and the silence becomes deafening.

After about five minutes, I can't take it any longer. "So how about those Dodgers?" I say with great enthusiasm which at least gets a laugh. But then Ryan falls back into silence, which is making me really uncomfortable. "I know what you're thinking," I tell him. "I'm guessing you're thinking that maybe staying in Florida and working on *It's a Mortician's Life*, would have actually been the better gig."

Ryan glares at me with total shock on his face. "How the hell do you do that? That's exactly what I was thinking!"

"Really?" I am as shocked as he is. "I ... uh ... was just trying to be funny," I stammer. "There was no psychic involvement on my part."

"So, you can't read my mind?" He sneaks a sideways glance.

I let out a big laugh. "No. Not at all." I don't share with him that I can see snippets of him in the past, like the time I saw him in the shower. And I most certainly don't share with him that I kind of concentrated on seeing more last night when I was falling asleep. I concentrated on the kiss we shared, and I suddenly saw our bodies entangled in each other's. That was a great snippet, though I glean it's more my wishful thinking than any future reality.

I pull into Ryan's driveway. "How's your back?"

"Still stings a little, but I'll live."

"Those scratches should be disinfected."

"Demons have dirt under their fingernails?"

I shrug. "You never know."

"I can tough it out." Ryan sits there for a minute, like he's about to say something. He is so different from Dean spilling his guts every second that I can't help but be drawn to his silence.

I suddenly feel like he's about to get out of the car, so I speak up. "Geoff told you to get someone to take a look at your back, and here I am."

Ryan smiles in spite of himself. "I think he meant a doctor."

"I know, but we should take a few still pictures for documentation."

He nods. "I guess we should." He grabs the door handle. "Too bad I can't sue the son of a bitch."

We go inside and head right to his bathroom where he pulls out hydrogen peroxide, cotton balls, and a tube of Neosporin.

I notice the energy in the room change, like the energy between us has become more electric. I take out my cell as he strips off his shirt. I try not to look at his muscular shoulders or his well-defined back, but I do and my breath hitches in my throat.

Focus! I force myself to concentrate on the three scratches which are long and bloody down his back. "It got you good," I say to Ryan, as I click off a few shots.

I set down my iPhone, douse a cotton ball with hydrogen peroxide, and gently begin to clean out the first scratch. There's a lot of dried blood and the hydrogen peroxide fizzles when it makes contact. Ryan doesn't move. He doesn't make a sound. "Are you okay?"

Still with his back toward me, he raises his head, but doesn't turn around. "That's a loaded question."

"I know tonight was ... well, it's a lot to digest." I take out another cotton ball, saturate it with hydrogen peroxide, and begin working on the second scratch.

"Just tonight?" He stiffens. "Try the last month."

The bite to his words keeps me silent. I begin cleaning out the last and deepest scratch.

"I'm not good with all this crazy stuff," he admits, softening. "People like me aren't."

"And what are people like you?"

"Organized, sensible, logical, knowledgeable. I had it all planned out."

"Had what planned out?" I start applying the Neosporin to his back.

"My life," he says. "I would move out here, work hard, get a good career going for myself. I'd meet a girl who shared my morals and beliefs. One day maybe we'd even get married, have kids, share similar interests, enjoy each other and have a simple, normal life … just like my parents did."

He finally turns around and faces me. "But my parents lived a lie, and the career I've embarked upon isn't at all what I envisioned. I'm filming things that aren't supposed to exist. I get attacked by something that should only be found in some horror film. I meet a girl who isn't even close to being normal. While other girls talk about how many shoes they bought on their shopping spree, you talk about how many dead people have contacted you."

"I didn't want this, Natalie." His eyes implore. "I didn't ask for his. I didn't want my normal life rocked. You've made me question my beliefs. You've made me question my sanity. You've made me see things, feel things, hear things."

He looks at me as if he's really seeing me for the first time. "You've made me think about you," he says in a desperate plea, "desire you, want you—"

His eyes are blazing into mine and I cannot move. The energy is crackling between us, and in a rush, he pushes me up against the bathroom wall, pinning me with his body. His lips are on mine, devouring me, and I'm welcoming it.

I grab onto him as he tears at my blouse, ripping it open. His warm hands touch my skin, searing it with heat as our kisses become deeper and more furious.

I zip down his pants and he pulls off mine. We are breathing hard, panting, pulling each other close. He kisses my throat, my breasts. I begin to moan. He finds my mouth again and kisses me hungrily as he rips off my panties, and touches me with such urgency that it almost makes me lose consciousness.

I kiss him harder, deeper. He lifts me up, and I wrap myself around him, begging him to take me. And when he does, the feeling is like ecstasy. We move as one, breathe as one, cling to each other as we let go of the anger, the frustration, the fear. We hold on, feeling sensations climbing, senses overriding, losing ourselves in the moment, and we explode together in blinding passion.

Ryan collapses on me as we remain standing against his bathroom wall. We hold each other up while our racing hearts begin to slow. Sweat is dripping from us, and when we both finally catch our breath, we look at one another, smile and laugh. Ryan holds me tight and I refuse to let go. I run my hand over his back, and only then do I remember the scratches. "I hope I didn't make your back worse."

"If you did, it was worth it." He pulls back and stares at me—a sense of peace, or maybe it's acceptance, washes over him. "What are you doing to me, Natalie Dalton?"

"Nothing your heart didn't ask for," I hear myself saying.

He chuckles, shakes his head, kissing me. "You are so different from me," he mumbles between kisses.

"Not as much as you think," I respond, running my hand through his hair.

And then, he abruptly glares at me. "You're not some kind of a witch, are you?" he asks me accusingly.

"What?" I say on a laugh.

"I mean, why wouldn't you be?" He steps away from me, as if he finally figured it all out. "How else am I to explain why I can't get you out of my head?"

"If you're going with that logic, then I can accuse you of the same thing." I pull him back, he calms down, and I begin kissing him again. "You've invaded my dreams."

He grins, lightly biting my lower lip. "I have?"

"Uh-huh," I say between kisses.

"What was I doing in your dreams?"

"What you just did in reality, so if anyone's the witch...."

"Hmm." He thinks about this for a minute, takes my hand, and leads me into his shower.

———

It's four in the morning before Ryan and I finally fall into his bed. I can't believe the range of emotions we've experienced together over the last twelve hours—from the frightening demon encounter to insanely awesome pleasure.

I'm very happy to report that there was no obsessive cleaning of my feet in the shower, only a shared giggle upon discovering a small piece of a condom wrapper stuck to the bottom of my foot. There was no awkward moment of debate on whether or not I should stay or drive home because Ryan passed out almost immediately.

Now, I'm staring at his face. He looks peaceful. And he really is gorgeous. I could get used to staring at this face. I rest my head on my hand and study his profile. A solid jaw, strong chin, a very straight nose. The guy even has perfect skin with tiny pores. How unfair is that?

I work my way down his gorgeous body and can't help but think back on the absolutely amazing sex we just had. I am still stunned at the level of intensity and the amount of passion between us. I smile, thinking about how much stamina he has. I high-five myself, acknowledging my own great stamina too.

Ryan is snoring now. I gently put my head on his chest and snuggle up to him. Okay, so he is super loud. Too loud to remain where I am, so I turn over, which wakes him up. He mumbles something incoherent, puts his arm around me, and pulls me close. We're spooning. Spooning! This is so perfect. I wish I could lie here forever.

———

I'm helping Ryan change his flat tire. Actually I'm not doing a thing. I'm just watching his biceps dance as he changes it on his own.

"Okay, that ought to do it," Ryan says as he gets off his knees, inspects his work, then puts his attention on me. "I really don't feel like running errands."

"I don't either."

He pensively studies my face, pulls me close, and gives me a long passionate kiss. "I think separating is a bad idea," he tells me before he finds my lips again.

Ryan and I have decided that we must physically separate for the rest of the day because we can't seem to keep our hands off each other. We had planned on running errands together, but when we tried to make out a to-do list, going back to bed was the first item on our list, so we checked it off immediately. Now it's early afternoon, and we've accomplished nothing.

The garage gate opens, startling us. We quickly pull apart, fearing it might be someone from the production office. We wait to see who it is, and when it isn't anyone we know, Ryan takes hold of my hand.

"I should be home in an hour," he says. "In case you get all of your errands done and want to come back over."

I flash him a coy smile. "I might just do that."

After another ten minutes of serious kissing, we finally manage to separate. When I return to my apartment, I have the best intentions of doing laundry, but it's difficult to stay focused on anything when I keep seeing flashes of Ryan's perfect body. Luckily my cell rings, jolting me out of my head. I glance at the phone's display and answer. "Hi, Carolyn."

"Oh, my God, Natalie." She sounds totally freaked. "This is just crazy down here."

"What are you talking about?" I ask. "Where are you?"

"The Brascias'. Geoff told you we were continuing, didn't he?"

"The investigation. Right," I respond, clicking in to work that seems like a distant memory. I can't believe it's only been twenty-four hours since Ryan and I started on the investigation.

"Geoff was attacked," Carolyn states with disbelief. "Just like it happened with Ryan. Three deep scratches down his back. We've had books flying off the shelves, dishes stacked up in a matter of seconds. The crew doesn't want to finish the job. Father Gerace, the demonologist, says it's the worst case he's ever known. We have so much footage, insanely scary footage that skeptics will be a thing of the past once this episode airs."

"That's great. About getting good footage, I mean. But maybe you guys should pull out of there and let the church take over."

"We are. I just wanted to tell you personally about this, and to also let you know that we're having a meeting tomorrow at nine."

"I'll be there."

"We left word with Ryan, but haven't heard back. In fact, I'm a little worried about him since he was attacked. I was wondering, since you live close by, if you wouldn't mind going over to Ryan's place to check on him."

A huge smile spreads across my face. "I'll be more than happy to."

———————

I don't remember the drive over to Ryan's because I spent the majority of it in my head. I cannot believe how madly in lust I am with him. I can't stop thinking about him, which is crazy since we only had one night together and a relationship can't be built on sex alone—though if asked, I'm most certainly willing to try.

As I pull into Ryan's driveway, I'm in such a hurry to see him that I throw open the car door, forgetting to put the car in park, or turn the engine off for that matter, and I find myself scrambling to slam on the breaks before I crash into his garage.

"Jeez, what's wrong with me?" *Disaster averted.* Forcing myself to concentrate on the matter at hand, I put the car in park, turn off the engine this time, and only then do I calmly walk to the door.

I can feel my heart thumping faster in my chest, which is ridiculous because he might not even be home. In fact, I'm hoping that he isn't because I really need to go to the grocery store and—

The door opens before I'm able to ring the bell and Ryan is standing there, shirtless in jeans, and I'm unabashedly drinking him in. My eyes finally make their way back up to his face. "Hi."

"Hi."

We continue to gaze at each other. The attraction between us is palpable. My mouth suddenly goes dry. "Carolyn said they've been trying to reach you, but you're not answering, so they sent me over here to check on you."

He doesn't take his eyes off mine. "My phone died. I'm charging it now. I'm glad you take your job so seriously."

I step closer. "We have a meeting at nine tomorrow morning."

"Maybe you can text Carolyn for me," Ryan suggests in a sexy, seductive voice.

I nod, pull out my phone, and type: RYAN'S PHONE DIED. HE'LL BE AT THE MEETING. HE'S FINE.

"Let me see."

I come even closer and hold up the screen so he can read what I just typed. He takes me in his arms and he pushes the SEND button before he stares at me with his gorgeous grey eyes and asks, "Am I? Fine?"

Scarlet colors my cheeks, and I can't help but laugh at his overt flirting. "You're more than fine," I say in a seductive voice, flirting back.

"Glad you think so." Ryan's mouth hitches into a half smile. "You're more than fine yourself." He stares at my mouth, slowly leans over and kisses me. Within seconds I am lost in him. I can feel his breath caress my cheek, and I can hear my own breathing grow ragged as he kisses me more eagerly and pulls me into his house.

I hungrily match his every move as we both heat up. He feverishly strips off my shirt, walking backwards toward his room. But we're still so far away. He picks me up, I hold him tight, and with two steps, we tumble onto his couch. He unzips my jeans. I pull them off as he slides his own to the floor.

Skin touching, my body is burning. Ryan's hands run all over me. With obsessive, fervent kisses, I urge him on, wrapping my arms around his back, pulling him closer. We explore, desire driving us. Intertwined, we breathe in rhythm as we so effortlessly move as one, building intensity until we both completely surrender to the waves of blinding passion that consume us.

Coming off the incredible high, we gaze at each other and start laughing. Ryan scoots off me to the side, misjudges the couch's edge, and lands on the floor.

"Oh!" I try not to laugh. "Are you okay?"

"Yeah, if you don't kill me first."

I help him up as I catch something out of the corner of my eye and scream.

Ryan jumps back, ready to do battle, but he doesn't see anyone.

"Sorry!" Tyler says, and immediately vanishes.

I groan, throwing my head back.

Ryan regards me with confusion. "What's going on?"

"Can I ever get a break?" I don't want to tell Ryan the truth, but I'd feel worse lying, and it's not like the topic of Tyler isn't going to come up again. I let out an annoyed breath. "Tyler was here a moment ago."

Ryan quickly covers up as he glances around his living room. "Are you sure he's gone?"

"Positive." I extend my hand to Ryan.

He hesitantly settles next to me, but the troubled look on his face isn't going away. "So, he can just come over any time he wants?"

I focus on him. "Would you like the truth or a more comforting lie?"

"God," he groans with disgust. "The thought that spirits are watching me ... it's so uncomfortable, so unnerving. Actually, it's disturbing." And then a worse thought crosses his face. "Was he watching us have sex?"

"No," I state emphatically. "Definitely not." I sit up. "But even if he had, you have to understand, once a person has crossed over, they are in spirit form and spirits don't judge. There is no envy or hatred or scrutiny or lust or any kind of kinky voyeurism going on. There's nothing but love over on the Other Side. They only want us to be happy, whatever that means for us."

Ryan scans the room suspiciously. "Well, what did he want?"

"I don't know. He was here for a split second. My scream made him instantly disappear."

I watch Ryan uncomfortably cross his arms, and I know he's wondering if he can deal with this.

"This doesn't usually happen," I try to assure him.

"Oh, really?" He gives me a strange look. "You do realize this is the second time that ghost has barged in on us."

"I know, but that's because his message to you was not … well received. Once he knows you understand, he will go away."

"But I told you," Ryan says, exasperation filling his voice, "I don't have a half brother named Tyler."

"Have you talked to your dad since your mom told you about his infidelity?"

"No."

"Then how do you know for sure?"

"I think I know what type of man my dad is." Irritation runs through is words.

"You know your dad from a son's point of view," I remind him.

"So, what are you saying?" Ryan asks, a little defensive. "You think my dad is the love 'em and leave 'em type?"

"I don't know your dad, so I can't answer that. But what I do know is that Tyler isn't going to stop bothering you or me until you know the truth."

Ryan stiffens, as if he just remembered why this whole conversation started, and before he can reply, his cell rings. Ryan goes to the kitchen table, grabs his phone, then stares at me, startled. "It's my dad."

I get up to give him some privacy. "I'll be in your room."

Ryan turns, answers his cell. "Hey, Dad."

I head down the hallway to Ryan's bedroom, and I'm about to step into his bathroom when Tyler appears. He's more transparent now, which makes me wonder if it's because he's been going back and forth between dimensions.

Before I can say anything, I hear him announce, "I'm a ten."

I give him a strange look, not sure if I heard him correctly. "You've come back to tell me you're good-looking?"

Tyler mirrors back my look of confusion. "No, I said I'm a twin. I have a twin brother."

My eyes practically pop out of my head. "Ryan has another brother he doesn't know about?"

Tyler smiles at me, relief on his face, and it seems like he's becoming even more transparent in just the short time I've been talking to him.

"I'll give Ryan your message, Tyler. I promise. And if I don't see you again, have a wonderful … er … afterlife."

Tyler fades away.

Holy crap! This message is *huge*. Why didn't he tell me this before? Why must it always be like I'm playing the board game *Clue?*

I sit down on Ryan's bed. *So Ryan has two half brothers. One named Tyler and one named…?*

I jump up. "Tyler, come back!" My eyes frantically search the room, but I don't see him anywhere. *Arrgh!* This is so annoying. Why couldn't he have given me a name or an address? Why isn't there a Facebook for spirits? Ugh! I pace off a few angry steps. When I cross over, I'm seriously going to put a few changes in place—the first one being that spirits should stop putting all their energy into manifesting and leave a frickin' note!

"Hey."

I turn around and see Ryan. He looks a little shaken. "Everything okay?"

He sits down on his bed. "My dad called to apologize about the divorce. Said it was all his fault."

"Did he say anything about his affair?"

Ryan puts his elbows on his legs, stares down at the floor. "It's been going on for years."

I gasp softly. Even *I* wasn't expecting that surprise. At least his father admitted it. Perhaps now Ryan will get validation of Tyler's existence.

"He asked if he could come out next weekend to talk to me."

"It will be good for you to see each other face to face."

Ryan nods.

"Did you ask about ... well, whether you might have other siblings?"

Ryan finally looks at me. "He said we'd talk about it next weekend."

Which means yes. I take a deep breath and let it out. I'm ready to explode with the news that he has another half brother, one that's still alive, but I wouldn't feel right beating his father to the punch.

I put my hand in his. "I know this is quite a shock. I'm here, if you need anything."

"Thanks." He caresses my hand. "I don't know what is more unsettling—discovering my dad has been carrying on an affair for years or finding out about it from a ghost who claims he's my half brother."

I don't say anything, but I'm relieved to know he's finally accepting Tyler's existence.

Ryan looks around, searching his room. "He didn't come back, did he?"

Why, yes. And you have another half brother alive and well. "He's not here, so stop worrying." I rub Ryan's back. Of course, I'm doing nothing but worrying, and I'm not sure why.

Chapter 16

———◆———

The following morning, I make my way over to the production office. I arrive a few minutes before Ryan, and when I see him come through the conference room doors, I realize just how much I have fallen for him. My palms are instantly sweaty and my pulse is already racing.

"Morning." He puts on his best face for me, but I can see pain in his eyes, no doubt from all that's gone on with his family.

"Morning." My voice is filled with empathy, and it takes all my willpower not to give him a big hug. "You okay?"

"Yeah." He slowly inhales. "Thanks."

"Hello, everybody!" Carolyn comes sauntering into the conference room, along with Adam trailing her.

I clear my throat, getting my head into work mode, as Ryan pulls out the closest chair to where he's standing. I go to sit in the seat next to him and suddenly Carlos takes it. I falter, feeling like I've been thrown into a game of musical chairs. I move to the seat on the left of Ryan but Haley plops herself down. *Grrr.* Sam sits next to Haley, Adam sits next to Sam, and I find myself on the opposite side of the conference table. Exasperated, I quickly grab a seat, which happens to be directly across from Ryan.

I glance at Ryan who's chuckling, having witnessed the whole thing, and I can only shake my head.

"Morning," Geoff says to the room as he is the last one in, and he immediately zeros in on me. "You have an amazing talent, Natalie. You called it and I should have listened."

I can only assume he's referring to the demon in the Brascia house. "I heard you were attacked," I say with concern. "Are you okay?"

"Yeah." He looks over at Ryan as he sits down next to me. "If Ryan and I were to compare scratch marks, I'm sure we would find they were made from the same creature."

Please don't, since I added a few to Ryan's. "I bet they were too," is all I can say, as I steal a glance at Ryan who immediately swivels sideways in his chair to suppress a grin.

"We documented everything," Carolyn says. "Marcus is assembling it right now, but we have well over two and a half hours of intense footage."

"That's fantastic," I tell her. "I can't wait to see it."

"Trust me. You are going to flip out," Carolyn remarks elatedly. "The Paranormal Network has seen some of the raw footage, and they went insane over it. In fact, they have just given us the green light to shoot another five episodes for the season!"

My mouth drops open. I'm too stunned to speak.

"Yes!" Carlos sharply pulls both arms into his side, like he's just scored a touchdown.

Sam high-fives Ryan as Haley cheers.

"I love the new promo for the pilot," Adam praises. "It's intense."

"Isn't it? It's crazy good!" Haley adds.

Ryan and I quickly eye each other and have to look away. The new promo has been airing over the last two days, but we've been a little busy.

"What did you think of it?" Geoff asks me directly.

"It scared me and I was there!" I embellish as I mug a look of terror.

Everyone laughs at my exaggerated expression—Ryan a little over-the-top, which I think Carolyn catches.

"First off," she begins, signaling us to settle down. "I want to thank all of you for your incredible dedication to this series. There's a lot of talent in this room, which I know is going to make our series a standout among the rest."

I glance around the conference table and everyone is beaming including Ryan, who finds my feet under the table and interlocks them with his.

"Once the pilot airs Thursday night, I really think *Super Natalie* is going to pick up serious momentum," Carolyn says, continuing, "especially since our show has broken the formulaic mold. With the pilot, right now we have four episodes, all different, and this last investigation is so scary that the network wants to make a two-parter out of it."

"Whoo-hoo!" Haley howls.

"Sweet!" Sam throws out.

Ryan squeezes my feet and a huge smile takes over my face.

"So, Natalie, for our next show, what would you think about the crew following you around on a typical day?" Carolyn asks.

My mind instantly goes to how I've spent the last two with Ryan. "Uh ... well." I swivel in my chair, forcing myself not to look at Ryan. "I lead a boring life for the most part. I'm not sure watching me clean my apartment or go grocery shopping is going to have the same scare factor."

Geoff speaks up. "What Carolyn means is, this next episode would be a video diary of a day in the life of a ghost whisperer. We would follow you into a hospital or a cemetery or a retirement home—or anywhere else you think would have a lot of spirits hanging around."

"I thought it cost too much money to get access to these places because of the liability issues."

"Not if we were shooting like that one show *Psychic Medium*," Haley interjects.

Carolyn sits forward. "Here's what we're thinking. After everyone is scared out of their minds from viewing the two episodes on the Brascia demon house, we'd like to make them even more uncomfortable by pointing out just how many spirits are around us all the time, in broad daylight and in public places."

I tilt my head and regard Carolyn speculatively. "So, you'd film me talking to them and to the people I need to give messages to?"

"Exactly. And as you've done on the other episodes, we'd like you to talk to the audience and explain what you are hearing and seeing, since we can't."

I nod, mulling it over. "Where are you thinking of shooting?"
Carolyn eyes Haley.

"We heard your grandmother is psychic," Haley says. "We can get clearance to film at her retirement home if she is interested."

"Meeting your grandmother and having the two of you work together would make for an exciting episode," Geoff maintains. "We'd then be able to talk about how the gift of the sixth sense often runs in families."

"Do you think she'd be willing?" Carolyn asks, folding her hands on the table.

I can't help but think back on how excited my Nana was for me when I told her about the series. I imagine she's going to love being on the show. Of course, I don't know that for sure. "Probably," I answer. "My nana's pretty spunky, and she's a better psychic than I am. Let me give her a call."

"That would be great," Haley says with appreciation. "And if she's okay with it, I'll see if we can get clearance for the beginning of next week."

"So, for story purposes," Carlos interjects, "I'm assuming we'll start with Natalie the moment she wakes up?"

"Absolutely," Carolyn replies, not giving me a choice. "Our video diary format is working incredibly well. So, Natalie, if you live with a boyfriend, or have someone who stays over regularly, you might want to give him a heads-up to clear out."

My eyes quickly skim over Ryan who has to look away to keep from laughing.

"Oh, um, no worries," I tell Carolyn. "I'm sure he'll have no trouble cooperating."

———————

It's amazing how fast time flies when life is treating you kindly. It's already Thursday, which means the *Super Natalie* pilot is airing tonight. Carolyn had originally invited everyone to her house to watch it, but this morning one of Carolyn's pipes broke in her house and flooded the entire downstairs. Now we are all doing our own thing.

I invited everyone to my tiny apartment, but my mom insisted we come over to her place since she has a forty-inch plasma screen TV, a far cry over my old fifteen-inch LCD. Ryan, of course, is invited. Matt, Lucy, my sister and Nana are coming as well. Peter was invited too, but he and Stephanie broke up.

Stephanie told me that she and Mikey now have a thing, though it's strictly for work. Apparently their "sexcapades" fuel their creativity to such dizzying heights that it would make Mozart proud. I told Stephanie to bring Mikey, but she declined, feeling it would define their relationship and potentially damage their creative process. I can't argue with her there. I might not be churning out lyrics after I've been with Ryan, but he definitely awakens every cell in my body.

It's already seven and I've been over at my mom's since five. We're putting together a few appetizers for the party. Ryan was going to come with me until I told him I needed to show up a couple of hours early to help with the food. Too much pressure, I guess, hanging out with me and my mom, so he'll be driving over with Matt and Lucy.

"If you leave the avocado pit in the guacamole it won't discolor," my mom instructs me as I'm about to throw it out.

"Thanks, 'Martha.'" I hold on to the pit as I mash the avocado, salt, pepper, garlic, and lime juice into a bowl. "How's your new travel company going?"

"Absolutely fantastic. All of my clients but four have come with me and I'm averaging a hundred new hits on my site a day."

"That's so amazing, Mom. I'm really happy for you."

She cuts up carrots and celery and puts them on a platter. "So, tell me more about Ryan."

"What do you mean?"

"I'm your mother. You practically levitate every time you mention his name."

I chuckle. "That's because he's different than anyone I've dated. He's smart, kind, a good listener ... very, very handsome." I flash a big grin. "He takes responsibility for himself, which is huge for me after Dean."

"And how is Ryan handling your talking to the dead?"

I open a bag of tortilla chips. "As you know, he was a big skeptic when I first met him."

"And now?"

"It's difficult to doubt the existence of the sun when you're sitting there nursing a bad sunburn."

She laughs. "So, he's had more experiences he can't explain."

"More than I thought he'd have."

"How did he handle them?" my mom asks, as she begins working on a fruit salad.

"Surprisingly well, but I can't say he's comfortable with spirits around, and I'm not sure if he'd be able to handle what I do on a twenty-four hour basis."

"Give him time. After all, it's taken you years to get comfortable, and you know they exist."

I smile. "Yeah, and at least he's not like Dad was, absolutely refusing to believe me."

"Well, I can't wait to meet him."

"Helllllooo," my sister calls from the front of the house.

"In the kitchen!" I yell back, emptying green and black olives onto a relish tray.

"Something smells good." Stephanie sticks her nose in the air. "What is it?"

"Nana's famous crescent cookies," I reply.

My nana gasps. "I haven't had those in ages. Are you really using my recipe?"

"Got the first batch coming out of the oven in about two minutes. Would you like to roll them in powdered sugar for me?"

"Oh, it would be my pleasure."

"You might have to try one or two, just to make sure they are good enough to serve."

My nana makes a little delighted squealing sound. "I'm more than happy to be your taste tester."

I pull out a bowl from the cupboard, throw some powdered sugar in it, and set it in front of my nana.

"What can I do?" Stephanie asks. "And remember, I don't cook."

"How about popping the popcorn?" my mom suggests.

"Sure." Stephanie goes into the pantry to find the box of microwave popcorn when her cell rings. "I gotta take this." She speaks into her cell, walking out. "Any news?"

I pull the cookies out of the oven and move them onto a cooling rack with a spatula. My nana starts to reach for one. "Ah-ah!" I chide her. "You know those are still too hot."

"Humph!" She grumbles, staring at them.

I hear the doorbell ring, and I immediately drop the pan into the sink with a loud clank. "He's here," I say to my mom, wiping my hands off on a towel.

"Who's here?" my nana asks.

"Ryan," I tell her. "And remember I work with him. That's all you know."

"So, I shouldn't mention that you are falling in love with him, and you haven't stopped thinking about him since the last time you saw him?"

"Nana, stop reading me."

My nana laughs as I hurry out of the kitchen to answer the door.

"Hi!" I say to Ryan, Lucy and Matt as I whip open the door. "Come on in. Did you have any trouble finding it?"

"Nope," Matt answers. "Drove right here."

"That's because I insisted he use the GPS I gave him for his birthday," Lucy tells me. "If we hadn't, I would have been calling you from God knows where in about an hour."

I laugh, then make eye contact with Ryan. "Hey."

He gives me a quick kiss on the lips, thinks better of it, then gives me a longer one. *Damn, he's a good kisser.* "Hi back," he finally says.

Lucy clears her throat and we both look up.

"Oh, right." I come to. "We're congregating in the kitchen." I bring everyone in. "Mom, Nana, you know Lucy."

"Good to see you again, Lucy," my mom says, as she wipes her hands off and gives her a hug.

"Oh, yes." My nana turns, her mouth covered in powdered sugar. "Of course I remember you, dear. And is this strapping man next to you Matt?"

"Hello, Nana." Matt leans down, all smiles, and gives her a delicate hug.

I quickly wipe my nana's mouth off.

"Oh, dear," she says, noticing. "The hazards of being the family taste tester."

We all laugh as my nana zeroes in on Ryan.

"This is Ryan Emery," I say. "He's renting Matt's duplex and he works with me."

"Well!" Nana says dramatically. "Seems like you're already family." She holds out both hands.

"Very nice to meet you, Nana." Ryan takes her hands, smiling at her.

She studies his face. "Such a good, sweet boy."

"Aww." Lucy lightly laughs.

"You'd make beautiful babies with my granddaughter here."

Lucy and Matt burst with a shocked laugh, and my mother and I gasp.

"Nana!" I chide.

"Mother!" my mom chimes in right behind me. "Why would you say such a thing?"

"Because I'm old and I can get away with it," she says, laughing.

"Betty White move over," Ryan remarks, taking it in stride.

"Welcome, Ryan." My mother officially greets him and immediately warms to him.

"Oh my GOD!!" Stephanie comes screaming in. "You will NOT believe this. The song, the one you insisted we play, Talie, the one I sang the other night that you all heard," Stephanie looks over at my friends, "is going to be the theme song for a new beer commercial, and they're going to pay us lots of money to record it and use it!"

"Seriously?" My face lights up.

"Yes!" she screams as she jumps up and down.

"Oh, Steph, that's fantastic!" I jump up and down with her.

"Sweet!" Matt yells.

"I can't believe it," she says, squeezing my hands. "You said the song would give us a big break and it has."

"And it's only the beginning," my nana adds. "Congratulations, honey."

"I'm so happy for you." My mom hugs her.

"Thanks, Mom."

"Yeah, Stephanie, way to go." Lucy smiles proudly.

Stephanie eyes Ryan, and I can tell she can't place him.

"Ryan was there the night you played, but I don't think you officially met. Ryan, this is my sister, Stephanie."

He nods hello. "Congratulations. The song sounded like a hit when I heard it."

"I hope you're right," she replies. "Mikey says he wrote it in five minutes. Woke up one morning and it was all there in his head."

"Not exactly," I inform her.

"What do you mean?"

"I think Mikey had some help," I enlighten her.

"What do you mean?" she asks, and then catches my meaning. "A spirit?"

"Yup."

"How do you know?"

"I saw him. He was an old guy, screaming at Mikey to play the song."

Stephanie sits down, a little stunned. "How about that!"

Ryan shoves his hands in his pockets, appearing uncomfortable.

"Spirits help all of us, more than we know," my nana whispers to Ryan, as if she's telling him a classified secret.

"I'm beginning to get that impression," he replies, whispering back.

"Well, this is certainly a night for celebration," my mom announces. "And there is no sense in celebrating without a bunch of spirits." My mom smiles as she holds up a bottle of tequila in one hand and a bottle of vodka in the other. "Name your poison."

As expected, the pilot was a tremendous success, which makes it all the sweeter to know that my nana will be working with me in the next episode. I ended up calling her right after we finished with our production meeting the other day, and my nana was thrilled. She became even more excited after she watched the pilot. Now Haley has secured her retirement home as our next on-location shoot.

I'm just as excited as my nana because this will be the first time we work together as psychic mediums, and I can't imagine what might happen. Who knows? Maybe with our collective energy, my nana and I might be able to help a spirit materialize for the cameras. Wouldn't that be something?

The *Super Natalie* crew pulls up to Willow Creek at ten in the morning. Because we won't be using any night vision cameras, we brought along lighting equipment just in case we need it as the day progresses. However, right now, there is no need for additional lighting since Willow Creek is almost too bright with all of its skylights and huge picture windows.

I jump out of the SUV, excited to get going. Luckily we won't have to waste hours setting up cameras because this is just going to be a single camera following me and my nana around the entire time.

"Do you want to go say hello to your grandmother first?" Geoff asks, as Shani touches up my makeup.

I laugh. "My nana is more psychic than I am. She knows we're here. Plus I talked to her last night and she thought it would be better if she met everyone while you were filming. She's not an actor and she worries that she won't be able to fake meeting everyone for the first time when it's the second or third time around."

"Understood," Geoff replies. "We'll try covering your greeting with the camera's microphone, but if the quality is poor, we'll have to reshoot." Geoff claps his hands together like he usually does when we are about to begin. He glances over at Carlos, Haley and Sam, who are already in the command post van, firing up the computers and equipment. "How's it going?" he calls to them.

"Looking good." Sam gives him two thumbs-up.

Geoff puts his eyes back on me. "Maybe we should film your intro over there, under that willow tree," he suggests, pointing to the largest tree on the property.

"That'll work," Ryan agrees as he pulls out his camera, checks it, and begins walking with me. "So, do you, uh, see anyone who's living here without paying rent?"

"Yup," I reply, matter-of-factly.

"More than one?" His voice goes unusually high.

"Quite a few."

Ryan stops walking and nervously glances around.

I get in front of him, suddenly remembering that this is the first time he's in a location with spirits since he was attacked. "I know you're a little apprehensive, being back on the job and all, but what attacked you that night in the Brascia house isn't on the same level as these spirits here. And I mean that literally. Please remember that the spirits we encounter today were once somebody's mom or dad or granddad or daughter. The reason they are here is because they are watching over their loved ones, so there is absolutely nothing to worry about. Okay?"

He finally seems to relax. "Okay."

"Great." I walk over to the willow tree and turn around, facing Ryan. "Where do you want me?"

Ryan puts the viewfinder to his eye and checks out the lighting and the frame. "A little to your right.... Too much." I take a step back. "Right there."

I firmly plant my feet as Shani once again does a final touch up. "You look radiant," she tells me.

And I can feel it. "This is going to be a great show." I clip on my radio mic, slide the battery pack behind me on my waistband.

"We're ready when you are," Ryan says into his walkie-talkie.

And over the walkie-talkie, I hear, "Action!"

I gaze into the camera and say, "Today, we're doing something a little different. So many people ask me what it's like to see ghosts and spirits on a daily basis. Well, today I'm going to take you with me."

I motion to the front entrance. "I'm standing outside my grandmother's assisted-living home. I'd really like to tell you the name of it because it's a very nice place. But I can't because there are as many spirits roaming the grounds as there are living residents, and let's be honest, that might scare away a few folks out there who might want to live here in the future." I smile into the camera. "I would, however, like you to meet my grandmother, who is an amazing woman and has a psychic gift that far exceeds my own. So, why don't we go inside."

I start walking toward the front entrance. Ryan is still filming because we are going to try to keep the camera rolling with minimal edits. I turn and look into the camera. "So, as we approach the porch, I see four spirits, well five actually, if you count the cat." I stop and point.

Ryan takes the camera off me and begins filming the porch area while I continue to narrate off-screen.

"There is a young couple walking down the steps. I have to tell you that I've seen them before, and they are not related to anyone in the home. They are wearing clothes from the turn of the century. She has a white parasol open and is holding the man's arm. They are laughing and smiling at each other, and it looks like they are out for a pleasant stroll."

Ryan smoothly pans the camera back onto me. "I cannot communicate with them because they are not here. What I just witnessed is a residual haunt, a loop of past energy," I explain. "But why don't I say hello to Mrs. Peterson."

I start walking up the steps with Ryan as he pulls back into a long shot of me so the camera can pick up anything around me. I stop next to a row of rocking chairs. "Good morning, Mrs. Peterson," I greet the woman that only I can see.

She peers up at me, still petting her cat. "Good morning, dear."

"Mrs. Peterson passed away last year," I inform the viewers. "Her sister still resides here. Mrs. Peterson is sitting in this rocking chair, petting her cat on her lap. She's enjoying the beautiful day and her cat is watching that bird there." I point to the bird sitting in a tree not far from the porch.

"What's your cat's name?" I ask.

"Mr. Tinkles."

I laugh, then I tell the audience, "His name is Mr. Tinkles, but I don't think he has to worry about that anymore." I put my focus back on Mrs. Peterson. "You have a very nice rocking chair, Mrs. Peterson. Is it comfortable?"

"Oh, yes, very much. And Mr. Tinkles likes it too."

"Can you rock Mr. Tinkles now?"

"Well, let's see. He might not want to rock since he's bird watching, but I will try."

The rocking chair begins to slowly rock, and then it abruptly stops as Mr. Tinkles jumps off her lap and runs toward the bird.

"Mr. Tinkles!" she scolds.

"Oh, I'm sorry. I shouldn't have asked you to rock him."

"Not your fault, my dear. He's still quite the hunter, though now nothing ever comes of it."

I smile. "Good to see you."

I walk away and say into the camera, "I'm not sure how many of you out there could see Mrs. Peterson's spirit, but I know everyone at least saw the rocking chair move. It stopped abruptly when Mr. Tinkles jumped off her lap. And for those skeptics out there, please take note that we do not have a breeze at all today." I gesture to the trees and Ryan zooms in on the motionless leaves.

When Ryan brings the camera back onto me I continue talking. "The other spirit who was here a moment ago has moved on, so why don't you meet my grandmother. We affectionately call her Nana."

I walk inside, and I immediately notice that we have an audience from several residents as well as from the staff. I spot the facility administrator who appears to be discussing something very serious with one of the staff members. When the administrator sees me, she starts to come over. I'm wondering if we should stop filming, but then I see my nana walking towards us.

I smile broadly, thinking that Nana is definitely the actress in the family. Her hair has been colored and cut in a hip style, and her makeup is so flawless that I swear she looks thirty years younger. I take her in and realize that she's walking beautifully and without a cane. "Nana! Oh, my goodness. You look amazing. Where's your cane?"

My nana is all smiles as she continues to walk toward me. "I no longer need it, Talie. I feel fantastic!"

"You look it." I laugh. "You're stunning. Nana, come closer. I'd like you to meet … well, the whole world."

I proudly turn and stare into the camera, but Ryan is lowering the viewfinder from his eye. I'm about to ask him why he's stopped filming when I hear an ambulance in the distance, coming closer. I assume Ryan is waiting for the ambulance to pass, for audio purposes, but a part of me knows that isn't correct.

And suddenly I can hear my heart pounding and everything seems to go in slow motion. I pin my eyes to Ryan's. He has this grave look on his face—the look I know so well because I've seen it on too many faces of former employers, co-workers, friends. That look of shock, mixed with disbelief, when they thought they were witnessing a crazy person talking to thin air.

My brain registers this familiar look—only on Ryan's face, it's much worse. I see pain and sadness. I notice how his eyes, locked onto mine, are filling with tears, and it is only then that I realize he knows what I have just figured out.

In a panic, I throw my arms around my nana, hoping beyond hope that I will feel flesh and bone, but I don't. I grab only air, and I suddenly feel myself weak in the knees. Tears are already stinging my eyes, and I hear myself cry out in a voice that doesn't sound like my own.

"Nana!!" I scream as I run as fast as I can toward her apartment, and as I get there, I notice that her front door is open. Inside, I see her lying on the floor with a bunch of personal care technicians surrounding her. Someone is giving her CPR. "Nana!" I run in, but a male caregiver blocks my way.

"You need to stay outside, Miss."

"I can't. That's my grandmother!"

"Make a path!" someone shouts, and I turn to see EMTs coming in with a gurney.

The male caregiver escorts me out into the hallway as Ryan and Geoff come rushing to my side.

"No," I tell them. "Just because I saw my nana's spirit doesn't mean she's gone," I say, vehemently shaking my head. "There are thousands of documented near-death experiences from patients all over the world," I explain, trying to hold it together. "They're doing CPR on her right now. They'll revive her any minute." I can feel my tears begin to flow again, and I quickly turn away.

The technicians slowly file out of my nana's apartment. Annie, one of the staff members I know, solemnly looks at me and says, "I'm sorry, Natalie. We all loved your grandmother very much."

I shake my head, not believing what I'm hearing. I run back into her apartment, and this time the male caregiver doesn't stop me.

My nana has been placed on the gurney. I keep blinking away my tears, so I can see her more clearly. My nana's face is serene. I hold her hand and tell her how much I love her. I'm certain her spirit will talk to me any minute now, so we can have a proper conversation, but she never materializes. I wait there, right by her side, talking to her until the male caregiver gently pulls me away. The EMTs take her out. I sit there on the couch right next to where she has died, trying to be with her, not understanding why I don't feel her presence.

Ryan quietly makes his way in. "Someone is calling your mother and sister," he tells me gently.

I nod, acknowledging that I've heard him. I keep wiping away the tears that keep running down my cheeks, but it's no use since they aren't stopping.

"Is there anything I can do?" Ryan asks.

I shake my head, and after several minutes of him sitting there with me in silence, I finally manage to speak. "Thank you for staying with me, but I think I just need to be alone for a while."

"Okay," Ryan says softly. He kisses me on top of my head and leaves.

I stay in my nana's apartment, talking to her without seeing her, as if I were devoid of my sixth sense entirely and I hate it. I wonder where she is, if she can hear me. I don't understand why she hasn't come back to talk to me. She knows I can see her. She knows I can hear her. Why won't she come?

Unless none of it is real. What if I really didn't see my nana's spirit today? It's quite possible that my subconscious created her when I noticed everyone staring at me as I entered the building, and when I saw the administrator walking towards me with a grave expression on her face. What if Nana and I and people like us only think we have communicated with the dead, but we really haven't? What if there really isn't eternity or God or Heaven? Maybe it's all just been wishful thinking. What if I really am crazy and all those spirits I've seen have just been hallucinations?

As I sit in my nana's empty apartment, it truly feels empty, and for the first time in my life, I have lost my faith.

Chapter 17

————◆————

It's been two weeks since my nana passed away. We had a beautiful service for her, and I was so happy to see such a large number of friends come to pay their respects. Every one of them had a great story about her, which only proves she had a life well lived.

Super Natalie is on hold. Carolyn has been incredibly generous to give me time to recover from my nana's sudden death, but now the network is freaking out because we haven't resumed shooting yet. They just aired the Musgrave Inn episode, which made *Super Natalie* number one for that time slot. Next week, they'll air part one of the insanely scary Brascia Demon House.

Carolyn told me that they have enough material to stretch the Brascia Demon House into a three-part special, but then we'd be out of shows because we didn't finish filming at Willow Creek. In order for the series to continue without having to air reruns, we will need to film the next episode by Friday, which means I have only three or four more days to get it together.

But how can I get it together when I'm questioning my own ability, my own beliefs? How can I continue when I haven't seen or heard from my nana? Not that I would believe my eyes if she showed up now. In these last two weeks I've become more of a skeptic than Ryan ever was.

I think back on all the spirits I've encountered. Not one of them gave me information I couldn't have found out myself. What if I had overheard Ed Cummings talking to his mistress before my TV appearance, and then under the pressure of people wanting me to see a ghost, I allowed my subconscious to manifest one?

Tyler is easily explained by the obituaries I was looking up and whether or not he's related to Ryan, remains to be seen. The spirit attached to Mikey in the club could have just been Mikey's strong projection of him wanting to play the harmonica, and I had somehow picked up on it.

And then there were all those ghosts at my many new jobs who got me fired. When I think about them, they all seemed to show up when I was under a lot of stress. I could have easily conjured them up as my way to deal with the stress.

I keep thinking about all of this, especially since I haven't seen one spirit since my nana passed. Of course, I've pretty much stayed in my apartment which seems to be ghost-free.

I know everyone is worrying about me. I've gone over to my mom's a few times for dinner, but that's about it. I've turned down Lucy's repeated invitations to have coffee or lunch or catch a movie, and as for Ryan, he's gone home. Not permanently. Just for a few days. His dad ended up getting into a minor fender bender on his way to the airport, so he missed his flight to L.A. Ryan's dad said he'd pay for Ryan to come back to Florida instead. Since our show was on hold, and since I haven't been very good company, he took his dad up on the offer.

So here I am, left with trying to figure out what it all means. My entire life changed in an instant when I went on *World's Weirdest Hobbies*. And now it has instantly changed again. The only time I find peace is when I'm asleep. I've been sleeping a lot. I don't have any energy to do anything, and nothing seems to hold my interest.

It's 10 a.m. I skipped breakfast after I skipped dinner the night before because I don't have an appetite. I know I should eat something, especially since I'm feeling a little light-headed, so I grudgingly reach for a bag of potato chips and flip on the TV. I scroll through the channels, but find nothing worth watching. I eat a few chips, but my usually favorite comfort food now tastes too greasy, so I set them aside. *Maybe I should just go back to bed.* If I sleep through the day, it will go by a lot faster. Of course, my going back to bed would require getting up off the couch, so instead I just close my eyes, and the last thing I think about is how much I need my nana.

I wake up with a jolt. I've fallen asleep on a bench in a park. It's a stunning park. Absolutely gorgeous. It seems like there are miles of deep green grass. Vibrant impatiens border a path that travels so far into the distance I can't see the end. Right in front of me is a lake lined with huge willow trees. Several pairs of white and black swans are leisurely hanging out in the pond.

"There you are."

I look over my shoulder and into the bright, cheery face of my nana. I jump up, run around the back of the bench and give her a sorely needed hug. This time it's not an empty hug like the one I was left with in her home. This time, I can feel her. Her love, her warmth. I can feel her hug me back.

I finally let go, pull back and take her in. My nana looks thirty years old. I'm not saying she looks great. I'm saying she truly appears to be around my age. Come to think of it, she looks exactly like the way she does in the picture my mom has of her sitting on a shelf in her living room—a strong, beautiful woman with bright eyes, raven-black hair and porcelain skin. The picture was taken when she was thirty-three. "You're so young, Nana."

She bubbles with a lovely effervescent laugh. "You've always told me that, so I guess I finally believed it."

I glance around the grounds. "Where are we?"

"In your dream, of course."

"So, this isn't Heaven?"

"This is your interpretation of it."

"Am I close?"

"For what your mind can accept, yes. But this is perhaps a tenth of its awe and beauty."

"Wow. That good? How come no one crosses back over to let us in on the secret?"

She laughs hard. "Mainly because there would be a major exodus from the planet, don't you think?"

I smile. "I see your point."

"Besides," she pats my hand like she used to do, "when we're here on Earth, we really do know how amazing home is. We know it in our hearts."

My nana and I start walking down the endless path, and the bordering impatiens turn to tulips, which happen to be my favorite flowers. "Nana, how come you haven't come to see me? I've been so upset."

"I'm sorry, dear. I didn't mean to leave you hanging. There's no time where I am, and as soon as I arrived, I walked into this huge party thrown in my honor. I spent a lot of time catching up with everyone I've ever known."

"The party must have lasted days."

"Funny you should say that. Since time isn't linear on the Other Side, when I think back on the party, it could have lasted two hours or two decades. I really can't say for sure."

I smile. "Well, we had a huge party for you down here too."

"I know," she says with a little chuckle as if she's holding something back.

"You were there?"

"Of course, and even if I hadn't been, I not only would have known about it, but I would have experienced it as well. On the Other Side, I know and feel everything." She picks a red tulip and hands it to me.

"Then you know how I've been doubting so much. I don't want you to take this wrong, Nana, but why didn't you just take two seconds to contact me?"

"You would have doubted seeing me if I had, so I thought I'd reach out the way most spirits do."

"Through my dream?"

"Yes."

I stop walking and give her a puzzled look. "But how can this be better? Because this is a dream, you know I'm going to doubt I've even connected with you when I wake."

She rubs my arms. "Then I guess you'll just need to have faith again."

I drop my head, shaking it. No matter what I do, I'm bested by spirits.

"Natalie, you need to carry on with your life. I'm happy and I have no regrets, so stop moping. In truth, I don't want to hang around on Earth. Where I am, it's beautiful beyond words. There is nothing but love and it's palpable. The feeling is ... well, it's indescribable."

"Is Grandpa with you?"

"Of course. Everyone I've ever loved is with me."

I immediately think of all the boyfriends from her past, surrounding her, vying for her attention. "How does *that* work?"

Nana giggles. "It's not like that. There's no jealousy, envy, hatred, or fear. We are pure in spirit. There is no ego. Only love."

"Sounds incredible." I search her face. "Tell me more."

"You don't really want me to. That would be like my telling you the ending of the best book you will ever read when you're only on chapter one." She takes hold of my hands. "Just remember, Talie, it's really very simple. There is love and there is fear. Life is supposed to be about love. It always has been. Fear will ruin that, so get rid of it. Throw it away. You don't need it, and when you refuse to be ruled by fear and all its complicated forms, you will find out how liberating that can be. Stop worrying about what you cannot control and let go. Live your life. Enjoy every minute of it. There are no missteps, only different paths. Take one, take ten. It doesn't matter. Just follow your heart. Love will never lead you astray. Do you understand?"

Tears are now streaming down my face, and I can only nod at my nana.

"Don't make me come back here," she says in a teasing fashion, and I can't help but laugh.

"Thank you for this gift, Nana. I love you so much."

"I love you too. Be happy, Natalie. We'll see each other again." My young, strong and beautiful nana smiles at me, and when she does I can feel her love touch every cell of my body. I squint at the explosion of pure white light as it surrounds her. The light becomes so bright that I have to turn away. When I look back, she's gone.

I wake from the most vivid dream I've ever experienced. As I sit up, I am suddenly filled with elation and incredible energy. "Thanks, Nana." I smile and burst with a laugh.

———

As I'm getting out of the shower, I suddenly feel light-headed, and I finally realize how hungry I am. *Maybe I could grab Lucy for lunch.* I finish toweling off and my cell rings. I look at who's calling and smile. "Now look who's the psychic," I say to Lucy. "I was just about to call you."

"Oh, yeah?" She sounds pleasantly surprised.

"How about lunch?"

"That's what *I* was calling about," Lucy remarks. "I love it when we're on the same page."

"Me too."

"Where do you want to go?"

"Well, I happen to have a gift certificate for the Terrace Restaurant at the Lindley Hotel."

Lucy gasps. "Who gave you such a nice present?"

"It was part of my payment for appearing on *World's Weirdest Hobbies.* Most of their guests live out of town, so they fly them in and put them up at a hotel for the night, but because I live here, they gave this to me instead."

"Nice!"

"So, do you want to go?"

"Heck, yeah! I'll pick you up in ten."

The Terrace Restaurant is one of those places you go to with your girlfriends. Small tables tucked away between ivy and flowers. Umbrellas overhead, a Tuscan-style water fountain nearby. The menu mainly consists of fresh salads, sandwiches and soups. They even have a formal tea menu which includes finger sandwiches and scones—a huge hit with bridal showers and birthdays.

Lucy and I are seated near the fountain. I take in the atmosphere and breathe deeply.

"I'm glad to see you're feeling better," Lucy remarks, sipping her iced tea.

"I finally connected with my nana," I inform her as I lean back in my chair.

"You did?" Surprise moves across Lucy's face. "When?"

"This morning."

"Oh, Talie. That's great news. Did you see her, hear her?"

"Both." I almost tell her that I saw her in my dream, but decide to leave that part out because I know it wasn't just a dream.

"Is she all right? What did she say? How did she look?"

"Lucy, she looked amazing." I take a mini blueberry muffin out of the basket of fresh bread and pick at it. "She was young again. Strong, vibrant. She's very happy, and she shared some pretty profound insights with me."

"Like what? If you don't mind my asking."

"She said we are either ruled by love or by fear, and I can't stop thinking about how true that is."

Lucy sits back and thoughtfully stares off into space. "She's right. There's an intention behind every action, and there are many shades of love and fear. You really do have to choose one or the other. Not both."

I immediately think of Ryan. "Well, I hope Ryan and his dad are coming from a place of love right now."

"Here you are, ladies." Our waiter ducks under the umbrella. "A Cobb salad...." He sets the salad under Lucy's nose. "And one roasted chicken sandwich," he announces, placing the plate in front of me. "Anything else?"

I catch Lucy's eye and she shakes her head. "No, we're good. Thanks."

Lucy mixes up the ingredients in her salad. "You know he's back, right?"

I perk up. "When?"

"Matt said he came in last night and looked exhausted."

"Did he say anything?"

"Not about his trip, but he asked Matt how you were."

I smile. "Really?"

"First thing out of his mouth."

"What did Matt say?"

"That you were still taking your nana's passing pretty hard."

"I need to call him," I tell her, taking a bite of my sandwich as I think back on that horrible day. "You should have seen him, Lucy. How sweet he was the day Nana died."

"Ryan's a good guy. He's sensitive without being ... Dean sensitive."

I laugh. "You have no idea." I wipe my mouth. "He's the antithesis of Dean in more ways than one."

"So does this mean that I have finally redeemed myself as your matchmaking friend?"

"Yes," I commend Lucy. "And I hope I'll never need your services again."

———————

I arrive back home from lunch with Lucy to find I've missed several calls from Carolyn. She not only tried my cell, which I accidentally left in the bathroom, but she left a few messages on my home phone as well.

If Carolyn herself called, it's important. I reach for my phone and dial. She answers on the first ring.

"How are you feeling?"

"Better, thank you."

"I'm glad to hear that," she says, a little rushed. "Natalie, I know I promised you could have a few more days off but we have a problem."

"What?" I ask, suddenly alarmed.

"The network is not allowing us to extend the Brascia investigation into a third episode...."

"Which means our shooting schedule has been pushed up," I finish for her.

"Precisely." She pauses, and then, "We need to start shooting tomorrow."

I inhale sharply. "Well, I guess there's no easing into it."

"I'm sorry."

"It's okay. I'm grateful for the time you've given me."

"So the million dollar question is, do you think you can handle it?"

"Emotionally, yes. But I have to be honest with you, Carolyn. I haven't seen a ghost or a spirit since my nana died."

"Well, maybe there haven't been any to see."

"I don't know," I say, uncertainty coloring my voice.

"How long have you had your gift?"

"I'm told I saw my first spirit when I was five months old."

"Then there is no way you can suddenly lose it," she remarks with confidence.

As much as Carolyn's words should comfort me, instead I feel a little bit of panic begin to prickle my skin. *What if I really can lose my ability? Maybe that's why my nana showed up in my dream instead of just appearing. Maybe she knew my sixth sense had short-circuited.*

"I might not be able to lose it," I agree, "But I ended up suppressing it for a while when I was a kid."

"And you think you might be suppressing it now?"

"Maybe. I was at the very old Lindley Hotel today, built in 1898, and I didn't see or feel any spirits or ghosts."

"Have you seen any there before?"

"Well, no, but I've only been there a couple of times."

"Not all hotels have ghosts, Natalie," Carolyn says through a light chuckle.

"I guess you're right."

Before I can make any more excuses, Carolyn says, "Now that we've cleared that up, I need to know if you're amenable to going back to a location where you have always seen ghosts."

My mind instantly flashes on Willow Creek. "I can't go back *there*." I hear my own voice cracking a bit.

"Aside from Willow Creek," Carolyn corrects. "Is there anywhere else you've been recently where you've seen a lot of ghosts or spirits?"

"Not like I do at Willow Creek."

There is a long pause and I know I'm not helping. "How about this? What if I have Haley call some other retirement homes to see if we can film in one of them tomorrow?" Carolyn suggests.

"You're thinking of using that footage?" I try to keep the outrage from my voice.

"No, of course not," she treads lightly. "I wouldn't allow anyone to air the part where you saw your grandmother. But the beginning is quite good. You are so vibrant and confident in your intro. Marcus started assembling a rough cut in case we were able to use it somewhere in an upcoming episode, and I'm telling you, Natalie, you are riveting. When you describe the couple walking down the steps, we can almost see them. And when you're chatting with the woman in the rocking chair, we can almost hear her. We didn't capture her image on film, but we clearly see the chair rocking."

"I don't know," is all I can say because the feeling I had when seeing my nana on the floor is still so raw.

"I'm thinking if, in another home, you could speak to a few more spirits and more importantly speak to their loved ones who are still alive, we could combine the footage and have this great, light, loving episode where our audience has a chance to experience another side of your work. They can see that what you do doesn't always have to be dark and scary."

"And what if I can't communicate anymore?" I say, fear rising in me. *Wait a minute. What am I doing?* And I can just hear my nana say, *Why are you allowing fear to affect your decision?*

I'm about to word things differently when Carolyn says, "Natalie, I have never seen talent like yours before. I have total faith in you."

If that isn't a sign, I don't know what is. "Okay, Carolyn. I'll do it."

———————

Before I can think about what I've agreed to, I call Ryan, but I get his voicemail. "Hey, Ryan. It's me, Natalie. I just wanted to thank you for being there for me with my nana and all. That was really sweet of you and greatly appreciated. Hope your trip went well. I just got off the phone with Carolyn. There's a good chance we'll be working tomorrow afternoon. Anyway, give me a call if you're around."

I wait another hour to hear back from Ryan and when I don't, I get back on the phone to call my mom and my sister. I share with them what my nana said and they seem to be as moved by it as I was—which gets me thinking. Maybe I should share what she said with everyone who watches our show. Maybe that's what she wants me to do. Everything she said was so incredibly profound. Why wouldn't people want to hear it?

I think about getting in my car and going to a cemetery or a hospital just to make sure I still have a sixth sense, but when I realize I've run out of clean underwear, I opt to do laundry instead. Before I know it, the whole day is gone. A little after eleven, when I'm really starting to wonder why I haven't heard from Ryan, he finally calls.

"Am I calling too late?"

As soon as I hear his voice, I realize just how much I've missed him. "Not at all."

"I forgot I had my ringer turned off," he admits, seeming a little embarrassed. "How are you?" he asks as if it's the most important question he's asked all day.

"Much better—now that I'm talking to you." And I know he can tell I'm smiling by the sound of my voice. "Did everything go all right?"

"Well, I can't say I've had as bad a shock as you did, but it was close."

"What happened?"

"You're not going to believe what my dad told me, Talie. *I* don't believe what my dad told me."

"What?" I demand, practically jumping out of my skin. "What did he say?"

"Shoot. That's Adam calling in. I'll tell you all about it tomorrow. Sweet dreams!"

He did NOT just leave me hanging. Arrgh! Ryan is as bad as disappearing Tyler. I shake my head. There is no doubt in my mind. They are definitely brothers.

———◆———

I'd like to tell you that with my advanced sixth sense ability, I meditate every day, but I'd be lying. I can't seem to do it. As soon as I clear my mind, I'm fast asleep, so instead, I walk. I take long walks to clear my head, and this morning I took an extra long one to release all of the anxiety I've built up in my body over the last few weeks. When I return to my apartment, I am feeling great!

And then Carolyn calls.

She tells me they can't get permission to film anywhere on such short notice—except, of course, for Willow Creek.

Seriously? I thought when a person is doing what he/she is meant to do, it was supposed to be easy. This was not going to be easy. Not even close.

"What if I shut down?" I ask Carolyn, anxiety building fast.

"You won't."

"What if I freak out?"

"Not going to happen."

"How do you know? I don't even know and I'm a frickin' psychic!"

Carolyn laughs. "Not knowing what's going to happen makes it exciting, don't you think?"

I sigh loudly.

"You have nothing to worry about."

"Thank you for your confidence in me. I hope I find some within the next few hours." *No fear! Nana would say.* "What time should I be there?"

"Two o'clock, so we don't interrupt lunch or dinner for the residents."

"Okay."

"Thanks, Natalie. You'll be great."

Chapter 18

———————

I'm a complete ball of nerves the entire drive over to Willow Creek. Even though Carolyn is confident nothing has changed with my ability, I've already convinced myself that I won't see any ghosts. And even if I manage to get over that hurdle, I'm faced with another. What if I see my nana? What if I don't see my nana? How am I to interpret either one? Ugh, I hate this. How could I have ever thought that hunting ghosts was a good career move?

I immediately think back on crazy camp counselor Heidi. I wonder what she would have done if I had said, "Yes, Heidi. Thank you for asking what I'd like to do when I grow up. I think I'll enjoy talking to the dead."

I drive down the road leading to Willow Creek, my hands trembling on the steering wheel. I take a big breath and let it out. "Okay. I can do this, I can do this."

I turn into Willow Creek's driveway, let out a horrified scream and slam on the breaks! A Border collie stares at me over the hood of my car, then runs off.

"A dog." I get control of myself. "I almost ran over a dog." I watch him trot out of the way, and when he looks back at me, he disappears before my eyes.

I smile. *I guess I can still see ghosts.*

As I approach visitor parking, I notice no one else has arrived yet. Right when I pull into a parking spot, I see Shani coming in behind me.

She parks and hops out of her car. "Hey, Natalie."

"Hey, Shani."

"I'm glad you're here early," she says, taking her makeup bag and chair out of the trunk of the car. "Now, I can spend a little extra time on your makeup. Carolyn said I needed you to look the same as you did the other day, in order for the footage to cut together."

"Guess that's why I was told to wear the same clothes."

Shani meets my eyes. "I'm really sorry about your grandmother."

"Thanks."

"So, how about if we set up over there under the tree?"

I look over and see a male spirit making his way down to the pond, and I can't help but notice how the pond with the willow trees around it is very similar to the dream I had with my nana. "Great."

About fifteen minutes later, the rest of the crew arrives. Shani waves to them, but I don't move since she's applying my mascara. She then removes a set of oversized curlers she put in my hair, does a quick comb-through and says, "You're all set."

"Thanks, Shani." I get up and make my way over to Geoff, Ryan, Carlos, Haley and Sam. They all give me a hug, each expressing their condolences.

"So, is it all working?" Geoff asks me awkwardly, then glances toward the porch, eyeing the rocking chairs.

"Yes, Geoff. I can still see spirits," I inform him even though I don't see any hanging out on the steps.

"Terrific!" He claps his hands together in his usual fashion. "Well, I'm going to let the administrator know we're here and then we can get to it." Geoff takes off toward the front entrance.

As Carlos and Haley head over to the command post van to fire up the equipment, Ryan stays with me. "You look great."

"Thanks."

"Sorry I wasn't able to fill you in last night, but maybe we can get something to eat after we wrap."

"I'd like that." We both stand there hesitantly, keenly aware that we're at work.

"I heard you thought you lost your gift."

"Yeah, kinda," I say, half smiling at him since it's the first time he's referred to what I can do as a gift.

"I'm glad you didn't because you were right about Tyler."

My face lights up. "Your dad told you?"

"That and ... well, I'll get into all that later, but Tyler was my half brother."

I see sadness in his eyes, and I get the feeling he's thinking about what it would have been like to have known him.

"I just wanted you to know how ... accurate you are. And I'm sorry I didn't believe you."

"Thanks," I reply, taking his hand. "Means a lot to me."

Ryan blows out a quick breath, as if trying to clear away the seriousness of the moment. "Well, I guess I better leave you alone, so you can prepare. I'll be by the van with my camera when you're ready."

After Ryan walks away, I take a moment. I center my energy and put protection around myself and Ryan, and like my nana said to do, I just let everything else go. Whatever happens, happens.

I find Ryan and we head on inside, ready to begin. As soon as we walk into the lobby, I see a few spirits I've spoken with when I visited my nana.

To continue with my video diary, I stare into the camera lens and say, "There's a spirit helping out on a checkers game we have going on over here. I've spoken with this spirit before. Her name is Mrs. MacMillan, and she is standing behind her husband, George. He's the player wearing the beige sweater. The other player is Leonard."

Ryan pulls out into a long shot so he can capture me approaching the checkers game.

I turn back and look again into the camera. "Mr. MacMillan is hard of hearing," I explain, warning Ryan and the rest of the listening crew that I'm about to raise my voice. "Hello, Mr. MacMillan! How are you today?" I yell.

Mr. MacMillan peers up at me, studies my face, trying to place me. He gives me an anemic smile before he goes back to his game.

"And how are you, Mrs. MacMillan?" I ask the spirit no one else can see.

"Frustrated," she replies. "How can George not see how he can beat Leonard in two moves?"

I quickly turn to the camera. "Mrs. MacMillan can clearly see how her husband could win the game, and though I've never encouraged a spirit to help a loved one cheat, this might be interesting for all of you to see."

"Maybe you should tell him how he can win, Mrs. MacMillan."

"I have," she spouts. "I've been yelling at him for the last hour and he can't hear me."

"If he can't hear you, then maybe you should move one of his pieces yourself," I suggest, and Ryan zooms in on the two men crouched over the board.

Just as George is about to put his hand on one of his front checkers, the left back corner piece flips up, shoots in a diagonal across the board, jumping over three of Leonard's checkers, and landing on the other side.

Leonard releases a startled, "Oh!"

George's mouth falls open in shock.

"Well, how the hell did you do that, George? I didn't even see your hand on it."

"Beats me." George sounds like he's hiccupping with laughter. "But that's a damn good move."

I peer at Mrs. MacMillan who's smiling.

"Now, George," Leonard waves a finger at him, "I don't think that counts if your hand wasn't physically touching the piece."

"Of course it counts. It was my turn!"

"Good to see you are keeping things lively, Mrs. MacMillan."

"I do try. Have a good day, dear."

"You too."

I glance over at Ryan as he quickly removes his eye from the camera and mouths *Whoa!*

I smile and venture into the dining room area where a few residents are painting or playing games with some of the staff members. I scan the area searching for spirits, when I see another ghost cat, not Mr. Tinkles, jump up on the table. But what's really surprising is that someone else sees the cat too. As I watch an elderly woman talk to the cat, I psychically pick up that the cat was her pet.

I stare into the lens and point. "See that lady over there wearing an orange sweater? Her deceased cat is with her and she knows it." I immediately head over there before the cat disappears.

"Hi," I say to the caregiver sitting with the resident. "I'm Natalie with the cable show *Super Natalie*." I shake her hand and her face lights with a smile.

"Why, yes, Natalie. Pauline was your grandmother."

"That's right."

"Oh, she had quite a gift," she recalls. "I suppose you do too."

"Not as good as hers, but I do all right," I tell her modestly. "I see you have another resident who's clairvoyant."

"Oh?" She looks around the room. "Who?"

"Well, this lady here."

"Mrs. Fenton?"

"Yes."

She leans in and quietly speaks to me as Ryan continues filming. "No, unfortunately, Mrs. Fenton has dementia. She often talks to herself."

"That may be so, but I just saw her talking to her deceased cat," I emphasize, pulling out the chair next to her. "May I?"

The caregiver nods. "Be my guest."

"Hello, Mrs. Fenton. My name is Natalie."

Mrs. Fenton doesn't look at me. She continues to search the room for her cat who has, as I feared, disappeared.

"Mrs. Fenton, I couldn't help but notice that you were talking to your cat."

Mrs. Fenton's eyes slowly drift toward my face.

"What's your cat's name?"

She mumbles something to me, but I can't understand it. "Pardon?" I say, leaning closer to her.

Mrs. Fenton says nothing, distracted by her search.

Darn it. If I knew what her cat's name was, I could call him or her. I close my eyes for a second, trying to psychically pick up on the name, and all I get is Whiskers, which is ridiculous. Of course, my mind comes up with the most popular cat name in history. I open my eyes and I can see Mrs. Fenton mumbling something again.

"I'm sorry?" I say, leaning even closer to her.

"His name is Whiskers," she answers, barely above a whisper.

I can't help but laugh. "Whiskers. How cute." I scan the dining room for any sign of him. No doubt Ryan and I scared him off.

"Whiskers?" I call. "Come here, Whiskers. Whiskers?" As I'm about to give up, Mrs. Fenton points to the ceiling and suddenly Whiskers comes running in. "Well, hey there," I say to Whiskers as he saunters over to his owner, purring. Since he's on the table, he sniffs her hair and nuzzles the side of her neck. Mrs. Fenton feels it and bends her head toward him.

"Do you see her cat?" the caregiver asks.

"Yes, he's rubbing his face on her cheek."

"That's so ... incredible," she remarks, not really knowing what to say. "What does her cat look like?"

"Whiskers is all white, except his right ear is black and his nose is black too."

"Mrs. Fenton, may I take out your pictures?"

Mrs. Fenton nods, still snuggling with her cat as the caregiver hops up, comes around to the left side of her wheelchair, and digs around in a canvas tote bag that's hanging to one side. She pulls out a tiny photo album, flips through the photos until she finds one of the cat. "Is that him?" she asks, pointing.

I glance at the photo. It's of a white cat with a black right ear and black nose. "That's him. That's Whiskers. When did he pass away?"

"Over three years ago, but as her dementia has taken hold, she's been telling us he's around all the time."

"He is. And that's not the dementia talking."

"Well, I'll be," the caregiver says, shaking her head.

"In fact, if any of the residents say they are seeing their deceased loved ones, take it from me, they are."

The caregiver stiffens a bit, looking around.

"Nothing to worry about," I assure her.

"I'll keep that in mind."

I glance over at Mrs. Fenton happily enjoying the visit from her cat. "It was nice meeting you, Mrs. Fenton."

She looks at me and mumbles something, but I only catch "you too."

"Nice meeting you as well, Whiskers."

The cat obviously doesn't respond. In fact, he completely ignores me, as if I'm the one who's the ghost.

"Let's head toward the sitting room," I say into the camera, really talking to Ryan.

As we make our way down the hall, I'm not seeing or feeling any spirit or ghost, but just as we round the corner, I see Mr. Bauman coming our way. He's still wearing all purple and has a flower coming out of his top hat. "Hello, Mr. Bauman."

Mr. Bauman doesn't acknowledge that I'm even there, and Ryan gasps.

"Mr. Bauman?" I try again, but he simply keeps walking as if I don't exist, and then I realize why Ryan gasped. I turn back to explain, but Ryan is now running down the hallway, filming the backside of Mr. Bauman. "He's not a ghost!" I call out to Ryan.

Ryan stops, turns, and is now filming me. "Mr. Bauman is not a ghost. He's very colorful and he's very much in his own world, but he is definitely not a ghost. Sorry."

Ryan stops filming and lowers his camera. "That sucks," he replies. "I thought I was actually seeing one."

"If it makes you feel any better, when I encountered him for the first time, I thought I was seeing a ghost too."

Ryan shakes his head and changes the camera battery since we've stopped filming. "We're getting really good stuff here, Natalie. Seeing the checkers move was insanely freaky!"

"I'm glad you got it on film."

"Yeah," Ryan trails off then looks around, and I can't believe I already know the guy well enough to spot his patterns. I know he wants to ask me something, so I wait. "Have you ... uh ... seen your nana?"

"No, and I don't expect to. Everything she needed to say to me, she said."

"That's a good attitude to have." He studies me and I can't help but notice that Ryan seems so much more open than he used to be when I first met him. "And you're feeling okay being here?" he asks with concern.

"At first, no, but now, it's helping to lessen the pain."

"I'm glad."

Geoff comes hurrying over. "Fantastic, Natalie. Terrific camera work, Ryan."

"Thanks," we both say at the same time.

"Why don't you guys take ten? After that, we'll grab one, maybe two more interviews, and then we can call it a day."

"Won't we need more footage than that?" I question.

"We shouldn't, now that we have the checkers moving on camera. You know Carolyn. She'll want to have experts on. She also told me not to push you."

"Thanks, Geoff, but I'm okay. Whatever you guys need."

———

After the crew takes a break, I end up talking to a deceased World War II fighter pilot who was the father of the man living in three-sixteen. And just as I'm feeling quite comfortable, I hear a siren coming closer and it's déjà vu all over again. Three caregivers rush by me in the corridor. They run into an apartment only two doors down from where I'm standing.

I start to shake, thinking about the day my nana passed. I feel like I can't breathe.

Ryan immediately stops filming. "I think you need some fresh air." He takes me by the arm and begins to lead me towards the front door.

"How did I get out here?" I hear someone saying.

I look back over my shoulder and I see Doris, my nana's best friend. She's wearing a bathrobe, and she's standing right outside the apartment where the caregivers are working.

"Oh, no."

"What's wrong?" asks Ryan, since he can't hear Doris.

"It's Doris Lawson. My nana's best friend."

"Hey! What are you doing?" Doris marches back into her apartment.

"She's very confused," I say to Ryan. "I can't leave her like this." And something tells me he should keep filming instead. "I'm all right," I say to Ryan. "You can keep shooting."

Ryan hesitates, searches my eyes, not sure if he should listen to me or not.

"It's okay," I reassure him, and Ryan turns his camera back on.

After he's set, I stare into the lens. "I'm seeing the spirit of Doris Lawson. The caregivers have just rushed into her apartment. She doesn't know what's going on."

I head toward the apartment and look inside, just as two EMTs come flying down the hallway and into her apartment.

"Coming through!" one of them says. Right as the EMTs disappear inside, two of the caregivers exit to give the EMTs more room. Doris is talking to the caregivers, trying to get some answers with no luck. "I'm talking to you! Why won't you listen to me?"

"Because they can't hear you," I interject.

Doris immediately pins her eyes on me. "Why not?"

"Because you're in spirit form now."

Doris shakes her head, squints at me. "You look familiar."

"I'm Natalie Dalton, Pauline Dalton's granddaughter."

"Oh, yes, Natalie." She offers me a warm smile. "Well, Natalie, can you explain to me why these caregivers that I'm paying good money to are ignoring me?"

"They're not, Doris. You're in spirit form," I say to her again.

She stares at me truly confused, and then she finally understands. Doris clutches at her chest. "I'm ... dead?"

I open my mouth to say yes when I think I can ever so slightly hear my nana say no. "I'm ... not sure," tumbles out of my mouth instead. "Can you tell me what you remember?"

"I just finished showering, put on my robe, and slipped on the wet tile. I think I hit my head."

"Do you see a bright light anywhere?"

Doris looks around. "No. Am I supposed to?"

And right when I'm about to ask her more questions, the EMTs come out with Doris on the gurney. She's unconscious and has an oxygen mask over her face.

The spirit of Doris puts her hand over her mouth. "Oh, no! That's me!"

We watch the EMTs carefully wheel her down the hallway toward the front entrance.

And then it hits me. I'm witnessing a near-death experience. I've read countless stories about people who have died and come back, only to claim they saw themselves outside of their body. I've also read accounts where patients in comas had similar out-of-body experiences. This has to be what is happening to Doris. Now certain I heard my nana say that Doris was not dead, I must do something.

"You're not dead!" I yell at Doris. "Go!" And I gesture to her body that's being taken away.

Doris runs after the EMTs and as she gets closer to her own body, it's like her spirit is pulled back in, and I hear one of the EMTs say, "We got her!"

The other one says, "Mrs. Lawson, can you hear me? Stay with me now."

As I watch her go, I am overwhelmed with emotion. My nana was here after all, looking out for me and her good friend.

"Could you see her?" I ask Ryan.

"No, but maybe the camera picked her up."

"I hope so," I tell him. "It would be undeniable proof that near-death experiences are real."

Chapter 19

———◆———

Even though I'm thoroughly exhausted from the shoot, I somehow find my second wind so that I can go out with Ryan like I'd promised. I'm not only dying to hear what happened with his dad, but I've missed him, and I hope he's missed me too.

We stop by a local burger joint on the way home. After we both order a beer, burger, and a side of fries to share, Ryan wastes no time in getting me up to speed.

"My dad has moved out of the house and is temporarily staying with his sister, so he picked me up at the airport and we went to a diner nearby."

"So, it was just you and your dad?"

"Yeah. My mom was invited but she hasn't spoken to him since she learned the whole truth."

I scoot to the edge of my seat. I already knew Ryan's dad told him about Tyler, but what about Tyler's brother? "What did he say?"

Ryan takes a big gulp of his beer, sets down his glass, thinks better of it, then takes another big swallow. "Basically," he sets his eyes on me, "for the last, oh twenty-five years, he's been telling my mom and me one lie after another."

I give him a perplexed look. "You mean he's had more than one affair?"

"No. Just the one," he clarifies as his voice fills with sarcasm. "Though I don't know if you can technically call it an affair since he was married to my mom and the other woman at the same time."

"What?!" I slam back in my seat, my eyes ready to pop out of my head.

"Good old Dad is a polygamist."

I regard him, completely stunned. "Oh, Ryan. I don't even know how to respond to that. No wonder your mom hasn't spoken to him."

"Yeah." Ryan takes another large swallow of his beer.

"How?" I shake my head. "How was it possible?"

"It was actually very easy for him. His job had him travelling almost six months out of the year, so he just created a second identity."

"Does the other ... wife know?"

"I don't know." He stares into his drink. "I assume she does, but he didn't say. He just kept trying to tell me how sorry he was and how much he loved me."

"Did he tell you why?"

"He gave me some lame excuse about how much he loved having a family and how he hated being away from us for so long."

"Then why didn't he just change jobs?"

"That's exactly what I asked him." Ryan meets my eyes. "He said he was going to quit the very week he found out that his other wife, but mistress at the time, was pregnant."

I shake my head, stunned by the truth. "So, he told you about Tyler."

Ryan nods. "His death was why he chose to come clean with my mom. He couldn't bring himself to pretend that he was going out of town for work when he was attending his son's funeral."

"Ryan, I'm so sorry."

"I still can't believe it. You think you know someone...."

"Especially when that someone is a parent," I reply, empathizing with him.

"Some great role model, huh?" Ryan attacks his burger, and I can see he's getting angrier and angrier as he thinks about it.

I'm thinking this is not the best time to bring up the fact that Tyler has a twin, but hopefully I won't have to. "Did your dad tell you whether Tyler was an only child or not?"

"We didn't get that far," Ryan says with his mouth full. "I just lost it." He swallows his food. "To think I had a brother I could have known but my dad, who I thought I knew, was too selfish to tell me. It just makes me sick." He sharply pushes away his food. "I don't care if I ever see him again." Ryan jumps up and he looks like he's ready to punch someone. I watch Ryan head toward the bathroom, and he slaps the wall hard as he rounds the corner.

Crap. How am I going to bring up that touchy subject again?

Needless to say, when Ryan returns from the bathroom he completely changes the subject. Strangely, he asks me if I think Matt and Lucy will get married. I tell him I do, but then we suddenly find ourselves on the topic of marriage and we both fall into an awkward silence.

Feeling like our night is going from bad to worse, I'm just about to suggest that we both go home and get some sleep when Ryan says, "You know, I've never been to your apartment."

Gasp! It's a wreck. "No, I guess you haven't." I'm mentally running through my apartment, trying to remember how much of a disaster it is.

"So, are you going to keep me in suspense?" Ryan asks, slightly bewildered by my response.

"It might be a mess," I warn him.

"I don't care about that."

As we head out into the parking lot, Ryan tells me he has to stop by an ATM first, so I give him directions to my place, and then I blast home. I buzz through my apartment like a chainsaw, shoving items into cabinets, straightening pillows on the couch and for once in—like ever, I make my bed. I hope I have time to wash the dirty dishes, but just as I pick up my clothes and shove them into the hamper, Ryan's calling.

I push on the intercom button. "Take the elevator to the fourth floor. Turn right. I'm in 408." I open my door and wait for him. A minute later, he walks off the elevator. "Find parking okay?"

"Right across the street." He comes in and looks around.

"Not as nice as your place," I admit, "but that's pretty much the case with a typical apartment."

"What? No crystal balls or séance room?" he asks teasingly.

"Sorry to disappoint, though I have a candle—just one—over on the bookshelf."

Ryan smiles, nodding.

"Let me give you the grand tour." I put on my best tour guide voice. "You're standing in the living room slash dining room slash family room built eons ago as evidenced by the prehistoric carpeting."

Ryan looks down, examining my grungy carpeting, which I suddenly realize I don't want him to do.

I quickly point behind us. "The kitchen." I head down my one and only hallway. "And we're walking, we're walking." I stop at the end of my very short hallway. "The bedroom." I spin slightly to the right. "The bathroom. And that brings us to the end of today's tour. Don't forget to stop by our gift shop on your way out."

Ryan chuckles, glances around. "I like it."

I shake my head in an embarrassed, dismissive way since I'm sure he's just saying that so I don't feel bad about living in a crappy apartment. I'm about to offer him something to drink when the look on his face stops me. It's not the lustful, I-must-have-you look, it's something much deeper.

"I've missed you," he says, studying my face. "I've missed you so much." He then kisses me. It's a very slow, deep, caring kiss full of emotion and tenderness.

I wrap my arms around him and we find ourselves moving toward my room, but when we get there, we don't tear each other's clothes off like the last time we were together. Instead we undress, climb into bed, and hold each other, not saying a word.

As I lie there, I think about how both of us have had to deal with such intense family circumstances over the last few weeks, and how it's been incredibly difficult to go through it alone. My nana was the only person who could truly understand what I deal with on a daily basis. And no one can understand the heartache that Ryan's been going through—to lose a brother he never knew he had, to discover his role model isn't as perfect as he thought he was. No one can understand, except for maybe Ryan's living half brother.

Ryan has fallen asleep with his arms around me. I finally realize that I have to tell him about his other brother as soon as he wakes. It would be nice to talk to Tyler first, so without any effort at all, I think of Tyler and he appears.

I'm about to get out of bed when I remember that I don't have any clothes on. *Let me get dressed*, I tell Tyler with my thoughts.

And then I hear Tyler's reply in my head: *I'll go hang out in the living room.*

I nod and he's gone. *Only Tyler can make that saying literal.* I ever so gently remove Ryan's arm from around my waist and slide out of bed. I throw on my robe, glance back at Ryan to make sure he's still asleep, and then I quietly slip out of my room, closing the door behind me.

I hurry into the living room and see Tyler—now more transparent than he's ever been. He seems to be pacing, though I can't see the lower half of his body. What I can see is his face and it looks very troubled. "I have an emergency," he blurts out.

I pause, slightly taken aback, since I thought I was the one who called him, and not the other way around. "What's wrong?"

"It's Connor."

"Who?"

"My twin brother." A shadow of concern haunts Tyler's face. "Why didn't you tell Ryan about him?"

"I was going to, but then life got complicated for both of us. Besides, you didn't help much. A name would have been nice."

"Sorry," Tyler apologizes, hovering closer to me. "Natalie, I need your help. Connor is way too depressed over my death. He's suicidal. I've tried to make my presence known, but I'm making it worse for him."

"Do you want me to call him?" I ask, alarmed.

"I don't know if he would believe you. But I think he might listen to Ryan."

"What are you doing?" I suddenly hear behind me, and I turn around to see Ryan standing there, rubbing his eyes.

"Sorry. We tried not to wake you."

"We?" Ryan's fully awake now. He glances around my living room. "As in you and a ghost?"

I nod.

Ryan inhales deeply. "I can appreciate that you have taken on this unusual job of passing on messages from the dearly departed, but have you ever thought that maybe sometimes you should turn a few down?"

"I couldn't with this one."

"Why not?"

"Because it's Tyler."

"My Tyler?"

I nod.

He throws me a suspicious glance. "I thought spirits moved on after they said what they needed to say?"

"They do, but Tyler still has unfinished business. He needs to talk to you."

Ryan looks around again, and he seems as if he's going to listen, but then he says, "Why? What's the point, Natalie? Don't you think I've been tortured enough? It was devastating to learn that my father had a secret life with a second family, that he's been lying to us for years and cheating on my mom. Now you want me to talk to a dead brother I was never given the chance to know?"

"But Ryan, you *can* get to know your brother. That's what I—"

"Stop, okay?" He cuts me with a curt look. "You might be able to talk to the dead, but I can't." He begins to walk away.

"Ryan, would you listen to me for a second?"

Ryan reluctantly turns back to face me.

"You're right," I calmly state. "You won't have the chance to get to know Tyler, but you will have a chance to know your half brother. Your *other* half brother. Tyler was a twin."

Ryan physically staggers back. The expression on his face changes from anger to shock to hope, and in a very small voice he says, "I have a brother?"

"Yes."

"A brother who is alive and well?"

"Yes."

Ryan's eyes get a little misty. "Are you messing with me?"

"I would never do that to you, Ryan. Never."

Ryan takes in a shaky breath. "You're telling me the honest to God truth."

"Yes." And now my eyes are getting a little misty.

Ryan rakes both hands through his hair. "I have two brothers. One named Tyler who is ... here right now, and another who is alive somewhere."

"Yes."

Ryan lets out an elated vocal breath and I can see that his mind is reeling. He smiles wide, gives off a little laugh, then pins me with his eyes. "Who is he? Does he know I exist? Does he want to meet me? Where is he? Does he live nearby?"

"Whoa, slow down." I glance over at Tyler, who is grinning from ear to ear. "Tell Ryan that his name is Connor. He lives in Myrtle Beach and is still grieving over my death. More than anything, Connor needs to know about Ryan. Today. Now," Tyler pleads. "Natalie, I can give you Connor's number, but you know he needs to get it from our dad."

I know Tyler is right. Whether Ryan forgives his father or not, he at least needs to try.

"His name is Connor," I relay to Ryan. "He still lives in Myrtle Beach. He doesn't know you exist, but he needs to talk to you now. It's critical, Ryan. Your father has his contact information."

All the joy that Ryan is experiencing quickly seeps from his eyes. "My father? You expect me to speak to him again?"

"There are always two sides to every story."

"The guy has been living a lie his entire life. How could any part of his double life be okay?"

"Ryan, I'm not suggesting that what he did was right, but he is your father and you should at least let him finish saying what he wanted to tell you when you went home to see him."

He shakes his head.

"Tyler says Connor needs you right now, more than anything."

"Then why doesn't Tyler tell Connor about me?"

"He's tried but he can't get through to him. Connor is still grieving. And to be honest, it's probably a good thing Tyler hasn't been able to make contact. If Connor saw his dead twin brother suddenly appear, it would probably put him over the edge."

Ryan says nothing, but seems to soften a bit.

"Why do you think Tyler made it his mission to contact you instead?"

"I get it." Ryan releases an irritated breath. "I don't want to, but I do."

"Thank you," Tyler softly says to me. "It's going to be okay now because I know he'll do the right thing. Thank you for your help."

I turn to him. "You're leaving?"

"Heck, yeah. It's so awesomely sick over here, you wouldn't believe it if I told you."

I smile. "I hear it's pretty incredible."

"Incredible doesn't begin to describe it." He puts his eyes on Ryan. "He'll be okay. Tell him his little brother will be watching over him."

"I will." I glance at Ryan who is staring right at Tyler but can't see him.

"Is he leaving?" Ryan asks.

I look back at Tyler, but he's already disappeared.

Uh-oh. Awkward. Since I know spirits can hear us when we're talking to them, I take the liberty and tell Ryan a little white lie. "Yes," I answer Ryan.

Ryan moves closer to where Tyler was just a moment ago. "Sorry I can't see you," he says to the empty space, "but the fact that I finally believe you exist and that you are here, right in front of me, is a big leap of faith for me."

Okay, now I'm starting to feel a little guilty.

"I just want to say thank you for not giving up on me and for … wow … coming back to let me know about my brother."

I guess this must be what it was like for my old employers, watching me talk to air.

"I really wish I could have known you." Ryan looks to me for Tyler's response.

Oh, right. I clear my throat. "He wishes the same," I reply, since I'm certain that would have been his response if he were still here.

"So, I guess this is goodbye," Ryan says to no one.

I can't let him continue. "Tyler says he'll be watching over you."

Ryan smiles at this. "I know I didn't want to talk to you before, but now…. Will you come back to see me? Natalie can be our translator."

Oh, crap. "He uh … he's gone."

"Oh." Ryan appears slightly hurt.

"He was fading right when he said, "Tell Ryan his little brother will be watching over him.""

Ryan smiles. "Yeah, I guess he was my little brother."

"And you have another little brother you need to meet."

Ryan releases a big breath. "Yeah. For the sake of Connor, I guess I'm going to have to talk to my dad."

"I'm sure if Tyler were here, he'd be very happy to hear that." I pick up his cell from the coffee table and hand it to him. "It's midnight there now. Do you think it's too late for your dad to answer?"

"There's only one way to find out." Ryan takes a deep breath, dials and starts pacing. "Dad? It's me."

I go into the kitchen and start washing the dirty dishes. As Ryan continues to talk to his dad, he migrates back into my bedroom. Thirty minutes later he reappears. His eyes are bloodshot and his face is a little blotchy, so I know the conversation got intense enough to bring on tears. "You okay?"

"Yeah, and so is Connor."

My brows rise in surprise. "You talked to him too?"

"Right after I hung up from my dad and before I lost my nerve."

"Did he believe you?"

"Strangely, yes. It helped that we have similar voices. We even said, 'I'm so blown away' at the exact same time."

"That's great, Ryan. Are you planning to meet up at some point?"

"He actually has a trip planned out here next week. Bought the ticket months ago to come hang with his brother."

"Though I'm sure it's going to be a tough trip for Connor, at least he will be meeting his half brother."

"It's sad that Tyler won't be with us."

"He'll be with you guys," I assure him. "That's one get-together I know he won't miss."

"I wish I could be as certain as you."

"Just have faith." I simply say as I take Ryan's hand in mine and lead him back to bed.

———————

For the rest of the week I'm working fourteen-hour days. The crew immediately shoots another episode, this one at a haunted high school. It turns out it really is haunted by a kid who was a track team star in the late '90s. There's also a student who committed suicide in the cafeteria after being mercilessly bullied. We end up getting some pretty good footage. One piece is of a chair moving on its own across the cafeteria floor. We also capture the voice of a male teenager on our EVP recorder.

After our haunted high school shoot, we're all working on post production for both episodes. Ideally we should be shooting yet another episode to give us some wiggle room, but our main focus has to be the Willow Creek episode. We're under serious pressure to get it ready in time to air.

Marcus has been cutting furiously, and has realized he needs some filler shots around Willow Creek, so Ryan was sent out to do just that. As for me, I'm laying down a lot of voice-over, explaining to the audience what the spirits were saying to me since no one heard the other side of the conversation.

As much as I wanted the camera to have picked up something, anything, of Doris's spirit, it didn't. Carolyn insists the footage will be riveting enough and that it will be, at the very least, one more documented case of a near-death experience.

Because this episode has evolved into a look at the spiritual world up close, I give Carolyn permission to use the footage where I'm talking to my nana. She's relieved since Marcus didn't want an unintended jump cut in the intro. Taking out all reference to my nana would have also affected my talking to Doris, not to mention why I knew so many of the residents. As Geoff points out, keeping Nana in adds serious drama to the episode by making it painfully real. The skeptics, he insists, will have a tough time taking it apart.

Though I told Carolyn I didn't want to view the rough cut, she calls me in to Marcus' cutting room and tells me I have to see something they just noticed. As it turns out, a tiny blue orb appears in the footage for one and a half seconds. The orb has blue light emanating from within the orb itself, and it appears exactly where my nana stood when I was talking to her. Of course, it will be explained away by skeptics as illuminated dust, but I know different, and the rest of the *Super Natalie* crew does too.

With so much that's happened—my nana whispering in my ear about Doris, her spirit in the form of an orb showing up on camera—well, I can't help but think I'm supposed to share Nana's message with everyone watching. It's too important to keep to myself. I'm beginning to think that's what she wanted me to do—share her message with the world.

After I tell Carolyn about my "dream" of my grandmother and what she said, Carolyn agrees, so I step into the studio and record one of my video diaries.

In my video diary, I tell the audience what my nana said about how we can be ruled by love or ruled by fear, and that our lives would be so much easier if we were motivated by love since love never leads us astray and Carolyn loves it, so she adds this video message on to the end of the episode, and when I watch the final version as it airs on TV with my mom and sister, their faces are wet with tears.

No one says anything for a few moments after the show ends. I can tell they are sitting with Nana's message, feeling its full impact. And finally my mom says, "Incredible."

Stephanie adds, "This episode might have changed the world."

I'm all smiles. "It is kind of cool how love and fear worked together in this episode to illuminate Nana's message."

Stephanie gasps and runs to my mom's computer. "I bet the website is on fire!"

My mom and I scramble over to Stephanie's side as she pulls up the *Super Natalie* official website.

The website is on fire all right—only not at all what any of us, including Carolyn and Geoff, expected.

By the massive amount of negative posts I can only glean that prime time is not ready for my nana's message. Though we knew the audience would most likely be at an all-time high, due to the two demon episodes catapulting *Super Natalie* into the most-watched cable show in that time slot, the Willow Creek episode was not well received. We got a lashing from the fans—everything from: WHAT THE HELL DID I JUST WATCH?; I THOUGHT THIS WAS SUPPOSED TO BE A SCARY SHOW; IF I WANTED TO THINK DEEP THOUGHTS, I WOULDN'T HAVE TURNED ON THE TV; NATALIE, ARE YOU ON GLUE? Followed by, ARE YOU ALL ON CRACK? Then, of course, my favorite: NATALIE, YOU LOOK LIKE A TOTAL PSYCHO TALKING TO NO ONE, which really has me baffled because apparently I look like a total professional when talking to no one in a pitch-black room inside an alleged haunted location where only a night vision camera can see me.

Needless to say, I realize a little too late that my nana's message was probably meant for just me. After reading about a hundred negative comments, I can't take it anymore and go sit back down on the couch.

My mom pours us a glass of wine and joins me. "Don't worry about all those negative comments. Did you know for every person who doesn't like something, there are ten who do?"

"Not according to those posts," I grumble.

"That's because the general public tends to complain rather than praise. Take it from me. Angry travelers are more apt to leave a comment than someone totally satisfied."

I tuck my legs up under me and stare into my wineglass. "I really thought Nana wanted me to share her message with the whole world."

"I'm sure she did," my mom replies. "Her message got through to the people who needed to hear it."

Stephanie shuts down the computer, grabs a beer out of the fridge, and joins my mom and me. "Everyone is a critic these days. Ignore them. Don't let anyone stifle your true voice."

My mom and I stare at my sister, surprised to be hearing her talk so sensibly.

"What?"

I give Stephanie a proud smile. "A pearl of wisdom from my very own sister."

"That's not wisdom." She snorts. "That's common sense."

My mom laughs. "So, what's happening with you and Ryan?"

"Yeah, now *he's* something to talk about. Ryan's hot!"

A huge grin takes over my face. "He is hot." I laugh.

"Did he ever believe his deceased half brother contacted you?" my mom asks.

"Finally," I tell her and Stephanie. "But that wasn't the entire message." I take a sip of my wine. "Ryan's deceased half brother was a twin, so Ryan actually has another half brother."

My mom gawks at me. "Are you serious?"

I nod. "Pretty crazy, huh?"

"It's like a soap opera with spirits." Stephanie takes a gulp of her beer. "Ryan's gotta be lovin' your gift now."

"Loving isn't exactly the right word. Accepting it, yes."

"But why? It's totally awesome."

"It can be, except for when spirits have *really bad timing*." I give my sister a look.

"Oh." She makes a face, getting it. "You're with a hot guy and three's a crowd."

"Exactly."

"So has Ryan met his half brother?" my mom asks.

"He arrived from South Carolina late this afternoon. I'm dying to hear how it's going, but it's not like Ryan can call me in front of him. I'll see him at work tomorrow, so I'm sure he'll tell me then." I'm expecting Stephanie to ask if Ryan's half brother is available and when she doesn't I know something is up. "What's happening with you and Mikey?" I ask.

Stephanie twists her hair around on her finger. "We're churning out songs like you wouldn't believe." And now it's Stephanie's turn to give me a look. We can't go into detail with our mom sitting there.

"I've always liked Mikey," my mom says. "He's a very polite boy."

"He's funny, too." Stephanie's eyes light up. "I never knew what a dry sense of humor he had, and he's so sweet to me."

By the look on her face I have my answer—that the two of them have a more serious relationship than they are willing to admit. I glance at my mom, who seems awfully quiet. "Now we just need to get you back to dating, Mom."

"No need. I'm saving up to go on a singles' cruise next summer."

"Right on!" Stephanie high-fives my mom.

I laugh. "That's great." I take a sip of wine, feeling my nana's absence, wishing she were with us.

My mom eyes me and must know what I'm thinking. "Nana's kicking up her heels right now."

"I know." I grab the wine bottle off the kitchen counter and pour us a second glass of wine.

"I bet she thought tonight's episode rocked," Stephanie adds.

"I'm sure she did." I inhale sharply, suddenly remembering the negative posts. "Let's just hope the majority of the fans did too."

———

With a bit of a hangover, the following morning I make a beeline for Starbucks before continuing on to the production office. In this state, I wish this Starbucks had a drive-thru. I'm a little nervous about today's meeting. Even though we'll be focused on prepping for our next investigation, I know we'll hear about the reaction to the airing of the Willow Creek episode. Was it favorable? Seeing as how I didn't get a call late last night telling me not to bother to come in, I'm taking it as a good sign.

I pull into the garage at the exact time Ryan does. I instantly forget my troubles and wonder what happened with him and his half brother. "How did it go with Connor?" I ask, getting out of my car.

He locks his eyes on me. He has a very serious look on his face, which is scaring me a little because he's not saying a word. Instead he marches over to me and just as he's about to grab me, a huge smile takes over his face. He picks me up, twirls me around and kisses me.

I bubble with a laugh. "I guess it went well?"

"We talked nonstop until three in the morning."

I get chills. "Oh, Ryan, that's incredible. I'm so happy for you."

"I can't believe how much we have in common, and how alike we are."

"I thought about the two of you a lot last night. I was hoping it was going well, but you never know. You guys could have ended up hating each other."

"I know—especially under the circumstances." He pulls me closer to him. He caresses my cheek and stares into my eyes. "Thank you. Thank you for making me talk to my dad." He lowers his head and kisses me again.

We walk toward the elevator, holding hands. "Connor and I watched last night's episode."

I gasp. "You did?" I'm very surprised to hear this, since it's not every day you meet your long-lost half brother.

"What did he think?"

"He loved it, and he thinks I have a stunner of a girlfriend."

I beam with a huge smile. "You told him I was your girlfriend?"

"Well, yeah. You are, aren't you?"

"Yes, I am," I proudly state, feeling like I'm flying.

Ryan pushes the button for the elevator, and my nerves about the overall reaction to the episode immediately come back. "I'm glad Connor liked our show, but did you see the nasty posts?"

"I never read those things," he admits honestly as we walk into the elevator. "It didn't go over well with the viewers?"

"It went over and off the edge." The doors close.

Ryan shrugs. "Some people just aren't ready to hear the truth." He looks at me and I burst with a laugh, realizing how much he's come around.

"I'd love to meet Connor. How long will he be here?" I ask.

"Just until the end of the week. I'm going to ask Carolyn and Geoff if he can come hang out on the shoot with us tonight."

"That would be great."

Ryan kisses my hand right as the elevator doors open.

Haley happens to be walking by and never misses a thing. "I knew it! I knew you guys hooked up." She hurries ahead of us and into the conference room. "Carlos, I won the bet! Pay up."

We walk in and the room erupts with applause from our crew. Ryan and I stand there completely stunned.

"It's about time," Geoff tells us.

"Yeah," Carlos adds, "I was like, 'Ask her out already, bro.'"

"You could tell we liked each other?" I ask in disbelief.

"Uh, yeah," Adam says, glancing up from his iPad but still typing away. "On day one."

"No way," Ryan argues confidently. "I was pretty cool about it."

"Men are so clueless," Carolyn interjects, which gets a laugh out of everyone.

I glance at Ryan and shrug.

Our crew has become a family, just like Carolyn and Geoff had hoped. Ryan immediately begins telling everyone about Connor and how I communicated with Tyler, and I can't believe how open-minded he's become. It's hard to believe how much we've both changed in just these few short months.

After the crew grabs some coffee and tea, we finally settle in for our meeting. Carolyn begins with the bad news. "For the record, I loved the episode. Unfortunately, the network did not."

Haley lets out a grunt of disgust.

"They signed off on it," Carlos brings up. "How can they suddenly not like it?"

"It wasn't the episode itself," Carolyn corrects. "The network didn't like the fans' feedback."

"Not all of the posts were bad. In fact, there were quite a few positive posts," Carlos counters.

"That's exactly what we pointed out to the network," Geoff relates. "I suggested we should do an episode on angels."

"How did that go over?" I have to ask, trying to keep the sarcasm out of my voice.

"Uh, it didn't." He quickly glances at Carolyn then gets quiet.

No doubt Carolyn was doing some fast dancing and smooth talking after *that* suggestion. Even *I* know that proving the existence of angels is far more difficult than catching a few ghosts.

"So where do we stand?" Ryan asks Carolyn.

"Luckily we've already shot the next episode, *Haunted High School*. I assured the network that it would be a typical paranormal investigation with lots of nail-biting moments and no feel-good messages delivered by Natalie from any feel-good spirit."

"So, it will be all about fear and death and anxiety and tragedy," Geoff pipes in.

"Just like the fans want," Carlos observes.

"Sorry, Natalie," Carolyn says.

"No, I read the posts and I get it," I say, a little deflated. "You don't have to worry. From now on I'll keep my warm and fuzzy thoughts to myself."

Because the Paranormal Network was worried we might stray off course, they insisted on approving each investigation before we committed to it. Even *Haunted High School* came under scrutiny, so Marcus had to send them an assembled cut of the show. Fortunately, they liked what they saw. In fact, they liked it so much that they encouraged us to find similar locations, which would keep drawing on the college crowd.

Haley found us a haunted college, which the network instantly approved, and a few days later, the *Super Natalie* crew was filming. As it turns out, the location did not disappoint. I was told by the network to stick to their paranormal investigation formula, and to keep it scary, and I abided by the rules on camera.

Off camera I talked to a ghost that was trapped there, and I shared with her what my nana said. The deceased college student actually listened and found her way home.

When *Haunted High School* aired, the website was on fire again, but this time most of the comments were positive. The momentum continued with each new episode and it wasn't long before we not only won back our audience but increased our viewers, making us number one once again. Because of that, the second season of *Super Natalie* was just announced. *Whoo-hoo!*

As for Ryan and I, we now spend more time together than apart. When we're not at work together, we hang out and stay over at each other's places. The only thing that bothers me is that we've never used the L word. I know I should just tell him I love him, but it seems like the time to say that has come and gone and now I'm afraid to say it.

Today, we're prepping for our ninth investigation and the first one out of state. I'd be more excited about it if I wasn't distracted by Ryan. He's been acting weird all day. Something is definitely up with him, and I can't figure out what it is.

Not being able to take it anymore, I stop packing up the equipment, turn to Ryan and say, "Want to fill me in?"

Ryan, who is just about to take two Pelican cases out to the van, gets a shocked look on his face, but then tries to act casual. "What do you mean?"

"You're acting weird, so just tell me what's on your mind."

Ryan sets down the cases, and meets my gaze. "Okay, if you really want to know, I've been doing a pro/con thing in my head."

"About…?"

"You."

I stiffen. "What about me?"

Ryan gets this tiny smirk on his face, which I'm not sure how to read. "Matt's biggest complaint is that Lucy spends too much time on the phone talking to her girlfriends. My biggest complaint is that the woman I love spends too much time talking to the dead."

Not sure if I heard him correctly, I focus on him like a laser. "You love me?"

"Obviously."

My face lights up. "Really?"

He stares at me, a little astounded. "You're a psychic. How could you not have known that?"

"One, you've never told me." I cross my arms. "And two, if you were expecting me to read your mind, it's a lot harder for us psychics to read the people we love," I say in my defense.

"So, you love me too?"

I do take note that he hasn't said the actual words. My mouth twitches into a half grin. "Looks that way."

"Well, that's pretty noncommittal." Ryan pulls me into his arms, and I swear I think he wants to hear it from me first.

"Okay. Yes," I say on a slow exhale. "I love you. I have for a long time."

"That's a really weird coincidence, since I've loved you for a long time too."

I break into a smile and he kisses me, and then I remember what we were talking about. "This definitely goes in your pro column."

He lets out a big sigh. "I suppose it has to."

I smack him playfully. "What was the previous point again?"

"Your talking to the dead?"

"Is that a pro or a con?"

He looks at me startled. "You have to ask? That's clearly in the con column."

"Hmm. I figured as much."

"Do you want to know what else is in the con column?"

"I don't know," I say, suddenly apprehensive. "Do I?"

"The biggest negative is the revolving door that your dead clients seem to use quite frequently. They come, they go, they come again. It's a little creepy to think that someone might be watching us have sex."

"Well, if you weren't so good at it, maybe you wouldn't invite an audience."

Ryan laughs, then kisses me before he continues, "I also hate your apartment."

"You said you liked it," I say, offended.

"I lied."

"Damn. Another con? I'm not doing so well."

"Actually hating your apartment is a pro."

"How so?"

"Well, it's the reason I started thinking about all of this in the first place."

I tilt my head. "You never did mention what has you so preoccupied."

"Oh, right. I didn't." He wraps his hands around my waist and pulls me closer. "I was wondering if you might want to move in with me."

My brows shoot up in surprise as a huge smile takes over my face. "You want us to live together?"

"Yes."

I just stare at him and I can't stop smiling.

"Reminder here. I'm not psychic. At all. So if you're trying to tele-pathically give me your answer, it's not going through."

I laugh out loud. "Yes." I kiss him on the lips.

"Cool." He flashes me a big grin. "After we get back from this investigation, we're going to have to figure out how to get all of your furniture into my place."

"Might not be so difficult," I tell him, sliding my arms around his neck. "Stephanie is moving out of my mom's and she hardly has any-thing for her apartment."

"Talk about serious hand-me-downs."

"What are sisters for?" I shrug. "Is there anything you want me to keep that you can't live without?" I ask him seriously, thinking about some of my framed artwork.

"Well, that would be you."

I bubble with another laugh as I realize how perfectly he answered my question.

He just stares at me like he's drinking me in. "I know what the super in *Super Natalie* stands for and it has nothing to do with seeing ghosts."

I shake my head at his corny comment, but Ryan remains serious and gives me the most tender kiss I've ever felt.

Haley clears her throat and we break apart as she says, "I was wondering what was taking you guys so long."

"We're just bringing the last of the equipment out now," Ryan replies as he picks up the Pelican cases and heads toward the door.

"Cool, I'll let Geoff know." Haley grins at me, then answers her cell on the go.

I pick up the last case, and I'm about to turn off the lights in the storage room, when I suddenly see my nana. She's hovering by the shelves, beaming a bright, beautiful smile at me. "See, Talie. I told you Ryan was a keeper."

"You're right, Nana. You are so right."

The End